THE FAULT

THE FAULT

The Knowing Saga Book Four

NINIE HAMMON

STERLING & STONE

The authors greatly appreciate you taking the time to read our work.
Please consider leaving a review wherever you bought the book, or
telling your friends about it, to help us spread the word.

Thank you for supporting our work.

Chapter One

THE ELECTRIC SHOCK of terror would light Denise Holterman up like she'd grabbed a high-voltage wire when the Ugly Man put his hand over her mouth, but right now she was still asleep, her breathing even and steady. It's possible she sensed his presence when he eased open the door and crept into her bedroom, though, because she stirred, mumbled something in sleep talk. Maybe she even awoke for a second or two, blinked, as the puddle of darkness in the doorway soundlessly became a deeper puddle in the shadows on the wall.

She wasn't afraid, though. Not yet.

Maybe that's what she was trying to avoid. Not so much the reality of his presence but the fear that would slice into her chest with a pain she didn't know existed in the world. Maybe some part of her mind did wake up, did know that a horror beyond her wildest imaginings had entered her world, but she didn't want to acknowledge it, wanted to stay in denial, shying away from reality, trying to grab those last few seconds of innocent sleep on the precipice of the abyss.

Maybe.

The Ugly Man understood fear. Oh my, yes, there wasn't anybody on the face of the globe who understood it better. He had made "intimate acquaintance" with a terror that'd stop your heart, except his kept right on beating. Oh, the many times he'd begged it to stop, begged his heart to give out and let him go. But after a while he came to understand that it wouldn't matter much one way or the other even if it did — that what was happening to him didn't have anything to do with being alive or dead. It'd be the same either way.

He took one quiet step. Then another. Wanted to get his hand over her mouth before she awoke — oh, not because he cared if she screamed. She could squawk her head off and nobody would hear her way out here. The nearest neighbors were three miles away. No, he didn't want to miss the sight of her eyes popping open in horror when she felt his hand on her. That was a delicious sight on anyone, but especially scrumptious tonight.

One more step put him at the foot of her bed. She stirred again, rolled over on her back so the puddle of moonlight from the window lit her face in gray light like she was already dead.

The Ugly Man froze. Stared at the form on the bed. Then he let out a wordless cry, a sound like a roar and a wail, a sound no voice should be able to make. The girl on the bed jolted awake — he didn't get to see the look in her eyes but he didn't care about that anymore. She screamed, and with surprising speed and agility leapt out of the bed and made for the door. The Ugly Man grabbed a handful of her hair and yanked her off her feet. She fell into her vanity, shattering the delicate mirrored table and sending makeup and perfume and hairbrushes flying. When she tried to stand, he backhanded her and she staggered into the night table beside the bed, knocking the lamp off onto the floor. She tried to keep her balance by grabbing the bedpost, but spun around it and clawed at the wall, pulling the framed cross-stitch of flowers off onto the floor.

He was still making that awful cry, and mingled with her screams it was a sound that would have curdled the soul of anyone who heard it.

But nobody did.

Her panic made her strong and she pulled herself upright and actually came at him, her nails bared, like some wild cat. He grabbed her right hand and flung her onto her back on the bed. Then he reached for his blade. It was always there, never so far away that he couldn't touch it. Because he had to touch it, had to feel the cold metal, had to watch the images dance.

He lifted it high in the air and brought it down in a slicing stroke that penetrated skin and muscle and bone.

She stopped screaming then, like he had flipped her off switch. But he continued to growl, to howl and roar, to vent the rage out of his soul into the world.

No, not his soul. The Ugly Man had no soul.

EVERY DAY that Natalie Karrick could remember had started the same way. Well, not every day. Not when she was sick, or visiting Grandma in Bradford's Ridge or when it was raining or snowing or sleeting or something like that. But every day that was clear and she was able to, she and Daddy climbed up to the top of the world to "survey God's whole magnificent creation." That's what Daddy said they were doing. Natalie just thought they were looking out over the hollow from the highest point around, the big pile of rocks on Rocky Top Mountain.

But maybe Daddy could see something she couldn't. Maybe it was possible to see everything God'd created from that one spot, but that didn't seem likely to her. She'd only just figured out there wasn't any Santa Claus. Once the teacher showed them a globe and said the world was round Natalie knew wasn't no way Santa could take presents to every kid on both sides of that globe on the same night. Of course, God was real and Santa wasn't, but she still didn't think you could see the whole world at the same time from anywhere on it. But she was only seven. Maybe she'd understand it better next week, after her eighth birthday.

"You sure you don't want to snuggle up warm in the covers and go back to sleep?" Daddy'd asked her. He asked her that every morning.

"I want to go with you to the top of the world," she said. She said that same thing every morning, too. But the question and answer were all part of the daily ritual and it wouldn't be complete without it all.

So the two of them set off when it was still dark, the sun glowing behind the mountain, already after "sunrise" out there on the flat where people didn't have to wait until ten o'clock in the morning for sunlight. The mist was still hanging gauzy over the creek when they crossed it on the big rocks Daddy'd thrown into it to make stepping stones. There was still dew on the leaves of the red oleander bush when they pushed their way past it and into the woods, climbing up the trail that wasn't really a trail, just the way they always came.

~

HE SHOULD HAVE LEFT her behind. She was going to die anyway. You couldn't chop off somebody's hand and

4

expect them to survive. He hadn't meant to cut her like that. She wasn't any good to him dead, had to be alive. All of them had to be alive until it was time.

He hadn't been thinking when he did it. The hot flame of rage, of seeing her there, seeing her face in the moonlight. He couldn't help himself. There was nothing in him that could curb or temper his rage. It was a force too strong, the force that drove him.

As he watched the blade rise up and slice down, cutting through her all the way, cutting it off, he became aware of the nearness of her warmth and then her blood. And he'd wanted that. He'd grabbed the tie off the bathrobe hanging on a hook in the bathroom as soon as he came back to himself, with her lying there in a puddle of blood as limp as a rag doll. He'd tied it around her arm as tight as he could. The blood stopped spurting out then, just about quit altogether, so she was not going to exsanguinate.

He paused at the word. He knew it meant bleed out, die from blood loss, but he couldn't remember how he knew that.

The blood wasn't as good as having her alive, but the Ugly Man liked blood. It was warm and had that salty taste. And he felt a desire in his chest for blood, briefly remembered what that was — desire, wanting something — but then it was gone.

Maybe it wasn't a bad thing that he'd carted her body off, brought it with him instead of leaving it lying there in a puddle of blood as morning light filled the room.

There was the blood, after all.

He'd had to dig around in her kitchen to find a garbage bag to wrap around her hand to keep from leaving a trail of blood when he carried her out and away. Bloodhounds could follow *her* scent, but they couldn't follow his. There wasn't a dog in the world that could follow his. But he didn't think they'd use dogs. As far out as the farm was, with nothing but fields around it — moonlit fields he'd had to cross before he made it to the trees — nobody'd think about a kidnapper on foot. They'd be looking for tire tracks, maybe setting up roadblocks, searching people's cars. Which they couldn't legally do, but nobody knew that so police got away with it all the time.

By midday, they might organize volunteers to search the woods *for her body*. They'd know as well as he did that she couldn't still be alive by then. Maybe he ought to do that, leave the body out there for them to find.

No, he wouldn't leave her. She was still alive, still warm. He'd keep her while she still had blood.

He traveled swiftly and silently among the shadows of the trees, a puddle of black moving from one to the next. The girl was small, weighed hardly anything, slung over his shoulder in a fireman's carry. That was a good thing because he had a long way to go. He didn't get tired or anything like that, but he had a sense of using energy and strength and there was only so much of both of them and he would use them until they were all gone. He suspected that would probably be a really long time, but there was no way to be sure of that.

Keeping to the woods, staying out of open fields and meadows, he was as swift as an owl falling down out of the sky on its prey. He never tripped or stumbled, as surefooted as a goat, and he never lost his way. He always knew where he was going.

It might have been a warm night. He didn't know about such things anymore but the girl had thrown off the covers as she slept and lay in a simple cotton nightgown that was now stained a crimson that looked black in the shafts of early light shining down through the trees. There might have been beginning-of-the-day sounds too, the ones others could hear that he couldn't anymore.

And smells. There was likely the scent of pine in the air, the aroma of wet leaves underfoot and flowering bushes and wildflowers whose names he didn't know.

He could almost remember those — warm air and birdsong and magnolias. Almost.

Now, his skin registered only the extremes, ice and fire. His whole being knew nothing but ice and fire.

When he got to the cave entrance, he passed from shadow into darkness and vanished altogether.

HARRELTON, Ohio, Police Department Major Charles Allen Crocker was Crock to his friends, and most everybody he met fell into that category eventually. Well, except those he informed solemnly that he was about to "deprive you of your freedom in a significant fashion" — which was what he told drunks, and sometimes he'd be able to get them all the way to the cruiser before they figured out that meant he was taking them to jail.

Crock was a round man without a hair on his head, and legs bowed out so far you could drive a rickshaw between his knees. One of those knees, the one where he'd taken a bullet through the kneecap years ago, was so cranky some mornings it wouldn't bend at all and others it would collapse right out from under him. In a couple of months, he was going to have to pass the department physical again. How was he going to pull *that* off? Getting old was not for sissies.

But if you had to do it, here was the place to do it and this was how.

He leaned back in the lawn chair positioned beneath

the oak tree in what would be a puddle of shade as soon as the sun cleared the mountain. Looking out over dawn mist rising up off the river, he let out a sigh of pure contentment. Yes sir, coming a week early for Saturday's festivities so he could get in some fishing was one of the best decisions he'd ever made, knew it the moment he hauled his suitcases into the house that had once belonged to Billy Ray Hawkins and had passed down to his daughter Becca when he died. It was an old farm house with two bedrooms upstairs and two down and, wonder of wonders, it even had two bathrooms, which wasn't common for farm houses as old as this one. Even one was a stretch, so he was grateful the three "bachelors" — he, Jack Carpenter and Daniel Burke — wouldn't be taking turns at an outdoor privy. He'd read somewhere that the incidence of black widow spider bites had tanked in the early 1950s and somebody somewhere figured out it was because of indoor plumbing.

Crock had moved his things into the smallest bedroom, the one directly behind the kitchen — figured Jack for the big bedroom that opened off the parlor. He was, after all, the main attraction here so his should be the most spacious digs. Daniel could have his pick of the upstairs bedrooms.

The women — Theresa Washington, Andi Burke and Becca — had arranged to stay at Ariel Murphy's house. Her father was a long-haul trucker who wouldn't be back home for a week. Linc had told Crock when they'd had a beer together his first day in town that Rita Murphy, Ariel's mother, was as excited as all the rest of them. Truth was, she probably ached to spend time with people who understood what'd happened last fall that had turned her eight-year-old daughter into a monster and shoved Rita so far down into a whisky bottle it'd taken six weeks in rehab to get her back on the wagon.

The others wouldn't start arriving until late tomorrow afternoon.

Crock closed his eyes and conjured up his fantasy, which technically wasn't a fantasy because all the elements of it were reality. He really was eligible for early retirement. He really did have sufficient resources at his disposal to pull it off. And the one-eyed man named Ike who owned the run-down bait and tackle shop at the top of the hill really would sell the place for a song and let you sing it yourself. Crock'd agreed to watch the store while Ike was out of town today and it didn't take as much imagination as you might think to consider the place his own.

He could almost see the new sign hanging over the door: Crock of Shad — shad being a bait fish nobody in Central Kentucky had ever heard of but he liked the alliteration and the play on words. He'd run the business just like Ike did — rural Kentucky style. When he wasn't there, when he went fishing as he had done today, he'd leave the front door of the bait shop open and a cigar box on the counter with twenty bucks in ones and a handful of coins in it. And a note pad beside the box instructing patrons to "Pay for what you got and make change or leave an IOU."

It was possible for Crock to hear the ring of the bell on the front door of the shop from right here by the river. He shouldn't have been able to hear it, of course. The oak tree on the bank of the Three Forks River was at least seventy-five yards from the shop and it was a small bell. Nobody could hear a bell ring at that distance — except Crock. And he wouldn't have been able to hear it without the assistance of Sonny and Cher. That's what he'd named the hearing aids that translated the garbled noise produced by his strange hearing loss into recognizable sounds and the staccato, missing-key-sounds of speech into words.

And protected him from speech he couldn't stand to hear.

He shook his head. No. Wouldn't go there. Absolutely would not go *there*.

A dead fish floating down stream bumped into the cork that hadn't bobbed once since Crock sat down. Looked like somebody's started cleaning it — a smallmouth bass, probably— and then threw it back in. Croc jiggled his line up and down.

"Here, fishy, fishy, fishy. Come to papa. I already invited Linc and Jenny over for supper and you wouldn't want me to serve them Charlie the Tuna, now would you?"

Crock fancied himself something of a chef, if he did say so himself, and he'd bought two bags full of groceries when he was in Bradford's Ridge on Monday so he could make his special Cajun rice dish along with a couple of other mouth-watering original concoctions. He wished Jack could have taken off early. Then Crock and Linc could have given him a real sendoff. Not that Daniel Burke — *Reverend* Daniel Burke — was a wet blanket or anything like that. Still, three off-duty law enforcement officers would bring their own special spin to the celebration. But Jack wouldn't have had his head in the game if he had come down early. Who could blame him? He was about to make his own fantasy come true.

Crock smiled at the thought. Jack Carpenter was about to make Becca Hawkins his bride. About dad-gum time!

The cork lay still in the slow-moving current as another half-cleaned fish, a yellow sunfish, floated by.

Chapter Two

THERE WAS a big pile of rocks on the top of the mountain — that's where it got the name, Rocky Top Mountain. The rock pile was right up next to the edge of the flat rock face that sliced down the mountainside all the way into the meadow a thousand feet below. She'd asked her daddy how it'd got there. He'd told her some fantastic story about giants fighting with slingshots and how one of them had piled up those rocks for ammunition. The pile was twice as tall as their barn, but it was easy to climb because it rose in a gentle slant in the back that ended in one really big boulder at the top that Daddy had to lift her up onto and then climb up behind her.

The view always took her breath away. Maybe this was all God's creation like Daddy said. He'd brought his Bible, of course, and read out loud from it — usually from the Psalms that he said were written by a young boy who herded sheep. Then they'd pray and Daddy would thank God for all that lay before them and for all that he'd provided.

They'd just got to the thanking-God part when the boulder started to move. It was only a small movement, not enough to make them lose their balance. But Daddy stopped in mid-sentence.

"Did you feel—?"

"The rock move? Yeah."

Daddy looked puzzled but not alarmed then. Not yet.

The next time the rock moved it was a jolting jerk that knocked them both down.

"Run!" Daddy cried. "Get off the rocks."

She hadn't ever got down off the big one by herself, but she jumped to another rock about three feet below it, then to another lower one and was scrambling down off it to the flat place where Daddy stood to lift her up. Daddy was waiting on the top rock to be sure she'd made it before he turned around and climbed down himself.

Then the rocks moved again, all of them, shook and trembled. Daddy had gotten to his feet from his knees and the movement knocked him off balance and he dropped his Bible. Natalie saw him reach for it and then the rocks began to roll and tumble and he was gone.

She didn't even have time to cry, "Daddy!"

The rocks were rolling around like marbles instead of boulders, rolling toward the edge of the cliff. And she tried to keep her balance, tried to jump from one rock to the next to get off the pile, but they were moving too fast and she wasn't quick enough.

She didn't see the pile of them sail out off the edge of the cliff, not *rolling off* but like … like they'd been shook off by the ground beneath, like they were water droplets flying off a dog when it shakes off after it falls in the creek. That's the way the other folks described it. Bob Young, who lived on the farm next door, heard a rumble and looked up and said he saw the mountain move, saw it shake and send the rocks flying off the edge. Beverly Bridges watched it from her kitchen window and described it the same way.

But Natalie didn't see that part. She'd been knocked down before she could get off the moving pile and was crushed to death by the avalanche that buried her daddy beneath thousands of tons of rock in the meadow at the base of the cliff face.

Caverna County Sheriff Hezekiah Lincoln pushed his hat back on his head and wiped the sweat off his forehead with the back of his hand. Linc was a stocky man, squat, built like a fire hydrant with reddish-brown hair in a semi-circle around a bald dome hidden by his hat, and deep-set eyes beneath heavy black eyebrows. Behind the affable, hound dog face was something approaching a photographic memory — in his line of work both a blessing and a curse — and a keen mind.

Jack Carpenter, a police sergeant in Harrelton, Ohio, just outside Cincinnati, had told him once, "Any man smart enough to realize he doesn't have all the answers is on an intellectual level way above the average person."

Linc certainly didn't have all the answers today. And right now he was having trouble even forming the questions. He only had a few seconds to pull himself together before the chaos. It would erupt like the contents of a soft drink can all shook up and left to sit in the heat as soon as his deputies got a look at this, unless he was settled and professional. He was in charge, or would be until the boys from the Kentucky State Police arrived. It was his job to keep the wheels on until then, to make sure everything was left just as he found it, nothing touched. This was no longer the bedroom where a sixteen-year-old junior at Caverna County High School, Denise Holterman, had been sleeping, a girl whose worst problem up until — how long ago? An hour? Two? — had been getting a zit on her nose on prom night. This was a crime scene.

And wouldn't be no prom night now. Not for Denise. No prom night or wedding or first baby. Not unless they found the rest of her — alive somehow — and he didn't have any hope at all that they would. You didn't chop off somebody's hand and leave it propped up on a pillow, with the fingers positioned in that universal gesture, if you intended to let her live. The wound was clean, slick. The blade that made it had been incredibly sharp. No, Denise Holterman was dead by now. And somewhere down deep in his bowels, Linc knew that was the good news. Because if she wasn't, he didn't like to imagine what was happening to that child.

Linc heard Deputy Carl Heff step up into the doorway behind him, heard the sudden intake of breath and prayed the boy wouldn't spray his breakfast all over the floor.

"What the—?" His speech was garbled after that but at least he was talking and not puking.

Linc turned to him, his face stern. And he gave the same look to the other two deputies who had appeared in the hallway but hadn't gotten as far as Carl.

"Stop right where you are," he said. He was grateful his voice was steady, didn't reveal the turmoil inside him. "Don't take another step."

The two deputies froze, but Carl was looking over Linc's shoulder into the room and Linc figured he probably hadn't heard a word.

"Now turn around and walk back out of the house just like you come in. Imagine there's flour on the floor and you're trying to put your feet right back in the tracks you made. You haven't touched anything — have you? Anything at all?"

"Well, I—" Bob Sirrine began and then stopped when he caught sight of the look on Linc's face.

"Spit it out, boy. What'd you touch?"

"Nothing — I mean, I just moved that vase."

Linc groaned. There had been a vase in the floor in the living room, flowers spilling out of it in a puddle on the carpet — the first sign that something wasn't right here. Maybe the killer had knocked that vase over, and praise God and all the archangels, it was even possible he'd touched it, tried to keep it from tipping over off the coffee table so it wouldn't make any noise to announce his presence. He'd come in the front door — had used a glass cutter to remove the middle pane of glass in the row of little windows beside the front door, then reached in and unlocked the deadbolt.

"I didn't touch it, though," Bob continued. "Not with my hand, I mean. I just moved it out of the way with the toe of my shoe, that's all."

Linc let out the breath he had sucked in for the tongue-lashing he'd been about to administer.

"Nothing else?" he demanded. "Not a door frame, the handrail on the stairs — anything?"

The front door was already a lost cause, unless the forensics boys from the state could lift the killer's fingerprints out from under his own fingerprints and those of Denise's father, who'd found the ... hand ... when he came over to get Denise for a dentist appointment. She'd been housesitting for her grandmother, Martha Holterman, looking after her tribe of cats and feeding her birds and fish while Martha was attending a wedding in Chicago. Her parents hadn't been sure about leaving a sixteen-year-old alone in that big old house, but they were just a phone call away, a couple of miles down the road, and Martha was only going to be gone three days. What could possibly happen in three days? Herbert Holterman had told Linc that in one long hysterical babble and then they'd had to haul him off in an ambulance. God only knew what all else he'd touched.

Both men shook their heads like little bobblehead dolls. And if he was lucky, they were even telling the truth. Not that they'd have lied, but it's hard to remember every little movement — when you were still so new at the job that nothing had yet become automatic. Linc had been nudging doors open with his elbow for years.

Carl was still looking past Linc into the room.

"You sure?" Linc demanded, a little louder than he'd intended. Another bobblehead wobble. "Fine, then get out of here — careful like I said." Bob and Thomas Conner turned on their heels and hurried back down the hall and down the stairs.

Carl remained where he was standing, looking into the bedroom at what he could see from the partially opened door — that Linc had nudged open with his elbow.

"Carl?" Linc said.

"Who does that? That kind of thing? Cut off a kid's hand and kidnap her or ..." His eyes raked over the shambles of a room that looked like it'd been the scene of the Texas Chainsaw Massacre. Blood everywhere, stunk like a jar full of wet pennies ... even a drip of it dried on the ceiling light fixture in the middle of the room. "Or take her *body*—?"

Linc took Carl by the shoulders and turned him away from the door and pushed him a step or two down the hallway.

"You don't suppose this has anything to do with Charlie or Miss Christine … I mean three disappearances in—"

"Time for those kinds of questions later and we won't be the ones asking them," Linc said.

But he'd already been asking them, of course. Other people undoubtedly would, too, as soon as word got out about what'd happened here. And given the grapevine in Caverna County, there probably wasn't more than half a dozen people who hadn't heard already. A lot of bad things happened in this county. Always had and it seemed to Linc that everyone in the whole county seemed to know all about whatever it was faster than there was any explanation for.

Charlie Brooker was a drunk but couldn't technically be called homeless because he did have a little shack out by the junkyard that had never had indoor plumbing and the electric company had long since cut the power to it. But he wandered the streets of Bradford's Ridge like he was homeless, slept in the alley behind the furniture store where there was sometimes a discarded couch or mattress and almost always big, sturdy cardboard boxes beside the dumpster. Or up against the building behind the bushes at the convent, where he could always count on food and usually a place to clean up and take a bath, if he was so inclined, which he seldom was. Linc had a soft spot for Charlie because the fall from accountant to drunk was a long one with a rock-hard landing at the end. Linc had stopped drinking years ago — because he sensed a growing dependence on it, and with the good judgment and strength of character that marked the rest of his life, he was determined to set it aside *before* he had a problem. Every time he saw Charlie, a little voice began the refrain, "There but for the grace of God …"

The thing was, Linc hadn't seen Charlie in a while — couldn't pinpoint exactly how long. Come to find out, neither had anybody else. There hadn't been a "missing person's" report filed or anything that official. But after four or five days, folks started remarking about his absence and Linc had spent part of an afternoon checking out his regular haunts. Charlie was nowhere to be found.

Neither was Christine Lajewski.

But what possible connection could there be between a missing Charlie, the bloodless disappearance yesterday of an old lady with Alzheimer's out of her front yard, in broad daylight, and the butchery that'd gone on in this bedroom in the black pit of night? Simplest explanation was that Charlie was sleeping off a drunk somewhere and Miss Christine Lajewski had just wandered off. Heaven knows he'd tracked down more than a few old people who thought they were walking home from school, or were out looking for the little dog they'd had fifty years ago that'd run away. What was it Crock always said, "Think horse, not zebra." No reason to go looking for some sinister plot …

But Miss Christine'd disappeared like a puff of smoke. Nobody'd seen her wandering down the road or across a field. They'd searched the woods for two miles in every direction from her house and found nothing.

She'd spent the night somewhere. Wouldn't have died of exposure even if she'd just curled up under a tree. But the hills was steep around her farm. He couldn't imagine her being able to climb them and get out of that hollow. So where'd she go?

His gut ... his cop's instinct ... had already been sending him signals before the dispatcher rushed into his office this morning before he'd even had a chance to drink his morning coffee and announced in something approaching hysteria, *Denise Holterman's gone, or dead, or been kidnapped or ... her daddy found her hand ...*

Now the buzz of the instinct was so loud it sounded like a bush full of cicadas.

"The state police will be the ones looking for answers," he told Deputy Heff. "Right now, our only job is to get out of here — we shouldn't even be breathing this air."

He'd said it for emphasis, but the truth was he wished they hadn't breathed the air, that when the team from the Kentucky State Police Forensic Lab showed up, the house and the air inside it had been just as the killer had left it. Because Linc had smelled *something* as soon as he walked into the house and the scent was much stronger in the bloody bedroom. It was an odd, unpleasant smell he couldn't place. No one else seemed to notice, but his deputies were on such sensory overload they could have stuck their heads into a bouquet of a dozen roses and not smelled a single petal. But what Linc'd smelled wasn't roses, not by a long shot. He inhaled deeply, struggled to smell it again, so maybe he could place it. But either he'd gotten so used to it he couldn't smell it anymore or the smell was gone. He hoped it wasn't gone. Linc dearly wanted the forensics team to get a whiff of what he had.

He heard them then. Sirens. The wail of multiple sirens in the distance getting closer and closer. Sometimes, Linc thought that was the most comforting sound in the world. Like a bugle announcing the cavalry's coming, help's on the way. Everything's going to be fine — you're safe now. But other times — and this was one of those times — he thought that sirens wailing when there was no hurry, when there was nobody to save … the only thing lonelier and sadder-sounding was "Amazing Grace" when they played it with bagpipes at the funeral of a police officer.

Without a backward glance, Linc followed Deputy Heff down the hallway, watching to make sure he didn't touch anything — in the normal automatic places like the knob of the stair railing — the killer might also have unconsciously touched. He didn't need to look back at the room. His mind had photographed it in minute detail, down to the fuzzy pink house shoe with blood smeared on it sitting at the foot of the bed and half a dozen white worms lying dead in the blood beside it. Maggots.

Maggots again.

He'd be able to reproduce the image of that room with the clarity of a digital photograph if he had to, which he wouldn't. His mind was like that. It helped a lot — *a lot* — in his line of work. But there were downsides to everything. He would also never be able to forget that room, either, would picture it every day for the rest of his life.

When he stepped down off the porch of Martha Holterman's house, he heard a sudden cry from the radios of all three of his sheriff department cruisers parked in the gravel driveway in front of the house.

"Ten-thirty-three," came the same voice from the three radios. "All units report to Rocky Top Mountain, ten-thirty-nine."

Ten-thirty-three — emergency. Ten-thirty-nine — lights and siren. The sheriff moved fast for a short, stout man and he was inside his crusader in seconds, the mic of his radio to his mouth.

"What do you mean ten-thirty-three?" he said. Using his radio to respond made their conversation private.

"That was all I knew to say," dispatcher Vicky Perkins

told him. "There isn't a code for … it's a landslide … or rockslide. On the south side of Rocky Top Mountain. Maureen Karrick called it in, hysterical, said to send help, that Aaron and Natalie were in it."

"*In* it?"

"Buried under the rock."

Chapter Three

Jonah Ballard seen it with his very own eyes, a pure-D miracle sent direct from God his own self.

He was out squirrel hunting when it happened. Best way to catch sight of a squirrel long enough to draw a bead on it was first thing in the morning, just after sunup and he surely did need some squirrel meat. Jonah lived off the land using the bounty the good Lord served up for him. The fat rabbits he'd got three days ago had just sat right there and let him shoot 'em, like they was bottles in one of them carnival shows he seen once in Taylorsville. But squirrels was different, couldn't count on them to wait for you to shoot 'em and if Jonah didn't get something there'd be no meat on his table for supper.

The woods was dark so he kept to the edge, out in the meadow, his eyes scanning the trees the sun was lighting up as it climbed up into the world on the other side of the mountain. He seen a squirrel, a big fat one, just standing on a limb looking back the direction Jonah had come, like he could see something there that so startled him he couldn't do nothing but stare. It was so odd, Jonah didn't even shoot the squirrel, just looked back over his shoulder to see what it was the squirrel was looking at. Wasn't nothing there but Rocky Top Mountain. He could see it clear from the meadow beneath where the cliff was sheared off on the side, like God'd took a butter knife and sliced down on it. The rock pile on the top of it as visible, too. And though it as too far away for him to see, Jonah knew that Pastor Aaron and his little girl, Natalie, was up there so the pastor could pray.

Guilt stabbed into Jonah's heart then. Pastor Aaron was a good man, a fine man after God's own heart, just like Jonah should have been, could have been if it wasn't for his weak will, for his lack of faith. He give in to the voices that whispered in his ear, give in to the sin of drink and the sin of lust and the sin of lying and the sin of … well, all the sins, and he didn't figure a man like Aaron Karrick ever give in to nothin'. Pastor Aaron was the minister of the Love of God Holiness Church where Jonah was just a deacon. But Jonah did aspire to be an elder someday, when he got his carnal urges under control like the circuit preacher said the last Sunday he'd preached in his six-week cycle, before Pastor Aaron took over. That preacher'd said carnal urges was the downfall of man and them that give in to 'em was lost.

It occurred to Jonah then that maybe he'd ought to start every day in a high place, talking to God the way Pastor Aaron done. Truth was, Jonah always meant to pray, but seemed like every time he tried he'd hear voices in his head directing him to do other things. Normal things like, "Not now, Jonah, you got them tomatoes to plant." But mostly it wasn't ordinary things. Mostly it was sinful things the voices spoke of, made the urges he felt seem almost good, certainly normal and nothing a man ought to deny, nothing God would want a man to deny. Maybe

Pastor Aaron was so holy because he got right with the Lord soon's he got out of bed every morning and let God take a hold of him and guide him the rest of the day. Jonah looked up at that pile of rocks that was all lit up by the morning sun and purposed right then to do what Pastor Aaron done every morning so's he'd be right with God and—

The mountains shook.

Jonah seen it shake!

The .22 in his hands slipped out of his grip and fell to the dirt as Jonah watched, looked at what the squirrel had been looking at. He'd have missed it all if God hadn't sent that squirrel to tell Jonah, *turn around, man, see my glory, my majesty, my power.*

The mountain shook again. It was the oddest thing Jonah'd ever seen. Wasn't no way to describe it — the mountain moved. The trees on the sides of it swayed with the movement and the rocks …

The rockpile. Jonah's eye shot to the pile of rocks where Pastor Aaron and little Natalie was praying and seen the rocks commence to roll from the movement of the mountain. Then it happened and Jonah lost his breath and fell to his knees in fear and wonder. The mountain shook and flung the rocks off the top. They didn't roll down the side like they shoulda done when the earth beneath them moved. That'd a'made sense. A pile of rocks would fall over in an earthquake.

That wasn't what happened, though. Them rocks didn't just roll away, or roll toward the edge of the cliff and fall off it. Them rocks was *flung off that mountaintop.* The movement of the mountain was so violent and abrupt that the rocks sailed out into the air like they didn't weigh nothing at all, like they wasn't nothing more'n a handful of marbles a little kid had tossed away.

Jonah watched in wonder and horror as the rocks sailed out away from the mountain, then dropped toward the meadow below, rained down on the meadow in a thunderous rumble.

The intake of air was so violent, Jonah began to cough and his eyes watered, so he was looking at the pile of rocks in the meadow and the dust rising up from them through a blur of tears. Voices in his head was shouting so loud it was almost like they was saying words he could hear with his ears. And maybe they were. They told him God hadn't just flung them rocks off the mountain. God had flung *Pastor Aaron* off the mountain. God had smitten him down in wrath, in an anger so powerful it moved a mountain.

Them voices was right. Had to be. That was the only explanation. Aaron Karrick wasn't the man everybody thought he was. His sins before the God of the Universe must have been vile indeed, his heart black as the coal they dug out of the mountain. He must have joined up with the forces of whispering evil in ways nobody ever saw. Nobody but God. God saw. And God punished.

Jonah had sat there on his knees, tremblin' and cryin' and listenin' to the voices in his head that told him God hadn't been pleased with Pastor Aaron's offer of goodness, that God had wanted more, that God was going to rain down judgement on all the world just like he'd done on Pastor Aaron, that God's wrath was going to smite the sinners and wipe them off the earth. Like he'd done Pastor Aaron Karrick. Even took the preacher's little girl with him to the grave.

Then Jonah went running, left his .22 there in the dirt and had to go back and get it later. He just ran to his neighbors — going from one member of the little congregation of Love of God Holiness Church to the next, telling them what he seen — if they hadn't seen it with they own eyes like Lee Wheatley had. He'd been coming in from milking his two cows and looked up and seen the same thing Jonah did. Not that Jonah needed a confirmation. He knew a miracle when he seen one and wasn't no force on the earth coulda done what he seen except God.

All the people he told could tell from the awe and wonder on Jonah's face that it was all coming to pass, that the end was nigh, that they had better get they hearts right and their souls clean and be ready to meet their Maker on Judgement Day.

The Day of the Coming of the Lord was at hand.

THE DARKNESS WAS as soft as a caress and the Ugly Man traveled through it as silently as a shark through a cold Arctic sea. He needed no flashlight, though he carried one in his pocket. He'd taken it out of a kitchen drawer in the old hag's house, but not for his own use. He could see after a fashion in the absolute blackness, like a blind cave fish or cave cricket. What his senses recorded were white objects on a black background, like a photograph negative. It was very little different from what he saw when he was outside in the moonlight. He avoided the sun. Hated the sun. Outside at night, he saw light and puddles of dark shadow, a black-and-white world. He tried to remember what color looked like, but couldn't.

The darkness itself was all the prison he needed for his victims. He needed no bars or handcuffs to restrain them because they couldn't go anywhere in the black. Just sat there, looking scared and confused. Huddled together the way they were when he left them.

A stinky old drunk all cuddled up with a crazy woman who probably thought she was Mary Poppins or the queen of England. At least the old drunk had wits about him enough to be scared, to know that what was happening to him was terrible and likely to get a whole lot worse.

He was right about that. Maybe the Ugly Man should have tee shirts made for the two of them — just the two, the teenager wouldn't live long enough to need one. He could print on the front in letters they couldn't read in the dark: "It sucks to be me."

Or he could print orders to the waiter, "Serve mine — *me!* — well done. Black and charred on the outside and pink in the middle."

He didn't know if their bodies would still be pink in the middle, though. Maybe. Hot dogs stayed pink in the middle when you held them over a flame — like he was going to do with these people, one at a time and watch them squeal. So did marshmallows — not pink, but still soft and gooey in the middle when the outside was charred black. That's probably how the people would be — still gooey in the middle.

He wouldn't have to wonder much longer. He'd find out for himself as soon as he'd gathered them all up, picked them off one at a time until he'd snatched the whole lot. As soon as he had sane people in his prison, they could talk to each other in the dark and he could listen in because they wouldn't know he was there. He could hear them talk about how scared they were, try to figure out what was happening to them — maybe even try to come up with a plan to escape.

Escape plans didn't work. The Ugly Man knew. He knew that, alright.

They might smell him, even if they couldn't see him, but that was part of the fun — them trying to figure out what in the world they was smelling.

He'd tell them before he burned them. He'd make sure

they knew exactly how they'd got where they was and what he intended to do with them. Then he'd leave them alone — at least they'd think they was alone because they couldn't see him in the dark — so they could think about it, picture in their heads what it was gonna be like to burn alive.

As he drew nearer to the spot where he'd left the captives, he began to hear it. A strange, keening sound, like some animal with its foot caught in a trap, the iron jaws biting into its flesh. It took him a moment to figure out what it was. The old lady was crying. Or howling. Or baying at the moon maybe. She could talk, form words and sentences, crazy stuff like she said as he carried her away through the trees.

"My dog will chew your leg off if you don't put me down," she'd said once. She had no dog.

"Are you the young man they sent to fix my cable TV box?" she'd said another time. And she'd asked him if the bus was late, said it better not be because she needed to go to the bathroom. Then she'd peed on him.

As soon as he had them in sight, he moved as silent as a breeze across a still pond, and they never knew he was there until he was only a few feet away.

Then he made his own horrifying sound, far more terrible than the old woman's tears. It was a garbled grunt growl, that carried in the sound hate and menace and corrupt intent as unmistakable as words would have been. He couldn't use words anymore.

And they jumped when they heard it, so terrified they crashed into each other in the dark and lay together in a tangled heap on the cave floor.

He approached the cowering pair and dumped the bleeding carcass of the teenage girl right on top of them, watched the old drunk scuttle away sideways like a beach crab he seen on a sandy beach in the Bahamas. In another world, another life.

"What is that? Who are you?" the drunk cried.

"What are we doing here? What do you want with us?" The old hag wanted to know. He'd have told them if he could have because the dreading it was as painful as the act was going to be. People suffered as much from being afraid as they did of whatever they were afraid of.

The Ugly Man grunted and rumbled and growled and the two conscious people on the ground turned toward the sound and began begging and pleading for him to let them go. He'd let them go when he burned them alive. But that was not now, not yet. He had invited others to this little party and it wouldn't start until every one of the guests was here.

Right now, there was the girl, though. The girl and her warm blood.

He picked her up off the floor and the tangle of bodies and carried her a short distance away. Then he sat down with her on his lap and loosened the tourniquet he'd put on her arm. When the blood began to flow again, he rubbed the warm liquid all over his hands and face. Then he began to lap it up with his tongue.

LINC DIDN'T HAVE much time to think on the drive to Rocky Top Mountain. It was only a couple of miles away and he flew down a narrow road that must once have been a cow trail ambling through the hollow — the only explanation he could come up with for the random twists and turns. The locals drove these roads at two speeds. Either flat out, pedal to the metal, because they'd driven them every day of their lives and could negotiate the corners in their sleep. Or so slow they'd have backed up traffic for miles, if there'd been any traffic.

Linc came up behind a pickup truck with a dresser, headboard and mattress tied down in the back. It was poking along, the driver ignoring the flashing lights and siren. Linc took his life in his hands and passed the truck in a blind curve, and received a toothless smile and a how-ya-doin' two-fingered wave from the driver.

What time Linc did have, he tried to order thoughts tossing around in his mind like clothes in a dryer, tried to figure out what it was about the "kidnapping" of the teenager that so unnerved him. It wasn't like he had never seen a grizzly crime scene in eleven years as sheriff. The bad ones always made him question his decision to run for the office more than a decade ago. It wasn't like he'd always wanted to be a police officer, studied and trained and prepared for it. He'd been an insurance salesman, for crying out loud. But he'd seen the corruption in county government, and it offended the unfailing sense of right and wrong planted in a young boy's heart whose bum had been on a church pew every Sunday morning, Sunday night and Wednesday nights for prayer meeting.

Linc had gotten elected on a "clean up county govern-ment" platform which absolutely wouldn't have carried the day, given that there were deputies at all the polling places reminding voters going in which side their bread was buttered on and coming out that there'd be free beer at the sheriff's victory party after the polls closed. But it was Linc's good fortune that the alcoholic former sheriff had been busted for driving under the influence of intoxicants — blew a 2.0, which was more than twice the legal limit — in a neighboring county the day before the election. Even then, he'd only been able to eke out a five-hundred-vote victory — with the incumbent in jail on election day.

Then Linc set about cleaning house, firing the deputies who'd all been related in some way to the former sheriff and turning the department into a real law enforcement agency — rather than the good-ole-boy, slap-you-on-the-back, we-can-fix-your-tickets sham it'd been ... which, in truth, mirrored just about every other sheriff's department in the state. The only real police force had been the Kentucky State Police, whose officers were spread so thin across their three- and four-county jurisdictions, rural citizens were heavily armed, knew they had to protect their own, couldn't wait for help from the state police or they'd be dead so long the bodies would be cold by the time a gray-uniformed trooper stepped out of his cruiser in their driveway.

He'd endured a four-hour round trip commute every night to attend classes at Eastern Kentucky University's famed school of law enforcement and earned a degree in only three years. After that, he'd attended every seminar, class and training program offered anywhere in the state, became something of a legend in the law enforcement community, who didn't grant respect to "elected" police easily. He'd gradually hired competent, trained deputies and ran his department "by the book."

Oh, he knew, just like everybody else in the county did, that Caverna County was the toughest, most violent, crime-ridden county in the state. He'd known the day he unloaded a moving van in front of the little house on Maywood Street, where he still lived, that there was something ... *bad* ... about the place. And he'd been fighting that "bad" every day of his life since.

And then, last fall, he'd discovered what he was really up against, had seen true, unmitigated evil in the face of an eight-year-old boy who had murdered one of his deputies *in his own office!* He'd helped ordinary people go to war against that evil, against demon-possessed children, and against some kind of devil hidden away deep in the caves under the county. He hadn't asked many questions about what'd happened when it was all over — some things in life you were a whole lot better off *not* knowing — but he knew enough to understand that they had somehow beat back an evil that threatened the lives of everyone in the county, the evil that had been the source of some of the most violent "badness" in Caverna County history. He knew they'd won, Jack, Daniel, Crock and the others. But there was still the lingering fear that maybe the evil might return someday.

That was what had so unnerved him about the bloody crime scene he'd just left. There was an evil … smell to it. Literally. He knew that was the source of the foreboding he'd felt from the moment he walked into that bloody bedroom. And he had to admit — it scared him to death.

Chapter Four

CROCK COULDN'T FIGURE it out. He'd always been able to catch fish here. Usually couldn't get his hook re-bated fast enough to haul them all in.

Today, zip.

Maybe some little bugger had nibbled the worm off his hook so carefully he hadn't detected the movement. He began to reel in the line so he could check as another dead fish floated by, its guts trailing along in the water, a big one, must have been ten inches long. Who throws a fish that big back into the river half-cleaned?

"See what happens when you don't eat the worms Papa so generously provides you?" he said to his unseen marine audience as the hook broke the surface of the water below the cork and he could see the worm still there, threaded on the hook like a sock on a foot.

He started to toss the line back out into the water.

Two more dead fish floated by.

That was odd. He looked upstream, but could only see about a hundred yards and then the river took a sharp bend to the right there.

Nothing.

He'd just have to come up with some bait more enticing, that was all. He laid the pole on the ground and turned sideways in his chair so he could see down into his bait can, where crickets of all sizes and all manner of other creepy-crawly critters were trying to get out.

Andi Burke, Daniel Burke's eleven-year-old daughter, had pronounced sentence on the whole sport of fishing the first time she looked down into the cooled metal boxes that held the bait in Ike's shop.

"Ewwwww." She wrinkled up her freckled nose. "That's gross!"

"Watch what you say, little girl," he'd told her. "Crickets are sensitive creatures and it isn't hard at all to hurt one's feelings."

"And you have to … *touch* those things, stick a hook in them?"

When he'd nodded his head, she dropped the lid back down with a clunk and announced that if her daddy and Uncle Crock wanted to go fishing that was fine with her, but *she* was going blackberry picking.

Crock reached into the can and selected a fat cricket and affixed it solidly to the hook.

And the look on that child's face when he and Daniel had *cleaned* the fish …

He smiled at the memory as he picked up his fishing rod and turned back toward the river to toss in the more enticing bait. The smile drained off his face and left it blank with shock.

At first, his mind refused to register what he saw.

It couldn't possibly be … what in the world …?

He closed his eyes and slowly willed the impossibility to be gone when he opened them.

It was still there. The whole river was full of dead fish. *Full!*

He dropped his rod in surprise and struggled to his feet, ignoring the stab of pain in his bad knee.

The river was *jammed* with dead fish, *clogged* with them, a solid mass stretching from one shore to the other. He couldn't tell what kind of fish they were — bluegill, channel cats, crappie, bass — because the only thing he could see was their guts. Somebody had ... but that was impossible. It was the only explanation, though — somebody had started cleaning the fish, got down to the guts, but instead of taking the guts out of the bodies, they's just thrown the fish back into the river.

Only that couldn't be. There were too many of them. Nobody could have ... why would somebody? He could make no sense of what he saw — which was a river so jammed with half-cleaned fish that they were piled on top of each other like cordwood, leaving a snail trail of dead bodies scraped off the mass along the shoreline where the water was shallow.

Crock's mouth went dry and a sudden irrational panic seized him and he backed up from the riverbank until he tripped over a tree root and landed hard on his backside in the dirt, watching the parade of death move inexorably past him.

Had something killed them all? Electricity? A power line down in the water would send voltage ... how far? He didn't know. Besides, wouldn't a downed line short out somehow? It wouldn't just continue to send electricity through the water until somebody turned off the power ... would it? It'd take a lot of shock to kill that many fish.

And that didn't explain the condition they were in — *guts hanging out.*

Poison, maybe. Some kind of pollutant? But what? As

far as he knew, and he wasn't a local so he couldn't be sure, but from what he did know there was nothing industrial anywhere upstream. The Three Forks River ran through farms and woods, no factories.

Some kind of disease? Now he was getting out there into the hinterlands, the far reaches of possibility. They all got a bad cold, like the germ that killed all the aliens in *War of the Worlds*, and died at the same time? Right.

Then he got hurriedly to his feet and ran — well, hobbled — toward the bend in the river upstream, where a stretch of river almost half a mile long would be visible. He broke through the trees and stood there, panting. Not from exertion. From ... what? Fear.

The whole river for as far as he could see was a solid mass of dead, *gutted* fish, looked like you could walk across them to the other side. He stood there until his knees gave way and he sank down in the dirt.

Time passed. How long, Crock couldn't say. He could do nothing but stare as the funeral cortege flowed slowly past. Eventually, the stream of dead bodies began to thin out. No longer a solid mass but islands, clots of bodies moving on top of the muddy water. Then the islands became individual fish. The spaces between them lengthened. Now, only a few.

Crock sat where he was until the river was unclogged again, the only indication that anything out of the ordinary had occurred were the remnants of the herd, dead fish stuck to brush or grounded up close to the riverbank. The line of them, matching silver stripes, stretched down both sides of the river.

The stabbing pain from his bad knee finally drove a nail into his consciousness, and Crock got slowly, laboriously to his feet, holding onto a low tree branch for support. He couldn't drag his eyes away from the river.

Something had killed those fish. And then … it had gutted them. Whatever it was, it'd killed them all. Crock was certain there could not possibly be a single live fish left in the whole length of the Three Forks.

He shook himself, reluctantly crawled back into the official "Major Crocker" so he could think strategically. That was *hard*. Here in the warm July sunshine, with a silly hat on his head where he'd stuck hooks like porcupine quills, his police officer persona fit strange and it didn't have anything to do with the ten or so pounds he'd gained that'd stretched his uniform jacket over his expanding middle. Yet another reason passing his annual physical would be a challenge this year.

He didn't have to revert totally to police officer mode. It wasn't his problem to figure out what was going on here. He just needed to report it to the proper authorities and let them sort it out.

The Three Forks River was the single largest tributary that fed into Rolling Fork Lake and if the dead fish were sick, they could infect the whole fish population of the lake. That would be catastrophic. The lake was huge.

He'd left his cell phone on the desk in the "office" of the bait shop, which consisted of a room roughly the size of a broom closet that had a stool in front of a small table and rows of wooden cubbyholes that'd obviously been lifted from a post office — maybe even acquired legally, though Crock doubted it.

He trudged back down the riverbank to the spot where he'd left his chair, fishing pole and bait can. Reluctant as he was to touch them, he went down to the edge of the water and selected several fish — different sizes, though it was impossible to tell what kind of fish they were by looking at their guts! He put the fish in the collapsible fish basket he'd planned to use for the fish he hadn't caught.

Gathering up his tackle box and rod, he slowly climbed the hill to the bait shop and went around to the back to the fish-cleaning table. It was equipped with a hose to wash guts off down a slanted chute at the end, made out of a house gutter, into a big bucket that usually smelled like it hadn't been emptied since the Eisenhower Administration.

He went inside and washed his hands after he dropped the fish on the table, even used a squirt of hand sanitizer — maybe the fish were sick — picked up his phone and googled the Kentucky Fish and Wildlife Department under state government offices. He had a hard time snagging the internet, and when he placed the call there was a spotty connection — sounded like his own hearing sans hearing aids.

When he was finally routed to the right administrator, the woman who took his call was professional and interested. Yes, they *did* want to know about any fish kill — especially one the size he was reporting. She'd even managed to keep the skepticism out of her voice when she asked questions about what he'd seen. Maybe it'd helped that he'd dropped into the conversation that he was a major in the Harrelton, Ohio Police Department — translate that: not some crackpot crying wolf over a dead minnow.

The woman took down his contact information and said they'd be sending out a ranger first thing in the morning.

Crock used the phone again to text the sheriff to suggest alternate dinner plans for him and his daughter, then dropped the phone into the front pocket of his shirt and went back outside to the cleaning table where he'd left the fish from the river.

He opened his tackle box and took out his fish-cleaning knife, a Dexter-Russell Model 1377, which was regarded as the workhorse of fish-cleaning equipment. Its seven-inch blade was long and flexible, to follow the curve of a fish's backbone and ribs, but stiff enough to cut through small bones and tough skin. Made of high-carbon steel, it was sharpened to a razor edge. It had been Crock's gift to himself for Christmas.

With a practiced hand, Crock slid the knife into the fish and sliced cleanly down it from one end to the other. Then he pulled open the sides of the incision to see what was inside.

Stared at what he found, gaping.

What the …?

He picked up another fish and did the same thing. With the same result. Another fish and another, half a dozen before he put the knife down and stepped back, breathing hard.

What he saw inside the fish, the same in all of them, was crazy impossible. He didn't know how to think about it.

What he saw *inside* the fish … was the *outside* of the fish. When he sliced them open, he found their outer skin, complete with scales, gills, fins and a tail.

The outside was on the inside. And the inside was on the outside.

Something had turned thousands of fish wrong side out.

BECAUSE HE'D ONLY BEEN a few miles away, Linc was among the first responders to the Code ten-thirty-three the dispatcher had sent out to the three community fire departments and the Caverna County Rescue Squad — all manned by volunteers and the Caverna County Ambulance Service to the scene that at least had paid, licensed paramedics, though the emergency medical technicians, EMTs, were volunteers. All the volunteers had been trained and certified and were surprisingly good at their jobs — but they still had to drop whatever they were doing on their day jobs — bagging groceries, or building houses or milking cows — to answer the call when their beepers went off.

Beepers had gone off in dozens of pockets and not one of the volunteers who responded was prepared for what they saw when they arrived. Neither was Linc. Lying in a meadow at the base of a sheer cliff face on top of Rocky Top Mountain was a pile of boulders, rocks and debris that wouldn't have fit on the football field at Caverna County High School and was piled up twenty, maybe thirty feet high. Shoot, the dust hadn't even completely settled out of the air yet.

Linc got out of his cruiser, shading his eyes as he looked up at the now bare mountaintop and crossed the grass toward the rock pile, where a handful of people — neighbors who'd seen or heard the landslide and members of one community's fire department — were digging frantically, trying to get to a man and his daughter they all knew in their hearts could not possibly still be alive.

A skinny man named Jack Baumgardner spotted him crossing the clearing and raced toward him, babbling as he ran.

"You never seen nothing like it in your life, Linc, I swear to God you ain't," he said, arriving in front of Linc breathless. "Them boulders come flying off that mountaintop like they's fired out of a cannon."

"You saw the landslide?"

"Wasn't no landslide, I'm telling you! Them rocks didn't roll down the mountain. They was … shook off it, like. I seen the mountain move. I ain't making this up. I ain't. The trees swayed. Some kinda earthquake, I guess, 'cause I didn't feel no tremor and I's less than a mile away."

"I didn't feel nothing neither," said Ryan Miller, who lived next door to Jack and had come up behind him to talk to Linc. Ryan had been in his front yard collecting yesterday's junk mail out of the mailbox with the house partially blocking his view and Jack had gone out back to take the remains of last night's dinner to the compost heap. "Close as we was, we couldn't see the rocks on the mountaintop. You'd have to be farther away than we was to see the whole thing."

"I didn't feel the earth shake or nothing, just looked up and the rocks was raining down out of the sky into this field," Jack said. "I think I hollered out—"

"You did. I heard you. That's why I turned around or I wouldn't have seen it at all."

"You're telling me those rocks—?"

"Come flying off the mountain, yes sir, that's exactly what I'm telling you," said Ryan. "They didn't *roll* — well, look, see for yourself."

He pointed to the cliff face, which wasn't a straight down drop-off from above, but it was close to it, so steep, the angle so severe, that Linc doubted anybody could climb it, even hanging onto the limbs of the trees and bushes growing there.

Trees and bushes.

"If them rocks'd come rolling down that mountainside, they'd a took every living thing with them," Ryan said. "I seen where a slag dump on the top of a mountain in West Virginia let go and slid down the mountain and wasn't nothing behind it but tore-up dirt."

He was right, of course. There was no way the cliff face could be unmarked, with vegetation intact, if a forty-foot pile of rocks and boulders had slid down it. But the alternative explanation boggled the mind. An earthquake under a mountain — nowhere else, just under Rocky Top Mountain, had shaken it so violently that rocks on the top of it flew out into the air.

"That's when I thought about Aaron and little Natalie," Jack said. "He goes up to the top of that pile of rocks every morning to pray. Has for as long as I've known him. And he usually takes his Natalie with him. She's seven."

"I hoped that maybe this morning he'd stayed home … sick maybe. Just hopin'. But Bill Showers went to check and Mrs. Karrick said they'd gone just like usual, both of them."

He turned and pointed to a woman dressed in nothing but a robe and slippers, digging at the rock pile, attacking it, throwing rocks off as fast as she could.

"That's her over there. She just come runnin', of course."

Firetrucks, rescue squad vehicles, and ambulance along with some of his own deputies and a Kentucky State Police trooper had pulled up while he was talking to the two men. Neighbors, too. Bad news spread fast in Caverna County. By now there was a crowd of maybe a dozen people, digging ineffectually at the pile of rocks. They were making minor headway with some of the smaller rocks, but you'd need a front-end loader to budge the ones that were the size of washing machines and Volkswagens, to say nothing of the two or three gigantic boulders Linc wasn't completely sure could be moved at all, even with a bulldozer. They'd have to get some heavy strip mining equipment in here—

Somebody called out and the whole crowd rushed to the spot. Then the woman in the bathrobe began to scream.

Chapter Five

THE CHOSEN ONE WALKED SLOWLY, deliberately out of the trees toward where Jonah was cowering on the ground in fear. Didn't have nothing on, *nekkid* as the day he was born, if indeed, the Chosen One had actually been born of woman like the rest of mankind. He walked right through the thorns on a hawthorn branch but them thorns didn't do nothing. He shoulda had bloody scratches all over everywhere — because *everywhere* was exposed — but wasn't no blood on him at all.

The most extraordinary thing about him was his color. He was black. Most of him, anyway — everything except his head and neck. But not ordinary black, like the skin of a black person.

Actually, his skin didn't seem so much black as it did *dark*. Dark as in no light at all anywhere. Coal mine dark. It wasn't the *color* of his skin, it was … what lay beneath his skin. Darkness. Nothingness.

Then, just for an instant, it was like a little bit of light blinked on inside and what it revealed was slimy worms and maggoty things, beetles and the like, right up underneath the surface of the skin! Then he was all black again, so Jonah musta imagined that part.

Jonah didn't look up, couldn't raise his gaze off the ground, didn't have the courage to look up at The One sent by God to prepare the way of His destruction.

"Jonah Ballard."

The Chosen One spoke just his name, nothing else.

At the sound of the word, the voices inside Jonah's head began to cheer, to rise up in a mighty roar of connection and approval so loud it would have drowned out any other words if the Chosen One'd said anything else. But he didn't. Just Jonah's name.

But that was more'n enough. Jonah Ballard had been called *by name*. He had been selected, just like the disciples was picked out, one by one and all them prophets in the Old Testament with names Jonah couldn't even pronounce. Jonah had been *called*.

He looked up eagerly into the face of the Chosen One then, took it all in.

The Chosen One's hair was as white as a blank piece of paper and it draped over his shoulders and hung halfway down his back. He was by no means a handsome man, but it instantly occurred to Jonah that the Scriptures said Jesus wasn't comely either and why would God send someone with a fine, unmarked face to warn people of the end of the world?

The Chosen One had a crushed nose, flattened onto his left cheek, and there was an indentation in his cheek, like maybe the bone had been smashed inward and never healed properly. The back of his head was oddly flat, like a baby that slept on his back all the time. He had a full beard that was pure white like his hair. But the hair on the rest of his body — and Jonah could see it *all* — was jet black. The mat of it on his chest stood in stark contrast to his beard, that hung down as far in the front as his hair did in the back.

Then Jonah looked into his eyes, and from that moment until Jonah took his dying breath, the naked man before him would be his master. Jonah would do his bidding, whatever was asked of him. Jonah was his willing slave.

The Chosen One's eyes were ... were ... there was *something* about them ... Jonah couldn't have said what color they were, only that they were set deep in his face beneath bushy eyebrows that were as jet black as the hair on the rest of his body. All Jonah knew was that looking into those eyes was the most terrifying thing he'd ever done. The jolt of fear that rocked him was more powerful than when he'd watched the God of the Universe fling a sinner off into destruction. The eyes drilled into him, like they could see into his soul, knew everything he'd ever done and every thought he'd ever had. Those were the eyes of judgement. There was no mercy there. No kindness. No love. No humanity. If the eyes of the Chosen One could strike such stark terror into his heart, what must it be like to stand at the seat of judgement and give an accounting of his every thought and deed — looking into the eyes of *God himself!*

Jonah's only hope of redemption lay in this being. If he could be true to the Chosen One, serve him faultlessly, follow his every command, maybe that would be enough to tip the scales in his favor when the judgement came.

"It's coming soon," said the Chosen One, "oh very, very soon. God is coming to destroy the world." He spoke like an educated man, his voice powerfully deep and melodious, and the rhythm of his speech kinda felt like he was singing his words. "I have come to lead the few, the faithful, out of harm's way on Judgement Day. And you are going to help me."

"Anything," Jonah stammered. "I'll do whatever you say."

The Chosen One smiled then but it wasn't a warm smile. It never made it all the way up to them eyes, didn't light his face, just showed perfect teeth like didn't nobody have that Jonah knew.

"Excellent," he said. "You may call me the Chosen One."

Jonah had known that! He'd known that's who he was, that that'd be his name even before he said the words.

"I want to speak to the faithful. Gather them for me."

"You mean the members of the church?"

"And anybody else willing to walk the narrow way."

"I'll go talk to every last one of them myself personally, tell them you're gonna be in the pulpit Sunday—"

"Not Sunday. Tomorrow. There's not time to wait until Sunday."

That soon. The end of the world was only days away.

"I'll tell 'em we're gonna have Friday night services."

"And Saturday night."

"Yes sir, Saturday night, too, like we's having a revival."

"It *is* a revival. The last one there will ever be."

Then the Chosen One seemed to notice for the first time that he was nekkid.

"I require clothing," he said. Jonah prayed he wouldn't ask for some of Jonah's clothes. He didn't have nothing clean. Not so much as a pair of underwear.

"You will go into town and purchase what I need. A black suit as befits the dignity of my station. White shirt, black tie and shoes with a shine you can see your face in. And gloves, pure white gloves."

Jonah nodded frantically, knowing it was likely to cost every cent he had.

"And sunglasses — Ray-Bans."

"Ray whats?"

"No … you won't find any of those in Bradford's Ridge, Kentucky." That seemed to strike him as humorous for some reason. "Just dark ones that wrap around."

"I'll go right now." Jonah got to his feet and stood on unsteady legs.

"One other thing," the Chosen One said. "I want you to get me a rattlesnake."

THE AGITATED VOICE of the man dressed in dirty bib overalls talking to John Sparks, his newest deputy, carried out into the hallway as Linc passed by, his mind spinning with what'd happened when the state police forensics team finally showed up at the Holterman house three hours after they'd been summoned. Or rather, what hadn't happened. He'd worked with crime lab techs on lots of occasion, Caverna County being the hotbed of crime that it was. He'd liked some of them, respected most of them and tolerated the handful who couldn't have found sand if they fell off a camel. Those were the guys who'd shown up today. Their work was cursory and slipshod, wrapped up snug in their own arrogance; they certainly didn't need some rube sheriff telling them how to do their jobs. He doubted anything they found would be any use to the state police detectives who'd be assigned the case — which meant, of course, that if there was any real "detecting" to be done, he and his department would be on the hook for it.

"I don't need you to send an officer or nothing like

that," the farmer in the office was saying. "I mean, exploding pumpkins ain't against the law."

Linc stopped in the doorway of John's still-bare office to listen. Sparks hadn't bothered to personalize the space yet — maybe never would, might be the kind of guy who was happy with a bare lightbulb hanging down from the ceiling and nothing else. But the man who'd had the office before Sparks had stuck something up on the wall in every square inch of available space. Ed Blackwell had University of Kentucky basketball team pictures dating back to right after the earth cooled off. He had pictures of Cincinnati Reds games, action shots like from *Sports Illustrated*, where some guy is stretching up as high as he can, his body frozen in some impossible contortion as a ball comes gliding out of the sky into his glove. He'd had pictures of his wife and kids, too. You could watch Allison and Andrea grow up through his pictures — he just kept adding to the collection as the children got older, didn't replace the former ones.

Linc winced at the familiar ache of sorrow that washed over him. He'd lost enough friends, in combat as well as a police officer, to know that time does NOT heal all wounds.

He glanced at the dark spot on the hardwood floor just inside the doorway of his own office. No way to get out the stain of blood. Nothing worked, soap, bleach, fancy cleaners, nothing. There'd always be a dark spot there where Ed's blood had squirted out of his chest after an eight-year-old boy named Russell Willis stabbed him with a pair of scissors.

"You're saying you got pumpkins that exploded and you want me to … what?" Sparks said matter-of-factly and Linc was proud of him that there was no derision in his voice. He might make a pretty good deputy after all. "Why don't you just tell me what happened."

Randy Nickel pushed the University of Kentucky ballcap back on his head to reveal the white line of untanned skin just under his hairline.

"That's the thing, Deputy Sparks," he said, his voice too high and strained. "I can't tell you what happened because I don't know what happened. I ain't got no idea. That's why I'm here. I figure you could request somebody from the University of Kentucky agriculture department to come down here and figure it out."

Linc stepped into the room.

"Figure what out, Randy?" he said. "This early in the growing season, I can't figure how you got pumpkin on the vine big enough to make much commotion if they all went off like nuclear warheads."

Nickel bobbed his head up and down in frantic agreement.

"I know. I know. These wasn't no bigger than tennis balls when I went to bed last night, swear to God they wasn't." Nickel took his cap off and clenched it in his dirty hands like a hound dog worrying a rag. "But when I got up this morning …" He stopped talking, either because he was gathering up the words he wanted to say or he'd run out of air to talk with.

Linc sat down on the edge of Sparks's desk and wiped all expression from his face and made his voice toneless. He'd found it was easier for people to answer questions that didn't have any feelings attached to them.

"Start from the beginning, from last night."

Nickel described in a breathless voice how he'd planted a couple of rows of pumpkins and squash and water-melons up by the house when he'd set out his tobacco in the field earlier in the spring. He passed by them every day going to and from the barn but paid them no heed, wasn't anything out of the ordinary. They'd started to put out tendrils and the little pumpkins were — best as he could recollect, they wasn't in no way peculiar so it was hard to recall — about the size of tennis balls when he saw them on the way into the house for supper.

This morning, he'd been awakened by a strange sound, odd like, not one he could say sounded like anything he'd ever heard before. It was a squishy, squirting sound, maybe like stepping on a grape, only way louder. He rolled over and tried to go back to sleep. He and Martha had been enjoying getting to sleep in ever since they sold their dairy herd and didn't have to get up for milking at 4 a.m.

Then he heard the sound again, twice in rapid succession. Martha heard the last one and she made him get up and go outside and see what was making the noise.

"I pulled up my pants, didn't bother with my boots, just went barefoot. It was just after first light and the morning mist was still hanging in the low spots. There's a creek right by where I planted them vegetables and it's always foggy there of a morning."

Nickel was straying far afield, hedging, putting off saying something he plainly didn't want to say.

"But you could still see, even dark and misty as it was, right?" Linc prompted.

Nickel sighed and nodded.

"Soon's I stepped out on the porch, one of them went off. I couldn't tell at first … it was a pumpkin, though, and it just … exploded, blew up, threw pieces of pulp and seeds everywhere, like some kid had put a firecracker inside … but it'a took more'n a firecracker to do that."

Nickel said hunks of pumpkin rind as big as his hand came flying out of the mist and splattered on the ground and the side of the nearby tool shed.

"Wait a minute," Sparks said. "As big as your hand? I thought you said they wasn't no bigger than—"

"They weren't. Last night, them pumpkins was little things you coulda picked up and thrown like a snowball. But this morning … they was huge. Biggest pumpkins I ever seen. Some of them was three feet across."

"You're saying that overnight, your pumpkins grew from the size of a baseball to—"

"I know it don't make no sense. I couldn't believe it neither, just stood there in my bare feet staring. I called Martha and she come out to look, but the first one that went off scared her so bad she run back in the house and called Luke, our son. He lives just down the road a piece and he come right over because his mama sounded hysterical. But by the time he got there, it was all over."

"What was all over?" Linc asked.

"The explodin' part. When I first come out on the porch, they was going off like kernels of popcorn in hot grease. Pop. Pop. Splat. Like they was bursting … like they got so big they just burst like a boil."

Linc looked at Sparks, who looked back at him with the same blank expression. Nickel caught the look.

"I ain't crazy!" he said.

Linc got up off the side of the desk. "I want to see them pumpkins," he said.

Nickel hung his head, sheepish. "You can't see 'em. They ain't there no more."

Linc sat back down like maybe his knees gave out.

"Not there?"

"Oh, they didn't just vanish or nothing like that. It's just … they ain't big ripe orange pumpkins no more. It'd already started before my son got there. The first ones that popped started turning black and mushy, like you'd left a jack-o-lantern out on the porch after Halloween until it rotted. Like that."

"So now, all the pumpkins are …?"

"Black, shriveled up and rotting." Nickel looked from Linc to Sparks, hoping for belief on their faces he didn't see.

"I don't have me one of them fancy phones with a camera on it, but Luke does. He started taking pictures soon as he got there. They ain't very good pictures — wasn't much light and the mist and all. And more'n half the pumpkins was already turned black before he rolled up." Nickel reached into the pocket of his overalls and pulled out an iPhone. "He got some of them, though. See."

He fiddled around with the phone, clearly didn't know how to pull up the pictures. Sparks took it wordlessly from him and tapped the right icons, and strange photos suddenly appeared.

Nickel was right. The pictures weren't great — just blobs of orange and black. But they were enough to confirm the story Nickel had told. Hunks of orange pumpkin rind lay all over the ground and the stringy seeds draped over nearby bushes like icicles on a Christmas tree. In one picture, Luke Nickel knelt beside an orange mess to give it perspective. It was clear from the size of the pumpkin remains that the gourd had to have been three, maybe four feet across.

Linc looked up from the pictures on the phone to Nickel's anguished face. He had absolutely no idea what to say.

"So …" Nickel began, "will you do it? Will you call the UK ag department and get them to send somebody down here to figure out what happened?"

"I'll have somebody here before sundown," Linc promised. But even as he said it he knew there might not be anything to see by then. If the pumpkins had gone from tennis-ball size to so big they burst open from the pressure in less than eight hours, and had already started to turn black with rot a half hour after that, there might be nothing left of them at all by sundown.

Nickel and Sparks had obviously come to the same conclusion.

"I ain't crazy! I swear I ain't. Them pumpkins exploded just like I said they did."

"I believe you," Linc said. And he did. God help him, he did.

Chapter Six

CROCK KNEW something was wrong the minute he saw Linc's face. It had a smile draped on it from ear to ear like a surgeon's mask as he made his way across the restaurant, greeting first one person and then another. The office of sheriff was, after all, an elected position in a small county like this, which required a level of responsiveness to John Q. Citizen that Crock was sincerely grateful he'd been able to avoid during his years in law enforcement. Both Chicago and Cincinnati were big enough that you could brush off the rubberneckers, the know-it-alls and the Saturday morning quarterbacks.

All the greeters launched questions that Linc quickly aborted with a pointed look at his eight-year-old daughter at his side.

"Linc, I heard you found Herb Holterman's daughter's hand— Why, hi there, Jenny. You doin' alright, sugar?"

Jenny was a shy little girl with straight brown hair cut blunt at her shoulders — like maybe Linc'd been the one who gave her the haircut.

"I'm fine," she said, snuggling up closer to her daddy and not quite looking the man in the eye.

Two steps later a fat farmer still wearing work overalls spotted the sheriff.

"'Zit true wasn't nothing left of that girl but—?"

Linc had to interrupt him.

"Me *and Jenny's* here to have a quiet dinner — not a good time to talk shop."

The man backed off and Linc made it the rest of the way to the table unmolested.

"Appears Boca might not have been a great idea," Crock said as he stood and shook the sheriff's hand. The best eatery Bradford's Ridge had to offer, it was called Boca on Bond Street, which sounded considerably better than "Mouth" on Bond Street, which was how the word translated.

Crock leaned over and stage-whispered into Jenny's ear.

"You better watch this guy, little girl. Last time I took him out to eat he ate all the food on his plate and all the food on mine, too."

Jenny offered the suggestion of a smile as she sat down.

"Given the day I've had, a quiet fish dinner at your place would have been easier," the sheriff said as he sat down.

"Given the day *I've* had, a fish dinner at my place was not an option," Crock said.

Crock could see that the sheriff picked up on his tone of voice — maybe had even figured out something was up when Crock left a voicemail cancelling dinner plans and offering to take him and Jenny out to eat instead. He was rapidly learning that Hezekiah Lincoln didn't miss much.

"I'm thinking that after dinner we ought to grab an ice cream at the drugstore for Jenny and have us a cup of mouth-watering-police-station coffee in my office while she watches a movie on her iPad out at the front desk," Linc said.

Crock nodded as the food began to arrive at the table. Boca was a mom-and-pop operation that served down-home cooking — country style, meaning the table was soon filled with bowls piled high with mashed potatoes, southern style green beans cooked with ham hock, fried okra, fried squash and, of course, fried chicken or fried fish.

"The last time I was here, I expressed sincere concern that if I held still for more than five seconds somebody'd pour batter over my head and plop me into a pan of hot grease."

Crock had said that to Jack Carpenter, Daniel and Andi Burke when they'd eaten dinner at Boca ... the night after Theresa Washington was attacked by rats ... the night before Daniel was kidnapped and ...

It was almost like he heard an audible "bang!" — and with his strange hearing, maybe he had — as he slammed the door on all thoughts of what had happened to him and the rest of his friends last fall. Yep, he definitely needed to get a padlock for that door. A deadbolt. Maybe two of them.

He hadn't had much trouble keeping it shut before he showed up in Caverna County. But here, where it'd all happened, here there was a sense of foreboding in the air so omnipresent it seemed at first that everyone he met was tensing for a blow, where he seemed to bump into some reminder of his waking nightmare everywhere he turned. Maybe it hadn't been such a good idea to come early to go fishing after all.

"My cholesterol spiked from the smell alone then, and it still does," he said, then studiously talked about the weather/school/sports/and any other innocuous subject while he and Linc made it through double helpings of almost everything on the table. And Jenny ate like a delicate little bird.

~

IT WAS cool when the two men stepped out of the restaurant. Felt like the temperature'd dropped ten degrees. The short walk down the block from Boca to the courthouse in the crisp night air had cleared Crock's head and the sense of unease — oh, come on, it was way more than "unease" — he'd felt all day was subsiding just a little. The normalness of it felt inexplicably comforting.

"Normal ain't nothing but a setting on a dryer," Theresa Washington said in his head and he smiled at the memory.

"First time I've seen a real smile on your face all night," Linc said.

"*Me?* You look like you learned to smile from a Smiles for Dummies book. What'd you do — spend the day assembling an IKEA wardrobe?"

"Wish that's how I'd spent my day."

Linc stepped to the door of his office and eased it almost closed, just left it open a crack so he could hear the background noise of SpongeBob SquarePants on Jenny's iPad. He'd set her up with it and an ice cream cone in the office of his dispatcher, Vicky Perkins, while Crock made coffee on the Bunn ten-cup Velocity Brewer coffeemaker — an anonymous gift the sheriff still suspected Crock of sending him. He might have if he'd thought about it, given that the old machine had looked like it'd been rescued from the landfill. During the Eisenhower Administration. But Linc had somebody besides Crock to thank for it.

Crock handed the sheriff a mug with a picture on it of two dinosaurs on the shore as Noah's Ark retreated into the distance. The caption said: "Was *that* today?" He'd picked it up from the assortment of mismatched mugs on the table beside the machine. He took the one that said "Touch my coffee and I will *bite* you," then sat down in the chair in front of Linc's desk. He jammed his shoulder against the door in his mind that needed a padlock and refused to picture the scene of an eight-year-old boy — who looked six — with brown hair and freckles plunging a pair of scissors into his leg.

But he pictured it anyway.

He figured Linc was seeing something similar on his own internal monitor.

"How about we play *Can you top this*?" Crock said. "You tell me about your day, and then I'll—"

"There's a teenage girl named Denise Holterman who's missing … and missing her right hand, too."

Crock hoped he didn't get it, but it was clear from Linc's face that he'd said exactly what he meant.

"Okay, you win the game," Crock said. "Tell me about it."

Crock listened in horror as Linc began to describe the scene. When he got to the part about the hand and the obscene gesture, Crock couldn't help voicing the gut-tearing fear in his belly.

"You don't think it was … you know …?"

Clearly, Linc wasn't surprised by the question. He'd surely been wondering the same thing himself.

"I didn't see a thing I'd call 'supernatural' about it — gross and strange but not supernatural. And believe me, I looked! If the killer coulda busted the door down, why'd he bother using a glass cutter to get in?"

The demon-possessed killers who had gone after Jack

and Daniel — and the demon-possessed children who'd stabbed Crock and killed Ed Blackwell — possessed super-human strength.

"The room was a wreck, but the kind you'd expect. Nothing the average 'madman' couldn't have done. The girl was a little-bitty thing — barely weighed a hundred pounds. Anybody coulda carried her off."

Crock visibly relaxed and the sheriff caught the movement.

"Yeah, looks like I just got your basic, garden-variety psycho on my hands." He paused. "A psycho with odd pets."

"Come again?"

Linc didn't explain, just went on with his story.

"And there may be more than one victim. Two other people are missing. I don't have any evidence to support it, but …"

"Your gut tells you there's no such thing as a coincidence."

Crock listened as Linc told him how a homeless man and an old woman with Alzheimer's had vanished without a trace.

"All that a coincidence? Might be able to swallow that if it wasn't for the maggots."

Crock was lost and must have shown it.

"Christine Lajewski was working in her garden the last anybody saw her. I checked the garden and the yard for signs of a struggle. Didn't find anything out of the ordi-nary except there were half a dozen maggots squirming around the rose clippers where she left them."

He paused and looked very old and tired.

"Charlie Brooker doesn't have a 'home' anywhere, but you can usually find him curled up in a refrigerator box in a lean-to shack he built out at the junkyard, or in the stairwell leading down to the basement of the convent, or on an old couch Robert Kurzweil leaves for him behind the furniture store — places like that. I checked 'em all."

"And didn't turn up anything."

"Nope ... nothing but a couple of maggots crawling around on his blanket in the shack. Of course, the place wasn't on the cover of *Better Homes and Gardens* in the first place, so—"

"And the girl?"

"Three maggots in a puddle of blood at the foot of the bed."

"If this is all connected—"

"Serial killer."

Crock nodded. "One who's seriously determined to make some kind of statement about *something*."

"And if I could figure out what that is ..."

"In my experience — I worked half a dozen serial killer cases in Chicago — their signature is usually their method of offing the victim: knife, hammer, gun. Had one where a dude killed three women three different ways — strangled one, shot one and hacked one to pieces with an ax ... but he was one of the lock-of-hair trophy boys. Got him with what he took with him. Might be you'll find yours by what he left behind. So what's he trying to say leaving behind bugs — specifically maggots? Symbols of rot and decay, maybe?"

"I might be running out past my headlights here, anyway," the sheriff said. Clearly he was not anxious to have the whole county out looking for Lizzy Borden. "Might be a reasonable explanation for all of it."

Linc sounded tired — the kind of tired you don't get from missing a night's sleep.

"But I can't for the life of me come up with a reasonable explanation for the sudden avalanche this morning of a pile of boulders that's sat on the top of a mountain for … oh, I'm no geologist but I'd hazard a guess at three, maybe four hundred thousand years, give or take a millennium. Aaron Karrick and his little girl fell with them … we had to dig out their bodies."

Crock started to speak but the sheriff held up his hand.

"Not done. Haven't got to the exploding pumpkins yet."

By the time he'd finished the tale, the pain in Crock's belly had ramped up so high he was unconsciously grimacing. Linc noticed.

"Either I'm about to have a serious attack of diverticulitis or … let's hope it's diverticulitis."

Linc took a sip of Crock's coffee and turned up his nose.

"It's not the coffee," he said. "If you can't even make good coffee with that whiz-bang machine out there, maybe Jenny and I avoided ptomaine poisoning by not eating your fish tonight."

"Oh, I suspect you might have got real sick if you'd eaten any fish I caught today. Real, real sick."

When he'd finished telling Linc about the fish, the sheriff looked like he was suffering from diverticulitis, too.

"Some kids were swimming at Moonstone and came by the station with a story about dead fish … and there were two or three other reports of a "fish kill" on my desk that I glanced at — didn't read them. Figured that was the state Department of Fish and Wildlife's headache … and I had bigger fish to fry."

"I already called them," Crock said. "They said they'd send a ranger down first thing in the morning to figure out what happened." He paused.

"But …?"

"I don't think there's going to be an explanation forthcoming that's going to satisfy the bureaucratic minds of the state wildlife department."

"You don't think they're going to be able to find out what killed them."

"Oh, they'll see right off what killed them. That's not the hard part. It's explaining ..." He cleared his throat. It suddenly felt as constricted as it did in the always too-tight collar of his dress uniform.

"I gotta drag it out of you?" the sheriff snapped. He wanted Crock to hurry up and tell him what he absolutely did not want to know.

"They died because they were wrong-side-out. Or maybe whatever killed them, turned them wrong-side-out."

"Wrong side—?"

"Internal organs on the outside, just hanging on the bodies — guts, lungs, heart. When I cut into them, I found the external — scales, fins, tails — on the inside."

Linc stared at him, uncomprehending.

"Think of reaching into a sock, grabbing the toe and pulling it back out. That's what they looked like."

"You think all them dead fish was like that?"

"They all had their insides dangling on the outside. I only cut open half a dozen of them to see if the scales, fins and all that was inside. But I figure I got a representative sample."

"But how ...?" He let the question hang out there in the air between them.

Both men fell silent then and the squeaky voice of Plankton drifted into the room, "That's it, mister. You just lost your brain privileges."

"You know what Theresa Washington would say about all this, don't you?" Crock finally said. Linc shook his head.

"Do I want to know?"

"She'd say, 'One robin don't make it spring … but a whole flock does.'"

"Meaning …?" The sheriff knew what it meant. He just needed to hear somebody else say it.

Crock heard his own voice, flat and toneless like it wasn't his voice at all.

"It's spring," he said.

Chapter Seven

JACK CARPENTER IS NOT aware of taking steps, can't feel his legs at all, as a matter of fact. But he's getting closer and closer to the tunnel that angles off this one to the left, where red, flickering light pulses.

And he is angry. He can't feel his legs but he can feel the rage boiling inside him. It rises up with the taste of bile in the back of his throat. He is flat-out done. Done with this monster from hell hurting everyone on the planet Jack cares about. Done.

Showtime, Pal, he thinks.

Then he turns the corner into the chamber where the red light pulses.

And his bravado drains out of him, water through a hole in a wading pool — leaving him parched, so dry and brittle a single touch would turn his whole being to dust. And something comes loose inside him. The essential Jack, the man who could get it done, the man you wanted to have your back in a firefight — that Jack had been held together with strong sinews attached to his bones. But at the sight that greets him when he turns the corner, the bonds go lax and essential parts of him come undone and float away like a helium balloon out of the hands of a kid at the county fair.

Lyla.

Her face — animated, not just a photograph — was as beautiful as it had been the last time he saw her. She'd been crying then, too.

Her words when she speaks drill down into his soul. She'd only wanted a baby, she says, but Jack doesn't like children.

The horror of her body below the beautiful face is more than Jack can bear. Broken arms and legs, shattered ribs, internal organs spilling out in a gelatinous mass down the front of her beautiful red dress.

She had fallen so far.

It was his fault, she says, and of course it was. She'd only wanted a baby but he had refused to give her the one thing her heart desired most. Jack had been selfish, self-absorbed. He had wanted life on his terms and hadn't cared a whit about the beautiful wife who only wanted to bear his child.

So she had died. She'd gone to work that morning in the tower instead of to the doctor's appointment she'd scheduled with a fertility doctor. She'd gone up in the elevator to the top of the building. And she had come down half an hour later, falling through the air, holding the hand of a man Jack didn't know, her red dress billowing around her like a parachute that failed to open.

Then Lyla begins to change. The color drains out of her black skin until it is milky white. Her curly black hair straightens. Before his eyes, it flows out over her shoulders and down her back, a pale blonde. Marilyn Monroe blonde.

She is still torn up, her body shattered, but now the body is no more Lyla's than the face. Both are someone else.

Becca.

Becca stands before him, her pale face every bit as lovely as Lyla's black one had been.

"Why did you let me die, Jack?" she asks him, and her pale eyes drill into his soul with the ferocity of a dentist's drill. "Why didn't you protect me?"

He has no answer. Can only look at her in adoration and shame.

"I counted on you, believed in you. But you let him come for me. The red monster with the scimitar, the horns and jagged teeth, you let

him take me while you ran away. You were scared and you ran away and left me there with the monster."

He wants to tell her it isn't true, that he'd never leave her, that he would stand between her and every evil thing for the rest of his life.

But he'd tried to protect her from the Bad Kids when they were children. And they were stronger than he was. The red monster is stronger than he is, too.

And he remembers the fear in his belly. The terror at the sight of the fifty-foot monster towering above them in the chamber. It eats his guts out …

Suddenly, he can't stay there another second. He doesn't care that Becca is there, that she needs him. He doesn't care that he's leaving her alone with the devil himself. He can't stand to be in the presence of the monster another second. And so he runs.

Becca cries out for him. He can hear her voice echoing in the dark chambers as he runs from the red glow. She begs him to come back, pleads with him to save her. But he just keeps on running, his heart thundering in his chest like stampeding elephants.

"Jack, come baaaaaaack," she cries.

JACK SAT bolt upright in the bed, shaking in the sweat-tangled sheets, crying. His heart hammered in his chest and he knew only that he had to run. Had to get away.

Slowly, the vapor of the nightmare began to fade. The black walls of the cave became the dark walls of his bedroom. The breeze blowing in his window was cool on his hot skin. His breathing began to return to normal.

Just a dream.

A variation of the dream that had attacked his sleep every night since Becca had said yes. Well, she hadn't actually said anything. She only nodded her head and he'd had to reach out tenderly and lift her chin so she was looking at him with those green eyes, the ones he'd said were "sea green" when he was twelve years old and had never seen a body of water larger than the Three Forks River.

You couldn't exactly call theirs a "whirlwind" romance since Jack and Becca were childhood friends. Still, it might seem like the few months they had actually "dated" wasn't very long. But the kinds of things couples did during the dating part of the relationship game, the two of them didn't need to do. They had been through the darkest hours of their lives together — *twice*. Their bond was already unbreakable, their love for each other unspoken for years even though it was the canvas on which both their lives had been painted. The "dating" part had been about transitioning from the Three Musketeers — Jack, Becca and Daniel Burke, BFF, best friends forever — to the twosome of Jack and Becca exploring their feelings for each other in a whole new light now that the danger was over and the rest of their lives stretched out there in front of them.

It could have been awkward. Daniel kept it from being so. Jack had admired Daniel's strength of character since they were children, but never more than the day Daniel had looked up over the can of bean dip he was opening as the two prepared to cheer for the Cincinnati Bearcats in the Liberty Bowl on New Year's Eve.

"Let's get the elephant out of the middle of the room," Daniel'd said.

"What? You're a closet Vanderbilt fan? If you are, that puts a serious strain on our friendship."

"No, what puts a serious strain on our friendship is you and me — *and Becca* — moving through life as the Three Musketeers, a threesome. And that's a whole lot easier to fix than me being a Vanderbilt fan."

Jack hadn't said anything. Gratefully, Daniel had the

conversational ball securely in his hands and had run all the way down the field and through the uprights with it.

"Ask her out on a date, dummy. Safe money's on she'll say yes. Surely, you don't need me to draw you a map of what comes next."

Jack still said nothing.

"Aw come on, Jack. You might as well write it in purple in the sky in Hebrew — you're in love with Becca and—"

"So are you."

"No, actually, I'm not. I love Becca, but I'm not 'in love with' Becca. Big difference. And it's going to seriously cramp your style if I'm the third wheel whenever the two of you are together. So I hereby officially bow out."

When Jack spoke again he was surprised that his voice didn't quaver.

"What do you mean, Daniel?"

Daniel rolled his eyes and feigned annoyance.

"How many things can 'bow out' mean? When we were kids I thought you'd get over being thickheaded." Daniel smiled and almost ... *almost* pulled it off as genuine. "Wrongo, moosebreath."

As Rocky the Flying Squirrel said so often to Bullwinkle the Moose.

When Jack hadn't ... *couldn't* keep up the ruse, Daniel dropped it. But he still kept a tight rein on his emotions, stayed matter-of-fact.

"I was 'in love with my wife.'" Daniel's wife, Emily, had been murdered by a demon when it all had started. "More than a year ... and I *still* wake up some mornings, and for a glorious few seconds, I forget she's gone. And when I remember ... it takes my breath away."

Daniel did get intense, briefly but fiercely. "Beautiful, fragile, wonderful Becca Hawkins deserves a man who can love her unreservedly, wholeheartedly without a pall of grief … a darkness. That man is Jack Carpenter. He is *not* Daniel Burke."

So Jack had asked Becca to dinner. It went from there. He broached the subject of Daniel once with her and was surprised to hear a variation of what Daniel had said to him. "I love Daniel. I'm not 'in love with Daniel.'"

And finally, Jack had said the words that had been in the back of his throat every second he had been in Becca's presence since they were children when he knew … *knew* she was the most beautiful girl he had ever seen. The words had hung there, like a suppressed sob, for so many years, he was surprised he didn't burst into tears when he said them.

"I love you," he'd said, his voice soft and tender. He would be that for her. Tender. Kind.

And he would never, ever let anything hurt her again.

The Lyla nightmares had started that night. They blew through his soul like a runaway train every night, leaving him weak and panting and ashamed. His fear of the monster had been stronger than his love for Becca. So he had left her there to die and run away.

A dream. Just a dream.

He got up out of bed and went to stand in front of his almost empty refrigerator, staring into the contents like something would magically appear there to replace the almost empty jar of mayonnaise, the almost full container of bean dip with suspicious white stuff covering the top, a container of eggs with one left and some kind of mystery lunchmeat.

Becca had taken one look at his refrigerator and pronounced it a biohazard and refused to go anywhere near it without a hazmat suit. It would be different when they were together, she'd promised, leaning into his embrace, moulding her body to his like warm clay. She would see that their refrigerator was well-stocked. She'd cook for him. She'd take care of him.

Becca would take care of Jack.

And Jack would take care of Becca.

That was the way it was supposed to be, right? The two shall become one flesh.

Only the dreams warned him that he wouldn't, that he would fail, that he would let her down.

The dreams—

"Stop it," he cried out in the dark kitchen, so much pain and emotion in his voice it didn't even sound like his own. Dreams ... nothing but dreams ... phantom synapses firing that bore no relation to reality.

He remembered the words of the angel, Andi's angel, as they approached the cave where the mother of all boogeymen lived.

"Remember who he serves," she'd said. "The father of *lies.*"

He went back into the living room in his underwear and picked up the picture of him and Becca — Theresa had taken it and had it framed for him. He looked at the man on whose face smiles did not sit naturally. He looked like the happiest man alive. And the beautiful woman at his side. She ... she took his breath away.

Jack was going to make Becca his bride. He had loved her his whole life and he would drive to Bradford's Ridge after his shift was over today and the day after that, *she would become his wife.*

He felt the joy of that wash over him like a warm tide. No dream was going to rob him of his happiness. Not now, not after all this time. He was the luckiest man in the world. His boyhood fantasy was about to be fulfilled. Life would be good.

He let out a sigh of indeterminate origin. Relief.

Happiness. Happiness felt so strange, it was like he was always walking around with sand in his shoe. But it was his and it would be hers.

He held the picture tenderly and it wavered in his sight as he looked at it through unshed tears. He would be a good husband. He would love her and cherish her and protect her.

He would.

The last of the dream floated away from him then, smoke from a guttering candle. He felt it, like a puff of wind that ruffled his hair.

But some part of him knew it would be back. That he would meet it again in the dark of the bedroom tomorrow night and the next and the next. No! He had to do something about it. He would not wake up in the bed beside his beautiful Becca, panting and crying over images that weren't real.

He needed to talk to somebody.

"Theresa."

He breathed her name aloud and felt comfort in his soul. Theresa would help. It felt a little like a grown man going home crying to mama, but he didn't care. She was his mama in every way that counted and she was the only person wise enough, good enough to assuage his fears.

He looked into the darkness outside his window. The sun wouldn't be up for hours but he was wide awake. He actually considered calling. She said she never slept, that she was up at all hours. He didn't, of course. He looked at the clock on the bedside table.

The flashing red letters proclaimed 3:30 a.m.

Might as well stay up. He was wide awake.

~

THERESA WASHINGTON LOOKED at the lighted letters on the bedside clock: 3:30 a.m.

Might as well stay up, she was wide awake.

So many things chasing each other around in her mind, it looked like the inside of a blender.

Flowers.

Make that little veil she'd seen a picture of in a magazine at the dentist's office.

And rice! Oh, Lordy, don't let her forget the rice. She needed to get some netting, too, and little tiny ribbon — blue, which was one of the colors Becca had chose. She still had time to make little bags of it so people could throw—

Folks didn't throw rice no more at weddings. Somebody figured out that birds was eating that dried-up rice and then it swelled up in they bellies and they died. Now people used birdseed. Fine, birdseed, then. There was a pet store next door to the cleaners where she'd taken her dress to be altered and she could get some there.

Jack and Becca hadn't done no formal invitations or anything like that — *Keep it simple*, Jack musta told her a hundred times. But even a simple wedding ought to be a celebration — and *this* one surely ought to be. And they was traditions you'd ought to abide by or later on you'd wish you had. That was what she'd said to Jack, musta been a thousand times.

Hadn't nobody accused her of going to all this trouble because this was the first and only time in her life she'd ever get to be the "mother" of the bride, and she was glad they hadn't because if they had she'd have been busted. Her Isaac was gone, but the good Lord in his bounty had given her Jack, Daniel and Becca. They were her family now, closer than family 'cause of all they'd been through together. And she intended to squeeze every drop of joy and happiness out of this holy occasion, was gonna chew all the sweet juice out of it till wasn't nothing left but the gum wrapper.

She needed to make herself a list of all everything she had to do, to make, to buy, and every time she done or made or bought something on the list, she could mark it off. Bishop had been organized. He had lists of his lists, stuck all over everywhere in the house—

Bishop.

She tensed for the staggering blow of grief, but it didn't smack her down every time now like it used to.

What was it Jack told Daniel after Daniel's Emily was murdered?

"Every morning, you'll open your eyes and it'll be the first thing you think about," he'd said. "And then one morning, it'll be the second."

"That don't mean you's in second place, though, sugar," she said.

She talked to him now any time she felt like it, didn't feel guilty about it anymore like she used to. In the beginning, she'd tried real hard not to reach out to him — he was in Heaven, after all, and folks in Heaven was in such perfect joy they didn't concern themselves with what was going on with the folks still on earth. She knew the One she'd ought to be talking to was the One who'd taken Bishop to Glory in the first place and was gonna take her home there, too, someday.

After a while, though, she figured out they wasn't the same things at all — talking to God and talking to Bishop. Talking to God was prayer. God listened to every prayer on a human heart, even the prayers wasn't never turned into words. And God had the power to do something about what you was praying about.

Talking to Bishop ... Shoot, just 'cause she was talking

didn't mean he was listening and if it made her feel better to talk, where's the harm? She always pictured him listening, though, taking in her every word, his big brown eyes full of love and care and concern. And one day when she got to Heaven, she was gonna ask him did he hear her all those times she talked to him. Of course, by then it wouldn't matter.

"I wish you's here to share all this with me," she said. "Sometimes my heart near bursts with the joy of it, 'specially since it was such a near thing. Remember how Jack come right up on the edge of not even asking her?"

Jack, Daniel and Becca had been friends in a childhood filled with monsters — real monsters. As adults they carried those scars — and the usual scars of living life. Daniel's wife had been murdered. Jack's had died in Tower Two on 9-11. And Becca ... Becca had took the worst of the abuse as a child and it tipped her over the edge into insanity for a time. Homeless, she battled episodes of PTSD flashbacks ... and perhaps real demonic attacks. Who could say?

When the Lord brought the three of them together, they survived horrific battles with Satanic forces and an encounter with a monster demon.

When that was over ... their lives returned to normal. For a little while, normal felt like walking around with sand in your shoe. But in "normal," sooner or later there were some issues they had to face. As twelve-year-old boys, both Jack and Daniel had been head-over-heels in love with Becca. Here the three of them were as adults. Unmarried. Their lives back on track again. Now what?

Now what, indeed.

Theresa sat up in bed and swung her feet out onto the floor. The ball of fur beside her bed was wagging his tail instantly, and going to town licking her feet — like he'd been sitting there all night just waiting for her to wake up so he could lick her. Shoot, maybe he had.

She reached over and ruffled the amber fur of the golden retriever — a birthday present last fall from her "kids." Now Cornbread was just about grown and if she'd known how much dog hair he was going to leave on every possession she had, she might have thought twice about the advisability of keeping the animal. A couple of days ago when Becca was finished sweeping the hardwood floors, she told Theresa solemnly, "We've just about got enough hair for a whole new dog."

Theresa smiled at the thought of Becca's face, so much now like she had looked as a child. She'd put on weight, didn't look like the first little breeze would blow her down the street, and once the tense, haunted look left her eyes and she relaxed, the beauty of the little girl she'd once been began to shine through.

A little girl *both* Jack and Daniel had been in love with. Didn't nobody ever tell Theresa how it came to be that Jack got together with Becca and Daniel didn't and wasn't none of her business to know anyway.

But she figured Daniel wasn't aware that it didn't matter what he said out his mouth, what he was feeling was written on his face. Oh, not everybody could read it. Maybe nobody could except Theresa. And what she read there whenever Daniel looked at Becca was the same thing she'd seen on his face when he was twelve years old. He still loved her. Hadn't nothing changed about that.

Chapter Eight

THE CLOCK on the wall in Becca Hawkins's bedroom was visible in the spill of light from a hallway lamp — 3:30. Might as well stay up. She was wide awake.

How were you supposed to sleep when the very best part of your life was out there only hours away?

She sat up, reached around and stacked the two pillows on the bed one on top of the other and then leaned back against them in the darkness.

If what she was feeling was happiness, what must it be like to feel this way day after day? Correction: what *would* it be like to feel this way every day, because she knew that her future would be very, very different from her past.

She took a deep breath and sighed and thought how peace and joy and well-being almost didn't feel foreign to her anymore. At first it'd been like trying to break in a new pair of shoes. The feelings were stiff, unfamiliar and uncomfortable, and she caught herself retreating into knee-jerk fear and apprehension just because those feelings were familiar.

But Jack wouldn't let her stay there long. He could spot

the hunched-over-waiting-for-a-blow body language from half a mile away. Sometimes, he'd just wrap his arms around her and hold her tight, wordlessly patting her back until the fear subsided. Other times, he would take her chin and lift it gently.

"Look at me," he'd say, and she would lift her eyes up to his and fall into the warm safety of them, eyes she said were the same color as Nutella, one of her all-time favorite new foods she hadn't even known existed until a few months ago.

Sitting propped up in bed in the darkness, Becca brought up the familiar images in front of her eyes, as she had done so many times over the years the color should be fading by now, like an old photo looked at so often the light begins to turn the colors yellow. But every time she saw it in her mind was like the first time she ever did, and the colors were as fresh as if they'd been painted on the world just moments before and the brushstrokes still sparkled wet in the morning dew.

Hope Chapel.

Becca had stopped dead in her tracks the first time she ever saw it. She, Jack and Daniel had stumbled upon it one day when they were in the woods engaged in the never-ending activity of searching for ginseng.

Daniel bumped into her from behind when she pulled up short, and Jack into him, a train derailed by Becca's gap-jawed wonder.

"Is that … a castle?" Jack had asked.

In truth, it had never looked like a castle to Becca. It had never looked like anything other than what it was, a little chapel in the woods, perfect in every way, almost like a doll house.

When you approached it, you felt like you were walking into a fairytale.

It was located deep in Queen Anne's Hollow, where the roadsides and meadows were blanketed in the pure white flowers that looked like snow. The chapel was so far back in the woods you had to park your car and hike the rest of the way, probably not more than two hundred yards as the crow flies, but the path hadn't been designed by a bird. A chipmunk, maybe. It wound like the Yellow Brick Road through the woods, a serpentine route laid out with stepping stones and lined with daffodils and tulips. At least there had been flowers when Becca was a child and the Tucker family still looked after it. Ancil Tucker had built the chapel right after World War I, fulfilling a promise he'd made to God that he'd build a church in the woods if God would bring his sons safely home from the war.

It would seat maybe thirty people on the beautiful hand-carved oak pews with ornate club feet set on the cold stone floor. Ancil had only intended it for his family — which had nine children — and a few neighbors close enough to attend. The lane leading to it from the road was not paved. The "parking lot" was merely a small plot of ground that had not been taken over by the bushes and brambles. Becca'd heard that Tucker preached from behind the little wooden pulpit in the chapel every Sunday — a variation of the same sermon for thirty years. God is faithful. God will protect you. God answers prayer.

The chapel had seemed magical to Becca then. The two stained-glass windows — one with a scene of Jesus with a little boy on his lap, the other a gigantic lily of the valley. The heavy oak door had only a latch, not a lock. There was an ornately carved stone altar down front beside the little pulpit. In the cool, hushed interior, they always whispered — nobody to hear, but it was a place that bespoke whispers from the trespassing children who had best not be disrespectful of the place. And they never were.

Becca never told Jack and Daniel about her fantasy, of course. They might have been the Three Musketeers, but sometimes a little girl had private thoughts she wouldn't share with a boy even if he was closer than a brother. The first night after they had discovered the chapel, she had lain in bed imagining herself a winged fairy princess in a beautiful white dress and ruby slippers — she mixed and matched her fairytales, but as she grew older, the fantasy solidified into a single scenario that played in her head every night as she went to sleep — she walks down the cold stone aisle in the magical chapel, a beautiful bride on her wedding day. In her fantasy, there are so many flowers in the little chapel there's almost no room for the crowd of people — anonymous fantasy placeholder people who would become all the people she loved in the world. As a little girl, she couldn't have filled a phone booth with all the people she loved in the world, but assumed that as a grownup she would have so many friends and family some would have to stand outside.

The daydream was centered around her. Oh, there was a groom. Couldn't have a wedding without one. She alternated imagining the groom was Jack and then Daniel. At the time, she couldn't imagine *marrying* either one of them.

Now, she couldn't imagine marrying anyone but Jack. He had been there for her — even if only in dreams or memories — her whole life. Once the terror that stalked their lives was beaten, falling in love with him had been the most natural thing in the world. Marrying him, with Daniel joining them together, was the fulfillment of fantasies so glorious she'd never even dared to dream them.

Tomorrow, she would become Mrs. Jack Carpenter. She would walk down the aisle *for real* in Hope Chapel.

THE CLOCK on the wall in the milking parlor said 3:30 a.m. Right on schedule.

Twelve-year-old Mark Durston stifled a yawn, but not because it was so early. Up way before dawn was how you did life on a dairy farm. The daily milking cycle was imprinted on the boy's DNA.

His great-grandfather had been the first of the family to sink his roots into the soil of Caverna County, carving a little farm out of the woods in the late 1880s, removing the trees one at a time, tearing the stumps out of the ground with a mule in a harness.

His grandfather had been the first *dairy* farmer, starting a small herd, adding to it one cow at a time, breeding carefully. Mark's father, Richard Durston, ran a good-sized operation with a herd of more than two hundred Holsteins.

Mark would be a dairy farmer, too, one day. He was mature for his age and at twelve didn't harbor grand dreams — like his brothers did — of going out into the wide world, maybe becoming a professional baseball player, or a ship captain. He had an innate understanding of where he fit in the grand scheme of things.

Every morning, Mark's first job was to clean the milking equipment. By 4 a.m., it was time to wake up the ladies — not all two hundred of them, some were nursing calves. The ones who weren't he'd bring into the holding area of a milking parlor that could milk eight cows on each side at the same time. After their udders had been thoroughly scrubbed, they were attached to the milking machine where a vacuum pulsated air to make the rubber insert inside the milking unit gently squeeze the milk out. The cows were only attached to the machine for about four minutes. Then they were moved out into the barn and the next group was moved in.

Mark could complete the whole cycle in his sleep.

Which he might have to do this morning. He was *so* tired, the kind of tired you don't get from missing one night of sleep or two, or three. It was the kind of tired that sets in when you haven't had a good night's sleep since … he couldn't remember when.

Not since everything had started to go … *wrong*.

His older brothers, Jason, fifteen and Eric, sixteen, had always gotten on each other's nerves. His mother said it was because they were supposed to be twins, but Jason missed the bus. It had always been annoying to listen to their constant bickering.

But then the bickering … *changed*. Turned ugly. Looking back, it seemed like it had only taken a few weeks. Now, they yelled at each other all the time, over everything and nothing, big stuff, little stuff, saying vicious, mean things they'd never said before. And their father always ended up getting into the argument whenever he tried to break them up.

Last night it had started over a video game and ended in the emergency room with Eric getting stitches in the side of his head.

Dad had barely gotten home in time to start milking.

Nobody spoke when Dad roused the boys from sleep. If either of his brothers looked like they might be about to say something, their father gave the boy a look sharp enough to cause internal bleeding.

Eric got out of milking because of the bandage on his head. Jason was furious that Eric got to roll over and go back to sleep when he had to get up in the dark and work. Mark could hear him mumbling to himself as he directed the cows one at a time into their stalls.

Only … it didn't sound like Jason was talking to *himself*.

It sounded like he was having a conversation with somebody else, only nobody else was there.

"If Dad hadn't pulled me off, I woulda. I woulda *killed* him."

Then he paused, as if listening to someone's response. Mark had known better than to get in the path of either one of his brothers this morning, had tiptoed around in the bedroom so he wouldn't rouse the sleeping Eric and had stayed well out of Jason's sight as he did his chores. So Jason didn't know Mark was anywhere near, had no idea the boy could hear what he was saying. But who was he talking to? None of his friends would be up at this hour and Jason was risking his hide bringing a cell phone into the milking parlor. Dad would skin him alive if he caught him.

Mark peeked out around the side of the milking machine that he was attaching to the teats on a black-and-white Holstein whose udder was so full it was almost dragging the ground.

"I should! He deserves it, the punk, gets to do everything first because he's the oldest, lording it over me when I'm the one does all the work, and then I get blamed when—"

Mark couldn't be sure his brother was on his cell phone without revealing his presence to Jason. But Jason was talking to *somebody*. Mark felt the same horrifying feeling he'd felt last night, when his mother and father had taken Eric to the emergency room and Jason was prowling around the house like some beast, making that sound …

It wasn't a growl. Like a cough, maybe, or he was hoarse, that's all.

But if Mark was anything he was an honest kid, and he didn't lie to himself any better than he lied to others. It hadn't been a cough and Jason didn't have allergies or a cold. He had been *growling*.

Like he was growling right now.

"No one will ever know. They'll just think he did something stupid — because he *is* stupid. They'll think he didn't turn the auger off. No way I could get caught."

Mark was afraid his heart was beating so loud right now that Jason would hear it, look up and see him, would know he'd been eavesdropping. Jason wasn't talking to somebody on a cell phone. He was talking to himself, only it wasn't the Jason Mark knew. His brother had become *somebody else*. Someone Mark didn't know at all.

If Jason caught him, he would do to him what he was planning to do to Eric. It wasn't hard to figure out what that was.

A grain auger was a long tube with a screw-shaped shank driven by a pulley that moved the grain from the ground to the top of the grain bin, or to load a truck, or a cattle feeder. Mark knew lots of farmers who'd gotten hurt on one, lost a hand or a foot. A spinning auger could chew off a limb in a heartbeat. Any time you worked on a grain auger, you were supposed to shut it off and lock out the power source — then tag the switch so nobody'd accidentally turn the electricity back on. But it was a lot of trouble to cut the juice every time the auger jammed. Most farmers didn't bother. If you were careful, you could kick loose whatever was stuck that kept the screw from turning.

… *they'll think he didn't turn the auger off* …

Jason was planning to push Eric into the auger with the screw *running*! He was planning to kill his brother.

Mark tried to back up from the reality, but there was no denying the … what was that sound … the *evil* he could hear in Jason's voice. What was wrong with him? *Kill* Eric over a stupid video game? That was crazy.

What could Mark do to stop him? If he told anyone, Jason would know Mark had ratted him out. He'd come after Mark then. Jason was big for fifteen, a strapping six feet with broad shoulders and arms made strong the way all farm boys' arms were strong. Not from working out in some pansy gym, but from lifting and hauling — from *work*.

Though Mark worked as hard as his father or brothers, at only twelve, he hadn't started developing any muscles. If Jason caught him alone somewhere, Jason would be the one walking away whistling, not Mark.

But Mark couldn't just *do nothing*! Pretend he hadn't heard … let Jason kill … *murder* Eric! How could Mark stop him without becoming a victim right alongside Eric, two brothers for the price of one?

What could he do?

Chapter Nine

Jonah looked at the clock on the wall before he stepped out into the darkness. It said 3:30 a.m. and the sun wouldn't come up for hours yet. But he needed to be in position when it did come up, be there ready and waiting.

He had spent all afternoon yesterday, and every dime he had in the world, purchasing the things the Chosen One had told him to get. The clothing was no problem. It was simple enough and easy to find. He'd had to go to only three stores to get it all, shoes to baseball cap — yep, he'd wanted a baseball cap and not just any team, had to be the Cincinnati Reds.

But he didn't get the last item on the Chosen One's list. Best time to find that was first light in the morning. He took a flashlight so he wouldn't break his fool neck falling over a tree limb or off a cliff, though he knew these woods so well he could about put on a blindfold and find his way. Of course, today was different. Today he was looking for the very thing he'd spent his whole life tryin' to avoid, checking the places they usually went, places he'd avoided all his life because his mama'd told him if he went there he was gonna get bit by a rattlesnake. Then he'd swell up and die. Wasn't nothing anybody could do — once you's bit, you's a walking deadman.

Had to wait until sunup, though. Wasn't no point in tryin' to find 'em in the dark. Snakes wouldn't be out till it was warmer and they could sun themselves on rocks. Least that's what his mama'd told him when he was a boy, and in his twenty-eight years of living he hadn't seen or heard anything to contradict it.

Truth be told, he didn't get up early. He never went to bed at all. How does a man take his boots and pants off, get in bed and start snoring when he'd just met the Messiah? He didn't reckon Peter got much sleep the night after they was took from the shore of the Sea of Galilee to become fishers of men. Or Matthew after Jesus called him out of the tax collector's booth. How was you supposed to turn your mind off after a day like that?

He had went to bed, hadn't paced the floor all night like he done the night before he was expecting that Drug Enforcement helicopter to fly low over his field near the riverbank and then officers would march up to his door and arrest him for the dope he was growing there. The next day he was exhausted, worn out as well as sleepy — when the rain kept the chopper out of the sky and didn't nobody come knocking on his door for nothing. Instead of walking a path in circles on the floor, he'd been content last night to lie in his bed and look at the stains on the ceiling where the roof had leaked and discolored the paint, not thinking anything much at all, really.

He might not be the sharpest knife in the drawer — had quit school in the eighth grade — but Jonah Ballard had managed to take care of himself for twenty-eight years, thank you very much, didn't depend on the government check that come once a month like most everybody he knew did. He managed on the farm that'd been his daddy's and his granddaddy's before him. Got paid for selling his little tobacco allotment, grew his own food — a neighbor lady canned his vegetables for him if he'd give her half — had a freezer full of venison from the deer he'd killed in and out of season and grew enough dope for walking-around money and to pay his electric bill and buy gas for his truck.

Jonah was a thief, too. Not to make money — just 'cause he wanted things wasn't his.

And he done … other things, too.

It had started out last winter as a whisper. The first time he heard it he was milking a goat and he turned around so sudden to see who it was had whispered in his ear the goat startled, kicked over the pail and run off.

The whispering come regular, then — too soft to hear the words — and it scared him so bad he went out into the woods and tore up his still, poured all his shine out on the ground, certain that the homemade hooch had done something bad to his brain.

Didn't help, though. Whether he drank or not, the whispering didn't go away. In fact, it came to him so often that after a while he realized that it was always there, that all the time every day, there was whispering in his head. In the beginning, he couldn't hear what the whispers were saying, but eventually he began to catch words, phrases, and started to piece it together. They was telling him there wasn't no reason he shouldn't have that shiny new knife Garland Jenkins had. Or the new axe Bert Pruitt bought in Louisville. Or the bills sticking out of that old lady's coin purse in the drugstore. So he took 'em. Stole chickens when he got hungry for something besides venison. Took a lamb once — almost got caught that time! — but it sure did taste good.

Then he overheard in a bar where he could get pictures he'd hadn't ought to look at. Pictures of little girls. And little boys. Once he got him some of them pictures, he couldn't think of nothing else, night and day, fingered them until there almost wasn't no image at all on them anymore. He finally decided he had to have what he wanted, satisfy that gnawing need, that *hunger* inside him, and he set to planning out how he was gonna do it.

Where he'd find a child.

… and what he'd do with them after …

Then he spotted the one he wanted. Had just about figured out how he was gonna pull it off, when elder Aaron Karrick took over as the pastor of their little church — they'd only had a circuit-riding preacher every six weeks before. Hadn't nobody ever heard Aaron Karrick preach, him being only an elder and all, but once he got into that pulpit it was plain to see preachin' was what he'd been born to do.

Jonah went to church every time the doors was open — his mama'd drilled that all the way down into his bones! Most everybody he knew did, too — didn't matter whether they believed anything at all.

Jonah'd listened to one bad preacher after another his whole life, sometimes fell asleep in the middle of the sermon.

But wasn't nobody sleeping when *Pastor* Aaron started preaching!

Sitting there on the back pew, Jonah started sweating bullets, listening to the man describe the hellfire and brimstone that awaited them as was living in sin. Wasn't like that was news to Jonah — every preacher said that. But this time, it was like the man was looking into his soul.

"Have you got sin written down in your calendar?" he'd asked. "You got your evil deed all picked out, have you? Planning to do something you oughtn't, scheming in your mind to disobey? You think God don't know what you're planning?"

Jonah's heart stopped beating right then and there. He couldn't breathe, couldn't move.

Pastor Aaron looked right at Jonah — right smack into his eyes, Jonah'd swear to it.

"He sees ..." the man roared. Then his voice got real quiet, but not so soft you couldn't hear. He said each word like he was tossing pebbles into a creek one at a time.

"He. Will. Make. You. *Pay!*"

Every one of them words was a nail driven all the way down into Jonah's soul.

He left church that day swearing he'd never look at another one of them pictures. Never have another impure thought. Never ...

But then the voices come. And he gave in to his urges again.

Then he was sorry ... *scared* ... and he'd purpose to throw them all away. Only he wouldn't.

Every minute of every day of Jonah's life became a battle. Them voices ... and sometimes his mouth watered with his need. Then his own conscience, beat up though it was, would stand up and warn him what kinda hell he was building for himself in the hereafter.

He took to reading his Bible every day. Wasn't no easy task since he could barely read at all. But he finally figured out from the Old Testament that there was a Chosen One coming, a Messiah on the way, that would save the people from their sin.

Pastor Aaron said that the Jesus of the New Testament was that Chosen One, but Jonah *knew* that wasn't the truth of it, couldn't be because Jesus talked about love and grace and forgiveness and God's favor and Jonah *knew* the one who was coming would bring judgement and God's wrath on them as was caught in sin. Jonah figured that since Jesus hadn't been the Messiah, there was another one out there somewhere.

So Jonah commenced to praying the *real* Messiah would come. Soon. Jonah couldn't hold out much longer. If he didn't, them voices was gonna convince him to do that unspeakable thing he wanted to do so bad that was gonna land him in hellfire all eternity.

Then yesterday, Pastor Aaron was flung off the mountaintop and that *proved* it, all the things he was saying was lies!

And the *real* Messiah had come.

Jonah'd done gone through all the stages — surprise, shock and terror — when he seen the naked man come walking out of the woods. And the Chosen One had left him with enough hope to hold the terror at bay so he could function.

And the thing was, them voices — whispering, bringing them bad thoughts to his mind — was still there. Only they wasn't no war in his soul no more. They musta recognized the Messiah, too, 'cause they was telling him he'd ought to listen to the Messiah, follow him, and to do everything the Messiah commanded him to do. The desire to follow the Messiah drove all his evil plans out of his head; he didn't have time to think of that now. His only hope of rescue from the fire of eternal hell was to obey the Chosen One and every minute of every day for the rest of his life would be dedicated to that one purpose.

As the sun warmed the morning and dried up the mists hanging over the creeks, Jonah tested the contraption he'd rigged up. He'd already tested it musta been a hundred times. He'd taken an old cane fishing pole fifteen feet long and run fishing line up through the hollow center. He made a big hangman's noose on the line at the far end. He wouldn't have to get no closer than fifteen feet — stick out the pole and slip the noose over the snake's head and pull the line tight.

It'd sounded easy enough, but when he tried it out on some sticks he stuck in the ground he couldn't even get the noose around them and they was standing still, which the snakes wouldn't be.

If his contraption didn't work, then Jonah was gonna have to come up with some other way to catch a snake. He would not show up before the Messiah empty-handed. He'd rather get snake bit than run afoul of the Chosen One of God.

WHEN MARK DURSTON got on the school bus after a breakfast eaten in cold silence, there was something like a brawl going on in the back two rows with boys throwing punches that mostly missed, but there soon were bloody noses and split lips all around. The bus driver looked in his mirror and watched the fight, actually seemed to enjoy it. Even looked like he wanted to join in.

Maybe Mark should have ridden to school like always with Eric and Jason in Eric's falling-apart old pickup truck. But he couldn't imagine sitting between the brothers, knowing what he knew, so he'd made up an excuse to ride the bus.

As the big yellow bus bumped along, Mark ignored the fighting all around him, just looked out the window, trying to figure out what to do.

At school, it seemed like half the kids in every class were in a bad mood and all the teachers had hangovers. Looking at all the ugliness around him, Mark began to relax. In truth, Jason hadn't been acting any worse than Bobby Settles when he threatened to push Paul Crawford down the stairs, or Melissa Walters when she said she'd claw Beverly Hastings's eyes out. Mark had just blown the whole thing out of proportion, that's all. Jason was mad and he was saying mean things. But *saying* wasn't the same thing as *doing*. Jason would get over it. He'd never really *hurt* Eric — that was crazy. By the time school let out, Mark was grateful he hadn't told anybody about the incident — and made a fool of himself.

Mark couldn't wait to get home to Cupcake, the fifteen-hundred-pound heifer he would be showing in two weeks at the Caverna County Fair. Just thinking about the fair put a smile on his face. He loved everything about it, the noise, the carnival rides, the smell of hot dogs and funnel cakes and popcorn … and manure, of course. But mostly he loved the show ring. Loved leading in the animal he'd spent hundreds of hours with — trimming and polishing their hooves, grooming them until their coats shone like a new penny and shining their horns. Jersey dairy cattle were polled — born without horns. On most Holsteins, horn-buds were removed when the calf was about a week or so old, so they never grew horns. But after Mark's father lost two calves to infections when their buds were removed, he'd stopped the practice. All the Durston cattle had horns — above their ears, sticking out at right angles to their heads. They all had ear tags, too, on their left ears to distinguish them from one another. Mark's father kept exhaustive records on every cow's feed consumption and milk output. The low performers he sold at auction alongside the farm's beef cattle herd.

His father'd never sell Cupcake, though. She was like a family pet. His brothers had raised her after her mother died, fed her with a bottle three times a day around the clock to keep her alive. Besides, she was a grand champion. You didn't sell a grand champion to make Big Macs.

Mark had put in his first appearance at the Kentucky State Fair when he was four years old. His father had let him lead Gracie, who was so gentle she was like a puppy, into the ring. If it hadn't been for her udder hanging down, Mark could have walked under her belly without bumping his head. A photographer from some newspaper spotted the little kid in bib overalls leading the behemoth dairy cow by a thin leather halter and snapped a picture. It was picked up by the Associated Press and published in newspapers all over the country.

Mark had started out showing rabbits at the fair. Then he graduated to lambs. Then to goats — not much bigger than a lamb but boy were they cantankerous. As soon as he was old enough — you had to be between nine and nineteen to join 4-H — Mark started showing cattle.

Technically, Cupcake was Eric's. But as soon as he got his driver's license and started chasing after girls, he didn't pay enough attention to her and their father gave Cupcake to Mark to show.

The bus dropped Mark off at the gate at the end of the lane half an hour after Eric and Jason had gotten home. Pitching his books on the kitchen table, he hollered out that he was home. No one answered. His father and brothers must be out working on a fence post, or maybe fixing that gate on the far side of the holding pen. Mom probably went into town for groceries for supper — yeah, there was a bowl half full of salad-makings on the counter.

Grabbing a carrot she hadn't peeled yet, Mark barreled out to the barn. It was dim in the barn, lit only by sunlight streaming in the open door and between the slats on the wall. And cool. Correction: cold. It was July, but Mark would bet Aunt Tillie's sneakers it was only fifty degrees outside. If it stayed this cold until the fair, Mark would be glad for Cupcake's warmth when he slept with her in her stall.

It was unusually quiet, too. But Mark couldn't for a moment track down what was missing.

Animal sounds.

Any place with a large number of great big mammals had a soundtrack of ambient noise that never stopped. The cows lowing at each other. Horses nickering. The pigs snorting and grunting in their pens, chickens squawking, the buzzing hum of green flies hovering around a recent, moist cow patty.

But today, there was only silence, an eerie silence that made Mark ridiculously uneasy — like he hadn't lived around animals long enough to know that sometimes they were strutting their stuff and other times they were off in a corner somewhere catching a nap. But all of them quiet at the same time …?

Cupcake's stall was on the end.

Mark began to call to her in an exaggerated high voice as he approached her stall.

"Hey Cu-u-u-u-pcake, guess what I-I-I-I-I-I got."

The big spotted Holstein usually stuck her head out over the stall gate when she heard him coming. Then he'd pet her pink velvet-soft nose until she bleated a horn-blast of "moooooah!" that was the dairy cow equivalent of a cat's purr.

Today, though, there was only silence.

Mark didn't open the gate, just climbed the slats to the top and hopped off onto the ground inside the stall. Cupcake was a darker shadow — that had white spots — on the floor in the corner of the stall. She didn't move.

"Cupcake, I brought you something." He held out the carrot.

The shadow in the corner moved then, but slowly, ponderously. Mark's mind flashed to the time he'd watched the elephant in the circus — how it rose so slowly when the ringmaster poked it with a stick, like it didn't like being poked. Like it didn't want to get up at all.

When she got to her feet, Cupcake turned around to face him. She was still in the shadows, but her head was mostly white so it was more visible than the rest of her in the gloom.

She just stood there. Then she took one step forward and her face came into a puddle of light from the fixture on the ceiling outside her stall.

Her eyes!

There was … something about her eyes.

She lowered her head. Pawed the ground once with her massive hoof.

And Mark was suddenly afraid.

Chapter Ten

Becca was glad she had demanded Theresa take the front seat where she could stretch out her bad knee, glad she was sitting behind Jack where he couldn't even get a look at her face in the rearview mirror. The joy and peace and sense of well-being that Becca'd been feeling for so long now began to drain out of her as she approached Caverna County, and if Jack saw her face, he'd know it.

Gratefully, he and Theresa were engaged in a some-times heated discussion about flowers — specifically, Jack's sense that flowers were the line of demarcation between a "small wedding" and a grandiose affair. Theresa wasn't necessarily arguing that. The point of contention was defining how many flowers it took to push small over the edge into grandiose. Theresa charged that Jack'd be happy if Becca carried a single rose and that was it. Jack countered that Theresa would be happy if she could back a florist truck up to the little chapel and dump flowers into it.

Neither of them was paying Becca any mind.

And that was a good thing, a very good thing indeed, because Becca felt the moorings that kept her tied snugly to the dock of a future reality filled with hope come loose and drop into the water with a plopping sound she could almost hear. Then a wave came in, and as it washed back out to sea, Becca was carried along with it into the vast, empty darkness there.

She never should have chosen *here* for the most important event in her life.

What a fool she'd been to believe she could just waltz in here, hang out, and then leave totally unscathed. Who'd she think she was kidding?

Oh, sure, she'd known that Caverna County would always have an evil feel to it — as Bishop said his grandfather had explained to him fifty years before that the veil between the demon world and the human world was very thin there. But the monster demon that had lurked in the caverns under the county for a quarter of a century was gone now. Jack, Daniel, Andi and Crock had sent it back to hell! There wasn't anything to be afraid of anymore.

The efreet was gone.

And the first thought after Jack proposed — well, maybe not the first … but one of the first coherent ones anyway — was that she wanted the wedding to be held in Hope Chapel. Jack'd thought that was a splendid idea — Theresa said that was only because the building was so small there wouldn't be much room to fuss around with foo-fy decorations.

She, Jack and Crock had made two trips to Caverna County in June — she and Jack to work on the chapel, Crock to go fishing.

And nothing happened! No sense of … oppression. No foreboding gloom. Nothing like that. If there had been *even a hint* of … they would have driven away and never come back!

That didn't happen. On the contrary, they had *enjoyed*

their time at Becca's farm — the one she'd inherited from her father when Billy Ray died. Laughing at *good* childhood memories. The tree they used to climb. The pile of rocks where Jack and Daniel used to play king of the mountain. She and Jack had cleaned out and cleaned up the chapel while Crock caught fish for supper every night. Everything was perfectly *normal*. They'd feared that vandals might have defaced the glorious old building over the years, partying teenagers and not-respectful neighborhood kids. Not. Maybe it was buried so deep in Queen Anne's Hollow, few even knew it was there and the world had mostly passed it by. Oh, someone had dug a fire pit lined with stones on the north side of the building and left a neat stack of firewood — not just kindling but some good-sized logs, for future use. She and Jack had tossed it all into the woods. And there were beer cans and miscellaneous trash both inside and outside. But a couple of weekends worth of cleaning, scrubbing and gardening had returned Hope Chapel to much like the fairytale-magical building Becca remembered.

They'd never even considered holding the wedding anywhere else.

Maybe they should have.

Correction — they *definitely* should have.

The closer they got to Caverna County, the more convinced Becca became of two things:

First, they should not have come here. Something *profound* had changed since they'd been in Caverna County a month ago. It was a *fundamentally* different place now than it'd been then.

Second, she couldn't let Jack know that. It was way past too late to change their plans now and she didn't want to bring him down just because she was.

"… asleep back there?" Jack asked.

"No, just daydreaming."

"You need to weigh in on some of this stuff," Theresa said. "You give this man his head and he'll—"

Theresa stopped mid-sentence. Jack had just rounded the final curve on US 31, revealing Bradford's Ridge on the road ahead. She made a sound like someone had punched her in the belly.

"What?" Jack asked. And when she didn't answer, he asked, "Do you smell … *demons?*"

The horror Becca heard in Jack's voice broke her heart.

"No …"

Demons were invisible. Except to people like Becca, Andi and Bishop. They had the knowing. When a demon entered the human world — by possessing a person — those with the knowing could see it. They could also see the ugly blinking green and yellow lights flickering around a person who was being dominated by demons — not controlled completely, but influenced. Listening to and believing the lies whispered in their ears by the demons always nearby.

Theresa didn't have the knowing as Becca, Andi and Bishop did. But in the presence of a possessed person, she could smell the demon stink and hear the otherworldly wailing of the spiritual world. She was also so tuned into the spiritual, that she could sometimes just sense the presence of a demon even if she couldn't see it.

"It ain't demon stink. But there is a … darkness, a heaviness to the air here. Don't you think, Becca, that—"

"All I see is a little town that a few hours from now we'll be seeing *in the rearview mirror.* Between now and then … if it's dark, we'll just light it up with our happiness."

She patted Jack's shoulder and he flashed her a brief smile.

A text pinged into Jack's phone and Theresa snatched it off the car seat before he could grab it.

"You oughta be ashamed of yourself. You a police officer and you text and drive."

She read the text and looked up at him.

"Crock and Sheriff Lincoln want to talk to you and Daniel soon as Daniel gets into town — at seven o'clock in Linc's office."

Jack was quick. "They must want to get an early start on the bachelor party."

Theresa pasted a smile on her face like a stick-on name tag and Jack's "I look forward to seeing them" was way too cheery. You didn't have to be as intuitive as Becca to realize they were apprehensive.

What was it that had made all three of them so uneasy?

She thought she knew.

≈

MARK SUCKED in a breath and held it.

He had never been as aware as he was right now of how big Cupcake was. She stood five feet tall at the shoulder. He had thought this thought before and it hadn't seemed sinister at all: at fifteen hundred pounds, Cupcake was the size of the black rhino at the zoo.

She didn't have the rhino's gigantic horn, of course. Hers were only about eight inches long. Sharp, though. Mark knew — he'd polished them two days ago to get her ready for the 4-H dairy show. The horns curved forward on the top of her head above her ears.

It had never once in his life entered Mark's mind to fear Cupcake. The worst thing she'd ever done to anybody was kick Eric in the shoulder when he pinched her udder attaching the milking machine to her teat.

Dairy cattle were gentle beasts that lived their lives eating grass and giving milk. They weren't hostile, aggressive.

Cupcake pawed the ground again, looking at him but not really seeing him, her eyes unfocused, locked in a thousand-mile stare.

Then three things happened at once.

Mark turned and leapt up onto the railing of the gate.

Cupcake lowered her head and charged.

And Mark spotted work boots half-buried in the straw on the far side of Cupcake's stall. Not just boots, though. There were feet in them.

THE REVEREND DANIEL BURKE had made it as clear as possible without being rude — well, maybe he had been a little rude. He'd told John Bleecker, pastor of the Covenant Church of Bradford's Ridge, that he would only agree to be the guest speaker at Men's Pancake Breakfast the Sunday morning after Jack and Becca's wedding if the minister stopped couching Daniel's appearance as "local boy comes home a big shot." Daniel had been born in Bradford's Ridge and lived with his family there until he was twelve. Now, he was the pastor of one of the five largest churches in America, the Voice of Hope Community Church in Harrelton, Ohio, a suburb of Cincinnati. If he remembered correctly, he'd told John: "I'm not going to be put on display like the blue-ribbon pig at the county fair." Yeah, he'd been rude.

"What's the matter, Daddy?" Andi asked. "You look like you just bit into an apple and found a worm in it."

Her voice surprised him. She had been unusually … uncharacteristically quiet the whole way from Cincinnati, but had brushed off his attempts t0 ferret out what was wrong with "I'm the flower girl … what if I drop the flowers? Or trip? I could ruin the whole wedding!"

That was a bit of an overreaction, and sounded a little off somehow. No, something else was wrong, but he had learned that she'd tell him what was on her mind when she was ready and not before.

He turned to the gregarious eleven-year-old in the front seat beside him and was struck, as he so often was, by how much the little girl looked like her mother. Minus the spray of freckles on Andi's nose and cheeks — that Emily always said looked like she'd been dusted with cinnamon — and the child's deep-dish dimples, Andi was so the image of Emily it was spooky. Her eyes were exactly the same light blue as Emily's had been, and if she'd had Emily's blonde hair — it was the color of honey — instead of chestnut braids tied with red ribbons, the resemblance might have been more than Daniel could bear. Emily was gone, dead, *murdered*, and he couldn't look at Andi without the pain of loss almost taking his breath away.

What was it Theresa Washington had told him? "Time don't heal wounds. It just changes that knife stabbing into your heart into a rusty Boy Scout hatchet hacking into your chest." Theresa got it. She had lost the love of her life, too. Bishop, her husband, had been murdered just like Emily had. Both of them killed by demons.

"I was thinking that I owe John Bleecker an apology for something I said."

"Did you tell him you'd changed your mind, that you didn't want to stay in Bradford's Ridge another day?"

"No … why would you think I — do you wish I'd said no? Do *you* not want to stay?"

Now it was Andi's turn to look like she'd bitten a worm.

"Come on, the truth now. Would you rather not be in Bradford's Ridge any longer than you have to?"

Certainly the child had every reason not to want to be there.

"I like to spend time with the people who live there — Ariel, Cassidy and Sheriff Lincoln and Jenny. But I don't like to *be* there. I don't like the place."

"Neither do I."

The two rode along in silence for a while.

"The last few times we've been there — like when you spent the weekend with Ariel Murphy — it wasn't so bad, was it?"

"No ... but it's never a happy place." She looked sheepish. "But I pretend I don't notice that it's dark and scary because that would creep everybody out. Ariel knows, though. We've talked about it. She sees how dark it is, too."

"Ariel can *see*—!"

"No, she can't see *them*. She just knows when they're around, that's all, even if she can't see them. Kinda like Miss Theresa, but not in the same way."

Andi *could* see them. Demons. Like Bishop Washington and Becca Hawkins, Andi had *the knowing*. And it shouldn't surprise Daniel that Ariel could sense their presence. The little girl had been possessed by one.

"I can call John Bleecker and tell him to find somebody else, that we're leaving town tomorrow as soon as the wedding is over. We don't *have to* do this."

"Yes, we do, Daddy. We *have to* do this. If we don't, if we run from them, then they win."

Andi was way older than her eleven years and it saddened him that her strange ability had all but robbed her of her childhood. It had certainly taken away her innocence.

He cleared his throat and changed the subject.

"Do you and your posse have special plans for tonight? Like binge watching *The Princess Bride* or something?" He called Jenny Lincoln and Ariel Murphy "Andi's posse" because they followed her around like puppies — and not just because she was two years older than they were. Cassidy Davenport rode with the gang, too, sometimes. She was Jenny's friend, though she'd once pulled up every rosebush in Jenny's back yard. She was a troubled little girl, whose possession by a demon had done her more damage than had Ariel's. The third member of the trio of possessed Caverna County children had fared even worse, though. Rusty Willis, who had stabbed Crock with a pair of scissors, was in a hospital or nursing home somewhere. He had fallen into a catatonic state moments after he murdered a sheriff's deputy, and had never come out of it.

Andi gave Daniel the look.

"Oh, Daddy … nobody says posse anymore."

"Says who? Where can I find the word police? I want to appeal my case to a higher court. And how do you *know* about such things anyway? Do they send out an email?" He made his voice pompous and authoritative. "To whom it may concern. Please know that the word 'posse' is no longer in vogue. Remove it from your vocabulary immediately."

Andi giggled.

"Not an email, Daddy. Emails are boring. A text."

As if on cue, Daniel's phone dinged with an incoming text.

"Would you read that to me, please, sweetheart."

Andi tapped the little word bubble at the bottom of the phone's screen.

"It's from Major Crocker," she said. "As the acting Grand Poo …"

"Spell it."

"P-O-O-B-A—"

"Poobah."

"Poobah of the Royal Order of What's Happening Now and Chinese Carry-Out Deli." She looked up from the phone. "What's *that*?"

"It's an organization Crock made up as he was typing that text."

Andi went back to reading.

"I hereby summon all minions great and small to a special session tonight at seven o'clock in the office of the sixteenth president. Be there or be square."

Andi looked at her father.

"That makes absolutely no sense at all."

"The sixteenth president … *Lincoln*."

"I thought the bachelor party was at that restaurant — Boca on Main Street."

"Change of plans, I guess. Text him back that round is my preferred shape so I will attend."

The little girl shook her head in mystified tolerance and then went to work, her thumbs flying over the keyboard at remarkable speed. Daniel was glad her attention was focused on the phone, that he had a few moments to rearrange his face before she looked at him. Andi was so remarkably intuitive that trying to keep anything from her was like trying to sneak dawn past a rooster. He didn't want her to sense his apprehension.

Crock's words had been silly; his subtext was dead serious. Why did he want to meet with Daniel and the sheriff?

In private?

Tonight?

Daniel would have to drop Andi off at the Murphys

and dash to the meeting to make it in time, wouldn't even get to go out to Becca's and unpack his bags.

Something was up. Had to be. A knot of anxiety formed deep in Daniel's belly.

MARK HAD one leg over the top of the gate when Cupcake slammed into it with such force it splintered the catch and sent the gate swinging around on its hinges until it crashed into the barn wall. Mark rode the gate around and barely kept his hold on the top slat when it banged into the wall.

He heard a sound, a popping sound like a far-off firecracker. Then another. Gunshots.

Cupcake's forward motion had carried her out into the center of the barn, but when she slid to a stop, she immediately turned back toward Mark, perched on the top of the gate.

Her ears were twitching so violently they looked like they might fly off her head. She pawed the ground again.

When she came at him this time, she'd crush him against the barn wall — if she didn't manage to impale him on one of the horns he'd worked so hard to file to a fine point.

If he leapt off the gate and tried to run, she'd trample him before he even got to the barn door.

The boots. Those were Jason's boots.

Mark's only hope was *up*.

A beam angled down off the ceiling to the wall about ten feet above him. If he could leap high enough to grab it, he could swing up and wrap his feet around it, then shinny up it to the ceiling joists. He could crawl along one of them to the ceiling above anywhere in the barn.

The massive Holstein started toward him. Mark

crouched on the top rail, poised to jump. The beam was way too high! He'd never be able to leap that—

Then he was flying, his arms outstretched, grasping at the air between him and the piece of wood above.

It was too far.

He wasn't going to make it.

When he couldn't grab the joist, he'd fall — and land on the barn floor right at Cupcake's feet. He prayed the fall would kill him.

Chapter Eleven

THOUGH IT WAS the middle of the afternoon and the sun was shining down into the hollow, it was still cool. Unseasonably cool. Should have been eighty degrees by ten o'clock on a July morning, but it was far from that. Jonah only had on a t-shirt and bib overalls and he was cold, gooseflesh all up and down his arms.

The cool ... that was a bad thing. Snakes wouldn't come out to sun themselves on the rocks if wasn't no warmth there. How was he supposed to catch a rattlesnake if ...

That's when he saw it. Saw them. He believed forever afterwards that it was because it had been chilly. That's why them snakes acted like they did.

Of course, at the time, he didn't care a fig about why they were behaving so peculiar. He was just grateful they were and tried to hurry as fast as he could to get his job done so he could get out of there.

He'd come over a rise and down into a gully at the base of a bare ridge. The sun shone there on the rocks from the time the sun cleared the mountaintop on the east until it went down behind the mountain on the other side of the hollow. He'd heard tell the place was plum broke out with snakes — all kinds, not just rattlesnakes. He'd never been curious enough to go find out the truth of that, but now Sugarloaf Rock was the first place he went looking.

He come up through the gully, tangled up with bushes and fallen rock, and it was a rough go, but when he spotted the rock face of the bare ridge, he knew he was almost there. He'd been thinking about something else. Something he'd oughtn't to think about. He was picturing a pretty little black girl with eyes like chocolate drops and a gap in the front where her teeth has come out and soon's he saw the ridge he started looking around frantically. He'd just come waltzing up on the back side of the rocks, casual as you please, and there could be snakes all over out there.

He listened for the rattle of a diamondback or timber rattler as his eyes raked the ground and the bushes nearby.

Then he stopped breathing. Probably stopped his heart beating, too. He'd come ambling along, not looking where he was going, and had wandered into a … a *den* of snakes. When you looked close, you could see them everywhere. On the ground beside the juniper tree was a black snake. On the big rock behind that hickory were two snakes, both garter snakes. And on the dirt near him, not fifteen feet from his foot, was maybe the biggest timber rattlesnake he'd ever seen.

He hadn't heard a thing. It was a quiet morning, and preoccupied or not, Jonah should have heard the warning rattle, and even from where he stood, Jonah could see the snake had a set of rattles on its tail six inches long.

Jonah was so scared he didn't dare move, froze up like an icicle instead of getting his cane pole snake catcher in

NINIE HAMMON

position to slip the noose over the snake's head. He wanted nothing in the world except to get out of here without one of the things sinking its fangs into his ankle and—

The timber rattlesnake started toward him.

Jonah started backing up. But a quick glance behind him showed him it was either the frying pan or the fire. Behind him, the way he was inching away from the timber rattlesnake was a diamondback that musta weighed three or four pounds. It was enormous. It didn't move, but Jonah knew it had to sense him, knew them little indentations on the sides of their heads was like noses that could sense heat. They had to sense him, all of them, close as he was — and this being such a cold morning, his warmth would be even more noticeable.

Blind panic took over, shoved Jonah out of the driver's seat of his body and took over. He dropped his snake-catching contraption in the dirt and turned to bolt — when he felt something on his foot. He looked down. A small, dark timber rattler was gliding across his shoe. Jonah leaped aside, kicked as hard as he could and the snake went flying through the air, landing with a plop in the dirt ten feet away … where it continued to glide along the ground and into the bushes like it hadn't seen him at all.

The big timber rattler that had been coming his way was only five feet away now, still sliding along like it hadn't seen Jonah at all. Didn't wrap up into a coil to strike or nothing like that. He'd heard a snake had to be all coiled up like that to strike and if that was true, wasn't none of these snakes ready for a go. Of course, if it wasn't true, Jonah Ballard was a dead man.

The snake got to him, glided up and over his foot like it was a log on the path, and just kept going.

Jonah reached down and picked up his snake-catching contraption where he'd dropped it in the dirt. There was what he was almost sure was a pigmy rattlesnake lying across it that he had to gently shake off onto the ground. It plopped into the dirt, not moving.

What in the Sam Hill ...?

Carefully moving the contraption from his left hand to his right, he began to swing the end of it carefully around, looking for a likely target. Truth was, most of them was likely targets — just lying there still, not wiggling or striking or sliding quickly for safety in the undergrowth. Half-turned around now, Jonah could see that the mother of all rattlesnakes he'd seen when he came in had stopped and lay now in the middle of the trail, not moving, just lying there.

With trembling fingers, Jonah maneuvered the noose part of the contraption slowly down toward the snake, expected it any minute to turn on him ... or at the very least run away!

He caught the big timber rattler on the first try. It didn't even struggle when he lifted it off the ground and swung the contraption in an arc like a crane looking for a load of wood. He'd dropped his sack in his hasty retreat a few minutes ago. Now he lowered the spaced-out snake into the top of the sack. Using a stick, he got hold of the edge of the sack, then shoved the snake dangling down into the opening. The snake put up no protest, might as well have been a garden hose with fangs.

He had what he'd come for and was turning to get out of the ring of snakes, when it occurred to him that the Chosen One might want an additional snake or two. For additional services, maybe, or just as backup. And if ever Jonah was going to gather up additional snakes, now was absolutely the time to do it.

Inside ten minutes he had four huge rattlesnakes in the

sack — not wiggling, squirming or striking at everything and nothing. They were just … lying there.

He pulled tight the drawstrings on the bag he'd used for the snakes and then tied the bag to the end of his contraption — so couldn't none of those suckers come to its senses and start attacking the side of the bag. Then he slung the cane pole over his shoulder and backed away from the rocks far enough that he felt safe turning his back. As soon as he did, he bolted down the gully away from Sugarloaf Rock, running so fast and out of control it was a wonder he didn't fall and break his fool neck.

By the time he got back to his house, he'd worked it out in his head why them snakes was acting so peculiar. They was just cold was all. And soon's they warmed up, they'd be a tangle of fangs and venom. He hoped he'd be able to hand over the whole bag to the Chosen One. He did *not* want to have to reach down in there to pull one of them out.

MARK MAY ACTUALLY HAVE CAUGHT himself with his fingernails, might literally have clawed his way to safety. It happened too fast to be sure but the fingers of his left hand were bleeding, the tips, and there were hunks of sharp wood under the fingernails of the other hand.

He only knew that he had jumped with every ounce of his strength and it wasn't enough. He hadn't reached the top of the beam to grab hold of it.

And then he was *there,* dangling for a breathless moment by one hand before he grasped firm with both. He didn't have to swing his feet up onto the beam because he was close enough to the wall that he could walk up it until he could hook one ankle over it and then the other.

He realized then that he wasn't breathing, had to yell at himself inside his head, "Breathe!"

He sucked in a gasp then, and another and then he was panting. And crying, maybe. Yeah, he was crying. He could feel the hitching in his chest and the tears streamed down his temples into his hair, but he made no sound.

"Climb!" he yelled silently at himself. Then he cursed aloud. Once he'd said that lone curse word, he couldn't stop. As he inched hand over hand up the joist toward the ceiling beams, he babbled out words that had never before come out his mouth, words he'd heard his father and the other farmers use, sometimes. And his brothers, too, when no one was around to hear them.

Jason. Those had been Jason's work boots!

His mind leapt away from the thought so violently that for a moment he almost lost his grip on the joist. When he made it to the ceiling beam, he had to pause and figure out what was the best way to clamber up onto it from below.

Without his own voice in his ears, he could hear her. Cupcake, down below him, lowing, bellowing, making a sound he'd never heard her make before. A sound he'd never heard any living thing make before. But he didn't look down until he was on top of the ceiling beam, hugging it so tight with both his arms and his legs that the rough wood scratched his wet cheek.

She wasn't looking up at him. She was just standing with her head against the broken gate smashed into the wall, one horn imbedded in the wood.

Hers was the only sound, though. Her lowing moan was the only noise of any kind in the barn — or coming in through the barn door. Where were all the other animals? Why were they quiet?

And the boots.

He couldn't not think about it now. His mind hauled

the image out of the depths of his soul and held it hot and stinking out in front of him.

He could scoot backwards down the beam until he was over her stall. Looking down into it, maybe he could see what had been lying in the straw back in the shadows of the corner.

No. He didn't want to see. And he didn't have to see. He knew. Jason had gone into Cupcake's stall to muck it out and she had … trampled him. Or gored him. He never even considered the possibility that Jason was still alive. He knew Cupcake had killed his brother. Just like she had tried to kill him.

But why would she do a thing like that? Why? Cupcake! He had slept curled up against her warm side in her stall at the state fair last summer, knew she must have been careful when she moved so she wouldn't roll over on him.

What was wrong with her?

Then a thought crashed into his chest with the force of a wrecking ball.

Whatever was wrong with Cupcake … was the same thing wrong with all the cows? *All two hundred of them?*

What kind of damage could a herd of two hundred rhinos do — two hundred *crazy* rhinos?

No, that was insane! The cattle wouldn't — why not? Cupcake had … *Go ahead, say it, say it out loud.*

"Cupcake tried to kill me."

The words came out like his nose was stopped up so he sat up carefully, his legs firmly hooked around the beam he was straddling, and wiped his nose and eyes on his sleeve.

Two hundred cattle. It was milking time — past milking time! His father and brothers — *brother* — would be out there with them. Eric guiding them into the chute at the end while his father opened the milking room door and lead the first six —

The first six *rhinos!*

No! *Stop it!*

It wasn't all of them. Something was wrong with Cupcake, only Cupcake. She was sick, that was all. They'd have to put her down.

Gunshots. He'd heard the sound of a rifle — his father's deer rifle, his .30-06. Two shots. Then silence.

Cupcake was still making the awful yowling, bellowing sound. Loud enough you surely could have heard her all the way to the house.

So where was everybody? Mom, Dad, Eric? Why didn't they come running?

Mark sat on the beam, dug his fingers into the wood, and started to cry again.

~

ANDI BURKE STOOD at the window and watched the tail lights of her father's car until he turned the corner and drove out of sight.

Maybe she should have told him.

Correction — yes, she should have told him. But the longer Andi lived with her strange ability — the knowing — the ability to see demons, the better she had become at keeping things to herself. It wasn't that she liked being secretive. No, she hated it. But it hadn't taken her long to figure out that the things she could see upset people — even the people she loved. Especially the people she loved. So she hesitated to share it, didn't like that she was about to ruin someone's day. Oh, she'd tell if it mattered that she tell — like when she had the vision of the shapes and it saved Daddy and Uncle Jack's lives. But last night's conver-

sation with Princess Buttercup … with the angel, wasn't
like that. The angel didn't ask her to listen carefully or to
remember what she saw. It didn't feel to Andi that the
angel was using her to take a message to anybody. The
angel had come to see *her*. The message, if there was one,
was for Andi.

Andi'd known she was there even before she opened
her eyes. The incredible brilliance that didn't look like any
light she'd ever seen before shone through her eyelids like
they were tissue paper. It wasn't a light you could look at
dead on. Probably wouldn't burn your corneas like looking
at an eclipse could, but you'd have to squint your eyes up
so tight to do it you wouldn't see anything anyway.

And as soon as Andi did open her eyes, the brilliance
dimmed. But didn't. It was just as bright as before, but
when she opened her eyes she was inside the brilliance
looking out instead of outside the brilliance looking in.
She'd seen a show about fiber optics and imagined it must
look like this. Millions of tiny points of light that formed a
single brilliance, but still stayed individual points of light.
At the same time. That was impossible, of course, but
apparently the words possible and impossible didn't apply
to angels.

She was standing at the foot of Andi's bed, dressed in
the simple white gown of Princess Buttercup.

"You don't have to do that anymore," Andi said. "The
Princess Buttercup thing. I'm not afraid of you."

"Oh, I don't do it for you," she said. Her voice was
silky. If you could see it, it would be the color of butter.
And she smelled of wildflowers in a meadow on a summer
morning. "I do it for me. I like playing dress-up."

She came around to the side of the bed to sit beside
Andi, with a second's hesitation to look at the blank space
on the bed that once was occupied by Andi's cat, Ossy.

"Have you thought about getting a kitten?"

Andi shook her head. She knew she was mistaken, knew that as soon as a little kitty snuggled up beside her and began to purr, she would melt in a puddle of love for it. That's what her head knew. What her heart knew was that there would never be another cat like Ossy — and that might actually be true. A male calico that wasn't sterile. You didn't run across one of those every day. Her heart believed that all her cat love had been lavished on Ossy, that Ossy had seen her through some of the most miserable days of her life. And then Ossy had attacked her and died because of it. A demon would never have bothered with simple little Ossy if it hadn't wanted to use the cat to get at Andi.

No, she didn't want another kitty, wouldn't put another simple little animal in that kind of danger.

Of course, as always, the angel seemed to know what she was thinking even when she hadn't said it yet.

"Loving always carries danger along with it," the angel said. "To love, you have to embrace the possibility of pain. Then you have to decide if the loving is worth the risk." She smiled. "It's always worth the risk. But you knew I'd say that, didn't you?"

Andi nodded. Angels were incredible, glorious, no-words-to-describe magnificent beings. But they were predictable. She didn't imagine they ever had bad days.

"You know about Uncle Jack and Miss Becca, don't you?" Andi asked. Duh. Of course she did. She was an angel. But she went on anyway and told her about it because she liked telling the story even to someone who already knew it.

"They're getting married Saturday. I'm the flower girl, Theresa's the matron of honor, Major Crocker is the best man and daddy's performing the ceremony. I know you'll be there, even if I can't see you. So will Becca's angel." It seemed awkward, sometimes, to talk about angels as if they belonged to you, like a pet turtle. But in Andi's limited experience, if an angel appeared to you — let you see them, in human form, in the real world — it would always be the same angel if there was a second appearance. Or a third. Andi didn't think anybody had talked to herds of angels — always just one. Becca's angel appeared to her as The Cat in the Hat.

"No, Andi, I won't be there. Neither will The Cat in the Hat."

"Why not?"

"We can't go there anymore, not to Caverna County. That's why I came to talk to you tonight."

Andi felt a chill down her spine as real as if a drop of melted icicle had dripped down the back of her shirt. Though she was shocked and dismayed, she discovered that she was not surprised.

"It's too dark for you there now, isn't it?" Andi didn't realize she was thinking the thought until she heard the words come out of her mouth.

"The darkness hates the light."

That was a Bible verse. Andi recognized it. She'd memorized it in Sunday School.

"It can't be dark and light in the same place at the same time, is that what you mean?"

"Or good and evil."

She reached out and took Andi's hand in hers. Her hand was soft, her fingers warm and clasped tight around Andi's.

"Be careful, Andi. I can't protect you there. Be careful who you trust and *what* you trust. Satan always masquerades as an Angel of Light."

Then the angel was gone, so fast it was as if she'd never

actually been there at all. And maybe she hadn't — how would Andi know? In the space between one heartbeat and the next, she vanished. There. Then not there.

Andi looked at where she had been sitting on the bed next to her. The sheets were not wrinkled. She reached out her fingers and touched the spot. The sheets weren't warm either.

Chapter Twelve

LINC HEARD his dispatcher on the telephone, trying to calm down whoever'd called, and his gut yanked into a knot. He stepped to his office door and called out to her.

"I'll take that call, Vicky!"

"But—"

He walked back to his desk and looked at his phone. Only one of the three red lights on the base of the phone was lit and as he watched, it went from solid red — someone was talking — to blinking red, indicating someone was on hold. He sat down before he picked up the receiver and put it to his ear and punched the blinking button.

"—right down the middle of the road!" someone was saying, obviously unaware that Vicky had hung up and Linc was on the line. "Like they owned it!"

"Who was walking down the middle of the road?" Linc asked.

"Linc? Is that you? Oh, Linc, I never seen nothing like it in my life. You gotta come now, quick. Them cattle's sick, got mad cow disease or something."

"Jude?"

Jude Green was a pig farmer who lived in the north end of the county — near Rocky Top Mountain, where an … an avalanche had killed Aaron Karrick and his little girl, Natalie. And where Randy Nickel's pumpkins had exploded … and all the fish in the river were … it wasn't that he doubted Crock's word, but Linc still couldn't bring himself to admit that the fish in the river had turned wrong side out.

"Just slow down, Jude, and tell me what happened."

"What happened don't make any sense! I was driving down Sawmill Lane when I come over a hill and the road ahead was full of cattle — not just one or two head but a whole herd. Richard Durston's dairy cattle."

"Cattle get out all the time," Linc said, trying — as unsuccessfully as Vicky — to calm the man down. "What's so strange about—"

"They wouldn't move! They was headed in my direction and when I come up on the first one, I blew my horn and she just kept coming like she hadn't even heard. I blew again and again. Nothing. So I stopped — what was I gonna do, run 'em down? — and got out to shoo them out of the way. All Richard's cows was out in the road. How do you not notice that every cow you got is—?"

"What happened when you tried to shoo them out of the road?"

"They come running at me! They charged! Like they was bulls and I was waving a red cape at 'em. Holsteins, for crying out loud! I jumped back in my truck and the one in the front crashed into my door! Tried to knock my truck over. The others was coming at me, too, so I slammed it into reverse and bailed!"

"When did this happen?"

"About five minutes ago. I'd a'called sooner but I had

trouble getting my phone out of my pocket and dialing. There's a road down the back side of Richard's corn field and soon's my hands stop shaking I'm gonna go tell him his cattle's—"

"No, you're not!" Linc hadn't meant to shout and continued in a calmer tone. "You don't go anywhere near Richard Durston's place, you got that?"

"Why not?"

Linc didn't know. He only knew that he had a horrible feeling in his gut that something really terrible had happened at the Durston farm.

"The way those cattle was acting — maybe they do have mad cow disease," he said, making it up as he went along. "I got to get out there and quarantine 'em, keep everybody away."

"You don't think I coulda caught it, do you? Standing that close to 'em. They say humans can—?"

"You can't catch mad cow disease like a cold, Jude. Now, you stay right where you are. Park your truck cross-ways in the road and don't let anybody go anywhere near that farm. You hear me?"

"I hear. But ... are you *sure* I couldn't a caught—"

Linc hung up the phone.

DANIEL BURKE PULLED into a parking space in front of the Caverna County Courthouse and killed the car engine. He paused, and very nearly started the car up again to move to a different spot. There were only a handful of others cars parked on the whole street and he was certain he'd pulled into the exact spot where he'd been parked last fall when Andi was attacked by her cat, Ossie.

His gut yanked into a knot at the memory. It had only

taken seconds. Andi had stepped out of the car and the cat had streaked across the street and leapt onto her chest. A big farmer standing nearby had yanked the cat off Andi and killed it before it could do her any great harm — just a couple of scratches.

But he would never forget the look of absolute desolation on the child's face or the feeling of impotent rage he had felt that beings out there that only knew ugliness and cruelty and hated all things good and beautiful had singled out him and his family for attack. His little girl! Leave her out of it, he'd raged in his head. You want me, you're mad at me because Jack and Becca and I kicked your butt twenty-six years ago — fine. Here I am. Take your best shot. Just leave Andi alone.

Of course the evil didn't leave Andi alone. And now that the child had the *knowing*, evil would follow her, dog her steps everywhere she went for the rest of her life.

He took a deep breath and let it out slowly. Struggled mightily get hold of his emotions. The same thing had happened every one of the few times he'd been in Caverna County since last Halloween. A darkness crept on rat feet into his heart, a sense of helplessness and hopelessness and fear settled around him like snow shaken off a limb overhead. Black snow.

It was over! The demon was gone. They had sent it back to hell. They had won.

So why didn't he feel like a winner? Why was he always cringing from a blow from the moment he set foot in Caverna County until he drove past the Bradford's Ridge welcome sign with the big picture of Chapman Whitworth — local boy makes good. Right.

And if this happened to him, he'd bet his gym shorts the same thing happened to Andi, too — but she kept it to herself because she didn't want to bring him down. Shoot, it might happen to all of them — Jack, Theresa, Becca — all of them who'd stood together against the efreet. Maybe they all fell into a black pit of despair every time they breathed the air here.

Why did Becca have to choose here for her wedding? But he knew why, of course. It was entirely possible that Becca was so sensitive to the evil around her that she felt what he felt in Caverna County no matter where she was. Maybe she didn't notice any difference because for her the world was often a very, very scary place. It was going to be … what Theresa called "a hard row to hoe" for Becca and Jack to get past the consequences/result of what had happened to Becca as a child that tipped her for a time over the edge into mental illness. Couple that with the fact that she had the knowing, could see demons no matter where she was … and they *knew* she could see them.

Jack would have to be there for her. She would need his strength. He would have to protect her from dangers both seen and unseen. And there was absolutely no doubt that he loved her; shoot, he'd loved her since they were twelve years old. But Jack wasn't exactly Mr. Sensitivity. He was sober, some would say stern, unemotional. Becca was going to need gentleness and kindness and Jack wasn't exactly poster boy for National Sensitivity Month.

"Stop it!"

He'd actually spoken the words out loud — he'd heard them. Now, if he could just get himself to *listen* to them and not just hear.

Becca belonged to Jack now. Period. He and Jack had both had a crush on her when … had *loved her* ever since they were boys. When the dust finally settled after their horrific encounter with the efreet last Halloween, Daniel had stepped up and eased what could have been an uncomfortable situation. He'd had the awkward conversation with Jack … telling him that there would no longer be a threesome — the three Musketeers — because he, Daniel, was bowing out. Oh, sure, he'd told Jack, he'd had a crush on Becca when they were children just like Jack had. But that was more than a quarter of a century ago. He said that the murder of his precious Emily by a demon had devastated him and he was far from over it. Might not ever get over it, in fact, but certainly was in no emotional position now to start a relationship with another woman.

"You love Becca, Jack. I don't. It really is that simple," he'd said.

And every word of it had been a lie.

IT WAS DUSK, that strange twilight time when the sun has gone down, but the light remains still, and the black canopy of darkness is gobbling up the sky, scattering stars as white and cold as chips of ice.

The Ugly Man never ventured out into the bright sunshine and even the failing light of dusk was unpleasant. He preferred the velvet darkness in the deepest, dark ditch of midnight.

But he knew he would have to carry his victim a long way, over rough terrain, and he needed as many hours of darkness as possible for that.

He glided from the shadow of one tree to the next, invisible even to some of the woods animals. He scared up a wild turkey that never saw him coming. Or maybe it did. He came out of the trees only five feet away from it but the turkey never moved. Either it didn't even see him or …

He circled the house once, staying in the woods, watching. The automatic light on the driveway that came on when it got dark blinked on as he watched. Then her car pulled up to the house. He saw an opportunity to leap out of the woods and take her there, but as soon as she pulled up, another woman the Ugly Man didn't know came to the door and the two women chatted as they walked into the house together.

Back to the original plan, then.

The sun went down. Puddles of gloom solidified into tar and as the light retreated, the Ugly Man felt stronger. He could do this. He would do this. They would pay. All of them. As he waited there in the darkness, he reached into his pants pocket and drew out the ring, felt the weight of it, the heaviness in his hand. He didn't know what the ring was or where he'd gotten it, only knew that it was *his*, the only thing left that belonged to him, and that it mattered to him in a way he no longer had the ability to understand. He squeezed it tight in his palm, just stood there holding it as he watched and waited.

All the light had gone out of the sky and the world was alight with starlight when the woman who'd greeted Cristina Trowbridge at her door came out of the house. Cristina stood at the door and watched her get into her car and drive away.

Then Cristina went back into the house and closed the door.

The Ugly Man would have preferred to wait until she had gone to bed, until she was alone, sleeping, vulnerable. He liked to take his victims then, loved the look of stark terror in their eyes when he clamped his hand down over their mouths.

But he would have to take Cristina now. There was no time to enjoy the delicious fear. But there'd be time for that later. Oh my, yes, there would be time to enjoy horror, fear, terror, to feed on them the way scavenger animals feed on a decaying corpse in the woods. He would suck every bit of pleasure out of it when he could, the only pleasure he would ever know … *ever.* But now was not that time.

He put the ring back into his pocket. Creeping from bush to shrub across the darkened back yard, the Ugly Man slipped as silent as a breeze up onto the back porch. He put his ear to the door and listened. He could hear her. She was in the room to the left of the door, the kitchen, and she was singing the Bonnie Tyler song, "Total Eclipse of the Heart." Her voice was pleasant though untrained, sharps and flats. She tried for the signature breathiness of the original and only sounded mildly hoarse. He knew a lot about music, but he didn't know when he'd learned it or why.

He tried the doorknob before he went to the windows to see if any were un—

The knob turned in his hand. He inched it forward, listening.

Keep singing, he thought. I will know exactly where you are as long as you sing and you won't hear me coming.

He eased himself inside and pushed the door closed but not latched. He was in a "mudroom" with a washer and dryer and water heater. An ironing board was set up in front of the washer. The iron sitting on it was hot. She'd been ironing and—

He heard the singing voice coming closer and just had time to step back behind the upright freezer before she came into the room. She went to the iron, lifted the lid on the water compartment and poured in the cup full of water. She set the cup aside and picked up the iron.

The Ugly Man stepped out, grabbed her arm and swung her around toward him. She gasped, then got a look at his face and began to shriek.

She still had the iron in her hand when she began to struggle to get free and she used it as a weapon, burning his arm and chest with a fiery sensation that was probably pain. He wasn't sure how pain felt anymore. He grabbed the iron, yanked it out of her hand and turned it on her. Shoving her up against the wall, he smashed the iron onto the side of her face. She wailed, fought and screamed, kicked and punched, but he was immovable. Just held the iron where it was, enjoying the cloying stink of burning flesh that filled the room.

Then she suddenly went slack, her knees buckled and she collapsed on the floor in a heap. Fainting saved him the trouble of having to knock her over the head. He dropped the iron on the floor and reached down to pick up the woman on the floor.

That was when he saw the little boy in the doorway of the utility room. He was probably five or six years old, wearing Spiderman footie pajamas and holding some kind of plastic gun that either shot water or Nerf balls out the end.

The kid just stood there, gawking at him. He dropped the gun to the floor and wet himself, the stink of urine mingling with the smell of burning flesh.

"Mommy." That was all he said.

The Ugly Man reached down to pick the iron back up and bash in the kid's head. But suddenly the child was gone. As fast as a baby rabbit, he darted out of the doorway and vanished. The Ugly Man stumbled over the body and the boy got a head start. He could have run outside, could be hiding anywhere in the house. Upstairs, downstairs, the garage.

The Ugly Man didn't have time to go looking for him. The woman would begin to come around any minute. She was the prize.

"Your lucky day," he called out. At least he tried to. No one could have understood the words, but he kept hollering anyway. "You tell them, boy. You tell them exactly what you saw. It won't matter."

Then the Ugly Man picked the woman up with a grunt of effort. She wasn't thin like the teenage girl who wasn't Martha Holterman as she was supposed to be. He threw her over his shoulder in a fireman's carry, opened the back door and was off the steps and out into the safety of the darkness in seconds. He never looked back. If he had, he would have seen a little boy in Spiderman pajamas standing in the back door. He was holding a cell phone. Punching buttons on it.

Chapter Thirteen

THERE WERE forty-five or fifty of them, filing silently into the sanctuary in groups of two or three. Not talking. Trying not to look like they were gawking at the Chosen One, who sat in a high-backed chair behind the pulpit in front of the baptistry. A scene on crumbling plaster, the paint flaking off into the water in a dusting of colored dandruff, was obviously supposed to be a river — the river Jordon, maybe.

The Chosen One sat with his back ramrod straight, surveying each person who entered the room. Lights flickered around them that only he could see. Not around all of them, though. A handful had remained unmoved by the whispering in their ears. He would convince them anyway, drag them along in a group hysteria. Or he'd kill them. One or the other.

They were desperately poor people, thin and hollow-eyed. It was in Martin County, less than a hundred miles from the spot where the church sat, that President Lyndon B. Johnson declared war on poverty in 1964. Twenty-two trillion dollars later — the Chosen One thought that was something like three times the expense of all the world's wars put together, but he wasn't sure of that — the proof of the pudding stood before him. Bare feet, tattered clothes, or mismatched outfits from some clothing drive in some wealthy neighborhood where the people had never gone to bed hungry a single night in their lives.

He couldn't even see desperation in their eyes. They'd passed that stage long ago. You still had to have some "wanting" left in you to be desperate and these people didn't even remember the yearning of want.

Most had been listening to the whispers for years, so what the Chosen One was about to say would have the ring of familiarity to it — like maybe they'd thought the same thing themselves. Like maybe it was their own idea in the first place.

When the last of the assemblage had found seats on the worn wooden pews, the Chosen One stood abruptly and strode with purpose to the pulpit. He didn't remove his sunglasses, though the cheap 40-watt bulbs in the overhead lights cast only a bilious glow and left the corners of the room in shadow. There was a Bible lying on the pulpit and he was careful not to touch it.

"I don't have to tell you why I've summoned you here tonight," he said. No hymn singing or Scripture reading. Right to the point. "You already know. You've felt the knowing of it in your chest for months, the pressure building until you're afraid you're going to explode. "

You could have heard a gnat fart in the room. Everyone was leaning forward, eager, hanging on his every word.

"The End is coming," he said, and somebody gasped. "Not just 'soon' either. The End of all life, of all hope, of all that exists or ever did exist is only hours away."

A woman whose pale frizzy blonde hair, Marilyn

Monroe blonde, stuck out around her head like steel wool, fell to the floor off the pew in the back of the church and began to twitch like she was having a seizure, the lights around her flickering like a Christmas tree.

Morag Heywood. Ah, yes — Morag was here. Good. *Excellent.*

He leaned forward and spoke the next words in a voice so soft you had to be concentrating really hard to hear. Everyone in the room heard.

"Are. You. Ready?"

He let the words hang out there in the air. One reason he didn't take off his sunglasses was that they afforded him the concealment to stare at anyone he chose, study them without their knowing. That was only one reason, of course.

He picked out a man sitting in the second row from the front, lights flickering around him like a dozen green fireflies.

He slowly lifted his finger and pointed at the man.

"You there."

The man looked terrified, tapped his chest and looked quizzical as he looked over his shoulder, praying that the Chosen One meant somebody else.

"Yes, you. Come up to the front here where everybody can see you, Brother Stedman."

There was a murmuring in the crowd. How did the Chosen One know Paul Stedman's name?

Stedman didn't move.

"Go on, now, Paul," said an elderly woman seated down the pew from him. You do what you're told to do, else he's gonna have you struck down with a bolt of lightning."

Stedman stood on trembling legs and staggered out into the aisle. He took a couple of steps toward the pulpit before he ran out of gas and stopped, swaying a little like he was standing on the deck of a ship in a storm.

"We don't have time to waste on doubt," the Chosen One said, though he knew there wasn't a man, woman or child seated in the room who harbored the slightest disbelief. Jonah Ballard had told them he was the Messiah, told them how he come walking out of the woods naked. And about the mountain flinging Pastor Karrick and his little girl to their deaths. They didn't need any convincing, but he intended to convince them anyway. He needed their absolute obedience and now was the time to secure that permanently. "I have come to save you, a small band of the faithful who will be spared the eternal judgement, who will be saved from the fiery furnace with singed coattails. You will live when all there will perish.

"But I will also save you from the doubt that can cripple you, the niggling disbelief that rests in the corners of all our hearts. You must *not* listen to that doubt. So I will prove to you today that you are indeed in the presence of divinity."

He gave Jonah the prearranged signal and he left quickly out the side door and returned in moments with a gunny sack tied with plastic insert-tab wraps. He set the sack on the floor in front of the terrified man standing before the Chosen One, used snips to cut through the plastic ties, then stood, holding the sack shut.

"I have dominion over the fowls of the air and the fish of the sea and the creatures of the earth." The Chosen One nodded and Jonah let loose his hold on the top of the sack as he grabbed the bottom. In one motion he dumped out the contents of the bag onto the floor as he leapt back out of the way.

Two huge rattlesnakes lay on the hardwood floor.

There was only one true scream, and the Chosen One

was almost sure the woman — her name was Lynn Geth — who emitted it, instantly swooned and lay sprawled next to Morag, who still appeared to be having a seizure.

The gasps, grunts, inarticulate cries and general horrified mumble came as folks came to their senses a moment after Lynn swooned.

The Chosen One took a couple of steps forward, bent and casually picked up the biggest rattlesnake, who had made no move to get away. He held it up in front of the man standing in the aisle and was afraid the man might also collapse from fear, too.

Come on, man, get it together.

"Fear not, brother," he said. "I have commanded these servants of the Evil One to be still and they will not strike at anybody."

He actually held the head of the snake up beside his own cheek.

"They are under my complete control."

He looked pointedly at everyone in the sanctuary, seeming to pause to stare into the eyes of every last one. "I command life or death here. I am in control."

He nodded to the man standing, swaying in the aisle.

"You may be seated, Brother Stedman. Your faith will be rewarded." The man looked like the only reward he wanted was a chance to go to the bathroom and clean out his pants.

The Chosen One knelt and picked up the second snake and walked to the pulpit holding them both. Neither made any move to try to get away.

"You will all be rewarded for your faith, which is the belief in something you cannot see. But there is still unbelief in the room. Still those who think the snakes are not behaving like ordinary rattlesnakes. Who think I drugged the snakes or something like that so they would not strike."

He dropped both snakes casually onto the pulpit, positioning them so they lay atop the Bible, holding it closed.

He took off his suit coat and laid it on the chair. Then he rolled up the shirt sleeve on his left arm, all the way past the elbow. That was the first sight anybody'd had of his black skin, and there was a stir in the audience though nobody said anything. Without another word, the Chosen One stepped back to the pulpit, picked up the larger of the two snakes and tilted its head back, pressing on its jaws to reveal its fangs.

"This," he said with dramatic flair, "is for the unbelievers. May you repent of your sin before Judgement Day."

Then he held up his bare left forearm, and stabbed the fangs into his own flesh. There were screams then from all over the sanctuary.

"Press here," he said, indicating a spot on the back of the snake's head, "and you can milk out the venom." Then he pressed hard on the spot.

Women cried out, men gasped, little children began to cry, but he wasn't done with them yet. He stepped back to the sack on the floor, placed the rattler into it, and picked up the second snake. Then he did the same thing to it he had done to the first snake. He jabbed its fangs into his forearm an inch or two below where he'd caused the first snake to bite him.

When he pulled the snake free, he dropped it back into the sack with the other and nodded for Jonah to take them away. He was only too happy to do that.

The Chosen One stepped back behind the pulpit. He had them now, every one of them, in the palm of his hand. They would follow him, the "Messiah," down the barrel of a Howitzer.

Holding up his arm for all to see, he pointed out.

"See, no blood." He paused and stepped back into

preacher mode. "Scripture tells us that without the shedding of blood there can be no remission of sin."

He paused dramatically.

"But our sins will be forgiven before we stand before God in judgement. Because we will shed blood to wash them away."

He leaned forward and spoke softly. "If you want to be saved from the fiery wrath of God, come back here in the morning, meet me here. We will shed the blood of the unbelievers. We will wash ourselves in their blood until we are clean."

WHEN DANIEL WALKED into the Caverna County Courthouse that evening, he was grateful for the warmth. It had turned suddenly cold and it'd not occurred to Daniel to bring a jacket. The smell of coffee — good coffee — wafted out into the hallway from Sheriff Lincoln's office and Daniel smiled. He'd heard Jack and Crock joke about how absolutely abysmal Linc's coffee was, so he'd sent the sheriff a coffeemaker, a Bunn ten-cup Velocity Brewer. Anonymously. Linc was certain it was either Jack or Crock — both of whom adamantly denied it — but he hadn't yet considered the possibility it'd been Daniel, who wasn't likely to hold up under close examination. But for the time being, the coffeemaker was a mystery surprise that delighted not only the sheriff but all who worked in the office and anyone who came to visit him.

Given all the sheriff had done to keep him and the others out of trouble with the federal authorities, it was a small gesture.

One look at the faces of the three men who turned to greet him when he walked into the sheriff's office and

Daniel's stomach fell into his shoes. He tasted fear in the back of his throat as bitter as the coffee that'd been dissolving the bottoms out of coffee mugs in the sheriff's office for years.

"What's wrong?" he asked, his eyes pleading with them to say it was nothing, to laugh it off, to smile and tell him not to worry, everything was hunky dory.

"And I'm glad to see you tonight, too, Reverend Burke," Crock said, stood and extended his hand. Jack was staring out the window with a look on his face Daniel hadn't seen since … The sheriff didn't even bother to put up a front.

"We look that bad, do we?" he asked.

"Like the Publisher's Clearing House million-dollar giveaway van pulled up in your driveway … and then the guys with the balloons got out and went next door."

"Wish we knew," Linc said, stood and crossed to the new coffee machine. "Want some coffee?" he asked. "It's not the elephant piss we used to drink around here."

"You didn't drag me down here tonight to show off your designer coffeemaker," Daniel said and realized his fear had made him sound harsh. "I'm sorry. Didn't mean to sound like a troll. It's just that …"

"It's just that this place gives you the willies and you'd rather get puked on by a little kid on an airplane than entertain the idea that something else is going on here — again," Crock said.

"Is it?"

There was a pregnant pause.

"Yep. *Something's* going on. Just don't have any idea what yet," the sheriff said and Daniel sank down into a chair. He wanted to put his head in his hands and cry.

"Tell me," he said.

"Yeah, let's hear it," Jack said, turning away from the window, his jaw locked and the vein on his temple pulsing.

Linc and Crock told their stories, then Daniel looked from one to the other.

"You think all this … is related somehow?"

"And you don't?"

"But how …?"

"There's more," Linc said, "since yesterday."

He told them that there had been a fourth kidnapping — and the number was pretty firm. It was clear by now that a homeless man named Brooker and an old woman with Alzheimer's hadn't just wandered off but really were missing.

"There's not but twenty thousand people in Caverna County and we just had four kidnappings in two days. We got there quick on this last one and sent out the dogs, but they couldn't pick up a scent. Nothing."

"And the bugs?" Jack asked.

"Yeah, there were bugs on the floor in the utility room where he grabbed her. This time, we got a witness." He quashed the bloom of hope before it had time to blossom on the two other police officers' faces.

"A little boy, Cristina Trowbridge's son. He's only five years old. He's the one who dialed 911. By the time we got there, he was almost catatonic with shock. Couldn't get anything out of him. He just kept repeating, 'The ugly man, the ugly man.'"

Then Linc fell silent, unconsciously flipping a pencil back and forth in his hands, staring at nothing.

"Spit it out," Jack said. Not mean. Matter of fact. One cop to another.

"A couple of hours ago, we found four members of the Durston family — Richard, his wife Lorene, and sons Eric and Jason — dead. Just one survivor — Mark. He's twelve years old."

"Cause of death?" Crock asked.

"The coroner will list blunt force trauma on the report."

"They were beaten to death?" Jack asked.

"Trampled." Linc paused and took a breath. "By cattle. Their own cattle — *dairy cows.*"

Someone sucked in a gasp. It was a moment before Daniel realized he'd heard himself.

Linc lost it for just a moment and his voice quavered, "We had to shoot them, probably two hundred head of them. Or they would have trampled us, too. Took two or three shots to bring some of them down. They just kept coming, charging, making this … awful sound in their throats. I never heard a sound like—".

He caught himself then. Stopped and regrouped. He finished the story in a police-officer, just-the-facts-ma'am monotone.

He and Deputy Bob Sirrine rolled up at the Durston farm in their cruisers at the same time. All the fences were down, had been knocked down and what appeared to be Durston's whole herd of dairy cattle were wandering around like they were lost. He could see they had to be in pain — their udders were swollen. They'd obviously missed the afternoon milking. He'd started to get out of his cruiser but paused instead — cop's gut instinct. He'd reached up and taken his service rifle out of the rack above his head and made Sirrine go back and get his when he saw that the deputy was armed only with his service revolver. Good thing, that.

After Linc called it in, other units showed up. His deputies and the state police. "The gunfire must have sounded like a practice range," he said. "Before long,

Durston's whole dairy herd — every last head of them — lay dead or dying in the dirt."

The sheriff said they found Lorene's body near the house, and Richard's deer rifle was lying in the dirt nearby.

"Lorene musta heard somebody calling for help," he said. "From what I can figure, she came out of the house with the deer rifle and started toward the milking parlor, shooting. She got off at least two shots before they got her."

"Mark heard the shots from the barn and started hollering. He'd got away by climbing up onto a roof beam. His brother, though …"

Linc said they found Jason dead in the stall in the barn. When they were finally able to approach the milking parlor, they found Richard inside.

"He'd been stomped so bad … if I hadn't known who he was, I …"

The other boy, Eric, was dead in the chute leading to the milking parlor.

"What about the other animals?" Crock asked. "There must have been more livestock — sheep, goats. Shoot, what about the chickens?"

"There weren't any other animals. I guess they scattered after the cows knocked down all the fences, sensed something was wrong with the cattle, maybe. I know he had pigs and we did find one dead piglet by the front porch of the house. There were rabbit pens in the back yard, knocked over and trampled, but I guess the rabbits got away because we didn't find any. He might have had some goats, too — for Mark to show at the fair. They must be up in the woods, or out in other fields. I didn't have a chance to look for them."

"So you're thinking … mad cow disease?" Daniel shoved the words out into the room the way you shove a paper boat out into a pond even though you know it's going to sink. He knew such a "city boy" question deserved a condescending answer but Linc didn't give him one.

"Mad cow disease has an incubation period of four, sometimes as long as six years. Calves get it from eating infected feed, but don't show symptoms until they're adults giving milk. A whole herd of cattle that all break out with the symptoms of advanced mad cow disease on the same day? Besides, infected cattle lose coordination, can't walk or stand, become agitated and disoriented, not ..."

"Homicidal," Jack finished for him.

"That's probably what they'll say, though," Crock observed absently. "The boys from the Kentucky Department of Agriculture. They'll come down here and poke around and then go back to Frankfort and concoct a story to explain it all away. The state Fish and Wildlife Department will likely do the same thing once they start digging into the two dead fish I gave them. I didn't cut those two open, but after the ones I did cut into, I'd wager they both had fins, scales and a tail ... on the inside."

"What could cause—?"

"Nothing could, Daniel," Jack said, in a voice that sounded both worn out and enraged at the same time. "Absolutely nothing. Let's get the elephant out of the room. There is no natural explanation for rocks flying off a mountaintop, exploding pumpkins, serial kidnappings, dead fish and murderous dairy cattle. There's only one way to go with that. The explanation is supernatural."

"Those ... demon things again," Linc said.

"Maybe."

"Appears to me we invited the wrong guests to this party," Crock said. "The four of us don't know squat and understand even less. We need to be talking to Theresa, Andi and Becca."

"No!" Daniel and Jack said the word at the same time with the perfect unison of a chorus line.

"Not this time!" Daniel said. "We are *not* going to drag my ten-year-old daughter—" Eleven. She was eleven now. "—into another nightmare."

"Becca has been through enough!" Jack said, and Daniel was proud of his protectiveness. "We came here to enjoy the happiest day of both our lives and that's exactly what we're going to do. Then we're leaving. And we're *never* coming back."

His voice grew quiet and he gave Sheriff Lincoln a penetrating look. "I'm sorry, Linc. But we don't have a dog in *this* fight. The efreet — that was our problem. We got tangled up with it when we were children. It never would have left us alone. It would have destroyed our lives unless we destroyed it first. But this — it has nothing to do with us."

"How do you know it doesn't?" the sheriff said quietly, and Daniel felt gooseflesh pebble on his arms. "How do you know it's not because you're here, or because of something you done ... before. Or maybe something you didn't do. You can't just walk away—"

"Yes, we *can* just walk away. And I absolutely plan to do just that." Jack stood abruptly. "We're not telling the others — Becca, Andi and Theresa. In just twenty-four hours, it'll be over and we'll be gone." He turned for the door, tossing words over his shoulder as he left. "We have sacrificed enough," he said. "This isn't for us to do! Not this time."

Daniel didn't think Jack was talking to anybody in the room when he said that last part.

Chapter Fourteen

BECCA WAS DRESSED in her nightgown with a dainty lace veil attached to a wreath of flowers pinned on her head, but she was wearing shiny white high heels so Theresa could judge how long to make the veil. Andi bet the t-shirt Theresa was wearing over her oversized, baggy pants had belonged to Bishop. Becca and Theresa were talking quietly while Theresa worked and Andi, Ariel and Cassidy Davenport — who'd come over for the slumber party — tried very hard to act like normal children playing. All of them were trying to pretend they were having innocent fun when all of them except Jenny were so weighed down by the oppressive darkness that nothing seemed like fun.

The girls had spread out on the living room floor all the furniture cushions — the couch, loveseat and chairs, and they'd been rolling around on them in a tangle, tickling each other and giggling.

Andi tried to shake off the gloom, determined not to let the oppressiveness suck all the joy out of getting to spend time with her friends. She whispered something into Ariel's ear. Ariel nodded and went to Jenny and started playing the handshake game — which was an elaborate sequence of movements that started with shaking hands and moved on to coordinated high-fives, elbow bumps, double-hand claps, pinky shakes and other stuff.

As soon as they were deep into the sequence, Andi got down on her hands and knees and crept toward Jenny until she was right behind her, crossways.

Then Andi cried "Three Stooges!" She'd picked that as the signal because they'd been watching videos of Moe, Curly and Larry after the Pee-wee Herman movie was over. Andi thought they were way funnier than Pee-wee Herman, the way they were always playing tricks on people, putting pies in their faces and things like that.

At Andi's signal, Ariel pushed on Jenny's chest and she stumbled backwards over Andi, landing in a sprawl on the big couch cushion on the floor in a burst of carefree laughter that sounded like tiny bells ringing in the gloom.

"I'll get you," she said, giggling, and tackled Ariel, who rolled up in a ball as Jenny tried to wrestle her onto her back so she could tickle her belly. As she threw herself into the pile, she noticed that Theresa and Becca were watching the game, with smiles that looked like they'd been stapled to their faces.

The joy of the moment evaporated like steam from a teapot. Within minutes, she, Cassidy and Ariel were somber again, staring into space, so preoccupied Andi didn't hear Jenny until she cried out.

"I said, you're no fun!" She looked from one to the other. "None of you. All you do is mope around like the sky is falling or something. I'm going downstairs to play a video game."

Andi watched her storm out and slam the door behind her. She felt bad for the little girl — all excited about a slumber party — a bachelorette party. She always identified with Jenny because Jenny didn't have a mother, either. Sheriff Lincoln's wife had died a long time ago, though. Theresa'd even brought a gag gift for Jenny to give to Becca — a wine glass, but there was a slit in it somewhere because it was impossible to drink from it without the liquid drooling down your chin. Andi wanted to have fun just as bad as Jenny did. More than Jenny did. But she couldn't; nothing was right. Ariel Murphy and Cassidy weren't doing any better job than she was of pretending they didn't know that, too.

As soon as Jenny was out of the room, they stopped trying.

"I'm scared," Ariel said, her voice soft, as a single tear slid down her freckled cheek. She had her long hair in a ponytail tonight, but it would be in braids tied with ribbons for the wedding tomorrow. Andi had talked Becca into allowing Andi's — what was it Daddy called it? — a posse — to be "assistant flower girls," tossing rose petals behind Becca as she walked down the aisle. Ariel would be wearing a pinafore her mother made for the occasion — making the child the image of a life-sized Raggedy Ann doll.

"I'm not scared!" Cassidy said and probably didn't realize that she'd reached up to touch one of the long scars that sliced across her face where she'd clawed it with her own fingernails. "Let 'em come. They won't get me this time. I'll show them."

She had struggled against the demon that had possessed her and that's what had earned her the scars on her face. Her kinky black hair had grown back in so the bald spots where she'd yanked out her own braids no longer showed.

"What's happening?" Ariel asked. "Why is it getting so … dim outside? It started a couple of days ago. I didn't even notice it at first, just kind of … gloomy, like on a rainy day except the sun was shining."

"I noticed it," Cassidy said. "It started Wednesday afternoon. I was in the back yard and the shadows under the trees got darker and darker until they looked like black holes, like if you stepped into them you'd fall down and down and …"

"Is it dark for everybody or just for us?" Ariel asked. "And it's so cold."

Andi wasn't sure whether "ordinary people" could tell it was dim outside. She called those without the knowing "ordinary" because if she called them normal, what was she? Besides, Theresa said normal was nothing more than the setting on a dryer.

But the cold — yes, the others could feel that. Her daddy said he might have to buy her a hoodie to wear over her flower girl dress and she'd told him she'd rather freeze to death.

"It's not like it was before," she said, struggling to find words to tack onto her thoughts, which were muddled and confused in her own head. "This is different, somehow. I don't think it's about demons possessing people. We sent the efreet back to hell. And you have to be inside the pentagram with it to be possessed. But … I think the darkness is about demons *somehow*."

Theresa put down the pincushion on the table, stepped back to survey her work. Then crossed the room and sat down on the couch beside where the girls were playing. The springs groaned under her weight.

"This here a private party or can anybody come?"

"Everybody's welcome, but it's not much of a party," Andi said miserably. "That's why Jenny left."

"Don't you worry about Jenny. She's just grumpy because she's coming down with something. Felt her forehead and she's got a fever. I give her two baby aspirins and looks like she's not going to make the wedding tomorrow. She's wrapped up snug in a blanket on the basement couch playing a video game. Now it's just us chickens." She cast a look at Becca. "The roosters is at they own party in the sheriff's office and I guarantee they ain't having any more fun than we is."

"Do *you* know why Sheriff Lincoln and Crock wanted to see Jack and Daniel?" Becca asked her.

"Nope. But it's something bad, else why the hurry?"

"If they knew that, why didn't they take us with them?" Becca said.

Theresa shook her head. "Child, you got a world of things to learn about men. If they could have, they'd have gone after that efreet all by theirselves, guns blazing. It's a macho thing. And next time we see them, they're gonna make like they rushed off to the sheriff's office so Crock could give them flyfishing lessons."

"Something bad's going on," Ariel said.

"We shouldn't have come," Becca said. "It's all my fault. But I never dreamed ... we've come to Bradford's Ridge other times since ... To bring Andi to see Ariel, to transfer the deed to the farm and to work on the chapel. Nothing out of the ordinary ... if I hadn't been so determined to have the wedding—"

"Things happen for a reason," Theresa cut her off. "Us being here right now — *all of us* — that ain't no coincidence." She looked from Becca to Andi and then back to Becca.

"When you come through town, did you see ...? Was they folks walking around with demons crawling all over 'em?" Becca shook her head. "'Cause I didn't smell nothing."

"It was just the lights," Andi said so softly everyone

turned to her. "They're easier to see when it's so dim outside."

"I saw the lights," Becca said. "Everywhere. I've never seen them so ... thick. Even in some of the bad places I've been in my life. Places like ... like Las Vegas where the evil's everywhere you look. Even there, they weren't like what I saw in town this afternoon. The lights were around almost everyone."

"Bishop's grandfather said them lights was demons that didn't possess nobody, but was trying to influence them. If Satan can't *possess* you, he'll try to *op*press you. Taking away your faith and joy by telling you lies. Getting you to do things you know you hadn't ought to do."

"I hear the whispers," Ariel said. "Can't you hear it? It's like if a huge crowd of people, a stadium full of people, were all whispering at the same time. None are loud enough to hear, but the sound of them ... buzzing."

"Not everybody's listening to the whispers, but some are," Andi said.

She turned and looked full into Cassidy's face, who hadn't said a word since her outburst of bravado before Theresa and Becca joined them. "You're listening, aren't you, Cassidy?" she said.

Cassidy was so surprised she merely gaped at Andi.

"They're bright, sparkling, swirling around and around your head. You can hear their voices, can't you? Telling you things, awful things, trying to get you to do things ... terrible things."

"No ... I—"

"We can see them, Cassidy," Becca said. "Don't listen to what they're telling you."

"When we were in the cave, the angel said, 'Remember who they serve — the Father of *Lies*,'" Andi said.

Cassidy exploded in rage.

"No demon's going to control me," she roared. "Not ever again. I'll fight. I'd rather die."

She jumped up and bolted out of the room. They heard the front door open and slam shut and Andi stepped to the window, and watched Cassidy run away down the street, trailing a string of lights like a tail on a kite.

～

No, no, no, *no!*

Not now, not *today.*

Jack Carpenter didn't believe he had ever — *ever* — been so angry. Blind rage flooded into his bloodstream, pure adrenaline pumped him up like a crackhead, made him as invincible as Cole Stuart had been when he'd chased Jack through all those warehouses a year ago. But Jack had beaten him. He'd beaten the efreet, too!

No, he didn't. Andi did. Andi and the angel. He and Crock were just along for the ride.

He leaned his forehead over on the steering wheel of his car and methodically beat it against the rubber surface.

He felt the rage begin to drain out of him and he fought to hold onto it. He wanted to be furious. He deserved to be furious. The fury was a powerful emotion and right now what he needed was power.

But the power ebbed as he sat there, and every vacant spot in his soul where the anger had been was filled up with fear.

You're going to die, Jack.

"Who said that?" Jack yanked around in the seat, prepared to beat whoever had slipped into his backseat to a bloody pulp. No one was there. But he heard the whisper, didn't he?

So is Becca. You're all going to die.

Jack looked all around him, stupidly checking under the seats and in the glove box — somebody was speaking to him, through a speaker of some sort. He yanked out his iPhone. Maybe he had butt dialed —

Unless you run. You have to run — run now!

Jack would have gasped but he was already holding his breath. He sat totally motionless, his heart jackhammering a hole in his chest as realization flooded over him. He knew who had spoken. Spoken to him, Jack Carpenter, the guy who a year ago didn't even believe demons existed.

The Father of Lies.

He recognized the voice, too. He'd last heard it in a dark cave deep in the earth where he and his friends had fought an epic battle with a prince of demons. And won.

Or had they?

MONSTERS ARE CHASING ANDI, Ariel and Becca through the woods and it's so dark Andi can barely see.

She's running wildly, can't see the others, only the white splashes of their dresses as they get farther and farther away until they're lost altogether in the gloom.

She tries to run faster, ignoring the stitch in her side, but she can't see where she's going. Trees suddenly appear in front of her out of dark mist and she hardly has time to dodge them.

Thorn bushes tear at her dress. She's wearing her flower girl dress, the one with the flowing white skirt that has little daisies on it, and the skirt snags on everything — the limbs of bushes and trees, tearing the beautiful fabric and yanking Andi off balance so she almost falls.

She has to get away! He's coming.

She doesn't know who he is, only that he is terrible, fearsome and somehow unnatural. But she doesn't know how she knows any of it or what it means.

In the weird way of dreams where impossible things can happen and seem perfectly normal, Andi is running through the woods in a panic but at the same time she is also watching herself run through the woods, from the outside. She tries to call out to herself, to the little girl running, that there's a low-hanging limb just ahead, but the running-Andi can't hear the watching-Andi and she plows right into it. It catches her in the chest with the force of being struck by a baseball bat. The running Andi feels it and the watching Andi does, too. It knocks the breath out of both of them and it hurts.

Running-Andi is not the only thing watching-Andi can see. She has a view of much more than a little girl in a white dress in dark woods. Watching-Andi can see all the woods as if she were high up in the sky, looking down into darkness — and there are blinking lights everywhere. Yellow and green. Ugly lights that blink but don't twinkle. Twinkling requires real light and these lights have no real light in them.

Then watching-Andi begins to get closer and closer to the blinking lights, like movies sometimes zoom in. She sees that the blinking lights are flickering around people, though she already knew that. She's seen those kinds of lights before.

The people are hurrying through the trees like they can see, like maybe it's dark for her but not for them. When she is up close and they're lit by the blinking lights that aren't light, she sees that the people are covered in blood, everywhere, clothes, face, hair.

One is a man carrying a bloody knife. Another is a woman holding something that looks like a hatchet — no, it's a meat cleaver. Blood drips off it onto the ground. Both of them are smeared with blood and they don't look injured so the blood must be somebody else's. Andi knows then, without knowing how she knows, that the blood is from the people they have murdered, butchered, stabbed and hacked to death.

A form appears who is there but not there. Running-Andi can't see him, but watching-Andi does. He isn't in the woods, but she can see him anyway. He is a shadow of great darkness, a black splotch that blocks out even the tiniest bit of light. She strains to see the shadow, but it's like she is looking into a black hole in the world.

Watching-Andi stops before the shape. Running-Andi keeps racing through the dark woods. There's a dark form in the woods, a man. He leans over her and his face is a nightmare …

Watching-Andi sees the other form and it has a face, too, and when she looks into his eyes, a black tide rolls over her, washes over her like a wave on the beach.

The dream stops there for both Andis, and she begins to scream.

ANDI JERKED VIOLENTLY AWAKE, an unreleased scream straining at the back of her throat. She was sitting up in bed breathing as hard as if she'd been running. And she *had* been running in the dream.

She looked over at Ariel, who was sharing Jenny's bed with her because Jenny was on the couch, propped up with a humidifier that was making the whole living room damp.

Ariel was awake, watching her. She didn't ask if Andi was okay. She didn't have to. Ever since the night an angel chased a demon out of Ariel as she lay crumpled and broken at the bottom of a gully, the two of them found that they understood each other's feelings without having to ask.

"Did you have a vision?" Ariel asked, sitting up beside her.

Vision?

It hadn't occurred to Andi that her terrorized flight through the woods was anything more than a bad dream, a nightmare. But nightmares always faded as soon as you woke up, so after a few minutes you couldn't even remember what it was about the nightmare that was so scary. This nightmare wasn't fading.

"I don't know. I don't think so. How could it be? There was no angel."

"Angels can't come here anymore. It's too dark."

How did Ariel know about that when Andi hadn't told anybody what Princess Buttercup had said to her? But Ariel just … knew things.

"How could I have a vision without an angel?" Andi asked. Ariel shrugged.

"It was just a nightmare, that's all," Andi said. The look on Ariel's face made it clear she didn't believe that any more than Andi did. "We need to go back to sleep."

Both the girls lay back down and closed their eyes. Neither of them went to sleep for a long, long time.

Chapter Fifteen

ALICIA DUNN HAD HEARD her friends talk about it with their new babies, but she couldn't believe it was actually happening to her. After all, she and Steven had waited so long for her to get pregnant.

Ali wouldn't let her mind go back to the rose bushes in the back yard. Three of them. She had been so surprised that first time. Couldn't imagine what was happening to her when she started to bleed. She and Steven'd decided to have kids and badda boom, badda bing, she got pregnant and she expected the basic happily-ever-after story.

She was four months along, only barely beginning to show, had just that afternoon gone into town and bought a maternity blouse, though she really didn't need it yet. Her older sister, Bonnie, had given her a dozen old hand-me-downs. She had six kids and the maternity tops had gotten lots of wear.

Ali Dunn wanted one of her own, at least one new one.

That night when she was shucking the corn for dinner, she'd felt something funny, something running down her leg. She'd started to bleed. She'd miscarried.

She'd been devastated. Maybe Steven'd taken it even harder than she had. He'd been telling all his friends how they'd soon be going to get the ultrasound that'd show his first baby boy and it'd been hard for him. He was the one wanted to plant a rose bush in the back yard, to remember the baby by.

The doctor told them both it didn't mean anything, that she must wait a few months, but then she could get pregnant again. That they'd have lots of healthy babies.

So they'd waited six months and she got pregnant again. She'd been a little nervous that second time, and had every right to be. She didn't even make it to three months.

The third time Ali'd got pregnant she was scared to death, just knew something bad would happen. And that time, she hadn't just miscarried. She and Steve had been in a car accident. Steve was hurt real bad, broke his leg in two places. All that happened to Ali was she had miscarried.

Folks told her how lucky she was, that she'd gotten out of that wreck without a scratch, how fortunate she was that she hadn't been "hurt" like Steve. She'd wanted to punch all of them in the face.

Ali wouldn't let herself get her hopes up with Kelly Ann. She didn't even tell Steve that she'd missed her period. Just kept on trucking, marking Xs on the calendar. She finally told him when she'd missed four periods, the two of them sitting in the living room, NCIS on television, and the both of them crying like it was bad news instead of good.

She hadn't had a single problem with her pregnancy. Everybody said she glowed. Steve wasn't even disappointed when they found out his little boy was really a little girl. In fact, by the time the baby was born she already had her daddy wrapped around her little finger. Steve had gone out and bought half a dozen newborn baby dresses, all pink with lace.

They brought the baby home, and everything should have been wonderful, right? She had what she wanted. Steve was the one glowing, held that baby like he was cradling a fragile ice sculpture in his arms. Ali's mother had stayed for a couple of days, then packed up and went home. Steve went back to all the put-off chores on the farm. Ali was all alone with Kelly Ann.

And she was *miserable*. All she could do was cry. This was absurd! Sure, other mothers had postpartum depression, but she just felt so utterly lost and alone she couldn't believe any other woman on the planet had ever felt such a thing. She was, of course, a lousy mother, would drop the baby or let her drown in the bathtub or poison her or something. She just knew it.

Ali'd tried yesterday morning for the first time to tell Steve about it. He not only didn't understand, he got mad at her for it.

"What do you mean, you're miserable? How can you be miserable — beautiful little baby girl like you got? What's wrong with you?"

Which, of course, helped a lot.

She had cried almost all afternoon off and on, felt so weighed down it was hard to find the energy to fix supper that night.

Then Steve came in the door with roses, said he was sorry, she'd cried then, too, but not because she was sad or depressed. And that night, for the first time in Kelly Ann's brief three weeks on the planet, Ali rocked her and sang to her … and she actually went to sleep!

Ali'd stood looking down at her in the glow of the Minnie Mouse nightlight, realized maybe for the first time how much she looked like Steve! She felt a single tear slide down her cheek as something shifted inside, and almost between one heartbeat and the next she fell madly in love with her precious little girl.

She'd been tiptoeing out of the room when she noticed the hole in the screen over the open window. Yesterday's storm had knocked limbs off some trees, but Ali hadn't noticed that one of them had poked a hole in the screen on its way down.

"Steve, there's a hole in the screen in Kelly Ann's room," she said when she went back into the bedroom. He'd just stepped out of the shower. Farmers showered at night — to get the day's work dirt off — not in the morning to look good for the cows when they went out to milk.

"A big one?"

"Big as a golf ball."

"I'll put some duct tape over it in the morning."

"Why not tonight? I don't want her to wake up in the morning covered in mosquito bites."

"You think the bugs are all lined up out there in the dark, waiting for their chance to sneak through that little hole and feast on baby blood?"

"Baby blood! That's not funny."

Steve held up his wet hands in surrender. "First thing in the morning. Promise. Just zip up the mesh for tonight, okay? I'm whipped."

They hadn't yet moved the baby bed into the house. Steve was still stripping the old white paint off it — probably poisonous lead-based paint — and refinishing it. Now Kelly Ann slept in a borrowed mesh playpen sitting on the half bed in the room.

Ali thought about going into the kitchen, getting a roll of duct tape — there was one in the kitchen junk drawer, wasn't there? — and fixing the hole herself. She didn't.

Maybe it wouldn't have mattered if she had. Probably not. But maybe it would have changed everything.

Tiptoeing back into Kelly Ann's room, she quietly zipped up the playpen's mesh sides, sealing the baby in and the mosquitoes out.

Ali slept deeply. For the first time since Kelly Ann's birth, she wasn't half awake, listening, thinking she heard the baby cry — so she never got any sleep even when the baby didn't wake up.

She fell asleep as soon as her head hit the pillow and only roused once. There was an odd sound from Kelly Ann's room. She wasn't crying, not even making the "I'm about to cut loose" noise she always made before she really started to bellow. It was a … metallic sound. Ali only woke up enough to be sure it wasn't a cry and didn't give any thought to what the sound had been.

A sound like a zipper maybe.

Or a screen tearing.

Ali sat bolt upright in the darkness, her breasts hard, full of milk because Kelly Ann hadn't awakened for her middle-of-the-night feeding. The digital clock said it was eight o'clock but it was still dark, so the clock had to be wrong. Steve was still asleep and he always woke up as soon as dawn light shone through the bedroom window. Ali leapt out of the bed, raced down the hall, just knowing something awful had happened … something had …

Sudden Infant Death Syndrome. The words pulsed like neon signs in her mind.

She turned the knob on the door to the nursery. It turned, but the door … wouldn't open. She let go then, the fear that had swallowed her whole had stolen her breath, but she screamed now.

"Steeeeeve! Come here. Steeeeve!"

She threw her weight against the door and it gave a

little. Like there was something holding it shut, but not something solid.

Steve was at her side, in his underwear.

"What the—?"

"The door won't open."

"What do you mean the door won't—?"

He pushed on the door and it gave a little more for him, but it still wouldn't open.

Ali flipped the light switch and flooded the hallway with eye-squinting brilliance. Steve threw his shoulder into the door and it opened maybe six inches.

In the crack between the door and the jamb Ali could see … leaves.

REBA KOLB LOOKED up at the sky and decided that was one of the things she was gonna miss most — the sight of starlings flying together in whirling, ever-changing patterns. Of course, she'd said that same thing about almost everything she'd looked at in the past three months.

Oh, I'm gonna miss bright yellow fields of ripe burley. And I'm gonna miss Friday fish fries during lent, and the tobacco spitting contest at the fair and the haze hanging low over the hills on a summer afternoon.

Truth was, she was going to miss it all, hadn't realized how much there was in a lifetime spent in Caverna County, Kentucky, that she loved so deeply until she'd found out she was going to have to give it all up.

Now, Mama, you know you'll find *new* things to love in Florida, Frances always said.

And the fact that she didn't *want* to find new things to love, that she was perfectly content with the things she had to love right now, didn't mean beans. What she wanted didn't mean beans. Once she started getting forgetful, couldn't find her glasses, missed taking her pills — the boys' wives hopped on that like white on rice. Your mother can't look after herself anymore, they said. She needs somebody to take care of her, they said. We need to move her into a nursing home, they said.

A nursing home *in Florida* — so they could come and visit her, which they never would. Before they retired, they lived thirty miles away and the only way she could have gotten their attention was to set herself on fire.

Oh, and they'd be put in charge of all her sweet Joe's real estate holdings — but that didn't have nothing to do with it. Oh, no, nothing at all.

Florida was a thousand miles from everything she had ever known or cared about, a dreadful place so hot you was always in a full body sweat but it never evaporated, with the sun glaring off the water so you couldn't see nothing without squinting. And palmetto bugs!

Now *there* was something new about Florida that she'd missed out on in all her eighty-six years of living — cockroaches big as rats that could fly.

It never snowed in Florida. The leaves never turned the color of red wine, or smiley-face yellow or so gold it looked like there was honey streaming down the mountainside.

Trading starlings for palmetto bugs — riiiiight.

The flank of thousands of birds like a solid blotch on the sky turned one hundred and eighty degrees on a dime and executed a figure eight movement that brought them swooping down over the heads of the workers getting ready for the annual Fourth of July parade, putting up barricades so wouldn't no traffic come down the street — not that there was ever more than a pickup or two, maybe, and a couple of cars.

Them birds come so close you could pick out individual birds — with their short pointed wings and pointed beaks that gave them their four-pointed star appearance.

That was odd. Reba'd never seen starlings do anything like that before.

The flock trailed along behind them, a strange song of chirping and trilling that sounded oddly foreign. Reba had listened to starlings in the trees her whole life and she'd never heard the birds make a sound like that. It was pitched lower than any bird tweet she'd ever heard, almost sounded like … a growl.

STEVE REACHED through the crack between the door and the jamb of Kelly Ann's bedroom and grabbed a handful of leaves, ripped them off and examined them in the hall light. Big fat leaves. Ali'd never seen anything … they were huge, the size of dinner plates.

"What is it?"

Steve threw all his weight against the door, grunted from the effort and it slid inward about a foot. Revealing a solid wall of leaves.

Oh, dear God, what …?

"What's in there, what's keeping the door closed?"

Instead of answering, Steve stood staring at the leaves in his hand. Then he dropped them and ran down the hall to the kitchen.

Ali stood helpless outside Kelly Ann's door.

"Ali!" Steve's voice sounded oddly high-pitched. "Ali, come—"

She ran to the kitchen where Steve stood beside the open back door, gawking. The whole doorway was blocked by leaves. Greenery. Vines of some kind.

Ali started to scream. She felt a great tearing inside her,

like a sheet ripping from one end to the other and she knew that when it ripped all the way across, she would come in two, come apart.

Steve ran into the living room, but she stood where she was in the kitchen, screaming, her eyes scanning the kitchen windows, which she could see now were covered over with … plants? That was why the sun didn't wake her up. The windows were covered with …

Steve came back into the kitchen, his face as pale as a gym sock. He began pulling drawers open, scratching through the contents. She put her hand over her mouth, clamped it tight to make herself stop screaming.

"Steeeeeve," she heard her voice, the sniffling quality. She sounded like a frightened child. She felt like a frightened child. "What is—?"

"It's kudzu!" he said.

"Kudzu?" Her mind refused to paint any picture in her head at that word.

Steve finally found what he was looking for in the bottom drawer by the stove. A meat cleaver.

"Stand back!"

Then he attacked the vines covering the door with the cleaver, hacking at them, making feral, grunting sounds as he cut the vegetation away.

Whack.

Whack.

Whack.

The vines fell away where he'd cut them and dawn light spilled into the room through the hole he had made. He kept grunting and cutting, hacking, inarticulate, angry sounds with no words accompanied every slash.

The vines were not thick. But the leaves on them were so enormous — Ali thought of elephant ears, the exotic plant Steve's mother grew in pots on her sunporch. These leaves were bigger than that.

When he had cut away a hole, he grabbed the vines and ripped them out of the way, tore a hole big enough to step through and he stepped out onto the porch. Barefoot, in a tee shirt and underwear, and then he was gone.

Ali followed him, her white cotton nightgown flowing around her feet. A cold wind hit her as soon as she stepped out of the house. It was freezing out here! Why was it this cold on the Fourth of July?

Steve had crossed the yard to the front gate and had turned around, looking at the house. She raced to him and he drew her into his arms, staring past her at the house.

The old farm house was a crackerjack box. Only the two bedrooms, a single bath, a kitchen/dining room combination and a small living room. It had a small back yard, but it was fenced in. Beyond the fence was forest.

When Ali turned to look where he was looking, she sucked in a breath to scream again, but no sound would come out.

The woods behind the house were covered in kudzu. Huge, distorted, misshapen kudzu, but plainly that's what it was. The vine was a nasty climbing perennial introduced into the country from Asia that had been terrorizing the whole southeastern United States ever since. It was roundly hated because it was almost impossible to kill, but it killed every plant it encountered. Wound its way up telephone poles, utility poles, fences and the sides of barns, it climbed up to the top of trees and covered them, blocking the sunlight, gobbling it up while the vegetation below starved for want of light.

Ali'd seen where kudzu'd taken over a stand of trees, or an abandoned building, here and there. Everybody in Kentucky'd seen it. But nothing like this, never like this.

The whole forest — acres of it — was covered. The fence and back yard of the house lay under a solid blanket of vines.

And so did the house.

~

"I NEVER DREAMED it'd be cold out here or I'd have brought a blanket to wrap around your legs," gushed Reba's daughter-in-law, Jackie *Jones-Kolb.* Her son's last name hadn't been grand enough to suit her. Jackie would not have spit on Reba if she *had* set herself on fire. "How could it possibly be this cold in July?"

The parade didn't start until nine, but Jackie had brought Reba early, so she'd be "right on the curb where you can see."

Reba shook her head. Like there was gonna be so many people standing on the sidewalk they'd get in front of her and block her view. How could there be a crowd *watching* the parade when most of the 250 people in town was *in* it? The Fourth of July celebration was one of a handful of things Reba would not miss about Caverna County. Silly contests — how far could you throw a hay bale? Like farmers spent their days throwing hay at their cattle. Or how many hot peppers could you eat? The celebration kicked off with this parade — floats with chicken wire netting stuffed with toilet paper for skirting to cover up the trailer wheels, carrying the homecoming queen and the cheerleaders and the football team. Boy Scout troops and the high school band marching by, followed by the fire trucks, the sheriff and his deputies and the rescue squad truck.

Reba watched Phyllis Weatherston making her way up the sidewalk on the other side of the street, piloting her walker decorated with balloons and streamers and a sign on the front that said, "Hot Mama!"

Yeah, it was Phyllis who Reba was going to miss most of all. They'd been friends since childhood, had walked through life together, celebrating births and weddings, mourning together at far too many gravesides and expected to be put in the ground beside their husbands on plots only about fifty feet apart. Though her sons had never said, Reba was sure that when she cashed in her chips in Florida, she'd be cremated. They'd scatter her ashes on some swamp to feed the palmetto bugs.

Phyllis'd started losing her hearing when she was in her forties and had learned sign language. Reba'd learned right along with her. It was like being able to speak a foreign language — they could say anything they wanted to each other and most of the people around them couldn't understand. Phyllis cursed like a sailor in sign, and Reba did a fair amount, too, sincerely believing that it didn't count as a sin unless she said the words out loud.

"I see Jackie-wacky dragged you out here in the cold," Phyllis signed. "She's trying to give you pneumonia to save them the cost of shipping you to Florida." Then she reeled off a list of obscenities to describe Reba's daughter-in-law that was magnificently creative.

"She's too dumb to think of it," Reba signed back. "Takes her an hour and a half to watch *60 Minutes*."

"I still got a car. How about we sneak off and do our Thelma and Louise imitation tonight? Drive off Lover's Leap into the sunset. Save all of them the trouble of killing us off."

Phyllis was only half-kidding. And maybe not kidding at all. She would be as devastated as Reba when they took Reba away.

The starlings swooped down over the street again, so

low this time that the men setting up barricades on the end of the street actually ducked. They were not a particularly popular bird, after all, given the incredible mess they made when the little poop machines decided to nest in one of your trees for the night, but Reba decided maybe they'd come to tell her goodbye.

Reba liked that idea. A ten-thousand-bird starling salute. All the workers had stopped what they were doing, watching now as the flock got to the end of the street and turned straight up, a solid wall of birds climbing like a rocket into the sky.

At a couple of hundred feet high, they changed direction on a dime again, flying high over the street, spread out like a blanket in the sky.

Then they turned again. And headed straight down.

Chapter Sixteen

THE KUDZU VINES that blanketed the forest and the backyard had climbed the back wall of the Dunns' little house, covered the roof, sides and front and grew out now halfway to the fence.

Something tickled Ali's bare foot. It was a kudzu vine. People joked that it grew so fast you could almost see it …

"It moved!" she screamed and jumped back from it. It had! She'd felt it … slither up over her foot! Instinctively, Steve brought the meat cleaver down on the vine, slicing it in two.

He was panting, sweating. The hand with the meat cleaver shook.

"What's happening?" she cried. "What's going on? Why is—?"

"I don't know."

And she thought about the time she had been creeped out when she passed an old abandoned car on the roadside, almost completely covered in kudzu. The vines had grown in through the broken windows, out the broken windshield.

"The hole in Kelly Ann's screen!" Ali screamed the words, except she didn't. They came out in a horrified whisper. "The vines grew in through the hole and … they're covering the door!"

"I'll climb in her window!" Steve started to run around the house, then turned to Ali.

"Go to the tool shed. Get … the scythe! And there's a machete, too, on that back wall, on a nail beside the horse blanket. Get them both and bring them here."

She stood looking at him. It was as if her will had come unhooked from her body. She intended to turn, run the quarter of mile to the big, black tobacco barn, and around behind it to the tool shed. But her limbs wouldn't obey the commands.

"Ali!" Steve yelled in her face.

She came back.

"The scythe and the machete," she repeated.

"Now, hurry. Go!"

She turned and bolted toward the barn. Steve turned with the meat cleaver and started around the side of the house toward Kelly Ann's bedroom window on the back.

Ali thought she heard … an odd sound behind her as she ran. A sound like … wind through wheat, or the way the leaves of the trees brushed against each other in a storm. Leaves against leaves, a swishing sound.

Cow patty. She only noticed it when she stepped in it, felt it ooze up between her toes. Didn't slow down. She had sensitive feet, never went barefoot, certainly not on the rock-strewn, potholed path from the house to the barn. Didn't matter.

She specifically didn't look back toward the house when she turned the corner of the barn that blocked it from view. The sight was too scary. And she couldn't start screaming, couldn't give in to the urge to burst into hysterical tears. There was no time.

Arriving at the tool shed door panting, her vision was distorted by the bead of sweat that'd coursed down her forehead and into her eye. But she wasn't seeing things. The tool shed was locked. A padlock fastened the rusty old hasp to the door. The key was in the kitchen.

Hearing herself whimper frightened her almost as much as … She'd sounded like a baby rabbit run over by a hay bailer.

There was no time to get the key.

She rushed to the back door of the barn and pulled it open. The morning sun had risen far enough now that a blade of sunlight sliced into the black interior of the building, igniting into sparkling effervescence the dust motes suspended in the air.

The Dunns lived on the top of a ridge, rather than down in a hollow, so they actually got to enjoy sunrises and sunsets instead of the pitiful cousins of them produced when the sun topped the mountain about ten o'clock in the morning and sunk down behind the mountain to the west by four.

Following the beam of sunlight into the barn, Ali found what she was looking for, leaning up against the wall beside the feed trough. A sledgehammer.

It was heavy and Ali was a small woman, but she barely noticed the weight as she ran back out of the barn to the tool shed beside it and slammed the business end of the sledgehammer into the rusty hasp on the door. It took three blows before it broke off and she could drop the sledgehammer into the dirt and step into the dark interior of the shed, her eyes raking the walls.

Where was the … the scythe, there it was, leaning against

the back wall. The machete was harder. It wasn't beside the horse blanket as Steve had said and she almost left without it. But spotted it on a nail by the door as she was leaving. Armed with the tools Steve had sent her to get, she steeled herself for what she'd see when she cleared the barn and the house again. Didn't matter, the sight still kicked her in the gut and knocked the breath out of her, how far the vines had gone in — what? Three minutes? Five? Impossible!

The house was not only covered in vines, but they were growing into the kitchen where she and Steve had left the door open. It was hard to run barefoot over a rocky path carrying a scythe in one hand and a machete in the other but Ali never noticed. Was aware only of the knot of cold terror that was growing bigger inside her with every passing second and the urgency of *hurry*.

"Steve!"

Gasping. Running, sobbing and crying out "Steeeve," she rounded the back corner of the house and—

Her legs stopped moving and so she stopped running but she hadn't willed it to be so. She had no will at all, had no voice and no being, was hollow and empty with a cold wind blowing through her soul.

"Steve."

She grunted the word, like she'd been struck in the chest with a wrecking ball and that was the sound of her pain. But he didn't hear her, of course. Steve didn't hear anything.

He was *attached* to the wall of the house beside Kelly Ann's window. The kudzu had grown around his arms and legs, somehow spread-eagling him against the building, holding him tight.

The vines wound around and around his neck were still moving. She watched them. Below his dark purple face the vines grew out across his shoulders and his chest, and started down the rest of his body.

He still held the meat cleaver in his right hand. It was affixed by vines to the wall, too.

Ali's heart stopped. Froze as solid as a glacier in the North Sea. She wanted to scream. Couldn't. You had to breathe to scream and she couldn't breathe.

Denial came galloping to the rescue in her mind riding a great white stallion.

A dream. A nightmare. She'd told her best friend, Kathy Manning, about her baby blues and Kathy had given her some of the medication the doctor had prescribed after her baby was born last Christmas. Ali hadn't taken any of it yet ... but, of course, she had, too. She must have. She had taken one of those little pink pills before she went to bed last night and that's what was happening. She was having a reaction to the drug, that's all. She'd wake up. Any second now, she'd come around.

The front of her white cotton nightgown was suddenly wet. The gown that was now filthy on the bottom where it had dragged in the dirt and through the cow patty. She looked down and saw that her milk had let down in response to her baby's cry.

Then she was aware of it. She could hear Kelly Ann now, crying, and her body had responded. The baby was zipped up tight inside a mesh playpen in her room, so the vines couldn't ...

The crying grew louder, along with the great roaring sound in Ali's ears. She felt the machete and the scythe drop out of her suddenly numb fingers as she backed away from the house, shaking her head.

No.

No!

Nooo—

The cry of her baby ratcheted into a wail and somewhere inside Ali something fundamental shifted, a gear clunked into place. Turning slowly away from the house, she walked back down the path. She had no clear destination in mind. She really had nothing at all in mind, was merely responding to the urgency in her belly she couldn't deny.

She felt neither grief nor fear. All that had burned away.

Her whole being was powered now by a pure blue flame of consummate *rage*.

She stepped through the puddle of sunlight into the tool shed. Heard nothing but the throbbing whump, whump, whumping of her heart slamming blood through her body.

She didn't move for a moment, a heartbeat. The world was about disturbed dust motes, floating away from her into the darkness, and the smell of her own breast milk.

It was quiet, still.

Then the silence was ripped open by the sudden rumbling *Grrrrrrr* of the chainsaw when she pulled the cord and brought it to life.

PUT ON A WEDDING DRESS, fix your hair up nice and add some of that sparkly eye shadow to your makeup — didn't take the whole day to do them things.

Yes, it did, too. At least the whole day was devoted to "getting ready" and that involved considerably more than petticoats and pantyhose. Mostly, it took all day because brides the world over wanted it to take that long. The happiest day of their lives — they wanted to squeeze every drop of sweetness out of it, make forever memories.

The Becca Hawkins who'd almost knocked Theresa off her feet, gasping like she'd run a marathon, laughing and crying at the same time, holding her ring finger so close to Theresa's nose she'd a'had to been cross-eyed to get a look at it … *that* Becca would have wanted the wedding to last *three days.*

The Becca who sat across from Theresa at breakfast this morning, with that cold, thousand-yard stare in her sea green eyes — *that* Becca'd been happy to have the ceremony in the living room right then, and her standing there in her pajamas before she even brushed her teeth.

Now, she stood like a marble statue while Theresa adjusted the hem on her dress. It was going to be a challenge to get that big old skirt with Becca in it into the back seat of Theresa's car, but wasn't like she coulda got dressed at the chapel. It didn't have no plumbing, no running water, nothing but a little anteroom on the back side where Jack, Daniel and Crock was gonna be waiting — along with three washtubs full of ice cooling bottles of champagne. Most of Theresa's sewing skills had been used to make normal-people clothing fit the big bear of a man she'd married, adding fabric to let them out in the shoulders. She'd asked Becca could she make the dress for her as a labor of love, hadn't sewed in so long she'd forgot how hard it was to get all the pieces-parts lined up. When she had the fabric cut, she basted it together to see how it was gonna look, and darned if she didn't get three or four stitches into it before she realized she was putting the sleeve in the neck hole. It'd took her two whole days to sew them little pearls one at a time in a pattern on the front of the skirt. It was supposed to look like angels' wings, but when she got them all done and stood back to look, the shape could have been mistaken for Viking horns.

She'd tore stitches out and redone them three or four

times — Becca never seen that part or she'd have gone out and bought a dress. Far as she knew, the flowing white gown with poofy sleeves and lace around the neck had come together as effortlessly as them little critters dressing Cinderella for the ball.

But the train she'd made for the dress ... well, that'd been a bridge too far. Some part of Theresa knew that when she was making it, but the woman at the fabric store practically gave her the material — likely wasn't selling well. Not many folks these days handmaking wedding dresses. Shoot, didn't seem to Theresa that many people these days was even bothering to get married at all, but that wasn't for her to judge. Her job was to take care of her own behavior and not sit around deciding what other people had and hadn't ought to be doing.

She'd done the best sell job she knew how to Becca for the train, how beautiful it would look trailing behind her as she walked down the aisle. She could ask Ariel and Jenny to walk behind the train, making sure it didn't hang on nothing, smoothing it all out pretty when Becca got to the altar and moving it so she didn't walk on it when she and Jack left the church as man and wife. Theresa had it all planned out. Of course, the original wedding dress pattern Becca had picked out hadn't called for a train, but Theresa put hooks and eyes all around so it'd fasten on — either at the waist or at the shoulder. Theresa thought the shoulder fit was the most regal, but looking "royal" ended up being what torpedoed the whole idea.

Becca hadn't said nothing at first when Theresa spread it all out on the floor of her living room for Becca to see.

"Oh, it's beautiful," she finally said, "but ... Theresa ... a *twelve-foot satin train*!" Okay, that probably had been over the top, and Theresa had gotten a bit carried away. "I bet Queen Elizabeth's train wasn't that long when she got married." Actually, hers had been a whole lot longer than that — Theresa had looked it up. But probably wasn't a good time to argue the point. "It's … too much. I couldn't possibly … Jack would have a coronary."

She'd probably been right about that part. Theresa had had to fight Jack every step of the way to do anything fancy. He was a plain man with plain tastes and anything beyond the absolute basics was labeled "foofy." Jack was not a fan of foofy.

Theresa didn't push it. After all, it was Becca's wedding and she'd ought to make all the important decisions about it. But Theresa had put the train in the trunk of the car and she was gonna give it one final shot when they got to the chapel. Ariel would be there to serve as a train-bearer. They'd probably like that part better than tossing rose petals. Maybe Becca'd get caught up in the moment and agree to wear it! It was worth a shot.

Theresa got up off the floor laboriously, holding onto a chair for support. Her and kneeling was not on good terms.

"Turn around, real slow like," she said, and went to the other side of the Murphys' parlor where she could see the whole of it better.

When she turned to look, Becca hadn't moved. She was just standing. Staring. Theresa didn't want nothing so much as she wanted to take that pour little girl into her arms and tell her everything was gonna be alright, wasn't nothing gonna go wrong, wasn't nothing gonna stop her from becoming Mrs. Jack Carpenter.

Trouble was, Theresa never had been a very good liar.

"Becca, sugar," she said, kind of loud. "I need for you to turn around so I can see if the hem's even." Becca turned like a robot. She'd basted that hem in place must be half a dozen times and every time it was either too short or too long.

This time — finally — it was perfect.

"B'lieve we got it, child. You gonna be such a beautiful bride you gonna take Jack's breath away."

"It's so dark," she said. "And so cold. How could it be cold in July?"

Theresa coulda come up with a pretty good guess, but now wasn't the time.

"If we have to, we'll wrap you up in that big afghan I keep in the car and won't take it off until you're standing at the front door of the chapel ready to walk down the aisle."

Becca looked at Theresa then for the first time, held her gaze.

"Something's *wrong*," she said, her voice small and soft. "And whatever it is, it's getting worse and worse."

"I don't smell nothing—"

Becca rushed across the room to take Theresa's hands. Becca's were small, cold and trembling, but she clung so fiercely the engagement ring Jack had given her dug into Theresa's skin.

"That ring of yours is nigh about to cut my finger off you squeezing so tight. Better than putting my eye out, though, which is what you almost done when you come running into the house with that ring on your finger, shoving it so close to my face I had to cross my eyes to focus on it."

Theresa was surprised that reminding Becca of that night didn't coax a smile. In fact, Becca seemed to sink deeper into herself.

"I never told Jack what a monumental fail his proposal was, taking me *there* that night."

"Where?"

"He wanted everything to be a surprise. Wouldn't let me look where we were going, made me keep my eyes closed and he led me. Had a buddy waiting there to take our picture. He got down on one knee, his friend snapping away, and he told me to open my eyes."

Theresa couldn't for the life of her figure out what could be sad about that.

"I never heard him ask me to marry him. I never even said yes. I couldn't talk, couldn't breathe. He still thinks that's because he proposed. Doesn't know that it was the *place* ... the Purple People Bridge."

Theresa knew the bridge, an old train trestle converted into a scenic walkway across the broad Ohio River in Cincinnati linking Ohio and Kentucky. The beams and girders on the bridge had all been painted purple — for some reason she couldn't remember.

"I'd been there before, went there ... to *die* because I couldn't live anymore in a world—" she made an all-encompassing gesture, "—like *this*! Full of demons."

A body had surfaced.

That's what she and Becca and the others had come to call those occasions when something from the "bad times" suddenly popped into their minds. Crock had coined the phrase, remembering working on the Ohio River after somebody'd jumped off the bridge. "The body'll surface in three days," his captain had told him. "And it won't be pretty."

Theresa saw that Becca had gone to that place, where they all had to go to deal with them memories.

BECCA WISHES the water were clear, like the pictures you see of coral reefs with colorful fish flitting here and there and the bubbles from your scuba tank, little round sprinters, racing each other to the surface.

She would lie back in the clear water, her hair floating like a halo around her head, and watch the bubbles of her last breath rush up to burst into the bright sunlight that filters down through the water's depths in rays like sparklers.

But the Ohio River is muddy, not clear. It flows lazily beneath the L & N Pedestrian Bridge, ugly brown water that will swallow her up with no bubbles or pretty fish or sunlight rays. Just cold, wet and dead.

Becca walks slowly up the Cincinnati approach to the Purple People Bridge, the purple beams and girders calling out to her with an air of silliness. Silly is a good last place to be in life.

She pretends to look down at the water as she studies the girders and posts and wires that fit around the bridge, a spider's silver steel web that holds it in place. As soon as there is a break in the foot traffic, she will hoist herself to the top of the railing, holding to a support post to balance on the narrow metal beam. She'll have to move quickly because if anyone spots her and figures out what she's doing, they would undoubtedly try to stop her.

No one is going to stop her this time. She'd tried before to escape the real-life monsters, the demons she could see slithering around on the human hosts they've possessed and crawling around in her head. She'd had her stomach pumped twice when she was in the sanitarium. After that, she'd tried to tough it out. She really had. She had lived with horror inside and outside, took every breath with her whole chest constricted, a guitar string pulled so tight you can't tell anymore if the sound it makes is music or crying.

Last night, the monster came to her. The efreet, buried deep in a cave under Caverna County and inside Chapman Whitworth at the same time. And he saw her, glided into her through the black spots in her eyeballs. Rumbling a mighty roar of rage inside her head, he had ripped her apart in a frenzy of destruction, shredding all she was, who she was.

Now, she is only the tatters of a person flapping in the wind. Ripped pieces with no substance and only the one thin cord of life holding them together. When that is severed, the pieces will float away free into oblivion. And whatever or whoever it was who had been Becca Hawkins would be no more.

She sees her chance, glances both ways and then hoists herself up onto the railing. She feels the sun on her face and a breeze lifts her hair off her neck. Down below is brown death, waiting for her, and Becca Jean Hawkins lifts her foot to step off into nothing.

That's when she spots the hat. Floating in the water below her is a tall, floppy hat with red and white stripes. She gasps.

The Cat in the Hat's hat.

The angel who'd come to her in the closet when she was a child didn't want to frighten her … so she'd appeared as the Cat in the Hat.

Becca looks at it in wonder, realizing as she does that it isn't moving. Sticks and other pieces of debris float along with the current under the bridge past the hat, but it remains steadfastly where it is.

That kind of hat wouldn't even float — would it? It would turn into a shapeless red-and-white striped lump. This hat doesn't even look wet. The muddy brown water hasn't stained the pure white of the stripes, either. And it is bobbing up and down … as if somebody wearing it were dancing.

"Hey, lady!"

Becca turns to see a man only fifteen or twenty feet away. He is big, with a huge chest and brawny arms, wearing a gray jumpsuit with his name and a logo — Harrison County Electric and Gas — stitched on the pocket.

The man starts toward her.

"What do you think you're doing up there?" he said.

"I … I dropped my hat," Becca hears herself say. She looks back down at the river flowing in an endless brown expanse, and sees the hat still bobbing in place where it'd been before.

"Well, it's gone now and you're going to go with it if you don't get down from there."

"No, it's not gone. See" — *she points to the hat in the river* — *"it's right there."*

The man glances where she's pointing. "Like I said, the hat's gone. Now come down off that railing."

The man doesn't see the hat. Can't see it.

Becca never takes her eyes off the hat as she climbs back down. When her feet touch the bridge floor, the hat floats slowly away.

WHEN BECCA COME BACK from that place, her eyes cleared and she looked deep into Theresa's.

"I never told you that the day I stole your car and drove to Daddy's farm, I had gone to the bridge to jump, to kill myself." She took a small sip of air, as if it was all she had room for. "I wanted to die. I didn't want to live in a world with monsters." Her fingers were trembling. "I still don't. I just want to run away and hide."

"If we run away, they win." The voice came from the doorway where Daniel stood, staring at Becca with a look of brotherly love pasted on his face. He held it there so tight it made the muscles in his temple throb. "That's what Andi told me yesterday."

As if on cue, the little girl came running into the parlor.

"Hi Daddy," she said as she blew by him on her way to Theresa. "The ribbon on my bouquet that's supposed to dangle down — it's all tangled." She held out the offending snarled bouquet. "How could it get tangled? They were fine when I put the bouquet in the box."

"I say the same thing every year about Christmas tree lights."

"Oh, Daddy ..."

As Theresa untangled the ribbons, Andi gave a report of the whereabouts and activities of everybody who mattered to this affair, like she had been assigned reconnaissance duties and was debriefing. "Okay, so Ariel's mostly dressed but her mother is still looking for her other shoe. Jenny has a sore throat and her daddy told her she couldn't go to the wedding — it's too cold out there. She's in her bedroom now sulking. Mrs. Murphy said she'd stay with her, said it gave her an excuse to not be around the "'celebration bubbly.'"

Andi wrinkled up her brow, and when she did Theresa saw Daniel in her — as a boy, he'd always done that when he didn't understand something. She might look like her mother, but her father was definitely in there, too.

"What's celebration bubbly?" she asked.

"It's the foam on the top of root beer in a mug," her father said.

Theresa nodded her admiration for his quick thinking and handed her back the untangled bouquet.

"I'll be ready for you to fix my hair whenever you want," she told Becca. She and Becca held a look a beat too long, and Theresa knew Daniel'd seen it. "I'm going to help Mrs. Murphy look for Ariel's shoe."

She blew back out of the room, and when she did it seemed darker for the absence of her light.

"You come to tell us what's going on here — right?" Theresa asked. "'Cause sure as Jackson there is *somethin'* going on here."

"I came to bring Andi's shoes that she left in the car and clearly hasn't even missed, probably won't until she finds Ariel's shoe." He held them out in front of him, then set them on the floor. "And to report that the men plan to leave in a little while. We'll get to the chapel in plenty of time to go around to the back to the anteroom before any of the rest of you show up. Wouldn't want Jack to catch sight of the bride."

"And you just gonna pretend you don't know things we don't know — that the way of it?"

Daniel held his ground.

"And I'll take Jack's wedding ring if you want me to keep up with it for you, Becca. I've done ceremonies where the bride got to the altar and … well, those usually didn't end well. Not many wedding dresses with a pocket."

"What's going on, Daniel?" Becca asked softly. "It's so dark … so heavy. It's almost hard to breathe."

Daniel crossed the room to her in two long strides and took both her hands in his.

"What's going on is this is your wedding day. And if you're happy about that you need to let your face know, because clearly it didn't get the memo."

"But—"

"As soon as the ceremony is over, we'll drink a toast to your happiness, you and Jack will leave … *and so will the rest of us!*"

Theresa stiffened. Whatever it was, it was bad.

"Change of plans — we're not staying the night. Bags are packed and in the car. I've canceled the speaking gig Sunday morning. Theresa, if you could have Andi's stuff rounded up, Crock will drop me here to get my car — and we *will all be out of Caverna County before sundown!*"

Chapter Seventeen

JONAH DIDN'T SLEEP at all on Friday night. At least he wasn't aware of sleeping. He couldn't sleep because the whispering in his head, that was the wallpaper of his mind, began to get louder and louder until it sounded like the swarm of black flies that filled the air around the carcass of a dog that'd got run over in the road.

And then he couldn't sleep because he began to hear voices in the buzzing — not just one, voic*es*. That's what the buzzing was — the hum of hundreds of voices, thousands of voices. No longer just the little whispers telling him he'd ought to look at them nasty pictures. The voices weren't whispering. They was talking right out loud and he could hear all of them and each of them — every individual voice separate from the rest of them. That didn't make no sense, but that was the way of it.

Who could sleep when something like that was going on in his head? Who would want to?

Men, women, black, white, young, old were speaking English and Spanish and all kind of other languages he didn't recognize — maybe Chinese or Russian or some-

183

thing like that. He hadn't never heard Chinese or Russian so he couldn't possibly understand a word of any of it, of course. But he did.

They were using sounds that made words he had never heard before and he knew what they were saying.

The voices filled his whole head and then seemed to seep down out into the rest of him until he was full of the voices. It was like his skin was the outside of a balloon that was full up with air, so full it was about to bust, and the air was voices. The air was words.

And all the words was telling him the same thing. In maybe every language on the face of the earth, the voices was telling him to kill.

Kill!

Kill the sinners! Shed their blood.

He was to bathe in the blood of those who refused to believe the day of judgement was at hand. Without their blood to wash away his own sin, he would stand before God a guilty man, condemned to burn in hell's everlasting fires for all eternity.

Jonah wasn't gonna let *that* happen.

He owned two guns — a .22 he used for squirrel hunting and a .30-06 deer rifle. He had disassembled them both during the night, cleaned every part, polished the metal until it shone. He had a bowie knife, too, that he sharpened until merely touching the blade opened up the end of his finger so he had to get an old sock to make a bandage until it stopped bleeding. He had a machete, too, out in the tool shed. He hadn't used it in years and it was all rusted up, the wood on the handle splintered. He cleaned that up, too, polished the blade and mended the handle with duct tape.

When the pale gray light of dawn began to filter down through the trees to the bottom of the hollow, Jonah was ready. He stuffed all the ammo he had into the pockets of his jacket, then slung one rifle over each shoulder. He stuck the knife in a scabbard on his belt and carried the shiny clean machete in his hand.

Though he hadn't closed his eyes all night, he felt strangely rested when the cold morning air hit his face as he started through the woods for the church where the Chosen One had instructed everyone to gather. It was cold. Forty degrees maybe. It shouldn't have been, of course, should have been sixty or seventy. This was July! The cold was a sign, Jonah realized. It was a sign of the coming of the end, of the day of judgement, of the final days of man upon the earth.

The Chosen One had told his followers not to come in vehicles and some folks had had to walk a sight farther than Jonah did to get to the church. It was still early when Jonah came out of the woods north of the church. He stopped in his tracks and marveled at the sight. There must have been fifty — sixty people. Maybe more. And there would most certainly be more coming as the morning wore on. All of them folks he had known his whole life and they was going to join him as one of the survivors, one of the handful of victorious souls who were ready when the avenging hand of God struck down the unbelievers. They was all gonna be like that camel in Scripture that went through the eye of a needle.

Every man and woman was armed with whatever they had. You could tell they'd done what he had — they'd cleaned up axes and scythes, hatchets, meat cleavers and butcher knives — any weapon they could lay their hands on. There was no shortage of guns, too. He didn't know anybody who didn't own at least one gun.

As Jonah approached the crowd, he could see the light burning in their eyes like he was sure they could see in his.

A light of passion and determination, a look others would have called wild-eyed, but it didn't matter what others would call it because before the sun set today the others would be dead and on their way to hell and he and the friends and neighbors gathered around him would be on their way to glory.

Bob Huddleston. He was a big, raw-boned man with strong hands and heavy, muscular shoulders. He'd got in a bar fight when he was fifteen, got hit in the face with a bottle, so he was blind in one eye. And the blow'd done something to his brain, too, and he fell down in foaming-at-the-mouth seizures sometimes, too.

His wife, Claudette, had come with him — a skinny woman with teeth that looked like the black stumps left after a forest fire.

Their 12-year-old daughter, Judith, was by their side carrying a scythe. She was a fat kid, her face so broad she almost didn't seem to have any features at all. Folks said she wasn't Bob's git and she surely didn't look like him, or like her mama neither.

The Cowdrey brothers were there. Don Cowdrey was the meanest man Jonah had ever met — a soulless monster who had beat his own wife to death and got away with it by saying she got trampled by their bull. He'd run off his kids a long time ago and had only been coming to church in the past six months — after the doctor told him he had cancer. His brother Colin was a drunk and Jonah was surprised to see that he looked cold sober, clear-eyed, though his hands had begun to shake.

David Lockwood, Jim Behning and Steve Hughes were there. Dave was a farmer who'd been raising dope on his few acres for ten years and had finally got caught. He was scheduled to go to trial next month but apparently he wasn't gonna stand before that judge but before another one altogether — and he'd be found innocent if he was willing to shed the blood of unbelievers.

Morag Heywood was there, too, the wild blonde hair around her face like the mane of a lion. She was grabbed-a-live-wire fried, couldn't stand still, kept fidgeting. He hoped she didn't throw another one of her fits like she done last night. He'd always figured her to be on drugs of some kind the way she acted, but might have been something else entirely. She carried butcher knives in both hands, gripping them the way you'd do if you was stabbing somebody with 'em.

Other women was there by themselves. Judith Blevins, Cheryl Kinest, Debbie Lloyd and Lauren Clough. Maybe their menfolk wouldn't come. It was that way with a lot in church — men stayed home and their wives went to church. Them men was gonna be powerful sorry.

No one spoke to Jonah. No one spoke at all. The crowd was as silent as church during the benediction. That's when Jonah noticed that the people wasn't talking to each other but they appeared to be listening.

The voices was talking to them, too! Jonah shouldn't have been surprised, but he was. And maybe just a little bit disappointed. He'd just assumed he was the only one they was talking to like that and he'd felt kinda special because of it. Now it was clear that every person standing in the growing morning light was there because they'd been sent. They'd show up because they'd been told to … and they'd listened.

Jonah had no doubt now, that the voices talked to lots of other people, too. Of course they did. But the thing was, not everybody listened! He'd barely been able to hear the whispers at first, but when he listened hard, paid attention, did what the voices said he'd ought to do, they got louder and clearer. Probably there was folks who'd heard the voices and shut them out by turning away from them. Them folks was gonna be sorry today. Them folks was gonna get dead because of their disobedience. And he, Jonah Ballard, intended to kill as many of them as he could. He had a lot of sin to wash away and he needed a lot of sacrificial blood to do it.

~

LINC STARED, blank for a moment, at the ashen-faced dispatcher standing in his office doorway.

"Starlings?" he said.

HALF AN HOUR LATER, when he stood on Main Street in Grant's Crossing looking at the carnage, he still had trouble processing it.

Starlings.

A sticky blanket of crushed and mangled birds covered everything. Black snow. In the street, on the sidewalks, awnings outside building, cars … and people. Bodies were everywhere. How many hurt? How many dead? It'd be awhile before they knew the numbers. He thanked God it had happened when it did — half an hour later, the street would have been jammed, probably five hundred people watching the parade — or in it. He doubted that any of them would have escaped untouched.

The birds had rained down out of the sky in a suicide dive, survivors told him. Just straight down, thousands and thousands of them, making a screeching, almost-a-scream sound those who heard would never forget.

Each individual bird probably weighed less than three ounces, but the combined force of so many of them pounding down from hundreds of feet up in the sky …

Linc was not particularly good at math, but even if he had been he wouldn't have bothered to figure out how fast the birds were traveling when they hit the ground. Didn't matter. They'd been going fast enough to kill.

As Linc got out of his cruiser, a crew of rescue squad personnel were lifting an old woman *beaten to death by birds* out of a wheelchair and placing her in a body bag. Reba Kolb. A nearby woman — couldn't think of her name but she was married to Reba's oldest son — was wringing her hands and babbling to a deputy.

"… looked up and saw them … I looked around, trying to find somewhere to … and they were coming and coming, then I saw the bus shelter …" She began to succumb to hysteria. "They hit the roof, thunk, thunk, thunk — hundreds, thousands of them. It was horrible. I'll never be the same."

Neither will the old lady in a wheelchair you abandoned on the sidewalk to fend for herself.

He turned away before he said something he'd be sorry for, grateful that the Kentucky State Police had arrived on the scene first and had taken charge. It was a hike from Bradford's Ridge all the way to Grant's Crossing, in the northern part of Caverna County, where the mountains rose so steep the sunlight only made it to the bottom of the hollows a few hours a day, a place so remote that only a few thousand people lived in the whole area.

And he'd made that hike three, four times in the last—

He froze and some tumblers slipped into place. He pictured a map of the county in his head, with Bradford's Ridge in the southeast corner and a handful of little communities scattered here and there. The murders. Then rocks that didn't fall in an avalanche. Right up by the northern county line. The fish in the river, the pumpkins farther south. Then Durston's cattle … and this.

If he'd put stickpins on every location on a real map, he'd have seen the pattern sooner. Whatever *it* was, *it* was spreading out south … and getting wider.

Hope Chapel, where Jack Carpenter and Becca Hawkins were to be joined in matrimony, lay directly in its path.

~

"YOU LOOK LIKE DEATH ON A CRACKER," Crock told Jack as he straightened Jack's tie, the gold one Theresa had knitted for him. "What time did you and Daniel go to bed last night?"

Jack dodged the question. Truth was, he didn't know what time it'd been, but it didn't matter because he didn't go to sleep once he did go to bed. He was working his way up to two sleepless nights and sleeplessness did strange things to you. What if he fell asleep beside Becca on their wedding night? *Not likely!*

"Asks the man who's so ugly he'd make a train take a dirt road," Jack fired back.

Daniel burped out a bleat of laughter in spite of himself.

The three men were jammed into the little anteroom in the back of the Hope Chapel — a space roughly the size of a British telephone booth, where a washtub on the floor held bottles of champagne and ice. They'd brought silver wine goblets, too, and they were … well, somewhere.

"No, Jack, we can't wait outside," Daniel said, reading his mind as he had when they were kids. He sounded all minister-official. "You and the bride can't see each other—"

"Says who?"

"It's written in the s'posta book, right alongside 'never

spit into the wind' and 'garlic makes a man wink, drink and stink,'" Crock said. "Oh, and don't step on a crack or you'll break your mother's back. That's in there some-where, too."

"Just go with it, Jack. It'll only be a few more minutes. This is how Becca wants it and it's her wedding. You're just a hood ornament."

Daniel seemed inordinately calm and chilled out. Like he was on Valium or something. After the tales they'd heard yesterday, and the hours they'd hashed and rehashed the information last night, he should be as wired as Jack. And maybe he was, but Daniel had never been much good at hiding his feelings — that's probably why he was such a terrible liar. Jack didn't like that thought because it begged a question he did not intend to ask. Not today, the day he would make Becca his bride.

Jack changed the subject.

"You got the rings, right?" he asked Daniel.

"Becca's is here." He patted his left coat pocket. Then he patted his right coat pocket. "And yours is … *not here*?" He patted around on all the pockets in his suit, like he couldn't feel anything in any of them. Then burst out laughing.

"I got this, bro," he said.

"I know you're in a hurry to get this over with and leave, but …"

Crock meant it as a veiled joke about Jack's wedding night, but all it did was bring up a subject they all had sworn last night they wouldn't mention.

"Oops," Crock said. "Stepped in it. I just meant … I got a hot date in Cincinnati tonight. We're going to eat Thai food and see which one of us throws up first, so—"

The wedding music began in the chapel.

"Showtime," Crock said.

Showtime. That's the word Jack had thought last fall before he turned a corner in a dark cave to face down a monster.

~

BECCA and her dress took up the whole back seat of Theresa's car so the two little flower girls was jammed together in one bucket seat in the front. All the bows and ribbons, flowers, corsages, bouquets, baskets of rose petals and little bags full of *birdseed* Theresa'd tied up with little ribbons to throw at the bride and groom were in the trunk.

There was no address to put into Theresa's GPS, but Becca had dropped a pin in her phone on the spot when she and Jack came down to check it out, so her phone could direct them.

Only it didn't.

"Lost signal," said the British voice on the phone — set to British because Becca loved the sound of a British accent.

"Figures," Theresa said. "Andi, honey, would you check my phone and see do I have any bars." Andi picked it up and shook her head at Theresa. "Didn't figure we'd be able to get coverage up here in these mountains."

"But Jack said there's a cell tower on the top of one of them and we got great coverage when we came here last month ..." Becca didn't finish, just switched gears. "We don't need a GPS to get us there — I know where it is, I can find it."

When they pulled up into the parking area at the end of the path leading to the chapel, Jack's car was there beside Crock's. The plan was that Jack and Becca would leave the chapel and go to her father's — no, *her* house — to change clothes and gather up their things. Becca had left a suitcase full of what she intended to wear on her honeymoon in Jack's car and he'd taken it into the house with his.

Becca told Theresa that Jack was keeping the location of their honeymoon a secret, that when she'd tried to wheedle the information out of him by pointing out she had to know what to pack, he'd said, "You can leave your Nanook of the North coat at home and your idiot mittens." When she'd looked confused, he'd explained. "Mittens you can't lose because they're tied together with a string that runs up through your coat sleeves. Daniel had a pair. I'd yank on one of them and he'd punch himself in the nose with the other."

"Well, 'pears he's actually gone do this." Theresa could hear the forced cheeriness in her voice.

The three in the front seat got out first. The instant they stepped into the outside air, Andi began to shiver.

"Why is it so cold?" she bleated. Her flower girl dress had spaghetti straps, was a summer dress — duh, it was summertime.

Becca and Theresa exchanged a look and fear passed between them as real as a breeze through wind chimes, setting off ringing and reverberations that became the canvas on which everything that followed was painted.

"I couldn't tell you, sugar," Theresa said. "Need to look on the bright side. You rather have cold or *rain*?"

"It wouldn't be rain." Andi shivered. "It'd be snow! Aren't *you* cold?"

"Old people is *always* cold. Takes a loooooong time for the blood to make it all the way 'round my body and by the time it does, I'm nigh onto freezing to death."

It wasn't really that cold, of course, but it was way too cold for the Fourth of July.

Theresa reached into the floorboard of the backseat

and retrieved the huge, multi-hued afghan she'd knitted with Joseph's coat of many colors in mind, using colors in a random pattern that — to her eye at least — made it look like the afghan was constantly billowing in the wind.

"You and Ariel can wrap up in this until the ceremony starts."

The afghan was only one of many projects Theresa churned out when she'd took up knitting after … last spring. She'd needed something to do with her hands and the needles was just the ticket. She'd made purses — hers first so if they was any lumps or bumps wouldn't nobody know it but her. She hadn't intended it to be so big, felt like a diaper bag. The purses she'd made for Becca, Andi and Ariel was white and dainty, and she'd put little pearls on the outsides to match the ones she'd put on Becca's wedding dress. She'd even made ties for both Jack and Daniel. Wasn't no ugly things neither, that you smiled when you got and then never wore. Jack's was gold on the top, and had a knitted lining that was white. Daniel's was forest green. They wasn't all that big but it took two skeins of yarn, 'bout 250 yards of yarn for each one. Daniel would be wearing his clerical collar for the service, but Jack'd said he was gone wear that tie she'd made him. She'd see about that.

Theresa and the girls helped Becca out of the back seat. Her hair was piled in curls on the top of her head and ringlet curls hung down her back. It sparkled like spun gold in the sunlight. Ariel marveled at her shoes — white satin with four-inch heels wasn't no bigger than a pencil. She'd put on the whole getup at the Murphys' house, and then tottered on those heels out to the car. It was gone be a challenge on that path back to the chapel, but Becca didn't care. She wanted it all.

Theresa took a deep breath. It was now or never.

"I's wondering if you might want to give that train a second thought," she said. "I brought it just in case—"

"A train!" Andi said.

"There's a train on your wedding dress?" Ariel asked. "Can I walk behind you and—?"

"No train," Becca said, firm but kind. "But as cold as it is, maybe I ought to wrap up in it like a mummy. There's certainly enough material."

"I want you to wear this today," Andi said. She reached off and unfastened the cross necklace that had been her mother's — the one she had not taken off since Jack put it around her neck the day of her mother's funeral — and held it out to Becca.

"Oh, Andi, no. I couldn't—"

"Something old, something new, something *borrowed* and something blue."

"And a penny in your shoe," Ariel added.

"Your dress is new," Andi began.

"And *I'm* old!" Theresa said. Then she reached into the pocket of her dress and pulled out a simple gold bracelet, small and delicate. "My mama give me this on the day I married Bishop. I been saving it … to give to my daughter on her wedding day."

She'd been determined to get the whole thing out without crying, but she choked up on the word "daughter" and sniffled out the rest.

Tears sprang into Becca's eyes so rapidly the sparkle of them in the sun looked like she had diamonds in her eyes. She said nothing, probably couldn't talk no better than Theresa could, just took Theresa into her arms and held her tight for a good long time.

"What about the penny and the something blue?" Ariel asked.

Andi had volunteered to handle that part of it and she

produced a shiny new penny out of the lace pocket on her dress, then looked sheepish. "But I forgot until the last minute — you guys were in the car waiting and I was looking around for something …" She paused, then pulled a small piece of blue duct tape out of her pocket. "It was either duct tape or a lampshade."

Becca lost it. She added tears of laughter to the ones already running down her cheeks. Theresa doubled over with mirth. Andi and Ariel looked at each other, not quite sure why it had struck them as so funny.

When Becca recovered, she stood for a moment, considering, then pulled up her dress and stuck the tape to the inside of the taffeta petticoat.

She was smoothing it back into place while Theresa and the girls got the flowers out of the trunk when another car pulled into the parking area. Sheriff Lincoln got out with a smile so broad it looked like the ends was gonna meet in the back and the whole top of his head was gonna fall off. He musta figured it made him look happy, but truth was he looked like a crocodile done seen something yummy floating in the water.

"Is anything—?"

"Wrong? No. I just …" He looked full at Becca. "We ain't known each other very long, but folks get to feeling close when they go through bad stuff together."

He paused, took a breath and continued. "I know you don't have anybody … was wondering if you'd do the honor of allowing me to walk you down the aisle."

For the second time in five minutes, tears sprang into Becca's eyes. She couldn't talk then, neither, but she nodded, gave him a brief hug and then reached out and took his arm, and the group headed down the stone path to the chapel.

Chapter Eighteen

LINC HAD BEEN COMPLETELY honest with Becca about why he was there. He just didn't tell her the whole reason. He'd been thinking ever since he heard about the wedding that the girl would have to walk the aisle alone, given that her monster father, Billy Ray Hawkins, was buried somewhere in the caves along with Jeff Kendrick. He wanted to offer his services, but that seemed forward so he kept his mouth shut.

But after the morning in Grant's Crossing, he was past the point of caring if he sounded forward. His cop's gut was tied in a knot, all the alarm bells were going ding, ding, ding. Something was bad wrong. He planned to ride shotgun on these five people until they could get safely out of the county.

And what did *that* mean?

Linc didn't really have any idea.

He could protect them from a serial killer who dismembered his victims, left worms behind, but no scent a hound dog could follow. That was in his wheelhouse. He resisted the urge to reach down and pat his sidearm.

But no matter how well armed he was, he couldn't protect them from an earthquake. He refused to think of it as a mountain shaking itself like a dog! His mind flat out wouldn't go there. Or from birds falling out of the sky. Not falling, *diving*. Or murderous dairy cattle — Homicidal Holsteins. Sounded like the name of a really bad rock band.

Or kudzu vines that …

Herb and Marian Cox owned the farm next to the Dunn place on Covered Bridge Road, and Marian had come over a hill early this morning and almost run down Ali Dunn. She'd been wandering down the middle of the road barefoot, in her nightgown, carrying her three-week-old baby daughter.

"All she'd say was 'kudzu, kudzu,'" Marian'd told Linc, holding onto her emotions with her fingernails while she was telling the story, her breathing shallow. "So I took her home so Herb could see to her." Herb was in the early stage of Multiple Sclerosis, could still get around pretty well but didn't leave the house much. "And I went over to their house … but I couldn't find it! Linc … it was gone. Just gone. Wasn't nothing at the end of the lane but … lumps, big things, the house and the barn, but it was all covered with kudzu and the leaves on them vines was big as dinner plates." The woman was right on the edge of losing it, but she held on.

"I run, scared me so bad … I hightailed it back home and Herb said Ali'd told him Steve was dead, that them vines had wrapped him up and choked him to death. She'd had to use a chainsaw to cut through them to get to Kelly Ann. That's when I called you."

Linc's deputies still hadn't found Steve's body. Linc planned to go there as soon as he saw these people safely across the county line. The deputies were using bush hogs to cut through the vegetation. The last report he'd gotten from Bob Sirrine was that the vines seemed to be growing back almost as fast as they could cut them.

Which was impossible, of course.

And heaven only knew what other random impossibility lay ahead.

All this had something to do with the group of people gathered here — whether they were willing to admit it or not — and he suspected that Theresa, Becca and Andi would be much more likely to consider that possibility than the men had been. Even if he didn't have any idea how it was expressing itself, Linc knew it was all about demons and those five people had gone head to head with a demon prince from hell and defeated it. No one else he knew, had ever known, had ever even heard about, could lay claim to that distinction.

Linc intended to see to it all five of them got out of Caverna County as quickly as possible. If he could manage to keep them alive and unharmed until — he glanced at his watch — it had stopped. Well, for just a couple more hours, then one of two things would happen.

One, maybe, just maybe whatever their presence had started would stop when they were gone.

Or two, it would continue, maybe even get worse, but then he would be alone, the only man in the whole county who understood the real source of what was happening — demons.

He figured the safe money was on Door Number Two. Maybe he was just listening to the voices of fear in his head. There was no reason to believe it, but he sensed that what had happened was nothing compared to what was going to happen. It felt like he'd seen the first shift in the snow, the first little movement that any second would become an avalanche that wiped out everything and everybody in its path.

What was it Crock always said? Yeah, right — *goody*.

He set out with Becca on his arm down the meandering path through the dense forest and undergrowth, thinking as they walked, that he'd forgotten how beautiful it was here, and how *long* the path was! At one time, the path had been stone, just like the chapel, with flowers planted along both sides. Ancil Tucker had had the stones set in place by the same masons who'd built the chapel. Now, more than half a century later, the flowers were long gone and the woods had encroached on the pathway — with branches dangling down over it so low you had to move them aside or duck beneath them, and places where oleander bushes grew right up to the stones on both sides, so you had to walk single file to make it through. Grass and weeds had found purchase in the cracks between the stones and the roots of nearby trees had bowed some of them up.

Linc suspected that the chapel had been in a similar state of disrepair, unused as it was for years until Jack and Becca came down to Caverna County in June to take a look at it — and that the two of them had spent a couple of weekends cleaning it up for the occasion. He knew that Rita Murphy, Ariel's mother, had come out here several times, too, to clean and decorate, so he had no doubt the chapel would be as shiny as a new penny.

Theresa walked behind him and Becca. The two little girls were in front, giggling, wrapped up in the afghan like they were in a sack race, trying to hurry to make sure none of the men was outside before they'd let Becca come around the final bend in the path and walk the rest of the way up the stone path to the chapel. Andi popped into the building briefly and did whatever it was eleven-year-olds knew how to do with an iPhone and a set of speakers no bigger than a Baby Ruth bar, and suddenly music filled the air.

Linc was so concentrated on being helpful to Becca, who had taken off her silver high-heeled shoes and was negotiating the rub-board pathway barefoot, that he was the one who stumbled. Must have turned his foot on a rock and lost his balance for a second. He and Becca both staggered a step. Linc turned and saw her looking around, eyes darting from the chapel to the woods to the path to the sky, a look of fear on her face.

"I'm sorry. I didn't mean to trip you," he said.

"What was that?" she asked him.

"What was what?"

"*That* … you didn't feel it?"

"What I'm gonna feel is my backside planted on these stones if I don't watch where I'm going. Getting clumsy in my dotage."

When they came around the last bend in the trail that hid the chapel with bushes and trees, Becca stopped so abruptly, Linc almost tripped again. Then she just stood there, staring at the chapel.

"It's beautiful … but—" Her face was aglow with wonder and some other emotion that looked a whole lot like fear. Andi was staring at the chapel with the same surprised/confused look on her face.

"It's scary," Andi said. "Why is it … the light …?"

"What is it you two can see that the rest of us can't?" Theresa asked, and Linc took a blow to the belly at the question. Oh, he knew that Becca and Andi could … that they could see an evil normal folks couldn't. Knowing it and seeing it firsthand were two different things entirely, though. He remembered the day in his office after Andi was attacked by her cat, listening to the child describe the creature that had possessed the animal. He remembered that he had broken out in gooseflesh all over. He did the same thing now.

"The light's ... wrong," Becca said, struggling for words. "It's ..."

"The windchime on our back deck, the one with a crystal in the center above the dangling chimes. It makes rainbows on the floor when the light hits it just right ..." Andi said. "And your keychain, Theresa. It's reflected."

All eyes turned to Theresa, who reluctantly stuck her hand into her huge knitted purse for her keys.

"*Refracted,*" Becca corrected. "All the different colors of the spectrum mix together to form ordinary white light. But here ..." She turned and looked all around her, up at the sky and into the woods. Andi did the same thing. "The light isn't solid. It's rainbow colors."

"Rainbows everywhere," Andi said, with none of the delight in her voice such a statement should provoke. "The light is *broken.*"

Theresa held up a set of keys dangling from a fob that was a crystalline Yoda.

Even Linc could see the rainbows it made in the air. But it almost hurt his eyes to look at them. Something about them was ... off.

"The color sequence isn't right," he said, studying the refracted rainbows from Theresa's crystal in wonder and horror. "All rainbows are the same, from the top down it's red, then orange, yellow, green, blue, indigo and violet."

He couldn't remember why he knew that, but he was certain. And they all could see for themselves that the color at the top of the rainbows refracted by Theresa's crystal Yoda was violet, followed by yellow, green, indigo, another red, then orange and blue. The light the rainbows made was odd in a way Linc didn't have words to describe.

"Might not be a plan to walk into them rainbows," Theresa said to the little girls. Then she asked a question to which she expected no answer. "What kinda power would it take to *break* light?"

The same kind of power it would take to drive thousands of starlings into a suicide dive or turn dairy cattle and kudzu vines into killers. But Linc didn't say that because Becca, Theresa and the girls didn't know what had been going on in the past few days in Caverna County. And right before Becca walked down the aisle to marry the love of her life was not the time to tell them about it.

THE UGLY MAN was as invisible in the bushes near the path to the chapel as an iguana on a rock. There was a sycamore tree with a root extending out from it about ten inches tall, snaking along the ground like a python into the bushes. He stepped over it, careful not to trip, and then took a couple more steps to a spot where an oleander bush concealed his feet and legs up to his waist. But from there up, he had no cover. Anyone who happened to turn his way would see him. Except they wouldn't, of course, because he blended into his surroundings, indistinguishable unless he moved. And he didn't. He stood motionless.

He hated being here, hated the noon-sun, hated all that wasn't dark and cold and silent. But she was supposed to be in the woods today and he'd come looking for her to take her back to the cave to burn.

Looking for *her,* he had stumbled upon *this.* The wonder of it stopped him in his tracks.

There were two little girls. The one with red braids

came within a few feet of him. He could have reached out and snatched her away before she even had a chance to scream. And it'd be a few steps before they even missed her, and by the time they turned around to look, he'd be gone.

He didn't, though. He just watched. This was such a delicious feast being served up for him that he had no intention of spoiling his appetite with a snack before the meal. He would have the one in the flowing gown and hair the color of corn silk, so blonde it was almost white. *That* one. He'd been sent for one like that and none of the others would do.

There was a longing ache in his belly and he struggled to remember what it was. Finally decided it was just need — hunger, the need to feed. It was probably more than that, though. Desire, maybe? No, something more. A flickering of memory, faces and people there and gone again in a heartbeat. He didn't often have memories, knew only the here and now. But he remembered ... *knew* these people — Then it was gone and he didn't care enough to puzzle it out, chase it in his head. What he did know and understand was enough. It was all he needed. He wanted the one in white. His mouth watered just looking at her, imagining the taste of her and the deliciousness of her screams.

Sure, there were the others. It was his way to take his prizes in the dark when they were alone, not in the daylight with other people around. But he could do it, already knew how he'd do it. He'd felt the movement they had ignored. Just a little one, but he could sense something was coming — something big. When it did, these people wouldn't be leaving like they planned. They'd be here for a while, here in his world. And out here in the woods with no "facilities" ... when a girl's got to go, she's got to go. And when *that one,* the blonde, stepped away from the others, just for a second, an instant, he'd be there waiting.

He'd have her then! She would be his, the Ugly Man's, to do with as he wished, and the imagined pleasure of what he would do to her built as an ache in his chest.

What passed for a smile spread across the Ugly Man's ravaged face. Drool ran down what was left of his chin and dripped onto the front of the shirt he'd stolen off a clothes-line somewhere. He took the ring out of his pants pocket, rolled it around on his palm, liked the feel of it and the almost-memories it stirred. But it also brought a yearning he no longer understood that somehow seemed more intense now than it ever had before. He dropped the ring into the pocket on the front of his shirt and patted it there.

~

"... THE WORST WEDDING I EVER OFFICIATED?"

Daniel thought for a moment. "The worse was prob-ably the one I didn't perform. The groom showed up drunk, wearing a wife-beater t-shirt, three days growth of beard and smelling like the bottom three floors of Noah's ark ..."

Daniel prattled on about the various disaster weddings of his experience after Crock cut his eyes at Jack, who was wrapped so tight his own eyes were bugging out of their sockets, then asked Daniel for war stories. The minister had understood instantly that his friend needed nothing right now so much as he needed distraction.

"... the one where the groom was supposed to sing 'The Wind Beneath My Wings' to the bride but he lost his nerve after the first verse ..."

Crock had been afraid when he first saw the closet-sized room where he, Daniel and Jack were supposed to wait for their music cue that it would get so hot in there they'd emerge looking like they'd just come out the business end of a car wash. But it wasn't hot in the room. That was the thing. It *should* have been. It was July, for crying out loud, and the sun was shining. How could it possibly be so cold he was gritting his teeth not to shiver? There was something profoundly *wrong* about that, though nobody mentioned it. Everyone was in 'ignore-the-elephant-in-the-room' mode. They would see Jack and Becca happily married and then *get out!* That was the game plan.

Don't mention that everybody in Jack's car suddenly lost cell coverage at the same time. Just bang, no bars. But they were in the mountains, after all, and …

Don't mention that the woods they walked through to get to the chapel were as silent as King Tut's tomb — breathless, holding-your-breath quiet. Not a single birdsong or tree frog or cicada. Of course, it was possible the others really didn't notice. Crock was a city boy and loved the sounds of the outdoors — which were often amplified in weird but usually pleasant ways by Sonny and Cher. Apparently the frequency of whippoorwill's cry — *whip poor will, whip poor will* — was in the sweet spot of his hearing range. It had sounded like the woods were full of them when he'd sat on the bank of the river fishing two days ago. Before all the dead fish floated by.

Don't mention that it had actually felt like … like the ground had moved beneath his feet a few minutes before. That was crazy. Of course, he was so bowlegged you could hang him over a door for good luck, so maybe he'd just tripped.

The introduction songs stopped and the classical wedding music started. They could hear Mozart. That was the music where Theresa would be seated as the mother of the bride. Next came Bach. That was the cue for the flower girls to enter and start tossing petals and their cue to open the door from the closet-sized room into the chapel and step inside. The music was long so they had plenty of time. They'd be in place, waiting, when Wagner's "Bridal Chorus" began so Jack could see his lovely bride walk down the aisle.

Crock glanced at Jack. He did not look good. Not good at all. He was sweating — even in the cold — and his eyes were darting around at the corners of the room. Everybody knew that something awful had happened to Jack the summer of 1985 when the three children had battled the efreet the first time. Jack couldn't remember what, but whatever it had been had left him with almost debilitating claustrophobia.

As THEY APPROACHED THE CHAPEL, Theresa heard "Everlasting Love" by Natalie Cole echoing off the stone walls inside and bouncing out the door to fill the little clearing with music. When Becca had happened to mention that she would miss walking down the aisle to "here comes the bride," little Andi'd been on it like white on sugar. A couple of days later she'd had a whole soundtrack recorded. Said she'd gotten "old songs" because Becca would like those best.

"Best of My Love" was followed by "All You Need is Love."

"Where'd you get that music?" Theresa'd asked and Andi had rolled her eyes.

"Off the internet." Which wasn't no answer at all, but Theresa'd wisely decided not to pursue the matter.

They had practiced how the procession would go, each different part of it cued by the music.

Theresa got all the flowers situated on the girls, they baskets of rose petals in they hands and her own bouquet all fluffed up as the introductory music played. When it changed to some classical music by Mozart — Theresa didn't know its name but she recognized the tune — that was her cue.

Theresa would be seated first, before the ceremony even started. Becca had asked her to be the matron of honor, but she'd had her speech already mapped out.

"I'll be whatever you want me to be, the matron of honor or the custodian sweeping up all the birdseed. But if it's all the same to you, I rather be the mother of the bride." Becca had teared up at that. "I been the matron of honor in a couple of weddings before this one and who knows — I might be one in some other wedding down the road. But mother of the bride … that's a one-time gig."

Now, Theresa glanced over her shoulder to make sure everybody was where they was supposed to be.

Becca had a firm grasp on Sheriff Lincoln's arm — almost like she didn't want to let go. Ariel was directly behind Theresa. Andi stood in front of Becca hopping from one foot to the other in excitement.

A body surfaced then.

Theresa was blindsided by the image of the little girl with missing front teeth who'd wanted to cross the street to the schoolyard the day that demon-possessed man tried to shoot up a bunch of schoolchildren. The day a demon killed her Bishop.

That little girl'd been hopping around from one foot to the other — like she needed to go to the bathroom. She had whined to Theresa that the bell was gonna ring and "we're all gonna be late." But Theresa hadn't let the child cross the street, of course, told her, "you stay right where you are" because she had heard demon wails and smelled demon stink and knew something real bad was about to happen that she didn't want that little girl to go waltzing into.

"Theresa …" Andi said, and the image of the little gap-toothed child popped and was gone.

Andi made a shooing motion with her hand. "We're all gonna be late," she said.

A chill ran down Theresa's spine.

But she shook it off, drew herself up straight and tall and held her bouquet out majestically in front of her. She had until the music stopped to get seated on the front pew, left side. The bride's side. But excited as Andi was, she might jump the gun and come in early, before her cue.

Theresa turned and whispered urgently, "You stay right where you are." She hated that those words echoed in her head, repeating again and again.

Then she began to march slowly into the building.

It didn't take long to get to the front of the small chapel. She sat down, dignified as she could — which sometimes wasn't easy because her bad knee would collapse halfway down in a sit and she'd plop like a beached whale. The knee held this time and she had time to spread her full skirt out and smooth it down — and then she noticed the afghan, neatly folded on the pew beside her. She turned and looked, and Andi winked. That sweet little girl didn't want an old lady to get cold.

Andi and Ariel were to walk in slowly in front of Becca, tossing rose pedals on the cold stone floor.

The music stopped, and there was a moment of silence before it began again, something by Bach Theresa also didn't know the name of. But she did know it was Andi's cue. Theresa turned in her seat to watch the children enter. But she never saw them. Suddenly, the ground groaned and shook.

Then the stone chapel that had been in the woods for more than eighty years swayed drunkenly and began to come apart. The floor sagged. The roof buckled and then the whole building collapsed into a hole that had opened up in the earth right below it.

Chapter Nineteen

SOMEBODY WAS SCREAMING, shrieking. Several somebodies. The shrill, high-pitched sounds bore into Becca's temples like a dentist's drill. Then she realized one of the voices was hers. She would have clamped her hands over her mouth to silence the sound, but she couldn't let go of the two little girls she had grabbed and yanked toward her when the building—

The building collapsed!

Theresa!

Becca had felt it. Only a tiny movement of the earth but she'd felt it just like she'd felt the one a few minutes before — the one that had made Sheriff Lincoln stumble. And a sudden certainty of disaster filled her whole body like inflating a Navy dinghy. She dropped her bouquet in the dirt and grabbed Andi by the arm and Ariel by the lace on her pinafore. She was already yanking backwards, off balance and falling herself before the building swayed, its foundation crumbling away beneath it. Then the sheriff's big arms were around her, dragging her and the girls back up the stone sidewalk, away from …

She watched in fascinated horror as the thick stone walls cracked and then crumbled, falling inward with what should have been a mighty rumble but wasn't. It hardly made any noise at all. The stained-glass window above the door on the front of the building popped and exploded outward, spraying shards of colored glass like confetti in front of the building. It rained out of the sky, sparkling in the bright sunlight, covering her and the others in a thin glaze of glass dust.

The roof disintegrated on top of the crumbling walls, sending roof tiles flying through the air, clay projectiles that wheeled off into the woods where Becca could hear them landing in the trees as the rest of the whole structure all but vanished into the ground.

Seconds. It had only taken — what? Ten seconds? Twenty? Maybe not even that long.

The chapel was there and then it wasn't. Where it had stood was a pile of rubble less than three feet high, the shattered roof tiles and beams. The rest was … *it had fallen into a hole in the ground.* It dawned on Becca ponderously, like lifting something heavy, that a sinkhole had opened up in the ground beneath the chapel and the building had fallen down into it.

Theresa!

Jack!

He and Daniel and Crock were in that little room in the back of the building waiting for their music cue. The song was after Theresa's, which meant the three of them were still in that little room at the back of the chapel when the building collapsed. A room that no longer existed, that lay smashed beneath the roof tiles and pile of rubble that was all that was left of the Hope Chapel.

"Jack!" she cried out. She screamed his name. Shrieked

his name. But no sound came out her mouth. Horror had stolen her voice.

JACK FELT an ache in his jaws and realized he was gritting his teeth so tight his whole mouth hurt. He tried to relax, release the pressure, but it was no use. He didn't intend to grit his teeth and tighten every muscle in his body. It was an automatic response he had no control over.

"… bride decided to recite a poem as her vow." Daniel's voice seemed to be coming from a long way away. "Nothing literary, mind you. Just 'roses are red, violets are blue…'"

He felt himself break out in a cold sweat.

Get a grip, Carpenter! he yelled at himself inside his head. That didn't do any good, either.

Jack didn't do elevators. Only managed to fly by gripping the armrests on both sides so tight he left marks and he'd prefer to have his bladder burst than use one of those little bathrooms. He didn't know the source of his phobia, only that it was something that happened the summer—

Images downloaded into his brain. It was what they'd all come to call "a body surfaced."

IT IS DARK AND TIGHT, cold and scary. Nothing but inky blackness ahead.

Jack is … somewhere with cold metal all around, pushing in at him, crushing him.

Terror wells up in his chest and he can't breathe. He starts to cry, to sob, but he continues to crawl forward into the darkness. He is in agony. His knees and legs are raw, on fire, and every movement scrapes away the raw, burned — burned, he's been burned! —

flesh. His hands are out in front of him, feeling his way along in the black nothingness, stretching out his fingers into … air. Terror grips his every move, fear that any second he'll touch something solid in front of him that he will be trapped in … a pipe, he's in a pipe!

He crawls and crawls. He has been in the pipe for — what? Ten minutes? Two hours? Each moment is the longest moment of his life — until the next. It feels like his time in the pipe is as long as the whole rest of his childhood, and with every scooting motion forward he leaves a piece of his childhood behind him. How far has he gone — thirty feet? Fifty yards? Half a mile? There is no gauge to use to measure anything, time or distance. He realizes he was still sobbing when he hears the sound and wonders for a moment what it is. When he stops crying, the pipe is still, silent.

A tomb.

Buried alive.

Panic rushes in, a hairy black monster gorging its belly full of the meat of his soul. The walls slowly tighten, begin to crush him, squeezing the air slowly out of his lungs.

"Let me out! I want out!" he cries, his voice ragged. "I'd rather die, burn — anything."

He fights the walls around him, tries to push them away, bawling in terror, kicking his feet and banging with his fists. He lifts himself up on his elbows and screams, "God, get me out of here!"

JACK WAS FLUNG VIOLENTLY BACK into reality. The real world was a small space, a room, where he was shoved tight up against Daniel and Crock — and he *had to get out!*

Daniel was standing with his back against the small door leading outside and Jack shoved him aside, fumbling for the doorknob in a panic. He grabbed it, flung the door open and lunged out into the sunshine, and gasping great lungfuls of the cold air into his chest, staggering away from the chapel.

Crock and Daniel followed him out.

Daniel took hold of Jack's arm gently and Jack realized he was holding on to keep Jack from falling, *not* to keep him from running away! Crock put his hand on Jack's shoulder.

"It's okay, Jack," Daniel said. "Grab some air. Bach is interminably long. We've got time to smoke a cigar and still—"

"Daniel," Jack cried, "I remember. I know how I got out of the nursing home that day! I remember—"

When he felt the ground move beneath his feet, he thought at first it was just that he was off balance — until he saw the looks on Daniel and Crock's faces.

Then there was a great rumbling sound. He turned back around to see — *it couldn't be!* — the chapel was collapsing!

The building ... imploded. It looked like the foundation fell out from under it and the walls collapsed inward, crashing down into the interior of the building with the grumble of rock against rock.

Jack saw the hole! The building was collapsing into a hole — a sinkhole. There was a rumble in the trees behind him and he glanced around to see trees falling, disappearing like the earth had been pulled out from under them.

The chapel roof crashed down on top of the collapsed walls, tiles clattering against each other in a sound like applause as they fell down into the hole with the remainder of the building.

In seconds — *seconds!* — there was nothing but a pile of rubble a few feet high and a cloud of dust in the space that had been occupied by the Hope Chapel. The building was gone.

Becca!

Where was Becca?

The thought formed in his head only seconds before he began to make out the shapes of people through the cloud of dust on the other side of the rubble.

"Jack!" Becca's voice, frantic. "Where are—?"

Then he was running, dodging around the still-settling pile of rubble toward her.

She was lying on her back on the ground. Linc — *when did Linc get here?* — was holding her and she had Andi by the arm and was holding onto Ariel by the back of her dress. The four of them were only about three feet from the spot where the ground had opened up and swallowed the building.

Jack knelt beside her and she let go of her grip on the two little girls — who were crying. So was Becca.

"Theresa!" Becca managed to gasp through her tears, pointing to the pile of shattered rubble. "Jack, Theresa's … in there!"

THE CHOSEN ONE looked out over the group of people assembled outside the Love of God Holiness Church building and a smile spread across his face. They had come. Oh, he'd known they would, but seeing them there outside the church was as close to a good feeling as he would ever have. That they were *outside* the church was not surprising. Nobody'd told them they couldn't go into the building, but not one person had even set foot on the church steps. They must have gone off into the woods somewhere rather than inside to the bathroom when they needed to go because he'd been inside the whole time. He'd spent the night there, watching and listening. Not planning, though. There was nothing to plan — it was all laid out on a simple path and all he had to do was lead his unsuspecting dupes down it.

They probably didn't even realize it — that they did not want to go inside the church, that they might even have refused to do it if they'd been told to. They'd have felt uncomfortable there, if they'd gone in. The voices that gave them such clear direction that it brought bright sparks to their eyes would be muffled in a church, maybe even silenced altogether. These people would never again set foot willingly in a church. But that was okay, of course, because none of them was likely to live long enough to see next Sunday. And any of them who did — well, church was the last place they'd want to be after what he had planned for them to do between now and then.

When he stepped out the front door of the church onto the porch, there was a gasp from the crowd. Several people jumped back from him, like he'd appeared out of thin air and perhaps they believed he actually had. When he'd instructed them last night to meet him here this morning, it clearly hadn't occurred to any of them to wonder where he would spend the night.

The Chosen One was a stranger, had come walking out of the woods naked. None of them had ever seen him before. Their singular lack of curiosity was testimony to one of two things: they were too stupid to wonder about him, or they really did believe, deep down in their hearts, that he had actually appeared out of thin air — or could have if he'd wanted to.

"Brothers and sisters," he said in his deep, resonant voice. Then he adjusted the sunglasses on his nose that he wouldn't take off — actually couldn't take off because he couldn't allow any of them to look into his eyes. They would not survive looking into his eyes, but that was for later. Not now. "It is time."

The expectant looks on their faces were almost comical.

He began a sing-song chant, swaying slightly.

"Time for the dying," he said.

Several in the crowd repeated his words, "Time for the dying."

"Time for the crying and the lying and the dying," he said.

"Time for the crying and the lying and the dying," more of them repeated.

"Time for the blood," he said.

"Time for the blood," they all chanted in unison.

"The cleansing flood."

"The cleansing flood."

The call and repeat was firmly established now and he ramped up the volume and the emotion.

"Time for the vengeance of the God on high."

After they'd repeated the last line, his voice fell to a whisper.

"Time for unbelievers to die ... die ... *die!*"

There was absolute silence then in the crowd of maybe fifty people — a handful of those who'd been at the church last night had not returned, but almost the whole congregation had come back and a few had brought others with them. They stared at the Chosen One with jaws set and eyes too bright."

"We will fall on them like locusts, slaying all whom the Lord shall place in our path. We will suffer none to live. Not man, woman, child. Not doddering grandmother nor suckling babe. We will lay into them with ax and scythe, knife and club."

He looked pointedly at Jonah and then his gaze swept the crowd.

"Lay down your firearms. Their lives shall not end with

a bullet to the brain. We must kill them with our bare hands." He almost said, "It's so much more fun that way." But he held his tongue.

His voice dropped again. "And when they are dead, smear their blood on your bodies. Let no part of you be clean."

The Chosen One watched as rifles, pistols and shotguns dropped to the ground. He'd gather them up after the people left, keep them safe for some future need.

"Spread out. Let the Lord lead you to his chosen victims. To escape the wrath of a vengeful God, cast into the firmament of flames to burn for all eternity, your act of absolute obedience is to slay everyone who comes into your sight — friend or foe, your mother or your child. None is to survive … save *one*."

He let his voice drop to almost a whisper, so the assemblage had to lean forward to hear him.

"Bring me back one for a special sacrifice."

The special sacrifice was just one more way to push them beyond the point of no return. Kill your neighbor, strike him down for no reason, and you didn't get a do-over. No oops, maybe I shouldn't have done that. But no matter what he told them, wasn't all of them gonna do that, commit murder. They might go along and soon's somebody else offed "an unbeliever" they'd participate in the blood-smearing. That wasn't good enough. He wanted them *all*. Every last one of them. Body and soul. He would settle for absolutely nothing less. The more heinous the crime, the more devout would be the people who committed it. Beheading a nun or a priest — shock and awe.

"A holy one," he said, the derision in his voice masked by the whisper. "Bring me back one of the nuns from the convent — preferably a young one and not some withered old crone. Or one of the brothers from the monastery. Alive and unharmed. I have a special fate in mind for imposters who lead others away from the true path, from service to the one all-powerful Lord who reigns supreme over all the earth."

He paused. "We will chop off their heads!"

That definitely got their attention. You coulda heard a mouse tiptoeing in house shoes across a cotton ball in the silence that followed.

"We will place the head of a deceiver on a stake." He reached down and picked up the one he'd brought along. It was a tobacco stake — one of the sticks used in tobacco fields during harvest. Once the leaves had been cut off a tobacco plant, they were stabbed down over a tobacco stick stuck in the ground to dry. The ends of tobacco sticks were sharp to cut through the tobacco stalks, but the Chosen One had sharpened the other end as well. He stabbed the stick into the ground, and reached out his finger and almost caressed the sharp point on the opposite end.

"The head will stare out with unseeing eyes at all who come near. But its dead stare will search out any unbelievers among us so we can strike them down. Then we will watch the birds peck out those eyes from their sockets, watch them dine on the flesh, and we will know the fate of any who turn their backs on the one true God."

Yup, a human head sticking on the end of that stick would be one more nail in their coffins ... so to speak. There'd be more nails. He'd be sure that before he was done with them, every man, woman and child would have committed some unspeakable act, that they all earned the blood they'd be smearing. Everybody who was here would be all in.

"Return before sundown covered in blood. Slathered in blood. Judgement Day is upon us. Your only hope of eternal salvation is the blood of your sacrificial offering to the Lord. Now go!"

A big man in a wife-beater t-shirt, a one-eyed man with a scar that slashed across his whole face, lifted up an ax into the air and gave a cry more feral than human and took off running into the woods. A fat girl with a scythe and a skinny woman carrying a meat cleaver trailed along behind.

Their movement freed the rest of them and in less than a minute the churchyard was empty, guns and ammunition lying on the ground.

The Chosen One went from one to the next, gathering up all the firearms in a burlap bag. He put the bag in the broom closet in the tiny church, stepped back out on the porch and drew out a knife from a scabbard hidden under his suit coat. It wasn't a kitchen butcher knife or a hunting knife to use skinning a deer. It was a dagger, thin and pointed, so sharp you could cut paper with it. The Chosen One had used it to slice up hymnbooks in the church after he'd spent hours sharpening it. The handle was made of black onyx, carved in the shape of entwined snakes, with their two heads forming the hilt. The snakes' fangs were bared. They were biting each other.

Chapter Twenty

IT WAS the oddest sensation Theresa Washington had ever felt in her six decades of living. She was sitting on the pew worn smooth by generations of backsides, listening to the music and thinking that she had to keep from crying. Well, not from crying. That wasn't gonna happen. But she did need to hang onto enough self-control not to burst out in big sloppy sobs the minute she seen Becca.

Jack, too, of course. Soon's she seen him all dressed up—

Then she felt a jolt, a little one, not even as jarring as a car hitting a pothole.

And the pew … fell.

The floor was suddenly gone — just not there anymore — and the pew she was sitting on dropped out from under her.

The only sensation she'd ever felt that was anything like it was when she was substitute teaching that rowdy Sunday School class that had them boys from Brewster Academy in it who thought the world belonged to them and you was lucky they let you breathe the air in it. One of them was standing behind her chair and when she went to sit down in it, he yanked it away and suddenly wasn't nothing there to sit on. Just empty air.

That's all there was now. Empty air.

She didn't have time to cry out, didn't even have time to get scared really before it was all over. She was sitting on the pew, and then she wasn't. There was the sensation of empty air. Then she was lying on broken-up pieces of rock, the stone floor, beside the pew, which musta turned in the air after it dumped her out and was standing on end like the pole of a beach umbrella.

What happened?

Theresa began to cough. The air around her was filled with so much dust she could hardly see. All she could see was broken-up rubble around her everywhere — pieces of ceiling beams and pews, the altar railing and rocks jumbled up like they'd been dumped into a blender, looked like there'd been a ... *earthquake!*

That little jolt she'd felt before. That musta been—

She tried to sit up and decided real quick that wasn't such a good idea. When she moved, that beach-umbrella-pole pew she was leaning up against wobbled. When it did, pieces of rocks began to fall out of the mess of debris that was up above it. So she got still, just lay there on her back looking around.

That was when it occurred to her that she was buried in rubble. Then the scared hit, smashed into her like she'd walked into a revolving door swinging the other way.

OH, Lord help me. I been buried alive!

. . .

AND THAT SOFT voice you could only hear in your head if you shut up your own mouth and listened, reminded her calmly that the key word in that sentence was *alive*. She was alive.

But was she hurt?

It was real hard to do a physical inventory lying on a bunch or rocks on your back and you couldn't even see your feet *because they was something lying across them*.

She tried to get a look at whatever it was that was on top of her feet, felt like all the way up to the knee, but movement made her umbrella pole wiggle and all the rocks and pieces of wood it was holding up wiggled, too, and Theresa might not know much about earthquakes and the like but any fool could figure out it wasn't a good thing for rocks and wood above your head to wiggle.

She did wiggle her toes, though, and they moved just fine — both feet — so whatever was pinning her legs down wasn't smashing them. That was a good thing.

She reached up to wipe the dust off her face and felt something wet on her forehead. Sticky wet. She looked at her fingers and there was blood on them, but it wasn't pouring down her face or nothing like that so it couldn't be too bad. She was lucky she didn't get squashed like a stomped bug, 'cause that's what happened to people in earthquakes.

No, it wasn't no earthquake because the roof and walls didn't crash down on her — the floor had fallen *out from under her* and then the building collapsed. A hole had opened up in the ground. A sinkhole! They was a cave right smack dab under that chapel and the roof of it collapsed and she and the building had fallen down into it.

I done ruined that beautiful mother-of-the-bride dress me and Becca seen in Macy's and they actually had it in my size.

Bride … Becca!

Was she down here, too, buried somewhere?

And the rest of them. The little girls — Jack and Daniel. Crock, Linc.

Where was everybody?

It don't matter about me, Lord, but you got to take care of them others.

"Becca!" she cried. "Jack! Daniel! *Andi!* Where you at? You answer me."

All she could hear was the hammering of her own pulse in her ears. If something had happened to any of the — to *all of them* — that'd be more than Theresa's poor old heart could bear. If they was hurt, or—

"Theresa!" Jack's voice. "Are you all right?"

"Would you be if the good Lord done dumped a whole building down on your head?" she called back.

He laughed. Everything was gonna be all right — he laughed.

Thank you, Jesus!

Jack heard a cry from the still-settling jumble of rocks and timbers and roof tiles, from deep beneath the pile of rubble.

"Becca! Jack! Daniel! *Andi!* Where you at? You answer me."

Theresa!

He had trouble speaking for a moment, only then admitting to himself how scared he'd been that she was—

"Theresa, are you all right?"

"Would you be if the good Lord done dumped a whole building down on your head?"

Relief bubbled out of his throat in a roar of laughter, and after a moment of shocked silence they all were laughing.

"You wouldn't think it was near as funny if you's the one down here," Theresa called back, but he could hear the same relief in her voice he was sure she could hear in his.

"Theresa, are you hurt?" Becca called out to her. Jack turned to where she was now standing near the edge of the sinkhole, peering down into the debris. Becca. In her wedding dress. She was so beautiful, she took his breath away.

It wasn't supposed to be like this! He was supposed to watch her walk down the aisle and into every moment of the rest of his life. They were supposed to be married! But the earth had opened up and swallowed their plans.

"Well, this sure screwed the pooch," Crock said. He looked directly at Jack then, almost like he knew what Jack was thinking. "But it could have been a whole lot worse. We could all be tangled up in that mess. *That* could ruin your whole day."

Stuff the self-pity, Carpenter! And use that energy to figure out how to get Theresa out of there.

"I ain't sure if I'm injured," Theresa said. "But I don't hurt nowhere so if I am, it can't be too bad. The thing is — I'm stuck. They's something — maybe one of them pews or a piece of the floor — on top of my legs pinning me down. And when I move, all that stuff piled up between me and you starts to wiggle."

Andi and Ariel started toward the edge of the sinkhole to try to get a look at Theresa, but Daniel headed them off.

"You girls stay back," he said. "This is a sinkhole, which means the roof of an underground cave collapsed and what was above it — the chapel — fell into it. That cave roof down there could collapse again and take you girls down with it."

So they sat down on the ground as close to the edge of the sinkhole as Daniel would allow them to go and began calling out to Theresa.

"I can't see you down there," Ariel said. "Is it dark?"

As the girls engaged Theresa in conversation, Linc spoke quietly so only the men could hear.

"Ever play pick-up sticks?" he asked. While Jack had been talking to Theresa, he'd been walking around the edge of the sinkhole, studying it. "Dump out a pile of toothpicks and then try to pick them up one at a time without moving the others? Almost impossible." He gestured toward the pile of rubble. "That's what we got here."

Jack wondered fleetingly when Linc had shown up. And why.

"If we try to get Theresa out of there, we'll most likely succeed in dumping the rest of the building down on top of her. And Daniel's right — the cave roof below us might not be near done collapsing."

Becca heard the last part.

"What are we going to do?" she said. "We have to get her out. She's an old woman with a bad back. She might be badly hurt and she doesn't even know it! People in car accidents sometimes climb out of the wreck without even realizing they're injured. She can't stay down there!"

"*We* can't get her out," Jack said. "We need help — lots

of help. The rescue squad and the fire department. We need—"

Crock had his cell phone out. "I don't have coverage," he said. "Which confirms my long-held suspicion that all things electronic are fundamentally magical and could vanish at any second. You got any bars?"

Jack shook his head. He'd already looked. Linc and Daniel pulled out their phones and shook their heads. Becca and Theresa's phones were in the purses they'd left in Theresa's car.

"I'll use the radio in my cruiser," Linc said. "Why don't you girls come with me," he said to Ariel and Andi. "Gather up the phones and you can help me see if we can get coverage out by the cars." He looked over their heads and caught Jack's eye as Jack handed Andi his car keys. "While we're doing that, I think you better bring Becca and Theresa up to speed." He paused. "Because there's more."

Linc and the girls headed back down the winding path to the spot where the cars were parked — a uniformed man and two little fairies, white dresses swishing around their legs. When Jack turned back to Becca, he noticed the flower girls' baskets and the rose petals scattered over the ground.

"What's going on, Jack?" Becca said, apprehension stapling a pleat between her eyebrows. Jack exchanged a look with Crock and Daniel, who nodded, then he moved as close as he dared to the edge of the sinkhole.

"Linc's gone to use his radio to call for help," he said, loud so Theresa could hear.

"You don't have to yell. I ain't deaf."

In truth, she wasn't more than fifteen or twenty feet away from them. It was what lay between that made it seem so far.

"There are some things you and Becca need to know about what's been happening in the past few days in Caverna County," Jack said, then nodded to Crock, who told how it'd started with dead fish in the river. Daniel took up the tale next.

Jack sat down on a big piece of the stone wall of the chapel that fell out onto the ground instead of into the hole when the building collapsed. He took off his tie and stuffed it into his coat pocket, unbuttoned the top choke-hold button on his shirt and was ready to take the hand-off from Daniel.

He had just completed the story of the attack of the dairy cattle when Linc and the girls reappeared at the bend of the pathway. He didn't like the look on Linc's face. He was carrying his M4 service rifle and his tactical vest with additional ammunition. Andi had a cardboard box that said "Road Flares" on the outside.

"Radio's as dead as the cell phones, nothing but static," Linc said.

"Great," Jack said. "Then we'll just have to drive down out of these mountains far enough to—"

"Car won't start," Linc said. "None of them." He tossed Jack back his car keys. "I tried all three. Dead. Turn the key, nothing."

Jack could have sworn he felt a sudden cold breeze blow on the back of his neck and he shivered.

Linc spoke the next words softly to the men standing nearby. "I'm no doctor, but I'm certified as an EMT. We trained a lot on the care of people who've gone into shock."

Jack knew where he was going. "That's what I've been thinking," he said and saw Crock nod that he was on the same page, too. "Whether Theresa's got injuries she doesn't know about or not, we have to get her out of there quick or—"

"How long?" Becca asked. Jack turned. He hadn't intended for her to hear. "How long before Theresa starts going into shock?"

"No way to put a number on it," Linc said. "We just need to be aware — there's a ticking clock."

THE GOOD LORD in his bounty had provided for Theresa and she'd ought to be thanking Jesus 'stead of being scared and worried and the like. God had known how cold-natured Theresa was and he'd made sure not to let her drop into a hole in the ground with a building on top of her 'thout making sure she could stay warm.

The afghan. The multi-colored one Theresa had knitted with Joseph's coat of many colors in mind had been lying on the pew and had literally landed right on top of her.

Theresa pulled the afghan around her and got as comfortable as it was possible to get lying on a pile of rocks. She'd squirmed around — careful not to disturb the beach-umbrella pew that was keeping the rest of the building from falling down on her head. As she snuggled up in the afghan's warmth, it occurred to her that it was probably a lot colder up there than it was down here in the cave. They needed that blanket a sight more than she did, but wasn't no way to climb up there and give it back to 'em so she thanked the good Lord for his provision and let it go.

Now, she lay with it pulled up to her neck, wiggling her toes that was caught under that piece of whatever-it-was every few minutes to make sure she still could. They worked fine. Soon's she'd calmed down and her heart started to beat normal, she'd realized she could move her whole leg around under the — she moved as slowly as she could and craned her neck to see. It was a rock, a piece of the stone wall that was pinning her down. The rock wasn't lying direct on her leg. It was lying on some rocks and stretched across her leg. She could have pulled her leg right out of there ... if she hadn't had a foot sticking up on the other end of it. 'Thout chopping her foot off, her leg was stuck there until somebody picked that rock up off it.

Ariel asked her if it was dark down where she was at and she told them it wasn't dark and wasn't cold, neither.

"Case you was wondering, I'm a lot warmer down here than you is up there. I got an afghan to snuggle in." She paused. "Thanks to God ... and his angel, Andi."

"I'm not an angel. I've seen one and it's *not* me!"

Then Jack hollered that Linc was gonna take the girls to the car, and soon's they was gone he finally filled in the blanks, dropped the pretense that wasn't nothing wrong and told her all the things that'd happened. She listened in growing horror, wasn't thinking about her leg or the rock or her foot or the umbrella-pew anymore. Soon as she heard them tales, she knew why it was that she was stuck down here in a sinkhole.

Oh, it'd take the others longer to get there. They'd likely deny it longer than Theresa done, but they'd all figure it out pretty soon. When all of creation is broke, ain't but a few possible explanations. They'd shy away from the explanations they didn't like for long as they could.

Theresa didn't shy away from nothin'. She hadn't yet puzzled out what exactly was going on, but wasn't no doubt who was responsible. It was demons at work here. Pure evil.

~

JONAH BALLARD REACHED his hand into the gory wound on the man's back and brought it back wet and slimy, dripping with blood and gore.

He found himself licking his fingers, putting each in his mouth and pulling it out slowly, the way you'd lick the grease off your fingers after you'd ate some fried chicken.

Finger-lickin' good.

That tickled Jonah and he giggled, a strange little laugh that sounded funny in his ears.

He'd found the man walking down the shoulder of the road away from a pickup truck that sat on the roadside with the hood up. He'd hid in the bushes, watching as the truck rolled to a stop right in the middle of the road and the man'd had to get out and push it off onto the shoulder so wouldn't nobody else come along and hit it.

As Jonah stalked him from the woods, he was glad the man was someone he didn't know. He looked like a Webster — had that black hair and them heavy eyebrows the Websters had. But Jonah hadn't never met the man and he was glad of that — his first kill — glad it wasn't somebody he knew.

Jonah'd waited for just the right moment, and when the man stopped, then leaned over to tie the lace on his work boot, Jonah leapt out of the trees, machete raised and brought it down with a kind of *twuck* sound right in the middle of the man's back. He screamed, fell forward on his face, but surprisingly he wasn't hurt so bad he couldn't try to fight back. Jonah'd figured with a machete buried in his back, a man would just roll over and die, but this one didn't. He rolled over onto his side and the movement yanked the machete out of Jonah's hand because the duct tape holding the handle together was wet with sweat.

Then the man had staggered, trying to get to his feet, and halfway up he lunged at Jonah, tried to grab him, caught him off balance and Jonah almost tripped over his own feet and went down. The man was slow, staggering, bleeding — still had a machete in his back! — and Jonah dodged out of his grasp. He sidestepped, shoved the man back down on the ground, grabbed a handful of the man's hair and slid the blade of his bowie knife across his throat — so sharp he couldn't even tell he was cutting anything.

The man went instantly limp and collapsed, with blood pulsing out his neck and spilling all over the ground and that's when Jonah remembered he was supposed to wipe that blood all over himself. That the blood was precious, that it was what was gonna save Jonah from the fires of hell.

He dropped to his knees beside the man, held his hands out and caught as much of the blood as he could, smearing it all over his face, his neck, into his hair. Jonah believed that if there was even one speck of clean flesh on his body when the day was over, one spot not covered in blood, he would be lost.

The gushing blood from the neck wound stopped when the man's heart quit beating, then it was just oozing out, so Jonah yanked the machete out of the man's back and stuck his hands deep in the wound — a big slice all the way down his back. He scooped out as much blood as he could get, smearing it all over his hands and arms, but there wasn't nearly enough because most of what'd come out of the man's neck had soaked into the dirt.

That was okay, though. This was just Jonah's first kill of the day. There'd be others. He'd find more blood, enough to cover over all his sins and make him clean.

Jonah got to his feet, shoved the bowie knife back into his scabbard and wiped some of the blood off the duct-taped handle of the machete because it was hard to hold onto when it was wet. He looked up and down the road and saw nobody. He could go to the Montgomerys' house. They was four of them — Rubin and his wife, Julie, and two kids. But they wouldn't be home. It was Sunday and they'd be in church.

Church. He wondered if maybe there might be a lot of people in church — people who wasn't armed, of course, 'cause nobody packed a gun into the sanctuary. There wasn't a church anywhere near, but the Hope Chapel was just on the other side of the mountain, in Queen Anne's Hollow. He didn't even know if people went there anymore, but it was worth a look. How he would love to be able to kill a chapel full of unbelievers and wallow in their blood.

Chapter Twenty-One

"How far are we from civilization?" Crock asked. "Anybody live nearby who is still living in the golden age of standard transmissions, televisions with dog-ears and telephones connected to each other by a piece of wire?"

"Most of the people who live up in this part of the county don't even have indoor plumbing," Daniel said.

Daniel saw Andi looking around at something he couldn't see.

"What is it?" he asked.

She told him about the rainbows.

"It's more than just the light that's broken, isn't it?" she said, drawing close to him and taking his hand.

He nodded, not surprised at all that she had picked up on the undercurrent among the adults. It was all but impossible to keep something from Andi.

"Other things … things in nature … aren't working right," he said. He told her abbreviated versions of what had happened to the rocks on the mountain, the fish and the pumpkins, didn't want to tell her about the cattle but she needed to understand that ordinary things might turn out to be dangerous.

"Some dairy cows killed people," he said simply.

"And some starlings killed people, too," Linc said.

Everyone looked at him. Clearly, Linc didn't like being the bearer of such bad tidings. Daniel figured what he told were sanitized versions of what really happened. The children didn't need to hear the gory details and the adults could easily figure them out. He described how kudzu vines had taken over the Dunn farm — that Ali had barely been able to save her baby daughter. After that, he told the story of the Fourth of July parade in Grant's Crossing.

"Are you saying that with that kind of craziness going on, our cell phones aren't ever going to work here?" Jack asked.

Linc shrugged. "I think that's why the *cars* won't start. A combustion engine works on certain principles of physics that might not be functioning properly right now. But the phones … it's reasonable that they're not working. I have driven through this part of the county lots of times and couldn't get cell coverage. That's normal around here. The mountains are steep and the hollows the road winds through are deep." He gestured up at the mountains around them. "We're in a hole here and cell phones are in a frequency that travels in a straight line."

Daniel continued to be impressed — and surprised, too — by Hezekiah Lincoln. Definitely *not* your typical good-ole-boy Kentucky sheriff! The man was quick, got there faster than most and seemed to know about a lot of different things.

"So you think maybe it'd be possible to get coverage if we were higher?" Daniel asked. "Like up on one of the mountains?"

"It's not just being higher," Linc said. "There's a cell

phone tower on one of the mountains around here." He pointed at the tallest mountain, Frog Croak Knob. "That one, I think. But it could be any of them."

"That's it, then," Jack said. He looked at his watch, and then back up in dismay. "My watch stopped on the way here. Anybody know what time—?" He looked at the shaking heads and didn't finish. "Okay, fine, it must about one o'clock, maybe one-thirty. I say we send somebody with a cell phone to the top of all three mountains."

"*Climb* the mountains?" Becca was dubious.

The Three Musketeers had played in the woods as children so they knew the mountains intimately. They understood that climbing one wasn't about how tall it was. Several Kentucky mountains topped 3000 feet, Black Mountain was 4100. These were smaller — 2000, maybe 2500. But height wasn't the issue — terrain was. The forests that blanketed the mountains had been logged at least once and maybe multiple times. Old-growth forests were so rare few Kentuckians had ever been in one. These woods were not populated by stately, fifty-year-old oak trees casting a canopy of shade that stunted vegetation beneath them. The forest floor under these younger trees was a tangle of brush, brambles and vines, with impenetrable windfalls of downed trees, broken limbs and branches knit together with creepers. The barbs of thorn and bramble bushes caught on your clothes, entwined grape vines as big as your arm dangled from tree limbs and the ground was slippery with fallen leaves and loose rocks. Not unclimbable by any means — they'd done it hundreds of times. But certainly not appropriate for dress shoes and suits.

"I could get to the top in an hour." Jack saw the look on Becca's face. "Okay, an hour and a half. That's three hours round trip. Remember, the sun doesn't go down until almost nine o'clock."

"In Cincinnati," Daniel put in. They were only a couple hundred miles south of there, but the shadows of the mountains darkened the hollows in between long before the sun dropped below the horizon "out there on the flat."

"We can be back down here by four-thirty or five. There'll still be plenty of daylight then. And *one* of us will find that tower and call for help."

"And if the phones still don't work on the mountain top?" Daniel asked.

"Eventually, somebody from town is going to notice we're missing and come looking for us." Jack turned to Linc. "When you're late checking in, what does your dispatcher—?"

"I'm not sure late applies anymore."

"What's *that* supposed to mean?" Daniel asked.

"What he's sayin' is if light can be broke, maybe time can be, too." The voice was Theresa's and the words were so stunning, nobody knew what to say.

"The car engines, watches, maybe the phones — especially the rainbows." Linc paused for a beat. "I'm just suggesting that … maybe time here isn't in sync with time in the rest of the world anymore."

"Are you saying …?" Becca's voice was very small.

"Just putting it out there. Maybe in the rest of the world—" Linc made a gesture back toward the highway and civilization, "—it's still the time it was when …" He stopped, regrouped. "Maybe our watches didn't stop. Maybe time did. Maybe it's still—" he looked at the watch on his wrist, "—11:34 in the morning out there."

That was a bridge too far for Jack.

"I cannot … I *will not* go there." Jack's voice had granite in it. "Until we know different, we will assume that we are still functioning on Eastern Daylight Savings Time

— just like all the rest of America between here and the Atlantic Ocean."

He was almost belligerent, daring anyone to challenge him. Daniel knew it was just fear taking the form of anger. That's how Jack processed things sometimes. They all knew that.

"We'll meet back here long before it gets dark," Jack said. "Help *will* be on the way." He looked at Linc, daring him to contradict. "Somebody will come looking for us by then or one of us will have found the tower and dialed 911. But either way, whoever comes here … they're going to have to start walking at some point if their engines won't run."

"We're going to be stuck out here all night, aren't we, Jack?" Becca said softly and she shivered. "It's going to get a whole lot colder." Her gorgeous wedding dress had bare shoulders and thin, poofy sleeves. Jack took off his suit jacket and draped it around her.

"I was never Eagle Scout material," Crock said, "but we might need a fire. Probably not, but still … There's already a fire pit."

"I'd share my afghan with you if I could," Theresa called out. "I's warm as a bug in a rug."

Thank God for the afghan … but she was still an old woman lying on cold rocks. Daniel didn't think it was possible for her to stay warm.

"There was a pile of small logs, too," Jack said. "Becca and I tossed them into the woods. Gather those up and other kindling around. Somebody'll come way before dark, but better to be safe than sorry." Jack's voice dripped optimism.

"Copy that." Linc's feigned optimism sounded as phony as Jack's.

Andi turned and started for the woods.

"No, Andi," Daniel said. "You can't go picking up pieces of wood. You'll ruin your dress."

She turned and looked at him.

Then it landed on him. Maybe it landed on the others then, too, or maybe they were quicker on the uptake than the right Reverend Daniel Burke ... or had a less severe case of denial than his.

They *had* to get Theresa out of that hole! And they had to get away from here — q*uick!* because something bad was happening. Something really, *really* bad. If they couldn't get away from it, whatever it was would gobble them up.

He waved Andi on and then turned to Becca.

"Do you have a change of clothes — at least some shoes?"

She shook her head. "Our clothes — Jack's and mine — are at the farm house. We were going to go there and change and then ..."

She looked at Jack, her face desolate. He crossed to her in two steps and put his hands on her shoulders.

"Listen, you," he said. "If you think a building falling into a hole and a wedding party stuck out in the wilderness dressed up like Barbie dolls is going to get you out of marrying me, you are sorely mistaken. You are stuck with me, Rebecca Jean Hawkins. We *will* get out of this. We *will* get married. And we *will* live happily ever after." He took her chin in his hand and kissed the tip of her nose. "I promise."

Daniel understood at that moment why he had not felt the kind of gut-clenching fear their circumstances certainly warranted. It was because he was too busy feeling relieved. He hadn't had to marry Jack and Becca. It wasn't over, final. Not yet.

It didn't take long to amass a huge pile of kindling beside the fire pit — large and small downed tree limbs with brown leaves still attached, and logs, some of them big enough to keep a fire going for hours.

"Smokey the Bear says it only takes one match to start a forest fire," Crock said, "but I used a whole box once and couldn't get a campfire going."

He lit the end of a rolled-up paper plate with Linc's Bic lighter and tossed it into the pile of dead leaves and small sticks beneath the bigger kindling. It caught immediately, sending up a pall of gray smoke that turned white as the flames began to catch the larger pieces of wood.

They'd assessed their situation dispassionately and certain unpleasant truths had become evident. Jack, Daniel and Linc would be the three mountain climbers. Crock wasn't suited for that duty, courtesy of a bum knee. He would remain with Becca, Andi, Ariel and Theresa and keep the fire going.

The girls were wearing filmy, gauzy, not-warm fairy dresses and patent leather Mary Janes. Becca was barefoot. Theresa had packed a meager store of supplies that consisted of cheese and crackers — "'cause we gone want to snack." And several bottles of champagne — "'cause we gone want to celebrate." And, of course, the wedding cake, which had been loaded up to be carefully transported to the chapel after the ceremony. It was huge — Theresa just kept adding layers and decorations.

Linc handed the M4 rifle to Jack, who took it wordlessly, slung the strap over his shoulder, then reached down and pulled his Smith & Wesson .38 caliber revolver out of the holster on his ankle.

Jack glanced at Becca as he did it, chagrined, a silent apology in the look for actually packing a gun to his own wedding.

"Habit," he told her simply, as he unfastened the holster. Then he turned and handed the pistol to Crock.

"There are only the five rounds that are in it. Don't spend them all in one place."

Linc carried a Glock 22 .40 caliber pistol as his service weapon. It held fifteen rounds plus the one in the chamber. He carried another magazine of fifteen. The M4 service rifle held twenty-eight rounds, with another 150 rounds in the tactical vest he set down beside the big rock Crock had staked out as the easy chair of the fire tender.

Crock stood talking to Daniel and Linc, with their backs turned to Jack and Becca while they said goodbye. Daniel had nudged the others to turn their backs, of course. Only courteous. Didn't have a thing to do with the knives it stabbed into his heart every time he saw the two of them together like that.

Best get used to it, Buddy-row, he told himself for roughly the one-thousandth time. But he knew that would never happen.

He took off his suit coat and draped it around Andi's shoulders. Ariel was huddled in Crock's; Becca was wearing Jack's. He gave Andi a peck on the nose and turned to head out up Tilman Ridge, the shortest of the three mountains. Nobody could remember the name of the third one, though, so Linc would be climbing No Name Mountain.

Andi grabbed Daniel's hand and wouldn't let go.

"Don't go into the woods, Daddy! There are crazy people in the woods, all covered with blood, and they'll try to kill you."

The others stopped what they were doing and looked at her. Daniel felt a lump of cold terror settle down in the pit of his stomach and spread tentacles of ice out through his whole body.

"Last night, I had another one of those … you know."

Yeah, he knew. A vision. If Andi was having visions,

there was no sense anymore denying that what was going on was being orchestrated by demons.

"I thought it was just a nightmare ... but I guess it might not have been."

Daniel knelt down on one knee, eye level, and took both her hands in his. Her little fingers were as cold as popsicles.

"I should have told you." Andi was fighting tears. "But it wasn't like the other times. There wasn't an angel. She said she couldn't come here anymore. It's too dark."

Daniel wanted to know what that meant, but he let it go for now.

"Tell me what you saw."

Andi told him about running in terror from monsters in the woods. Every word scared him worse than the last. By the time she was finished with the story, he realized he was holding her hands so tight his grip must hurt. He released it and drew her into his arms.

"They had blood all over them?" Linc asked. "Like maybe they were hurt, had been in a fight or an accident?"

"No, not like that. It was smeared on them. All over them, their hands and arms — everywhere. You could see it in the blinking lights."

She looked down and her voice got quiet.

"It was the blood of the people they killed — stabbed and hacked to death. Murdered. Then I looked into the eyes of the dark shape and I could see ..." Her voice trailed off.

"What could you see?"

"It was like ... dead things, worms and bugs and stuff." She shuddered and shook it off. "Then a black tide, like an ocean of ink flowed over everything. Over me and the woods, everywhere for as far as I could see. There were blinking lights in the darkness."

~

BLOODY LUNATICS in the woods with hatchets and knives.

Jack barely caught hold of the bleat of hysterical laughter that almost escaped his lips.

This was crazy! Nuts.

He had come here to get married, for crying out loud.

But instead of taking the most beautiful girl in the world as his bride, he and everyone he cared about had walked smack into a buzz saw of evil.

Jack made himself a solemn promise. No, *a sacred vow.* When they got out of all this, when they were all safe, he would never set foot in Caverna County, Kentucky again as long as he lived!

Logic informed him calmly that there was no escaping evil. You couldn't run away from it because it was everywhere.

He fired back at logic that there was a whole lot more of it here than in most of the rest of the world and he *could* get as far away from *here* as it was possible to get.

Jack thought all those thoughts between one heartbeat and the next. His mind — his law enforcement and soldier mind — had been busy processing information at the same time.

"Wackos in the woods puts a different spin on things." He turned to Daniel. "Not too keen on you wandering around out there in the trees unarmed."

"Want to give me a gun so I can shoot my foot off?"

"I'm thinking maybe *I* ought to climb a mountain by myself — armed — and you and Linc ought to stay with the others — to protect them."

"That gives us one chance in three of being able to summon help," Crock said. "You can get better odds than that in a back-alley crap game."

"Are the things Andi sees in these visions always accurate?" Linc asked.

"Sometimes they're vague and hard to figure out, but they're never wrong," Daniel said, and briefly told Linc about the descriptions she gave of the kidnappers that enabled Jack to find them. "... all the way down to the beads of condensation on the water bottles."

"But sometimes her visions are warnings so you can prevent what she sees," Becca said. "Like the explosion at the Wingate Hotel that *didn't* happen."

"What she saw ... it was dark, right? She couldn't see," Linc said.

The others nodded.

"The sun doesn't go down until nearly nine o'clock. We've got plenty of time to get to the tops of those mountains and back before it gets dark. Then we'll all be back here together to defend ourselves, if we have to."

Jack didn't like leaving Becca and the others unarmed while he, Linc and Daniel climbed the mountains to find cell coverage. But he didn't see any way around it.

"If we're going, let's *go*," he said and took off toward the mountain to the north. He didn't look back. He was afraid if he did, he wouldn't be able to leave Becca behind.

245

Chapter Twenty-Two

LINC HAD fifty pounds and fifteen years on Daniel and Jack, but he moved with surprising speed through the trees. The slope wasn't steep, at least down here at the bottom it wasn't, but it would get a whole lot steeper higher up. You could see from down in the hollow that there was a bare meadow about halfway up and beyond that the going would be rough. At the edge of the meadow was a steep, rocky hillside with only broken trees and stumps. A fire a few years back had taken the trees from the north side of No Name Moun— no, Creasser Mountain, that was its name — and the south side of Tilman Ridge, the one Daniel was climbing. From what he could see from below, the hillside looked unstable enough to slide right out from under him as soon as he stepped out on it. Didn't matter. He'd find some way up it. Failure wasn't an option.

Hezekiah Lincoln was a bull of a man, wide and strong, and he plowed ahead with a determination born of desperation. A gray sense of foreboding had been gradually settling around him in the past few days. Each new catastrophe tightened the knot of fear in his belly. Oh sure, he had believed the others when they'd told him last fall that Rusty Willis was possessed by a demon — wasn't the least hard to believe when he saw what the child had done to Crock and Deputy Ed Blackwell. He had believed them when they told him about the efreet in the cave and how they had defeated it. He'd believed them when they told him about the angels, too.

But what had happened then — horrible as it was — at least *made sense*. The demons had skin in the game. They wanted to stay in the physical world where they could work their evil through the human beings whose bodies and souls they'd hijacked. The efreet was trying to protect itself when it sent the demon-possessed children after Daniel and Andi. That was logical. *Horrifying*, but logical.

What was happening now in Caverna County made no sense at all. He could see no plan, no order, no purpose in the random acts of violence. What was the endgame? What did the demons want that making cattle murderous or killing people with birds diving out of the sky would get them?

Sure, he understood that the nature of evil was that Satan wanted chaos in the world. He wanted to inflict pain on humanity. He wanted to thwart the purposes of God and destroy the beauty God had created.

He could understand demons controlling humans and making them do horrible things. He had come to believe that the serial killer was someone possessed by a demon, and the crazy people in the woods had, in fact, made a kind of sick sense to him.

But the rest of it …

How did demons make pumpkins grow and explode? Or kill fish — turn them wrong side out? Or send a flock of birds in a kamikaze dive into a crowded street?

If it was possible for a mountain to shake and throw

rocks hundreds of feet into the air ... what else was possible?

If docile dairy cows could massacre a family ... what other animals might go nuts and go on a killing rampage?

Why was it happening?

Why was it concentrated here in the northern part of the county ... but spreading out south?

And most important of all ... how could the craziness be stopped?

If it could be stopped.

The thoughts were making his heaving chest tight, making it even harder for him to gasp in enough air to keep climbing, and he tried to banish them from his mind. He could see a break in the trees up ahead, but didn't make it all the way to the clearing before he had to stop, lean over, put his hands on his knees and get his breath back.

Something hit him in the side of his head, something small and soft like a kid's spitball. He reached up to feel what it was but there was nothing there. He looked down and didn't see anything at first. Then he noticed a bee on the ground at his feet, squirming around in the dirt. Had the bee just flown into him? Another one hit his leg and dropped to the ground.

Neither stung him. They weren't crawling around in the dirt, either. He knelt to get a better look. Both were spinning around on their backs, their wings cutting tiny furrows in the dirt.

He stood slowly. A sudden irrational fear gripped him and he looked around frantically, trying to see ... what?

He didn't know. The break in the trees ahead of him was a meadow and he set out toward it — walking, not running — with a sickening sense of foreboding sitting unquietly in his belly.

As he approached through the thinning forest, he could make out nothing unusual about the meadow — weeds, wildflowers, just an unimpressive expanse of —

He stopped just inside the tree line, reluctant to step out into the sunlit field. His heart began to jackhammer a hole in the side of his chest, the pulsing blood drumming into the veins at his temples so that his vision throbbed with each beat. The meadow before him was a tangle of unrecognizable vegetation, much of it blackened and wilting. Flowers that might be daisies — *were* daisies, only the blossoms were the size of frisbees — sunflowers and buttercups and Queen Anne's lace had grown into something that looked like the jungle in a rainforest. No, something out of a science fiction movie. He thought of Randy Nickel and the pumpkins.

The stink of rot in the air was overwhelming with tendrils of dying plant life slimy with decay glistening wet in the sunshine. Everything was so … outsized. *Wrong.* Too big, or — he could see a dandelion plant with a stem the size of his arm and huge buttercup blossoms, asters and bluebells. There was something that looked like a purple primrose growing out of a malformed black-eyed Susan the size of a washtub.

Was it a trick of his pounding vision or was there, could he see … movement? No, there was nothing wrong with his eyes. The movement, subtle but ever-present, spread out across the whole field so it seemed to be writhing somehow. Growth. He was watching the plants grow. And die. A purple milkweed plant standing as tall as a basketball goal in the center of the field collapsed — maybe from the weight of the blossom it held up that was as big as a chest freezer.

Then he saw actual movement off to his right and he spun, automatically pulling his sidearm from its holster and drawing down on … kudzu. It was a kudzu vine. He returned his gun to its holster with trembling hands. He thought of the Dunn family. Steve strangled to death, Ali cutting through the horror with a chainsaw to rescue her baby daughter. As Linc watched in growing revulsion, the vine twisted slowly in the dirt like a turgid snake, moving relentlessly toward the trees. Not just one vine, two — three of them.

In a sudden rage, Linc reached out and grabbed it, yanked it off the little tree it was winding around and stomped it into the dirt in a frenzy of semi-hysteria, slamming his foot down again and again until the vine was nothing more than smashed green goo. He stood looking down at it, panting, tears blurring his pulsing vision.

And he watched as the broken end of the vine he had stomped began to slowly slither out over the part he had smashed and moved toward the sapling again.

Linc staggered back in horror and gawked at the field that should have sported the accompanying array of bugs — bees, butterflies, dragonflies — whatever. He wasn't an entomologist and had never stopped to consider the exact nature of the "buggage" in the ecosystem of a meadow. He did now, though. Felt bee after bee dead-head into his chest and legs and drop to the ground to spin in spastic circles. He saw a lone butterfly, a monarch, lying dead on the ground near the spot where the kudzu was attacking the forest.

What had happened to the rest? The beetles and ants and—

He turned away, unable to consider the nightmare possibilities, and started to continue his climb, making his way *around* the meadow. He couldn't have been dragged *into* that field by a team of Clydesdales and the Budweiser beer wagon.

That's when he saw it.

With no trees to block his view, he could see across the meadow to Tilman Ridge, the mountain Daniel was climbing. The cell phone tower was sprouting on the top of the mountain.

Though he was still far below it, Linc took out his cell phone and gave it a shot.

No bars. This one was Daniel's baby. At least that meant Linc's afternoon jaunt up the mountainside was over and he turned and started back down again.

That's when he saw *them*. Figures on Tilman Ridge in a small clearing where the woods thinned out about a quarter of the way up the slope. Though he could only make out shapes at this distance, he had no doubt what the shapes were, *who* they were. They were the "crazy people with blood all over them" from Andi's vision. They were gathered behind a jumble of boulders on the downhill side of the clearing close to the trees. The way past it was narrow. It was the perfect place for an ambush. Lying in wait. Daniel might make it to the top to try to call for help, but he would never make it back to the Hope Chapel alive.

There was a tall ridge of hills that connected Tilman Ridge and Creasser Mountain. If Linc could get there before Daniel had climbed all the way up the mountain and started back down, he could flank the attackers and get the drop on them. But it was a long way across those hills, and then back up the side of Tilman Ridge.

And he had no idea where Daniel was.

He might already be walking into an ambush.

JACK MADE his way up a narrow ravine cut by a creek coming down from the top of the mountain. He had made a judgement call when he happened upon the creek and decided to climb the creek bed — which would be open, no brush and bushes to block his way, instead of powering his way up the mountainside. Trouble with climbing a creek bed was the possibility — likelihood? — of coming to a dead end at some point where the water flowed out over a rock embankment and dropped in a waterfall thirty feet down into the creek bed below.

There was only about six inches of water in the creek but it quickly soaked through his dress shoes, by no means the proper foot attire for mountain climbing or creek walking. It was cold. Jack could tell the temperature was continuing to drop even though he was covered in sweat.

In some places, the creek bed was overhung by grapevines dangling down from the trees above. He and Daniel had played Tarzan as kids, swinging around, dangling on the vines and trying to make that idiot Tarzan yell perfected by Johnny Weissmuller in the old black-and-white movie. It would certainly be handy right now to have the apeman's skill. If he could travel through the forest swinging from one vine to the next — as if that were possible and not just some trick of movie camera angle — he wouldn't have to slog along through the cold water of the creek in soggy dress shoes.

And the woods were silent as a tomb. Not a single bird called out to its mate across the sunlit dappled forest. No cicadas hummed. There was no sound of some small creature scurrying off through the bushes at the sound of his approach.

The quiet was unnerving. Like the whole world was holding its breath, waiting for something, and he flat out did *not* want to know what that something might be.

He was as careful as he could be, but with no tread on his shoe soles, it was almost impossible to keep from slipping and sliding. He went down on one knee, twice, soaking the bottom portion of his dress pants. And he remembered the day he, Becca and Daniel had gone for a walk in the woods up to Red Rock. The day Jacob Dumas and Victor Alexander killed Becca's dog, McDougal. He could still hear the sound of her heartbroken sobs as she cradled the bloody, lifeless body in her lap.

He and Daniel had spent that day playing in the creek, pushing, shoving, wrestling, trying to trip each other — anything to get the other off balance and down into the water. All of it, of course, in an effort to impress Becca. He'd spent his whole childhood trying to win her attention, and her affection. He and Daniel both had. And when Jack had finally managed, after a quarter of a century, their wedding had been hijacked by … yeah, by what? Evil, of course. Demons.

Why?

He shoved his way through a tangle of dangling grapevines, trying to puzzle it out, perhaps not paying as much attention as he should have been to where he was placing his feet on the slick rocks. When he came around a bend in the creek he hit a particularly slimy spot. His feet flew out from under him, depositing him on his backside in the six-inch-deep water, soaking him to the skin.

He sat for a second, getting his breath and cursing his clumsiness. But the truth was, if he hadn't fallen, he wouldn't have looked up. He'd have kept his eyes on his feet to keep his balance and he never would have seen it. In fact, if constantly examining his environment weren't second nature to Jack, he might not have seen it at all. Kentucky bobcats were so well camouflaged you could walk within a few feet of one and never spot it.

But no, he'd have seen this one because it wasn't standing still, blending soundlessly into the background foliage. It was standing out in plain sight on a rock six feet above him, not even looking at him, just staring straight ahead.

This was a big one, a male, probably forty, maybe forty-five pounds of coiled-spring agility, with a short, broad face that had ruffs of fur on both sides extending from the pointed ears down to the lower jaw. Its body was reddish brown with black spots, a white belly and a bobbed tail.

Jack sat perfectly still, staring up at the big cat, frantically summoning from the memories of boyhood science classes, and every other random source, everything he knew about bobcats. It wasn't much. They hunted small game, he thought — rabbits, mice, squirrels and birds — wild turkeys and chickens when they ventured out of the woods to hunt on nearby farms. He remembered hearing farmers complain about losing lambs to them, too, though — baby pigs and goats.

He thought bobcats hunted mostly at dawn and dusk. It was the middle of the afternoon and this fellow didn't look like he was *stalking* anything — not even Jack. He was just standing there, glaring, making a strange sound in his throat that definitely wasn't a purr and couldn't even legitimately be called a growl. It was a kind of whining, moaning sound Jack suspected might not be a sound the average bobcat on the street was capable of or inclined to make.

Bobcats were solitary creatures. He remembered that much, for sure. The only cats in the wild that lived and hunted in groups were lions. Which meant that while Mr. Bobcat was standing sentinel up above, there wasn't a Mrs. Bobcat somewhere nearby, preparing to attack.

But it was entirely possible that Mr. and Mrs. Bobcat — and other members of their extended families — had taken leave of their senses on this day, and were about to engage in totally un-bobcat behavior.

Like a dairy cow turning violent.

Or a flock of birds committing mass suicide.

So what might a bobcat do if it were not constrained by hundreds of thousands of years of evolutionary bobcat-ness?

He slowly got to his knees, then slipped off the rifle slung over his shoulder as he stood, aware that he only had a few rounds of ammunition so he couldn't waste them. He had to see if this creature were aggressive. Shoot, it might not even see him. Right now it seemed so catatonic, Jack might have been able to throw a rock at it and get no response. He'd just back away slowly, ready to drop the animal if he had to — with one shot, which even Andi could have done at this range with the cat standing still as a hood ornament. The cat kept making that odd noise, shaking its head, a little like a drunk trying to get his bearings when he wakes up in an alley beside a dumpster. Jack carefully nestled the stock of the rifle in his shoulder, took a bead on the animal's chest, and took a step backward. Then another.

The animal didn't move.

But *something* did.

In the bushes on the creek bank to his right he caught sight of motion as Mrs. Bobcat and assorted uncles and cousins stepped out of the undergrowth and lined up like cadets for inspection on the riverbank. Then they all started to make that strange whining, totally un-bobcat sound.

Chapter Twenty-Three

DANIEL WAS IN GOOD SHAPE, the three-times-a-week-at-the-gym good shape he'd cultivated most of his adult life.

Andi had asked him one morning a few weeks ago, "Are you training for one of those tin man competitions?"

He had assured her that a *tin* man competition was more suitable for him than an iron man, but he wasn't actually training for anything.

"Then why do you work so hard, Daddy?" she had asked. "You run so fast on that treadmill you could go a hundred miles if you were really going anywhere."

That was the perfect metaphor for Daniel's workout routine. He was running as fast as he could to get nowhere. It was a pretty good metaphor for his life, too.

Of course, he wasn't actually running *to* anywhere. He was running *from* … from all manner of things that nipped at his heels if he so much as slowed down or paused to take a break.

The beep, beep, beep of Andi's heart monitor growing weaker and weaker until a flat green line replaced the shrinking mountains and valleys on the black face of the screen.

The sound of the gunshot from inside the church as he frantically struggled to get inside the building in time to—

The sight of Emily lying in a pool of blood on the floor of the sanctuary.

The little girl who looked like a life-sized Raggedy Ann doll — sweet Ariel — baring her teeth and attacking him with a rock.

Jeff knocking him off balance. "Take good care of Emily's little girl," he'd said.

The red monster in the sea of flames. The sound of it. The stink.

And Jack's face so transformed by joy it was hardly recognizable. "I've asked Becca to marry me," he'd said. "She said yes."

All those memories — individually or in groups — chased him down the hallways of his mind night and day. He couldn't outrun them. He'd never be able to escape them. And one day, he would have to stop running, turn and face them all. But he wasn't ready for that yet. And so he ran. On a treadmill. Going nowhere.

As he scrambled for a foothold on a patch of slippery leaves, it occurred to him that at least right now, he was running somewhere. Unlike his futile treadmill flight from nowhere to nowhere, he had a purpose this time.

He had to get to the top of the mountain to summon help.

And he had to get back to the ruin of the chapel to protect … well, everybody he loved in the whole world.

Linc and Jack had given Daniel the shortest mountain, Tilman Ridge, which was neither as tall nor as steep as theirs. But the mountain had become far steeper than it looked as he got farther up the slopes. Now, going was rough, slipping and sliding on loose rocks and dried leaves, clambering over rockfalls and beating his way through stands of mulberry bushes — so thick in one spot that he had to retreat and go around before he could continue to climb.

He had stopped to catch his breath briefly farther down the slope and thought he might have seen ... no, he couldn't be sure. But as he broke into a small clearing and lifted his eyes to the top of the ridge, he was sure. He had drawn the ace. High above him stood a tall black tower with wide, silver panels facing in all directions. He reached into his pocket and pulled out his phone. After all, he didn't have to climb all the way up ...

Still no bars.

His blank phone screen ran a chill down his spine.

What if ...?

Nope, not going there. What if's will drive you daft — that's what Theresa had told him when he was a kid.

He shoved the phone back into his pocket and continued to climb. He'd know soon enough. One way or the other, he'd know soon enough.

Fifteen minutes later, he leaned against one of the support poles of the cell tower, gasping for breath, so winded he was seeing spots in front of his eyes. He had sprinted the final fifty yards — running full out. Now, his hands were trembling as he again removed his phone from his pocket. He closed his eyes before he looked at it, clearing his vision. Then he opened them and stared at the screen of the little machine he held in his hand.

No bars.

Like an idiot, he shook the phone, banged it against his palm and looked again. Still no bars.

With hands shaking — from fatigue and from ... fear

— he turned the phone off and then powered it back on again.

Nothing.

He fiddled with the device for five minutes or so, knowing his fiddling was futile but unable to help himself. He certainly was not the man to fix the phone if, indeed, something were malfunctioning. After all, Andi had been trying to teach him how to use an iPad when he came upon the email Emily had sent to Jeff. About the lacy negligee.

The image of those words swimming in the sudden puddle of tears in his eyes still had the power to sucker-punch him and he almost went down on one knee from the force of the blow.

When he shook his head to clear it, he flung drops of sweat off onto the metal struts of the tower.

After one last try, he turned the phone off again, slipped it into his pocket and headed back down the mountain. He wasn't looking forward to delivering the devastating news that even beneath a one-hundred-foot-tall cell phone tower, the phone didn't work. The signal was blocked … somehow.

Or maybe there just wasn't a signal at all. What if … in the screwy New Normal that had materialized out of nowhere in the past few days, cell phones had gone the way of combustion engines. The principles behind them didn't apply here. The natural laws that enabled all electronic devices to operate were just … gone. Or blocked. Or dead.

He didn't like the sound of that. Not one bit.

That's what he was thinking about when he emerged into a clearing about a third of the way up the slope. There was a pile of rocks at the far end of the clearing and there was only a narrow space between them and the trees.

When he stepped into that space, he felt a sharp pain at the base of his skull, and he dropped in an unconscious heap in front of a man holding a machete, whose hands, arms and face were smeared with dried blood.

JACK FROZE IN PLACE, trying to look around him moving only his eyes instead of turning his head.

How many were there — and what difference did *that* make? Wouldn't take more than three or four of them to make a fine breakfast out of Jack Carpenter. He couldn't possibly drop them all before they got to him.

The collective — what? Wail! — of the bobcats gathered around him rose in volume and intensity. The strange head-wag he could now see afflicted all of them grew more and more pronounced.

Jack tried to dispassionately assess his situation, which was seriously hard to do when any second he could be ripped to shreds by a pride ... herd ... tribe ... gaggle ... *murder* of animals with inch-long claws and teeth they seemed to be baring at him. Though it was hard to tell how much of the look on their faces was natural, how much was threatening and how much was deranged lunacy.

He didn't know how long they'd stand there wailing at each other until one of them got an itchy trigger finger, but he suspected he had seconds rather than minutes to come up with some kind of defense.

Or escape.

The grape vines.

A tangle of them hung down from the big elm and oak trees only a few feet to his left. Not a single vine but several wound together like knotted pieces of string. He could leap for them, use them to swing out of the cats' way, or at least give him leverage to kick at them. One problem with that plan. He was holding the rifle in both hands. Perhaps he could slowly slip the strap back over his head ...

He never actually saw movement, just felt the impact of the pouncing bobcat that caught him in the shoulder and sank its teeth into his upper arm. The force of the blow knocked the rifle out of his hands and it clattered on the rocks in the riverbed at his feet. Jack screamed and staggered sideways.

Instinct took over.

With every bit of strength Jack possessed, he lunged upward, catching hold of the grapevine and shaking loose from the attacking cat, whose claws sliced down his back as it fell away. In the same motion, he swept both feet forward out of the creek, which gave the vine's swinging motion momentum so that it carried him forward. Another cat launched itself at his leg, its claws digging deep into the flesh of his calf. He slammed his foot — the one still wearing a shoe — into the animal's face, knocking it away as he let go of the vine with his right hand, reached up and grabbed it farther up — hauling himself upward even as he let go with his left hand and did the same thing again. Another cat, or maybe the same one he had kicked in the face, leapt at him, only managing to claw the side of his foot before falling away. One more heave upward and then he pulled his knees up to his chest and kicked off his remaining shoe. There was a bit of a knot there on the end of the vine, enough that he could cling to it with his toes and shove himself upward, grabbing hand over hand — moving his feet upward and shoving again — and then he was above them, hanging about ten feet off the ground, swaying gently back and forth on the vine.

He could see all of them now, seven, eight — *nine* of

them lining the creek bank below him and one other one — smaller, a cub maybe? — lying on its back, either playing roll-in-the-dirt or having a seizure. Only two had attacked him, and those two stood beneath him now, leaping upward at him like Ossie used to jump at the catnip-filled ball on a string Andi dangled over his head, trying to sink his claws into it before she yanked it away. It occurred to him that the cat's reflexes had usually been faster than Andi's.

Then Jack felt the vine above him give way as it came loose from the tree.

JONAH BALLARD HAD OPTED to go around Frog Croak Knob rather than over it. Steep near the top, the mountain would take longer to climb than it'd take to go out of his way through Cedar Hollow and into Queen Anne Hollow from the south and come out on the other side of Hope Chapel.

As he walked along he listened to the melody — it was a kind of melody, it seemed to him now — of the voices in his head. Listened to each individual voice and to the hum of all of them together — which wasn't possible to do at the same time but he could. He listened to the sounds that made words in languages he'd never heard before and understood what they were saying.

The voices had become a part of him and even though it had only been — what? a day? — Jonah couldn't even remember what it had been like to be alone in his own head. The presence of the voices gave him a sense of belonging he'd never experienced before. He was one with the voices and that oneness gave him a power he could not describe and a sense of purpose that he had never known before.

Jonah replayed the scene with the man on the side of the road, only then stopping to consider that he had put his own life at risk when he'd attacked the other man. Oh, the guy wasn't armed. But he could have been. Jonah hadn't waited to find out, just rushed at him at his first opportunity. He'd so totally surprised the man that he wouldn't have had time to get to a weapon even if he'd had one. Still … what if?

The horror of the thought stole his breath and he stopped in his tracks.

What if somebody killed Jonah before he had a chance to earn his salvation?

What if he were suddenly thrust before a vengeful God without the protection of the blood of the unbelievers?

He actually shuddered at the thought. He'd be lost, condemned to an eternal hell to burn forever for his sins. He had to be more careful! Sure, he had to do as he was commanded — butcher all those the Lord brought into his pathway. But he needed to consider his own safety while he did it. He was down to the wire now. The end of the world was at hand. God was coming to judge mankind — soon, that's what the Chosen One had said. Soon. As in only a day or two. Or maybe less time than that.

Between now and then, he had two jobs. His whole world, whole existence, every fiber of his being was to be expended in accomplishing those tasks. He had to slay the unbelievers and cover his whole body in their blood. And he had to stay alive!

Voices.

Up ahead, around the pile of rocks at the base of Tilman Ridge, he could hear people talking. He stopped, listened his heart tripping up into a gallop in his chest with excitement at the thought of blood on his hands. It hadn't occurred to him as he stood listening to the Chosen One tell about it on the church steps, but he would *enjoy* the killing. The voices in his head had cheered when he plunged the machete into the man's back and their applause sent a thrill down his spine he ached to feel again. And again. And again.

Then he recognized some of the voices, heard Bob Huddleston and his wife, the Cowdrey brothers, Colin and Don, David Lockwood and Lauren Clough. Not unbelievers.

The killing lust had grown so hot in his veins that he almost loosed it, swallowing it back with great difficulty. He wanted to kill and keep killing — even though these were believers, he wanted to shed their blood. He didn't, though, just stepped out into the trees near them. And he watched looks cross their faces and realized they felt just like he did. They would have liked to kill him as much as he wanted to kill them.

"David," he said, "What—?"

"Shhh," Lauren said. "Get down or he'll see."

Don Cowdrey grabbed his arm and yanked him down behind the rocks, whispering harshly, "There's a man coming, the one the Chosen One sent us to fetch."

There were more than a dozen people and they all got quiet and hunkered down behind a rock. Jonah did likewise when he could hear the man approaching.

The moment the man stepped into the narrow space between the trees and the pile of rocks, Colin Cowdrey leapt up behind him and hit him in the head with a rock. Jonah stepped out then, blood lust in his veins, and raised the machete over his head.

"No!" Claudette Huddleston said. "Don't kill him!"

"We are supposed to kill them all, all the unbelievers."

"Not this one," Don Cowdrey said. "The Chosen One wants him alive — wasn't you listenin'?"

Other voices piped up then but the loudest was Claudette, who pointed at the man's neck and Jonah noticed the clerical collar.

"He's the pure lamb, the sacrifice," she said. "We ain't supposed to hurt him. The Chosen One's going to sacrifice him for us all."

~

LINC HAD MOVED AS FAST as he could through the trees. Couldn't run, couldn't go loping through here or you'd catch your foot on a tree root and break an ankle. But fear for Daniel drove him to the limit of his endurance and the outer edge of prudence, and it had carried him across the connecting string of small hills and to Tilman Ridge faster than he'd ever dreamed possible.

But he was still too late.

He'd slowed, approached the rocks carefully, struggling to get his heaving breathing in check before somebody decided there must be a water buffalo in the woods. Slipping from one tree to the next, he got within fifty feet of rocks. And what he saw froze his breath.

Daniel was lying on the ground, surrounded by people who fit to a T the description Andi had given of the "crazy people in the woods covered in blood."

He recognized several of them. Jonah Ballard. The big man in the wife-beater t-shirt was Bob Huddleston, and his wife and daughter were there, too. He spotted Paul Stedman and ... was that the Cawdrey brothers?

Though he couldn't see all of them, one thing was clear. If they charged him, there were too many for him to drop before they got to him, even if he dropped each one with one shot — and a handgun at this distance would be so inaccurate he'd be lucky to take them down with two or three attempts.

But when Jonah Ballard lifted the machete into the air to bring it down on Daniel's head, Linc took a bead on his chest anyway and—

One of the others — it was Don Cowdrey — grabbed his arm and shoved him aside, snarling at him words Linc couldn't hear. The man lowered the machete, reluctantly. Linc crept closer. If he had to, he'd drop the biggest one, Huddleston, and Ballard — cut off the head of the snake so to speak, and though these guys didn't look like they were in charge, they did appear to be meaner and stronger than the others. Linc crept from a sycamore tree to a nearby oleander bush, peering out through the leaves at the blood-splattered — no, blood-*slathered* — people now only a few feet away.

Jonah Ballard was arguing with the others. He wanted to kill Daniel and they didn't. Colin Cowdrey said "the Chosen One" wanted him alive to use as a special sacrifice.

"We done been to the convent," said Lauren Clough, who had blood splatter on the front of her dress — the kind of splatter you get when you cut an artery. "Ain't nobody there but the caretaker." She held up her bloody hatchet. "And I got him."

Linc felt relief flood through his body. The Sisters of St. Thomas Convent wasn't actually a true convent anymore. With so few young people going into the ministry, it had been turned into a retreat center operated by a skeleton staff of nuns from Holy Trinity Church in Bardstown. Obviously, there'd been no retreat scheduled for this weekend, and since the archbishop was scheduled to speak in Louisville today, the good sisters must have gone to hear him. There were only about half a dozen of them — including Sister Mary Margaret, who'd been Linc's first grade teacher and who was so gentle she'd allowed her students to skip the whole part of science class about dissecting a frog. She and the other sisters would never have been able to defend themselves against these Looney Tunes, even if they'd tried. And they wouldn't have tried.

"What's the convent got to do with him?" Jonah Ballard was determined to bury his machete in Daniel's face at the first opportunity.

"You blind? Can't you see what he's got around his neck?" asked a woman Linc didn't recognize.

She gestured at Daniel's clerical collar.

"He's a priest, moron," she said. "We got to take him back for the special sacrifice."

It was obvious the dude with the machete was not down with what the others were saying. It appeared he was out-voted, however, because he finally gave it up and the Cowdrey brothers lifted Daniel off the ground, with Colin holding his hands and Don his feet. But they didn't make it fifty yards before they figured out they couldn't move him that way, dangling like a hammock between them. They set him back down on the ground then and summoned Bob Huddleston, who had been watching the proceedings leaned up against a rock smoking a cigarette.

The man tossed the cigarette to the ground, crushed it into the dirt, then bent down and lifted Daniel up onto his shoulder in a fireman carry as effortlessly as tossing back a twenty-pound grain sack. Then the group set out through the woods.

Linc had no choice but to follow along behind, and hope for an opportunity when he wasn't so outgunned to get Daniel free.

Chapter Twenty-Four

CROCK LOOKED AT HIS WATCH. It had stopped somewhere along the road on the way here and still said 11:15 in the morning. Of course, he didn't need a watch to know that it was getting late. In fact, a watch might have argued with that fact. It seemed to be "getting late" awfully early.

Oh boy, don't chase that bunny down a hole.

The mountain climbers should have been back by now. Crock couldn't imagine what had delayed them, but knew it had to be something bad, really bad, because Jack would run through a brick wall to get back here to Becca. And if Crock's antennae were delivering accurate messages, and they usually did, Daniel would do the same thing. He hoped the others hadn't picked up on the vibe he had, hoped they'd been too caught up in the excitement of the festivities to notice the way Daniel had been looking at Becca.

She sat now on one of the rocks Crock had dragged out of the rubble to place around the fire pit as "chairs." He'd selected the biggest and ugliest as his own easy chair.

But she wasn't facing the fire. She was facing the

woods. She'd been watching for the guys' return since five minutes after they left.

"Is it my imagination or is it getting … late?" Theresa asked from beneath the rock pile. They'd tried to engage and include her, keep a conversation going, but it kept fizzling out. "It hadn't ought to be so dark, or has it got cloudy?"

"Not a cloud in the sky," Andi said. "But it sure doesn't feel like a sunny day." She shivered.

Becca caught Crock looking at her and said quietly, "Something's happened, hasn't it?"

Andi and Ariel were on the other side of the fire, the spot nearest the edge of the collapsed building, so they could keep up a running prattle with Theresa. They should have been engaging in the universal kid activity of poking sticks into the flames. Instead, they sat huddled in their oversized jackets, staring sightlessly into the flickering light.

"Maybe. Hard to tell how long they've been gone, though, with a bunch of dead watches." He tried to shift attention away from the obvious. "Anybody want some wedding cake?"

It was clear none of them had any appetite at all.

"I was thinking we could—"

A sound from the distant woods stole his words. It was a howl.

They all turned toward it, but it was impossible to see anything in the dense foliage, particularly in the failing light.

Which shouldn't be "failing" this early!

"Are there wolves in the woods?" Andi was clearly terrified.

"Not wolves," Crock said. "Coyotes."

"I thought coyotes lived in the desert — with jackrabbits and cactus and stuff," she said. "Like Wile E. Coyote and the Roadrunner."

Ariel spoke up then.

"When I was in the second grade, Greg Little brought his pet coyote to school for show and tell — its name was Wiley ... of course," Ariel said. "His daddy found the cub after he shot its mother for killing his chickens. The teacher said that coyotes had spread all over the country when people moved in and killed wolves."

"So coyotes aren't just small wolves?" Becca asked.

"Nope," Crock said. "They're entirely different species. Wolves hunt in packs, but coyotes are solitary — more like dogs than small wolves."

Another howl sounded, but this time it was coming from the woods on the other side of the chapel.

Well, so much for "solitary."

In truth, Crock had absolutely no idea what the difference was between a coyote and a wolf other than he thought wolf packs tracked down and attacked big prey, deer, antelope and such, while coyotes lived on gophers and jackrabbits — and apparently chickens when some farmer's back was turned. But he'd bet his pension it didn't mean a hill of beans anymore what wolves *normally* did or what coyotes *normally* ate.

"But they're afraid of fire, right?" Andi said, clearly unconvinced the animals were harmless.

"Yup, not a wild creature in the world will come anywhere near one," he said. Total bluff. He didn't imagine a flamethrower would have stopped those Holsteins from trampling that farmer and his family.

"The woods are full of them," Ariel said, gesturing out into the gathering dusk under the nearby trees. "Can't you see the sparkle?"

Not sparkle, eye shine. He could see it now and the

sight raised the hairs on the back of his neck. The flickering flames were reflecting off sets of shiny circles in the trees.

Trees that now formed great puddles of shadow. It was dusk. It couldn't be ... but it was.

There was another howl, followed in quick succession by a series of yips and barks and then another howl.

And that was bad enough. Scary enough. But then came a sound Crock had never heard before. A kind of yowling wail, a cry that set his teeth on edge. He would have blamed Sonny and Cher for some malfunction, that he wasn't really hearing what he thought he was. But one look at the faces of the others told him they were hearing the same thing and that none of them had ever heard such a sound before.

Normal animals didn't make sounds like that. Which meant, of course, that the coyotes in the woods weren't normal coyotes.

FOR A HEART-STOPPING MOMENT, Jack was sure he was about to be dumped unceremoniously into the claws and jaws of the big cats beneath him. A thought flashed through his mind like a meteor: it's supposed to be Daniel who gets tossed into the lion's den. If there was some dude named Jack with him, Scripture failed to take down his name for posterity.

But the tangle of other vines held firm. He dropped a few inches, maybe a foot, and as his heart jackhammered a hole in his chest, he realized several things.

One, he was not nearly high enough above the cats' heads. If he weren't so close, dangling here like a carrot, maybe they'd lose interest and go away.

And two, the vines above him could give way at any time. The biggest one was wound tight around the limb of an oak tree. But the limb itself was not thick enough to bet your life on — though that's exactly what he was doing whether he liked it or not.

Three, he had to get to the place above his head where the tangled vines joined, so he could stand, crouch, straddle, *something* where the vines held together and then balance there. All his daily chin-ups notwithstanding, he would not be able to hang here for long holding all his weight with his hands and arms.

He had to climb, but carefully.

Slowly and gently, he pushed upward from the knot in the vine he had grasped with his feet, and grabbed the vine farther up with his left hand.

The cats below him continued to jump at him, and the ones on the shore kept making that eerie keening sound. He distracted himself by engaging in a one-sided conversation with the felines.

"See, here's the thing." He grunted with the effort of hauling himself, inch by inch, up the vine. "The order of the universe granted you guys claws — all the better to rip you apart, my dear."

He shoved carefully upward again, holding his breath.

"But in the distribution of survival apparatuses, *I* got these." He wiggled the thumb on his right hand. "Prehensile thumbs trump claws every time."

The cats' only response was to continue leaping up at him, and to continue their eerie wail that had begun to sound like some kind of strange song in his ears.

When he finally made it to the juncture of vines, his arms were trembling from exertion. He pulled upward on the big vine, reached out with his left leg and hooked it over one of the tangles of smaller vines. He carefully allowed the vine to hold his weight. It creaked and pulled taut, but it held. With careful wiggling and repositioning, he finally sat astraddle a tangle of vines that reached out to several trees. He slowly let out his breath and relaxed.

He hadn't even been aware of the pain of his injuries until that moment. The sedative effects of adrenaline. But he could feel them now and it took his breath away. He surveyed them dispassionately.

The most concerning were the wounds on his right leg, three gashes, each six or seven inches long, starting just below his knee and extending down the back of his calf all the way to his ankle. Blood was running down his leg and dripping off his foot. And the cats below him were going postal over it, lapping it up where it had splattered on the treebank rocks, then jumping up, trying to get to the source, catching drips in their faces.

They'd stay here forever, as long as he was enticing them with the drippings.

He unbuttoned the starched white shirt the cats had shredded in the back — painful scratches, but not deep — took it off and peeled off the t-shirt beneath it. Then he ripped the t-shirt into strips and used them to wrap around the leg wounds to stop the bleeding.

The puncture wounds where the cat had bitten his upper left arm were bleeding badly too, but if he could put pressure on them, he could staunch that flow. So he took spare pieces of torn t-shirt, wadded up his handkerchief, put it on top of the holes and held it tight in place by wrapping the t-shirt strips around it.

He put his shirt back on — ripped or not, he needed the warmth. He'd done all the first aid he could do, though he could tell the leg wound was slowly soaking the fabric of his t-shirt. The two cats remained beneath him, looking up expectantly to catch the drips of blood.

He was safe from attack, at least for the time being. Safe, but stuck here. He was not climbing the mountain to find the cell phone tower and he wasn't back at the chapel, helping get Theresa out of the wreckage of the chapel and taking care of Becca.

The image of her in her wedding gown, the bottom filthy from where she had fallen into the dirt, literally took his breath away. Who knew what might be happening to her and the others. Shoot, they might be fighting it out with wacko foxes, or squirrels or … there were bears! Black bears in these woods.

He swallowed hard, willed himself to calm down. He couldn't do anything to help anybody until he could get away from the snarling cats below him. And he had absolutely no idea how he could pull that off.

A PACK OF LUNATIC COYOTES.

Five helpless civilians, one of them buried under a collapsed building.

A fire that would likely be totally useless as a defense.

A five-shot revolver.

And night roaring into town way ahead of schedule.

Crock had been dealt worse hands than this and somehow managed not to lose all his chips. But right now, he couldn't recall what those worse hands had been.

In less than a minute after he heard the first coyote howl, he had already formed and discarded half a dozen *Now-What?* plans. In truth, there was really only one thing he could do. No way to protect the others out here in the open if the psychotic dogs came after them. The only place they'd be safe was in one of the cars.

Two flies quickly plopped down into the buttermilk of that plan and started doing the backstroke.

The cars were a looooong way away, at the end of a winding path through the woods.

And he'd have to leave Theresa here alone.

Another strange, whining yowl came from the trees to the right and he and the others watched in fascinated horror as a coyote emerged from the woods. It wasn't in stalking, crouched-and-about-to-attack mode. It didn't even appear to notice them, just stood there, shaking its head in a jerky-jerky, side-to-side motion.

A second coyote stepped out of the woods beside the first, its head hanging down. Neither of them looked dangerous.

Which sounded like famous last words.

Time to bail.

The two little girls were seated on a rock between the fire and the debris of the chapel, where they could talk to Theresa — though they couldn't see her. Crock stepped up to Becca and spoke quietly.

"We can't stay here," he said.

"You want us to *leave*?" Becca was incredulous. "Theresa's—"

"Listen to me," Crock said, employing his most officious, police officer tone of voice. "We have to go, and we have to go *now*, before ..." He let his voice trail off and cut his eyes toward the dogs near the trees and then to the girls.

Becca looked like he'd slapped her.

"You think those coyotes will—?"

"Who knows what they might do. But last time I checked, dogs can't open car doors. You'll be safe there."

"*The girls* will be safe there," Becca corrected. "I'm not leaving Theresa here by herself."

"So you want to leave Andi and Ariel in a car by themselves — in the *dark*?"

Dark. Acknowledgement of the impossible reality passed between them. It didn't matter what time it was — it was getting dark.

"But—"

"When you guys are safe in the cars, I'll come back here and stay with Theresa."

Becca didn't like it one bit, but her argument died in her throat when the coyote whose head had been hanging down looked up, suddenly alert. And snarled.

THERESA HAD BEGUN to shake and she was having trouble keeping the trembling out of her voice.

And she wasn't sure anymore she could move her toes. She'd been wiggling them every so often, making sure she still could. But a kind of numbness had set in — the kind that sets in when your butt goes numb from sitting in the same position too long. Not like when your legs go to sleep and you can't feel anything, but when you stand up and realize your backside don't appear to be connected to your brain anymore.

She wasn't sure why she was shaking, but she suspected it didn't have nothing to do with being cold. In fact, she didn't even feel all that cold. That afghan pulled up around her neck had ought to have been enough to keep her toasty warm. It was getting colder and colder up there where the others were, but down here, she was in a cave and caves was always fifty-four degrees, year round.

So the shaking had to be something else and whatever it was, she knew it wasn't good.

An old woman couldn't lie on her back on a pile of

cold rocks not moving for hours and not have something start to malfunction. And on top of all that she needed to pee and couldn't for the life of her figure out how she was supposed to pull *that* off.

"… sure it's not cold down there where you are?" Andi asked.

She and Ariel were keeping her company and they was both trying to be real chatty.

"I've just about broke out in a sweat, sugar, with this afghan wrapped around me." It took an effort to keep her voice level. "You two need to stay snug up against that fire where it's warm. We ain't got no marshmallows or you could put 'em on sticks and roast 'em."

"I guess you can't roast a piece of wedding cake," Ariel said. "It probably wouldn't stay on the stick—"

There was a strange, howling sound. Whatever had made the sound was nearby. Theresa heard Andi ask Crock about wolves and coyotes. She could hear in his voice that he was bluffing most of his answers but she hoped the girls were buying what he was selling.

There were more howls and yips and strange animal noises. They all sounded so unnatural, like wasn't no sound any animal had been created to make.

"Theresa," Crock called out to her from above. "I'm going to take the others to your car. It'll be warmer there."

And safer, but he didn't say that.

"Once they're squared away, I'll come back—"

"You think I need a babysitter? You go on along with them to the car and stay there. I'll be just fine here by my own self."

"And leave this roaring bonfire I've worked so hard to get going? No way."

She wanted to argue with him, but he was gone before she had a chance. The coyotes took up howling again and

Theresa kept shaking. Maybe she was scared. Or maybe she was going into shock. She didn't really know for sure what that was, but people in the movies was all the time doing that. And when they did, it didn't usually end well.

She pulled the afghan tight up under her chin and began to consider how she was going to pee.

Becca loved dogs. And these animals were dogs, scrawny little things, looked half starved, probably didn't weigh thirty, maybe forty pounds. She'd been heartbroken when Victor Alexander killed McDougal, the mutt from the animal shelter she'd had as a kid. Theresa's dog Biscuit had saved her life, had died trying to protect her from a rattlesnake.

She looked at the coyotes standing near the trees and tried to summon some of those warm, fuzzy McDougal/Biscuit feelings for them. She might have been able to pull it off if these had been garden-variety coyotes, but they weren't.

They were — what? She didn't know, but it was clear that something had happened to them to make them totally uncoyote-like. They might as well have been rabid — no possible way to tell what they might do. They were small, but there were a lot of them. If they …

"Girls, I need you to listen to me," she said, keeping her voice low and soothing — she was certainly no expert on dogs but she figured loud noises or abrupt movements were probably not a good idea. "We need to go get in Theresa's car — you left it unlocked, right?"

"But we can't leave—"

"She's safe where she is down there. We need to go where we'll be safe."

The girls probably wanted to argue but more and more coyotes began emerging from the woods. Just standing there, watching.

Crock drew his pistol out of his pants pocket. Becca picked up her long skirt so she wouldn't trip over it.

"Get behind me, move slowly and don't turn your back on them," she said. "And don't run. If you run from a dog, it will chase you."

The girls did as they were told and together the three of them and Crock began to back toward the path. Becca ignored the sharp rocks that her bare feet stepped on because she couldn't watch where she was placing them.

The coyotes stood unmoving in front of the tree line. It was impossible to see if they were watching or just standing there blank-eyed. There were more of them now and Becca didn't know when they had come. The light was failing, fast. It was getting dark.

She and the others kept backing slowly away. They were on the path and inching backward down it. Even from this distance, the flickering fire was growing dim, difficult to see.

"Becca," Andi whispered, and Becca felt a small hand take hers. "Do you see … is it getting dark … *that kind of dark?*"

Andi was right. The light wasn't failing just because it was evening — which was impossible but clearly reality. But that wasn't the only thing that was happening.

"Crock, can you see … is it getting dark?" Becca asked quietly.

He had positioned himself between her and the coyotes as she positioned herself in front of the girls. He didn't turn around to speak to her.

"Yup. Shouldn't be, but it is."

"I mean … darker than it was two or three minutes ago."

Even as she asked, she knew the answer. The sun didn't go down this fast. Night didn't gobble up the day in a matter of minutes.

"Why do you ask?" he said. "What's the matter?"

She had to swallow hard and breathe in before she could speak. Sudden terror had so tightened her chest she was breathless.

It was like black ink began to settle down out of the sky around her, blotting out everything. She felt Andi gasp and knew she was experiencing the same thing. Staring in terror, Becca watched the light of the blazing campfire grow more and more dim, hidden behind a liquid gauze of darkness. It flickered, a match flame, then went out.

"Andi and I …"

One of the coyotes on the other side of the fire let out a long, plaintive howl. Then another cried out. And another. She and the others involuntarily froze. There was a beat of breathless silence, then the howls were answered by another howl, a lone, warbling wailing cry that sounded like a bad imitation of a coyote. But this howl didn't come from in front of Becca — beyond the fire. It came from the trees surrounding the trail *behind her*.

Chapter Twenty-Five

CROCK EDGED SLOWLY BACKWARD, his pistol in a two-handed grip pointed at the ground, his head on a swivel, looking around 360 degrees, panning his environment so his mind could create a mental map, positioning everything in its spot.

Coyotes lining the edge of the woods beyond the fire, which was blazing next to the pile of debris that covered Theresa.

The safety of the cars still much too far away.

The four of them were on the trail near the point where the trail took a sharp right turn and was hidden behind trees and undergrowth the remaining distance to the parking lot.

Apparently, Wiley had invited all his rowdy friends to the party because shapes continued to meld into the dappled light beyond the fire, their eye-shine flickering like fireflies in the evening light.

Several things happened then, one right after the other.

Becca told him she and Andi couldn't see — that they were almost *blind.*

The phalanx of coyotes that had been standing still and apathetic in front of the trees was on the move, seeming to match their backward movements step by step. And spreading out so that the once-straight line of them was now a letter C, curving around in a motion it was hard to mistake for anything except encircling.

So much for coyotes don't work together as a pack.

And after the coyotes had them trapped, boxed in on all sides? Probably weren't making a circle around them to play dodgeball.

More *Now-What?* scenarios downloaded into his brain and he liked his options now even less than he'd liked the other options — which he hadn't liked at all.

They could break and run full out for the cars — maybe get a surprise step or two head start on the coyotes — which might just stand there with their tongues lolling out and watch them go. He didn't believe for a New York minute that'd be their response. But that option wouldn't be open to them much longer. With the quickening advance of the coyote pack it wouldn't be long before the coyotes had them penned. And running probably wasn't the best strategy anyway, given that one of them was barefoot, two of them couldn't see where they were going, and another had a collapsible knee.

He could drop a couple of the creatures, see if the gunfire scared the others off. Or waste bullets he might need badly later.

Then he noticed that the advancing phalanx of coyotes had split in two and were cutting a wide berth around the campfire. Might be some part of their addled brains had remembered mama coyote telling them not to play with matches after all.

All the animals were making strange sounds now that raised the hair on the back of Crock's neck. Some were whining, like a dog begging for a treat, others cried out like puppies their first night home from the pet store. But even those sounds were off somehow, not the right tone, with a kind of intrinsic lunacy that set your teeth on edge. Others were simply making sounds that didn't sound like any kind of dog or animal sound at all. A wailing that made Crock wonder if what he was hearing was accurate, and if it might be the sound Theresa had tried to describe to him, the one she heard when possessed people were near, the sound of the demons who held them captive.

Then one of beasts tilted its head back in a classic howl-at-the-moon motion and emitted a cry that sounded like the screech of a harpy, sharp and jagged and horrifying. The cry was answered by another one *behind them, between the back-stepping humans and the cars.*

The coyote trap was about to slam shut.

Err on the side of action. Do something ... even if it's wrong.

"Ariel, take Becca and Andi's hands," he said, keeping his eye on the advancing coyotes, not turning to look at her. "Then I want the three of you to freeze. Statues, okay? Don't move until I draw them off. Then Ariel, you lead Becca and Andi to the car."

"What are you going to—?" Becca began.

"Don't run from a dog," he repeated. "If you do, it'll chase you."

He took a deep breath and took off at his best approximation of a sprint back toward the campfire.

ARIEL FROZE. Like she'd frozen that day as she lay in the hospital bed, watching Mr. Jack through a forest of eyelashes, pretending she was still unconscious and couldn't see Cassidy with the scalpel, ready to stab Andi in the back, and then kill her, too. She'd been so scared that day.

But she hadn't been as scared as she'd been all the days before that when the monster had wandered around in her head, screeching at her, making her do horrible things she didn't want to do but couldn't help herself. The prospect of being attacked by a pack of coyotes was scary, but not *that* scary. Nothing would ever be that scary. She knew that didn't make her brave — it was just that whatever happened to her for the rest of her life, whatever terrible thing she had to face ... well, she'd seen worse.

That's why her hand didn't shake when she took Becca and Andi's hands in hers and stood as still as she could — a statue — while Mr. Crock turned and ran back to the fire, hollering and waving his arms.

Nothing happened. The coyotes just looked at him, watched him go. Several turned to face him, but none of them followed.

"What's happening?" Andi asked.

"They're not moving," Ariel whispered back.

Mr. Crock skidded to a stop in front of the fire, put his hands on his knees for a moment to get his breath, then reached down and picked up a rock and threw it at the coyote that was the closest to where she and the others were standing. It was skinnier than the rest and its coat was patchy like maybe it was molting or something.

Mr. Crock's rock missed by three feet. He didn't seem to care, just reached down and picked up another rock and another and another, throwing them as fast as he could at the coyotes closest to them. He finally hit one — the skinny one — and it yelped and jumped back.

And it was like that flipped some kind of switch. The weird wailing sound stopped like you'd turned off the TV in the middle of somebody's song. The silence following it was so creepy that Becca's voice seemed loud even though she was just whispering.

"Why'd they stop wailing?"

Ariel realized then that she needed to describe to Andi and Becca everything that was happening.

"Mr. Crock hit one of them with a rock and—"

A coyote lifted its head and howled — a normal coyote howl, and the others took up the cry. So many of them gathered around that the howling was booming. The wailing had been continuous, but they hadn't all done it at one time. A couple would wail, then another would start and the first two would stop — like that. But they were all howling at once now, making *woof, woof, woof* — *arooooo* sounds that went on and on, so loud Ariel wondered if Mr. Jack, Andi's daddy and the sheriff could hear it way off where they were in the woods climbing the mountains.

Then she could hear a different sound — a growl — mixed in with the howls. Slowly, the howling faded away to the rumble of growling. She'd seen mean dogs growl — teeth bared, ears flattened on their heads. The coyotes weren't like that. They didn't have any "expression" at all on their faces — not vicious or angry. They might as well have been whistling.

When the growling started, Becca and Andi had started squeezing her hands. "They don't look mean," Ariel whispered, trying to sound as reassuring as she could. "And they're still not moving—"

But they were. One of them about twenty feet away — not the skinny one Mr. Crock had hit with the rock but the one next to it — began that tired-looking walk like before, slowly coming their way. And the others that had turned to watch Mr. Crock turned back and did the same, growling, some of them with their heads down, shaking them back and forth.

Mr. Crock watched them for a few seconds, then dropped the rocks he was preparing to throw. He pulled out his pistol, took aim at the coyote closest to him and shot it! Becca and Andi jumped at the sound of the gunshot. The coyote collapsed to the ground with blood pouring from its side, twitched once and was still.

The coyotes were startled by the gunshot, too, and backed up a couple of steps. Then the coyote closest to the one Mr. Crock had shot leapt to its side — the first fast movement Ariel had seen one of them make — and began sniffing frantically at the blood puddling in the dirt. He put out a paw and prodded the dead coyote — then grabbed its leg in his jaws and began to tear at it. Another coyote — a bigger one — took three bounding strides and crashed into the one with the leg in its mouth, knocking it down. The big coyote was snarling and this time it did sound mean. Its teeth were bared and its ears were laid back flat on its head. The first coyote let go of the dead coyote's leg, rolled over on its back and stuck its feet up in the air like a dog that wanted its belly rubbed.

The bigger coyote turned away then and began tearing at the body of the dead coyote, ripping open its belly with its teeth. It got a mouthful of guts — gross! — and was dragging them out of the body when another coyote attacked it and tried to snatch them away.

Then they were all into it. The coyotes near the three of them dashed to join in the fight and in moments there was a tangle of snarling biting coyotes, not trying to get to the body of the dead one anymore but attacking each other, barking, snarling, snapping and growling.

Mr. Crock had backed up closer to the fire after he shot the coyote, and now there was a tangle of angry, mad dogs rolling in front of him. He looked up at her and motioned for her to go, to take the others and make for the car.

"The coyotes are all fighting each other now," she told Becca and Andi. "We need to go."

"Walk backward slowly," Becca said, "until we're around that bend in the path where they can't see us anymore.'

Ariel began to move slowly backward, looking over her shoulder. She was so intent at making sure there wasn't anything behind them that Becca and Andi could trip over that she didn't even look up from the ground until they had rounded the bend in the path and the attacking coyotes were out of sight — the sound of their snarls and yelps and growling so loud they could still hear it.

Then she lifted her eyes and saw it. Standing in the middle of the path was a lone coyote. Just standing there, wagging its head from side to side like the others had before Mr. Crock had shot one and they'd all got into a fight over who got to eat it.

She stopped abruptly.

"Wait," she said. "There's a coyote … one of the coyotes is standing in the trail between us and the car."

"Does it look like it's about to …?"

"It just looks stupid, like the others did at first. What should we do?"

"Go around it," Becca said. "You said the others didn't attack when Crock ran away from them — so this one isn't going to attack us either if we just move slowly." She was trying to sound like she was sure of that but Ariel could hear a little tremble in her voice. It occurred to her then that even as scary as it was to stand here looking at the coyote, it was probably a whole lot more scary to stand here in the dark, knowing it was there, but not being able to see it.

"We'll need to go single file," she said. "Andi in the middle. Give me her hand."

Ariel did as Becca directed. She took Becca's hand and placed it in Andi's. Then she moved slowly to the other side of Andi, took her hand, and began to lead the others toward the trees, stepping sideways because she didn't think it was a good idea to turn their backs on the coyote. It didn't move, didn't even appear to be watching them, just stood there, head down.

It hadn't been hard to lead Becca and Andi by the hand on the trail. But the woods would be different. There'd be roots and bushes and rocks and things to trip over. She'd have to be very careful to make sure nobody fell down.

She kept her eyes on the coyote. When she got to the tree line, she turned away from the animal and stepped carefully onto the carpet of leaves between the trees. Andi turned to follow her. Becca followed Andi. She knew she needed to go far enough into the forest that the coyote couldn't see them before she turned and headed back in the direction of the car.

There were bushes here that helped. She had to go around them to get into the trees, but once she was on the other side of them, they would shield the three of them, so they couldn't be seen from the trail. She took each step carefully, quietly kicking sticks out of the way, avoiding tree roots, winding slowly back into the woods. She kept looking at the coyote as long as she could, until the vegetation hid it from view — then she went a little way farther just to be safe.

Finally, she stopped and peered through the leaves. Though the coyote and trail weren't far, they were concealed. In order to turn and head toward the car, she'd have to lead the others over a tree root big as a fire hose, twisted like a snake. There was no way around it — but then the way would be clear.

There was a footprint in the dirt in front of the tree root — a big one, like a man's shoe. But Ariel was so intent on making sure nobody tripped, she hardly noticed it at all.

LINC WASN'T A LOCAL, so he wasn't as familiar with these particular woods as the people he was following through them. But he had grown up hiking and hunting in the Daniel Boone National Forest, 700,000 acres of natural woodlands that he had come to know like his own back yard. He had come close to trying to get on as a park ranger. Hadn't worked out and he ended up selling insurance — which had never required he take out his woodsmanship skills, blow the dust off and put them to use.

But being county sheriff had. He'd tracked down many a dope grower guarding his marijuana patch or a bootlegger looking after his still back in the woods, courtesy of his tracking skills, so he allowed himself to stay far behind the band of murderers to be sure he remained undetected. If he got caught and they decided to fight it out, he and Daniel Burke were toast.

In truth, all his care wasn't necessary. The group of people tromped through the woods, wildebeest on the way to a waterhole, and never looked right, left or behind. It didn't occur to any of them there'd be anybody out here but them. He had stayed so far behind them, in fact, that he'd been unable to hear what they were saying that might give him some idea why they had gone on a murderous rampage. It could be that they were just the human equivalent of the cows that had attacked the Durston family — that they had just lost it for the same reason all the plant and animal life around here had lost it. But theirs was not just random killing.

Somebody had sent them out — with instructions — and they were now dragging Daniel back to whoever it was to use in a special sacrifice that Linc didn't allow his mind to conjecture. So there might genuinely be a head on this snake and taking him out might very well leave the others disoriented and directionless long enough for him and Daniel to get away.

And back to the chapel where, oh by the way, Theresa lay buried in a cave beneath a collapsed building.

Daniel had been to the top of the mountain and was coming down when Linc saw him — so he'd been to the tower to call for help. Maybe some guy on a white horse and cavalry were on the way.

And maybe not.

Not ordinarily a pessimist, Linc was certain the safe money was on not. Mainly because … it was getting late. It couldn't possibly be approaching sundown, but it undeniably was. At least *here* it was. The implications of that took Linc's breath away. He shook off all such considerations or they'd have expanded in his head like a navy dinghy and he'd have been unable to think at all.

Approaching a big juniper tree, he could see the figures he was following well beyond it. The only thing out here that Linc knew about other than farm houses was the Love of God Holiness Church. And when he thought about it, that lone thought ran chills up and down his spine. These folks were so far from civilization in the mountains and hollows that everything got concentrated, by which he meant that it wasn't just people's genetic code that over generations had become so blended they all had a common look, even if they couldn't or had never bothered to trace their lineage back more than a couple of generations. And Linc had often thought what a shame it was their common ancestors hadn't been more attractive people. Big ears and broad, flat faces, with short upper lips — when they smiled you could see an inch of gum above their teeth — abounded. So did the mentally deficient. Yes, there was a lot of mental retardation, but Linc suspected it went deeper than that — that nobody in the north end of the county had gotten any farther than the eighth grade, would have trouble making change for a dollar and believed the whole man-landing-on-the-moon thing was a hoax.

The same thing had happened to the church here. It had morphed through time into something no church should be about. Besides the wailing, speaking in tongues and falling down on the floor in spiritual fits, the church and its congregants slid farther and farther out there on the edge where delusion and reality had so blended most folks really didn't know what was real and what wasn't. Traveling evangelists who used snakes in their services to slide an icy finger of dread down your neck became more and more difficult to pick out of a crowd of normal people because just about everybody in this part of the county was a bubble or two off plumb.

It seemed to Linc they were traveling in the general direction of the church and that suspicion was confirmed when he came around the bend and there stood the little building with a small cross on the roof, nestled in a small meadow surrounded by trees.

As the group who'd kidnapped Daniel approached the church, the front door opened and an old man Linc didn't recognize stepped out onto the porch. His white hair was long and he held it back in a ponytail at the back of his neck. From this distance Linc couldn't tell much about his features — white man, small, dressed in a suit and tie. That was about it.

Linc decided to trade video for audio. He had to know

what was going on and he could get close enough to hear what was being said, but to do that he'd have to crawl on his belly through the bushes and he would chance being seen if he tried to lift his body to get a look at what was going on. So he stayed low, crawled closer and began to catch snatches of conversation.

Chapter Twenty-Six

THE WORLD WAS ALL WRONG, upside down. Daniel's blood had run to his head and he felt like his head was about to explode.

Pumpkins. Pumpkins exploded.

What pumpkins?

The world grayed out and there was a great buzzing sound in his head. The pain and the jolting movement were wrapped up in cotton, happening to him but not really happening to him — happening to the rest of him but not to his mind.

The world re-formed. His face was smashed into fabric that stank — sweat, the kind of body odor it took a long time to accumulate.

Moving.

Jolting.

Somebody was carrying him!

As his mind began to actually focus it became clear quickly that somebody had slung him over their shoulder and was carrying him. Over rough terrain.

There were voices, more than a couple, a group of

people were nearby, walking along with whoever was carrying him, talking.

He could hear them clearly like they were only a few feet away, but it took awhile for his hearing to hook back up to his intellect and process the sounds into words.

"… kill a man quick and there's hardly any blood at all," one of them was saying. "Have to split him open to get enough."

"If you don't kill them outright, just hurt them bad and let them live for a while, the blood kinda squirts out — like from a cut-off hand. You can squirt it all over you, don't even need to smear it."

Smeared blood.

Andi'd seen that. In the vision she told him and the others about right before they left. She'd seen people in the woods smeared with blood.

Daniel hadn't been scared before, just hurting and dizzy. Now, terror joined pain and fear in a pounding lump in his belly that made him instantly nauseous. He swallowed hard to keep from vomiting, and concentrated on trying to figure out what was going on.

He opened his eyes a little, not enough that anybody could see, and from his limited range of vision, he could see that the stinky dude who was carrying him and his murderous companions were carrying him through the woods.

It was impossible *not* to hear what they were saying but he quickly wished he could be struck deaf. Tales of carnage, horrible murder and mutilation, the mother of all slasher movies.

As horrible as their words were and the acts they were describing, even more disturbing was how they were doing it. They sounded like a group of excited ten-year-old boys who had just gotten dirt bikes — bragging about their proficiency and trying to one-up each other with tales of their performance. They were excited, thrilled, babbling in a non-stop stream none of them was listening to. Giggling when somebody came up with something particularly gruesome, like the dude describing his murder of a nun.

At first Daniel was terrified these people were possessed and he screamed a silent *noooooooooo* in his head. It was supposed to be over! They killed the bad kids, banished the efreet. But he soon realized the man who was carrying him was not superhuman. He was strong as a bull, but he had to stop every now and then to adjust the load on his shoulder and to get his breath. And the others' descriptions of the horrors they had committed had been delivered with as much enthusiasm as any demon-driven soul. But the scenes they described involved normal mayhem. Stabbing people and slitting their throats — not ripping off their arms or throwing them up into a tree.

Then the conversation stopped altogether, words bitten off in mid-sentence. He wondered if they were even aware that they had slowed down together at that moment, weren't walking with a purposeful stride anymore but creeping along in kid-dragged-to-the-principal's-office speed. He heard a door open and close and heard treads on a wooden porch.

Suddenly, he was falling through the air as the man carrying him leaned over and dumped him on his back on the ground.

The crowd laughed when the sudden connection with the ground forced a grunt out through his lips, a grunt he was sure sounded as pitiful as a baby rabbit.

Not joyful laughter. He'd heard this kind of laughter before, years before when the Bad Kids had tormented the Three Musketeers. It was a good enough imitation to pass, fooled most people. It was in the eyes, though. If you looked in the eyes, you knew.

"Well, would you look what we have here," said a voice out of the laughter, which was dying away to a chuckle.

Daniel had never heard the voice before — it was rich and melodious, but there was something familiar about the tone. He lay as he had fallen, peeking out through the forest of eyelashes of his closed eyes. The man who had spoken was standing on the porch of a building and Daniel was lying on his back on the ground in front of him.

The man had white hair, a beard it must have taken him twenty years to grow — all the way down his chest to his waist — and was wearing sunglasses. He wasn't a big man, at least he didn't appear to be from Daniel's perspective, and he was dressed in a suit and tie — even had a white handkerchief in the top pocket — and white gloves. His nose had obviously been broken more than once, and lay off center on his left cheek. He walked slowly down the steps until he was standing beside Daniel's head. He appeared to be smiling a kind of half smile, but maybe not. With all that hair it was hard to tell.

"Stop acting like you're asleep, Daniel," he said.

THE ECHO of a distant gunshot disturbed the unnatural silence of the forest and Jack jumped at the sound. Crock. He had Jack's back-up weapon, a Smith & Wesson .38. Sheriff Lincoln was packing a Glock 22, .40 caliber — which would have made a louder, harsher sound.

What had Crock shot at?

The door to a million terrors flew open in his mind. The crazy people covered with blood had attacked! Andi had described seeing in her dream a lot more people than Crock had bullets to kill.

Or something else? *What?*

It could be anything. Something as harmless as ... well anything, deer maybe. If cattle could turn deadly, so could deer.

Jack's heart labored on, thundering as he held his breath, listening. Nothing. No more gunfire. Whatever Crock had shot at, he'd dropped with the first shot so maybe there was only one of something.

A bear! You couldn't stop a charging bear with one shot from a .38.

Stop it!

Jack grabbed his panic in a stranglehold and quickly choked the life out of it. He'd been a soldier in combat and a police officer. He'd spent his whole life fighting to protect others, but the others had never been *Becca*. He felt a surge of the helpless rage he'd felt when they were children and came upon the Bad Kids in the woods trying to kidnap Becca. He would have ripped out their throats if he could have. So would Daniel. But they were no match for super-human demons. Now Becca was in danger again — from *what?* — and he was just as powerless to do anything about it as he had been then.

He had to get out of this tree!

... because it was getting late.

Much as he was trying to deny it, Jack couldn't ignore the reality that the light was failing. The woods were falling into shadow. He didn't know what time it was, but he did know it *couldn't possibly* be late enough for ... He shoved Theresa's words out of his mind ... but not before she whispered them in his ear.

If light can be broke, maybe time can be, too.

No. Not going *there*.

Jack concentrated on surveying his environment, looking for something, *anything* — he was open to all options — he could use to escape the cats without being ripped to shreds.

All but the two bobcats beneath him had wandered aimlessly away. Those two had tasted his blood and apparently liked the flavor. They'd stopped jumping at him as soon as he got the bleeding stopped, but it was clear they weren't going anywhere.

Two bobcats — one probably forty pounds, the other smaller — maybe thirty. Could he possibly fight them unarmed and survive? Not likely. And once the carnage started, the remainder of the family might return to join in the feast.

His only hope was the rifle. The M4 had twenty-eight rounds. He could drop these two and if the others returned …

How could he get the rifle? It was lying on the rocks in the creek — gratefully not down in the water — directly below him. Right there, so tantalizingly close. But he'd have to fight his way through the two bobcats that were practically sitting on it to get to the weapon and kill them.

Possible … last resort possible.

What else could he do? As long as they were sitting there right beneath him, waiting for another blood-drop treat, he couldn't—

What if they weren't right beneath him? If he could get to the rifle, he wouldn't need but a few seconds. He'd once had to dive for Sergeant Benson's rifle, turn and shoot two Somali rebels charging at him with machetes. He'd managed.

So how could he make the cats move far enough away that he'd have a chance?

How could he distract them? Scare them? Entice them?

The image of Andi and the catnip ball flashed through his mind. She'd tease Ossie by dangling it just out of his reach — then she'd throw it *and he'd chase it.*

Could he get the bobcats to chase something? What did he have they'd want bad enough to go after?

Not catnip. Blood.

WELL, he'd stepped in it now.

The slack-jawed, dead-eyed coyotes had snapped and were slashing and tearing at each other, as crazy as nuclear waste dump rats.

Crock was an audience of one at a command performance of Charles Darwinism at its finest and he figured it wouldn't be long at all before the fittest survivors noticed they hadn't dispatched *all* the lessor creatures to that great coyote heaven in the sky — that there was one more, a two-legged one.

He had four rounds left.

Of the two or three dozen coyotes who'd gone postal when he shot the first one, fewer than a dozen remained — hard to tell with them rolling around snarling and biting and generally being horrifying beasts. He'd cherished the hope when they tore into each other there wouldn't be a single one left standing, or at the very least they'd narrow the field down to a number below the number of rounds he had to shoot them with.

That wasn't how it was turning out. Amid the carnage of dead and dying coyotes that spread out all the way to the tree line beside the collapsed chapel, the survivors stood panting over their last kill, looking around, not immediately leaping into another death match with the nearest still-breathing creature. The frenzy appeared to be ending.

Had the alpha males thinned the pack down to some genetically coded perfect size? That was lunacy, of course. Coyotes didn't hunt in packs to begin with so it wasn't likely they were following some instinctual program. They were just as bull-goose looney as the murderous cows and suicidal starlings, that's all. Which meant, of course, there was absolutely no way to predict what they might do next.

They could all attack him together in a rush, in which case he would take out as many as possible before they got him, diminish the potential threat to the others as best he could.

Or they could all gather around the campfire, clasp paws and sing Kumbaya.

It had appeared to him that the girls got away. He hadn't heard any screams and surely if … no, not going there. They were fine. They'd made it to the car. Barring information to the contrary, he intended to continue believing that … for the rest of his life, which might not be long.

"What's going on up there?" Theresa cried.

Crock had edged up so close to the fire he could smell his suit pants singeing. Now he stepped around it closer to the collapsed chapel's pile of debris and called out softly.

"Shhhhhh. Probably not a plan to call attention to yourself." Actually, he figured Theresa was the safest of the lot of them. Unless these dogs started digging …

"Where's Becca and the girls?" she asked, quieter. "I thought you said you's gonna take them to the car?"

"I stayed to keep the coyotes occupied. They're safe in the car now, snug as bugs in a rug."

Two of the remaining — he counted … seven, eight,

nine — coyotes were now feeding on the carcasses of the fallen. One was licking his own wounds. Four more still seemed restless, eyeing each other and snarling, ready to pounce.

Come on guys, don't give up now. Go for Olympic gold!

"You don't know that," she said. "You ain't hardly no better at lying than Daniel is."

"I'd call that the pot calling the kettle black — metaphorically speaking. You're not fine down there and you're getting more not-fine by the minute. How about a *reality* check."

When she spoke again, her voice was trembling.

"I wish I's up there by that fire. I can't seem to get warm, even snuggled up in this afghan."

She sounded old and tired.

"… and it don't help that now I'm … wet."

Wet?

"I didn't mean to say that. Course it was warm to begin with, but now—"

"When I was a wild kid, I was riding a motorcycle at night in a monsoon out in the middle of nowhere — peed my pants on purpose just for the warmth."

He heard a small chuckle.

"Can you still feel your feet and legs, wiggle your toes?"

There was a pause.

"I ain't sure no more."

The nearest survivor coyote had turned at the sound of Crock's voice and now began to advance on him slowly. The others looked up when he did. One dropped a leg bone he was chewing on. Another got up from where he was seated, licking his wounds. In short order all nine of them were on the move, headed his way.

Showtime.

EVEN FOR ARIEL, who wasn't almost blind, the forest was dark and gloomy in the failing afternoon light. She couldn't believe it was that late, but it was obvious the sun had gone behind the mountain, sending its shadow down into the valley below, edging across it and then up the side of the mountain on the other side. Andi's grandmother had warned her about "The Shadder."

Her father joked that Granny Stevens lived "so deep in the mountains the sun can't get there but about once a week." Though he had always poked gentle fun at his wife's hillbilly relatives, he'd encouraged Granny to pass on to Ariel mountain traditions and heritage. She'd taught her how to spin yarn from wool, using a contraption like the one Ariel had seen when they went to the Great Smoky Mountains on vacation. In the Ye Olde Antique Store in Gatlinburg, Tennessee. It was selling for fifteen hundred dollars. She'd taught Ariel how to churn butter, too, how to cook on a wood-fired stove, how to knit and do needlepoint and even how to make doll clothes using tiny stitches you could barely see.

In the evenings when she stayed with Granny, the two of them sat on the porch and watched the fireflies and Granny told her stories — that Ariel's father made sure she understood were just superstitions. That's where she heard about The Shadder.

"The Shadder's what comes for ye when ye die," she'd said one evening, rocking back and forth in her rocker. "It's big as the mountain."

They were deep into the conversation before Ariel realized her grandmother's mountain dialect had translated "shadow" into "shadder."

"When it's yore time, ye kin watch it a'comin' fer ye

through the trees," Granny had said. "Comes ever day, lookin' to take them as is ready to go on to glory ... and the rest on to hell."

After that day, Ariel never watched a mountain's lengthening shadow through the afternoon toward evening without being just a little apprehensive, like maybe she didn't want it to touch her.

Then last summer, the monster had come for her, had taken over her will and body, her whole being, filling her mind with shadows where a thousand terrors lurked. Even when Andi and the angel had helped her banish the demon, the shadowy places he'd created remained behind. That's where nightmares lived.

And hurrying through the dim woods right now, holding tight to Andi's hand, terrified of the coyotes they'd left behind, felt like running through those shadowy corridors in her mind.

She expected any second some monster would jump out from behind a tree.

And then one did.

Chapter Twenty-Seven

As SOON AS Jack removed some of the strips of blood-soaked cloth from around his leg, the blood began to drip, and the cats beneath him came to life, jumping at the droplets, trying to catch them in midair.

He remembered reading a gross story once about a tiger that had killed a man in front of his wife and kids and then proceeded to eat him — *including* his blood-soaked clothing. So in theory, at least, this should work.

Fashioning the bloody bandages he'd removed into something more or less ball-like at the end of a long strip of t-shirt fabric, he took off his belt and tied the strip of fabric to the buckle.

It was probably long enough to reach from here, but he had to get closer, position himself on the end of the vine so he could leap off it and grab the rifle if the big cats took the bait.

It was entirely possible, probably likely in fact, that his movement back down the vine would dislodge it from the tree it was attached to — thereby dumping him in a heap on top of the cats. He'd try to be prepared for that, somehow manage to fight them off long enough to get at the weapon.

Definitely not best-case scenario.

It seemed to take an eternity to ease off his perch and begin to shinny down the vine to the spot where a large gnarl gave his feet purchase so he wasn't holding his weight with his arms. That was as low as he could go because there was nothing to stand on below that, but the drop from here was definitely in leg- and ankle-breaking range.

Jack had not been a paratrooper, but army rangers trained in everything. He'd learned the PLF — Parachute Landing Fall, a clumsy-looking roll where you lock your knees and ankles together, land flat on your feet, then "push, turn and roll over." Ideally, the roll should see to it that your feet, then ankles, then calf, thigh and then back rolled on the ground — dissipating the force of the fall. A fully laden paratrooper's landing was the equivalent of jumping off a second-floor balcony.

The problem was, the guys in airborne school spent two weeks learning that one technique — out of a four-week training schedule — practicing it off two-foot platforms, then four-foot platforms and eventually a two-story mechanical simulator.

Jack's team had spent three days. He'd actually jumped out of an airplane a whopping one time. And that had been years ago. Well, the skill had better be like riding a bicycle or he might survive the fall, kill the bobcats and then have to crawl back down the mountain with two broken legs.

The cats had come alert as soon as they saw movement above them. He'd seen how high they could jump, but had been too busy at the time not being eaten to measure the distance. And he had to dangle the ball close, above them far enough to be enticing but not so close that they'd grab it and yank it out of his hands, and yank him off the vine in the process. For now, they stood in the creek below, just watching him.

Would they actually take the bait?

As soon as he positioned himself on the knot in the vine and got his balance, he held onto the vine and began to lower his dangle ball down toward the cats.

Lower.

Lower.

Houston, we have liftoff.

The bigger of the two cats leapt at the ball — way higher than Jack had anticipated it could jump. One of its claws actually caught in the fabric and almost pulled the whole apparatus out of Jack's hand.

Now both cats were crouching.

He lowered the ball again, but not quite as far.

The big cat jumped again, missing by a few inches.

Jack left it where it was and the other cat lunged at it, too.

Then he began to swing it slowly above their heads, back and forth. They followed it like locked-on missiles.

Carefully, no sudden movements, he made the arc of the dangling ball bigger and bigger.

The big cat followed it several feet upstream. When it swung back down, the smaller cat followed it downstream. Not good. He'd never be able to drop them both with them on both sides of him.

He slowed the swinging and the cats returned to their position beneath him.

Then he swung the ball out again. The cats had figured out the drill and this time they both followed it immediately, jumping and falling, jumping and falling.

Good boys.

Now farther.

It was a delicate maneuver, keeping the ball just out of reach, but low enough to entice them to follow it as it rose higher in the air at the apogee of its swing.

Down and back up again.

He let out a little more line so the ball would go farther, then had to yank it quickly upward as it slid beneath him where the distance to the ground was shorter.

The cats were fully engaged now. When the ball swung out, they followed it, then raced back, following it on the downward swing, frantically leaping into the air, batting at it with their claws.

Back and forth. Three feet. Five feet. Ten. It had gained momentum, swinging fast now. It wasn't likely to get any better and every swing risked losing the bait or falling off the vine.

Now.

When the ball swung out the next time downriver, Jack gave it all the momentum he could muster going back upriver … and let it go.

The ball and belt went flying through the air.

The cats dashed after it.

Jack let go of the vine.

WHEN THE NEAREST coyote was about fifteen feet away, it growled deep in its throat and crouched, ready to spring. So much for maybe they're just looking for a scratch behind the ears and a belly rub. Crock snapped the cap off a flare, scraped the end of it with the cap and pointed the flames that erupted at the coyote.

It stepped back. Didn't leap back in terror, put its tail between its legs and run for the woods, though, which was the response Crock had hoped for — was banking on, actually.

"Yaaaaaa!" he yelled, swishing the flare back and forth in front of him. He lunged it at the coyote, then turned and tried to spew flames on the others. None of them bolted.

Lions and tigers and flares, oh my!

Three flares, forty-five minutes. Then what?

Now, sometimes a flare'd last a lot longer than that, an hour maybe and—

And sometimes they got stopped up and lasted a lot less — like five minutes. One way or the other *Then-what?* was out there waiting for him so he might as well face it now, figure out what he was going to do.

He'd shoot them, of course. At least four of them. He harbored no illusions that they'd all bolt at the sound of gunfire. They hadn't when he dropped the first one.

Then?

He'd grab a flaming stick out of the fire — which was likely to be the next thing to useless given their reaction to a full-bore, spitting fire flare.

And then?

He'd … throw the gun at them!

And when that didn't stop them, he'd …

Die.

Little word. Three letters.

It was small comfort that he'd seen worse, faced a more horrifying death. Snarling coyotes paled in comparison to the fifty-foot red demon that had risen with its black wings furled out of the fiery sea.

He could still hear the sound of its roar. Some part of him had heard it reverberating behind every breath he'd taken since that day, not with his deaf ears but with his bones and his skin and his blood. The roar had been more than sound. It'd been a single corrupt thing that would have shattered glass, clear and horrible beyond description. It was the sound of pure, consummate evil and to hear it was to die. And some essential part of his humanity had done just that.

He'd checked out when he heard it, collapsed to his knees, with all his circuits fried. The man who'd been Charles Crocker turned away, put reality firmly behind him and selected a corridor in his mind that led to the deepest part of himself. Decided it was time to pay a visit to the sub-basement, take a look at the HVAC unit there.

He had known he was going to die that day, remembered hoping it wouldn't be a brutal death. A man should be allowed to die with some dignity — as much as the situation allowed, anyway. He'd been in for dying, just not for horrible dying.

He definitely harbored no illusions about what the coyotes'd do to him when they got to him. He'd watched them rip into each other and it was the kind of horror he'd been spared that day.

Death by being ripped to pieces. Eaten alive. But he wouldn't scream! Well, he'd try not to scream. He didn't want the girls to hear him. And Theresa … she'd be able to hear enough of what was going on to know. He'd die … quietly.

Or not. He didn't *have to* go out that way. He could shoot the first three coyotes but save the last bullet.

Was that being a coward?

He'd prayed in that dark corridor, with the light of the angel in front and the sound of crinkling tissue paper behind, told God he was a coward, that he wanted to run away, that he'd have left all them behind in the cave and bailed if he could have. And maybe he actually would have done that. Maybe he wouldn't. But he couldn't bail then and he couldn't bail now.

The big question now was not how to stay alive but how to die. Did he have a right to pick? And it was likely the others would never know what he'd done. Once those coyotes got through with his remains, it probably would be no simple task to confirm cause of death.

… but if he wasn't ashamed of what he was considering, why was he glad nobody would ever know about it? And if there weren't something wrong with doing something like that — good Catholic boy notwithstanding — why was he ashamed?

The flare began to sputter and he picked up the second flare, popped off the cap and lit it off the first. The coyotes had been edging closer and he used the brighter flare, yelled and lunged at them to drive them a back couple of steps.

Theresa must have heard him shout.

"What's goin' on up there?"

The flare, the one he'd just lit, suddenly began to sputter! He pulled the last flare out of the box, popped off the cap and lit it from the dying flare in his hands — then he heaved the sputtering flare at the nearest coyote. When it struck him in the side it must have broken open and spilled the backed-up flammable contents all over him. Within seconds, the dog was a torch — dancing in agony, shrieking the most penetrating cry, writhing on the ground. Then it was still, and the flames continued to consume its body, the stench of fried flesh and fur filling the night air.

"Major Crocker, what you doing?"

"Just about to feed the coyotes a little supper." There was a pause. "Me."

"You think that's funny, do you?"

"You hear me laughing? There are ten coyotes circled

around for dinner. I'm more frightened of athlete's foot than these guys are of this fire and I have four rounds left and no flares. Do the math."

THERESA SUCKED IN A GASP. What Crock was saying seemed to swell up inside her chest like a balloon when you squirt helium into it. They was wild dogs up there — she'd heard the battle they'd already waged with each other, the sounds of snarling and howls of pain didn't even seem muffled by the distance. It'd sounded like them coyotes was killing each other right in front of her.

And now Crock was about to face the ones that won that fight. Alone and unarmed.

OH, Lord, don't let them tear him apart. He's a good man who don't deserve to die like that. I know we don't get to pick how we'll leave this world, but please not that way. And not today. Besides him being a good man and all, we need him here. The world's done gone crazy and I think you and me both know why that is. But in this little bitty part of it right here, I'm asking for your help. Please keep him safe.

ARIEL'S HAND was sweaty and Andi was having trouble hanging onto it as Ariel pulled her and Becca along behind her, dragging them through the woods toward the cars to escape the coyotes.

There wasn't anything to be afraid of here — well, except it was a dark woods full of demons and all sorts of normal creatures that might turn deadly and attack them. There was that. But the only obvious threat was behind them — the coyotes, and if they could get to the car and close the doors, they'd be safe from them there.

Still, Andi was growing more frightened with every step.

There's something else here.

The thought stole her breath so she stumbled and almost took Ariel and Becca down to the ground with her. It was one of those things, like so many others, that she knew without knowing how she knew. Something evil was here, in the woods with them. She only knew what it *wasn't*. It wasn't a demon. But what it might be …

It was after them, too. It wasn't just some random bad thing nearby. It was chasing *them*. And whatever was out there in the woods wasn't one of the coyotes from back at the chapel, either. It was stalking them, following them through the trees, getting closer and closer.

Andi wanted to warn the others, but she was too breathless to cry out and besides, what good would it do? They were already trying to get away as fast as they could. Knowing that something much closer than the coyotes was chasing them wouldn't make them move any faster.

A plan, then. What should she do, what *could* she do if the thing caught up with them? *When* it caught up with them?

Suddenly, Becca's hand was ripped out of hers. She turned, tried to see what had happened but all she could make out was a dark shape, a man maybe, holding Becca by the arm, shaking her and making an awful sound in his throat that might even have been supposed to be laughter.

DANIEL'S EYES popped open and he stared up at the white-haired man in astonishment. There was a beat of silence

— barely time enough for Daniel to wonder how in the world—?

Then the man burst into laughter, clearly understanding some cosmic joke the rest of them had missed. It was real laughter in that whatever had struck the man funny had genuinely delighted him. But there was no joy in it.

Daniel made to rise but the man pushed him back down on the ground with an expensive shoe polished to a shine he could see his face in.

"How do you know my name?" he asked. "What with one thing and another, I must have missed out on the introductions."

The man ignored him as if he hadn't heard a word. He turned toward the crowd and began to speak in a deep, impressive, powerful voice, spoke as one who was accustomed to others listening to him when he spoke and he commanded their full attention.

"Where did you find this man?"

"We found him wandering around in the woods," a man replied, so sycophantic he was almost licking the man's shoes.

The white-haired man turned back to Daniel.

"And why is it that a man like yourself is wandering around all by your lonesome?" He paused. "You are all by yourself, are you not?"

Daniel wasn't about to give up the location of the others, so these maniacs could do to them what they had already done to— But what could he say? What possible reason …?

"I got lost," he said. Lame, but the best he could come up with. "I grew up around here — well, not in this part of the county, in town — and I brought some out-of-town friends to show them where I used to play when I was a kid. City folks who've never seen woods like these."

"*They've* never been in the woods but *you're* the one who got lost. Am I getting all this?"

"Well, I … one of them forgot their cell phone and I went back—"

"You can't get coverage way out here."

"Not to call — for the camera. And I said I'd go back to the car for it. I took a shortcut, and …"

The man didn't believe a word Daniel said. Why did he ever bother lying? He had never in his life been any good at it.

"So there are other people out here — all dressed up in Sunday best wearing shoes clearly unsuitable for walking in the woods?" the man said. "Where are they?"

"A few … men … as a matter of fact, one of them is a police officer. We parked about a mile from the Grafton Bridge." Which was the opposite direction from the chapel.

"And walked this far?"

The man was playing with him.

"I don't know how far they walked," he said. "I've been lost for several hours … and they were going the other way."

The man was tiring of the game.

"Well, you walked right into a buzz saw," he said. "We're getting ready to celebrate the end of the world." The man leaned closer, his eyes invisible through the dark tint of his sunglasses. "And you, Reverend Daniel Burke, are going to be the guest of honor."

Daniel knew none of these people. How did they know him? He had no idea who they were, but he suspected the sight of them wouldn't have surprised Andi at all. She'd have recognized them from her vision. Andi's visions always came true. And that thought knocked the breath out of him for a moment.

"Yes, sir, you turned up right at the most opportune moment." The man leaned closer and Daniel tried to see his eyes through the glasses but couldn't. "You of all people understand the significance of blood sacrifices. The Israelites went to the temple once a year with their perfect lamb and the priests sacrificed it to atone for the people's sins. 'For under the Law almost everything is purified by blood, and without the shedding of blood there is neither release from sin *and* its guilt *nor* the remission of the due *and* merited punishment for sins.' Hebrews 9:22."

He continued in a solemn tone that somehow managed to sound mocking at the same time.

"The Lord God on High has revealed to me that the time of judgement is at hand and we will *not* be left behind when the train leaves for heaven because we didn't make a proper sacrifice."

He took a step back and said, "On your knees." Daniel rolled over in the dirt and got to his knees.

"It's going to be your privilege, son, your honor to serve as the sacrifice for all of us. Our many sins and sacrifices will be wiped away with your blood and we won't burn in the fiery furnace of hell for all eternity."

Sacrifice. Daniel was to be a *blood* sacrifice. A death sentence. He was reasonably certain none of the lambs in Israel walked out of that temple alive.

Again. Here he was again facing death, knowing his life was about to end. He tried not to flash back to that time in the dark in the cave with Jeff Kendrick waiting for Billy Ray to come with his sword and slice off their heads. He'd had hours … days … years … he had no idea how long to think about what that meant, to get himself prepared to

315

NINIE HAMMON

die. And what he figured out down there that day had changed every day of his life since then.

As you sucked in your final breath at the end of all things, love was what mattered. It was all that mattered.

Love was true.

Love was good, too, the force that stood against the evil Daniel had not wanted to know existed. The evil he'd caught glimpses of — in the eyes of the madman who'd butchered Emily, and distorting the innocent features of a little girl who looked like a life-sized Raggedy Ann doll.

If good really existed, were true, all the rest of it was true, too — all the things he'd said Sunday after Sunday about good versus evil and light against darkness. And about love that was pure and good. He hadn't really believed a single word of it when he'd said it — in feigned faith and counterfeit humility. But his glib insincerity didn't change reality. It was still true.

Daniel didn't know the exact nature of the evil that had tangled up these people's hearts and souls, or that drove the white-haired man to madness. But the exact nature didn't matter much at this stage of the game. What was happening here was evil. He was still battling evil. And if evil really existed, so did good. Since the day he had thought those thoughts in the black depths of a cave, in a boxcar filled with gold bars, he had felt a kind of peace he couldn't explain. It might be fourth quarter, behind fifty to nothing. It didn't matter. His peace came from knowing in advance who was going to win the game.

His own terror-filled thoughts had consumed his attention and when he tuned back in, the white-haired man was still speaking to the crowd.

"… stuck right there on that stake for the world to see. For unbelievers to know the wrath of a righteous God."

What was going to be "stuck right there on that stake?"

316

A horror began to well up in Daniel's belly. It couldn't be. It couldn't possibly be.

The man turned back to Daniel then, leaned close.

"Grab a handful of hair — get a good hold on it — then bring the sword down hard, slice across the throat, just one clean blow so you're left holding the head in your hand."

He leaned even closer and whispered.

"You got to follow the instructions, do it the way The Man says."

Chapter Twenty-Eight

CLEARLY, the flares weren't going to dispatch the coyotes into the woods with their tails between their legs. Crock was going to have to shoot them, so he decided he'd be better off taking them out now, pick off the biggest and meanest, than waiting until the final flare died and they all jumped him at once. He studied the animals. They were roughly the same size — about as big as Lassie but without the gorgeous fur. They were all mangy-looking, their brown fur that was streaked with black and gray was patchy. They looked malnourished, too, like they hadn't had a decent meal since ...

He shuddered. After they killed him, would they ... *eat him?*

The thought was so horrifying he felt vomit rise up in the back of his throat and had to swallow hard not to splatter the remains of the morning's McMuffin all over his shoes. How could he wrap his mind around such a thing? Even if he was dead when they rang the dinner bell — and he *would* be dead, one way or the other he had no intention of hanging around for that part — how could you think about an animal tearing your body apart?

What was it Woody Allen had said? He didn't mind dying, he just didn't want to be there when it happened.

How could he think about …?

He realized he was gritting his teeth so hard his jaws were aching, and that tears were running down his cheeks … from the smoke in his eyes, of course. Who was he trying to fool, he'd probably been crying for half an hour and hadn't even noticed. The prospect of being ripped to pieces by wild dogs would likely have that effect on anybody.

And his hands were shaking.

He stiffened his muscles, willed the tremors away. But he might not be able to keep a steady aim for much longer. He pulled the pistol out of his pocket and studied the pack, searching for his first victim. Biggest and strongest would draw the first short straw. That dog had already captured his attention. He wasn't a notably brawny specimen of coyote manhood, but Crock had watched him kill several of his brothers or sisters or cousins or whatever.

The dog was standing off to Crock's left, staring at him, making that weird cry. He took dead aim and pulled the trigger and a red blotch appeared in the fur on the animal's forehead between his ears and he collapsed like the puppeteer had dropped his strings.

So there, Mr. Darwin. At the end of the day, blind luck had more to do with surviving than being the meanest dog in the junkyard.

The other animals were startled by the sound and jumped back, but they didn't bolt.

He swung the pistol toward victim number two. It was a female who'd held her own against all the males, and from the look of her he was about to make a litter of puppies orphans.

Bam.

Beyond those two, it was a crap shoot, no pun intended. The other dogs were indistinguishable from each other. He dropped one more. Well, that was all the damage he could do. Now, there was nothing left but to wait.

When the final flare began to spit and fizzle, Crock spun the cylinder of his .38 with his thumb. Counting the rounds of ammunition … like maybe a brand new one had appeared out of nowhere while he wasn't looking. Or maybe he'd miscounted — shoot, it happened all the time when there was *only one round left*, easy mistake to make. Maybe there really were three. Or five.

One.

The flame on the final flare was spitting out more sparks than flames now.

His mouth was dry, his heart was pounding but his breathing was normal. In and out. One breath. Two.

The flare died.

There it was, then. The end of all things.

He threw the smoldering flare at the nearest dog, hoping maybe it'd catch the animal's fur on fire, but it didn't. There was a breathless moment and then, as if a starting gate had suddenly slammed open, they all came at him.

He put the pistol under his chin.

And instantly yanked it away again and fired, catching an attacking coyote in the face at a range of about ten feet.

Nope, these dogs were going to have to earn their supper. He would go out fighting.

He didn't throw the gun at them, just dropped it as he stepped back and grabbed the end of the burning branch he'd left on the edge of the fire for just this purpose, clutched it in a baseball grip and swung in what would surely have launched a ball over the centerfield fence. It caught a coyote broadside and knocked it into the fire, where it yelped and cried, staggering out of the flames, its fur on fire.

He didn't have time for another swing before the others were on him. He tried to grab one by the scruff of the neck to fling it into the fire, but it caught his hand in its canine teeth and hung on, dangled there.

He saw the one that would take out his throat coming, watched as it leapt into the air, fangs bared. He lurched away to avoid the blow, knew he wouldn't be fast enough, and closed his eyes for the impact of it slamming into his chest.

A VICE GRIP of fingers closed around Becca's upper arm and yanked her backwards. She'd have fallen if the hold on her arm hadn't kept her upright and for a moment she hung from it, dangled from it until it pulled her upright and set her on her feet, facing a man she could only see as a darker shadow on the shadows of the night.

Andi's vision, crazy people in the woods. And maybe this man was covered in blood, too. It was too dark to make out anything but a shape.

He stinks.

The random thought blew through her mind, one leaf among others scattered by an autumn breeze.

… now there'll just be two musketeers …

The dark shape grabbed her shoulders and shook her so violently her head snapped back and forth on her shoulders.

He's going to give me whiplash before he kills me.

Then he made a horrible sound, the sound of mirthless laughter, vicious bloodlust laughter. It froze her breath in her chest, a cold splash of reality that ordered her thoughts again as he let go of her left arm and pulled from a sheath at his side a huge blade — it seemed as big as the blade in the efreet's hand, a scimitar. But it wasn't shiny. It was stained dark and she knew what those stains were. The man began to draw it back slowly, over his head, still laughing. There was no angel here to stop him, to tell him "you can't harm them."

Seconds to live.

Ariel and Andi!

"Run!" she cried out, her last words. "Hide!"

❧

"Run! Hide!"

Another voice, another time:

"When I close this door, you run. Up the ladder into the pageant storage room. Don't close the trap door behind you, he might hear it. And you hide."

That's what Mommy had said to Andi the day she shoved her into the storage closet so the man possessed by a demon that looked like a lizard — with red eyes that didn't have a black spot in them and no eyelids at all — wouldn't shoot her. That was the last thing Mommy ever said to her. Then the man had killed Mommy.

He'd have killed Daddy, too, if Princess Buttercup hadn't told Andi what to do to stop him.

This man was going to kill Becca — but Princess Buttercup wasn't here to tell Andi what to do this time.

In her mind, Andi's voice sounded strangled and tear-clotted and terrified. But she thought maybe when God heard prayers, they didn't have a voice.

HELP ME. I have to help Becca get away — how?

IMAGES FORMED in Andi's mind as instantaneously as touching the little arrow on an iPhone screen.

JACK HIT the creek bed hard and collapsed in a PLF, rolling on the calf of his injured leg with a lightning bolt of pain, then his thigh and over onto his back.

He never stopped moving, just turned the motion sideways and rolled over the rifle, grabbing it in the process, right hand on the stock, left on barrel. But this time the surge of adrenaline into his brain didn't crank the world into slow motion as it had that day in Andi's classroom when he had killed the demon-possessed school shooter and shot Andi in the process.

It was real-time speed.

The small cat comes into view, lunging at him.

His fingers scramble for the trigger.

The cat's too close, so he uses the momentum of his roll to bring up the barrel of the rifle and slam it into the side of the cat's head. It's a glancing, off-balance blow, not a lot of force behind it, but enough to knock the cat sideways, off its feet.

The motion of the blow carries Jack sideways along with cat and he lands on his shoulder in the water.

He has one second, maybe two.
The trigger guard's wet, slick.
Bam!

The bullet strikes the cat in the chest in mid-pounce from a range of about ten inches.

With a strangled sound, not a cry, the cat crashed into Jack, knocking his rifle barrel sideways before splashing down into the creek. Jack yanked the rifle back in the direction of the other cat, finger firmly on the trigger now, ready to …

The other cat was tearing at the ball of bloody bandages, trying to free it from the bush where it had landed, paying him absolutely no attention at all.

As he moved in slow-motion, carefully getting his feet under him, his eyes made a full, 360-degree sweep of the shoreline and the creek up and downstream. None of the other cats reappeared. He waited maybe half a minute, prepared to take out anything that moved. Nothing did. The only sound was the snarling of the cat trying to tear the bloody bandages out of the bush. It's ball-like structure had disintegrated into strands of bloody cloth that the cat batted and snapped at.

Standing carefully, Jack stepped over the carcass of the dead bobcat, its chest ripped apart and its blood staining the creek water red. He didn't want to draw the attention of the other cat. If it attacked, another gunshot might summon the others. He walked backward one step at a time, head on a swivel, his eye on the other bobcat that appeared — at least for the moment — to have no interest in him. That could change in a heartbeat.

When he was a good distance downstream from the bobcat and saw no sign of any family members in the woods, he stepped out of the creek and began to move faster, turned sideways, looking back. A cat could move as silently as … well, as a *cat*, and he wouldn't likely hear an attack coming.

He moved as quickly as he could without making noise.

Downhill through the rapidly darkening forest.

The priority was no longer finding a cellphone tower — which might not do any good anyway and might be on some other mountain.

Jack was going back to the chapel. And Becca.

It was painful going, making his way down the mountainside on his injured leg. It was bleeding freely again and even if the wounds were not life-threatening, bleeding to death was! It seemed to take hours, but Jack no longer trusted his sense of time. It was already almost dark! It couldn't possibly be, but it was. He had to get out of the woods while there was still some daylight to see. And he had promised to be back to the chapel before nightfall.

Then he heard more gunshots. He froze for an instant and then started to run, heedless of the pain or the blood or the bobcats behind. The one gunshot he'd heard before had been concerning, but Jack knew Crock was a crack shot and had dropped whatever he'd taken out with one bullet. But Crock began firing what had to be the last rounds in Jack's Smith & Wesson .38 and Jack was certain he must have encountered some of Andi's 'bloody people in the woods."

He should have approached the chapel carefully, but his fear overrode his training and he burst out of the trees at a dead run. He took in the whole scene in a single glance. What he saw froze his blood. The carnage was astonishing. Dead, mangled corpses — dogs … *coyotes!* — were everywhere. Crock was backed up against the fire, holding off an attack with a burning stick.

Becca, Andi and Ariel were gone.

He was shooting before he told his mind to lift his rifle.

Caught one coyote in mid-pounce, but it slammed into Crock anyway and knocked him over. Then he picked off the others rapid-fire, dropping each with one shot.

Bam! Bam! Bam! Bam!

LINC THOUGHT he heard gunfire in the distance. Three shots — maybe four. A rifle. An M4? The sound was faint, and no one turned to look, but the people here couldn't have heard the sound over their own voices. He lay on his belly, looking out through a small opening he had made in the dense branches of a wisteria bush. He could hear from this spot most of what was said. Certainly, he could hear that the man intended to sacrifice Daniel by chopping off his head!

Linc didn't have any idea how he could stop them, though none was carrying a weapon of any kind that he could see except, knives, hatchets and the like. There must have been fifty people, maybe more, whipped up into a mindless mob if ever he'd seen one, by the words of the white-haired man in the suit, who had descended the porch steps and come to stand next to where they had dumped Daniel's body in the dirt. The man who had seen some kind of cosmic joke in the situation that escaped Linc and the rest of them.

Who was this guy? Where did he come from? Linc had never seen him before — he wasn't somebody you'd likely forget if you ever met him. He had to be new in town — Linc would know if he were a local. Oh, not that Linc recognized everyone in the crowd. He didn't. These people in the north end of Caverna County kept to themselves, didn't come into town often. You'd see them sometimes at the county fair — particularly the tractor pull. There was something about tractor pulls that engaged people who wouldn't climb out from under their rocks for anything else. But even if Linc couldn't have called them all by name, he recognized them … or the look of them, the family resemblance. And he actually did see people in the crowd of blood-smeared people whose names and families he did know. The presence of some of them shocked him. Others … well, mass murder and blood-smearing definitely fit in with their skillsets.

He could see Bob Huddleston, whose claim to familiarity was that he was the only man Linc had ever seen at the fair who could hit the platform with a sledgehammer and ring the bell every time. Even with the game rigged. He was the one who had carried Daniel through the woods. He had brought his wife and daughter with him. Well, the family that prays together …

Steve Hughes was an out-of-work coal miner, as were half the other men in the crowd. His wife was so severely dish-faced that both her chin and forehead extended farther than her nose.

There were Jim and Jerry Hayes. No surprise there. He'd last busted Jerry when he got so drunk one night at the Last Man Standing Saloon — which had since burned to the ground, to the dismay of not a single soul in town except its patrons — that he had stripped buck naked and run down Main Street in the middle of the night, peeing on every parking meter. When Linc arrested him, he had protested that if they weren't properly watered, they would never grow big and strong.

Judith Blevins and Jim Behning. Lauren Clough and Debbie Laseter Lloyd — who was either her cousin or her sister-in-law. Maybe both.

He could name others in the crowd, but the white-haired, white-bearded guy in a black suit fit for burying was a stranger.

So how had he gotten all these people to follow him down the barrel of a cannon in a matter of days? He was captivating, his voice almost hypnotic. But not supernaturally so. He was no Chapman Whitworth! Linc had listened to one of Whitworth's speeches on television and found himself agreeing with everything he said, admiring and respecting him — until he'd changed the channel and couldn't believe he'd bought what Whitworth was selling. Jack and the others said Whitworth had been possessed by a monster demon.

This guy wasn't possessed. As far as Linc would tell, none of them were. He'd need Andi or Becca to confirm that, given they could see demons and he couldn't, but none of them had superhuman strength. Huddleston, who had carried Daniel through the woods, had had to stop and get his breath several times and was panting and sweating when he dumped Daniel on the ground. And they were cooperating with each other, not snarling and nasty as Jack had described the Bad Kids from when he was a boy, who had attacked each other at the drop of a hat. These people seemed to get along just fine, were only hostile to the poor, unarmed victims they butchered.

He wasn't dealing with possessed people but he *was* dealing with a mob, a crazed mob that was being whipped into a frenzy by the white-haired man. He was dealing with mob mentality, too, and maybe he could use that. Mobs could be like a cattle stampede. It was possible to stop one and when you did, the cattle lost that herd instinct and wandered off by themselves. Trouble with trying to stop a stampede was you had to stand right out in front of it. Turn the lead cow. And if you failed, they would mow you down.

Chapter Twenty-Nine

JACK COVERED the distance between himself and Crock in
what felt like two giant leaps, knelt beside Crock and rolled
him over onto his back. A head wound — a slash across his
forehead that'd likely leave a permanent reminder of this
auspicious occasion. And a hand wound — nasty one.
Neither was life-threatening.

"Where are the girls — where's *Becca*?"

"They're in the car, safe," Crock gasped.

Jack felt like collapsing beside Crock in relief.

"Daniel and Linc?"

Crock just shook his head and shrugged.

"What's going on up there?" Theresa cried. "Major
Crocker! Crock! Is you alright?

"He's fine!" Jack called out to her.

"Jack?"

There was surprise, wonder and relief in her voice.

"Don't you go telling me he's fine when he ain't," she
said. "Me and the major done worked all that out. I want a
reality check."

"Reality is …" Crock said, his voice airy and shaky, "I'm fine."

"You boys either need to take some classes or just give up lying altogether 'cause ain't neither one of you any good at it," Theresa said as Crock sat up. Jack stood and offered his hand to pull Crock to his feet.

Crock shook his head.

"Scenery's pretty good down here right now so I think I'll just sit for a while and wait for the tour bus."

Crock wiped the blood out of his eye and it promptly refilled. He felt his forehead for the wound, found it and winced, and said, "I bet *this* looks waaaay worse than it is."

He looked at his hand then. A coyote must have buried its fangs in the meat of his palm, bitten all the way through, then the puncture had ripped sideways when Crock flung the animal off, maybe tearing out ligaments and tendons.

"Now this puppy, no pun intended, *is* as bad as it looks."

And when the painkillers in his adrenaline high wore off, it was going to *hurt*, too. A lot. Jack could have given him a pretty good estimate of how *much* it was going to hurt if he'd let himself feel the agony of his own leg wound.

"You look like you've been in a catfight," Crock said, grimacing as he cradled his left hand in his right. "And lost."

"Final score: Carpenter one, bobcats nothing."

"Bobcats? I wouldn't want to cross one of those even if it was in a good mood."

"Have you seen the girls, Jack?" Theresa called. "Did they make it to the car safe?"

Make it to the car?

He shot a look at Crock, confused and frightened.

"I thought you said—"

"It started getting gnarly, so I sent them to the car while I entertained our guests here. I'm sure they're—"

His words were cut off by a sound from the woods. It was a sound Jack had heard before and an echo from the past joined it to make it ring like a bell in his head.

A scream, a wail of terror, a wild angry cry from the nearby woods.

Becca!

Jack turned toward the sound, but Crock grabbed his ankle before he could move.

"Take this," Crock said, reaching for the end of a burning branch that was propped up handily on a rock. "It'll be dark soon."

No, not soon. Now. The gathering gloom of twilight had darkened but the fire was so bright Jack hadn't noticed. Night had come.

THE SHAPE in the forest that was a man backhanded Becca when she told the girls to run — not even hard, but casually, the way you slap a bug off your arm at a picnic.

Even so, the blow was staggering and she lurched backward a step, went down on one knee. She stumbled upward, trying to stand. He towered above her, watching her as he took the blade in both hands. She cringed backward and screamed a long wailing cry of fear and anger and loss for all that would never be.

The man lifted the blade high above his head. He was holding it at an angle, like maybe he intended to strike Becca with the hilt and not the blade. Becca raised her arm to ward off the blow, and he began to bring it back down—

Andi suddenly cried out: "Three Stooges!"

Becca's response was a reflex. She lurched at the man, put her palms on his chest and shoved as hard as she could. He tried to step back but instead he lost his balance and fell over backwards.

"Run away!" she cried out to Andi, who had rolled as the man fell over her and was now stumbling to her feet. Becca barked out a contemptuous laugh at the man sprawled on the forest floor in front of her.

"Hey you, pathetic troll — catch me if you can!" Then she turned and bolted away into the darkness. She called out over her shoulder. "Come and get me!"

She'd never escape, of course. That was out of the question — she could barely see where she was going. But she could draw him away from the girls if she could stay free for a little while, make it far enough that the girls would have a chance to hide.

Her billowing skirt became a streak of white, moving through the trees like a ghost, a splotch of light on the gray-black canvas of dark fog and night shadows. Walls of trees materialized out of nothingness in front of her, the stalks of saplings rose up out of the forest floor, black fingers reaching for her, catching her long shirt, pulling at it, dragging her down.

Becca stumbled, went down on one knee, lurched to her feet, staggering, tripping over her skirt, her bare feet cut and bruised by stones and tree roots on the forest floor. At first, she heard no pursuit. Did he not take the bait?

~

Andi never even made it a full step. She got up but felt the man's hand grab her ankle before she had a chance to move.

332

She fell back on the ground, wiggling and squirming, trying to get free, but his hold on her was a metal band — solid and unbreakable.

He was still on the ground and he sat up, never releasing the pressure on her ankle. Then he got to his knees. She rolled over onto her back and kicked at him, but she might as well have been kicking a barn door.

Andi's heart was banging so fast she could feel only a solid hum in her chest and she was so scared she couldn't breathe at all.

Terrible things had happened to Miranda Elizabeth Burke in her short life. She had been frightened before, terrified. But this time was different. She was utterly alone, in the dark woods of a horror nightmare. It was like she had seen it in the vision. And then the vision just stopped.

Now, she understood why. It stopped because there was *nothing* after — she was dead.

Uncle Jack had been there to rescue her when the men kidnapped her and took her to that cabin in the woods.

Now, Uncle Jack was climbing a mountain, miles away.

The angel had walked with her, held her hand when she had to enter the horror of the cave and face the monster.

The angel couldn't come here. It was too dark.

The man's face was worse than any horror movie, any Hollywood animated mask. It was mashed-in, flat, no ridge with eyebrows on it or holes where eyes fit. It was like all the bones in his face had been crushed, shoved inward. Most of his lower jaw was crushed over onto the side of his face so his tongue hung out like a dog's between his broken teeth.

He had a huge knife in his hand that he'd drawn to use on Becca. Now, he raised it above Andi.

This was it. Andi Burke was going to die.

~

FOR A TIME, she thought maybe … just maybe she'd gotten away. She heard no pursuit and surely she'd hear—

And then she did. Branches behind her snapped. The bushes rustled. He was back there, coming. She could smell him. He was very close and she knew any second she would feel his fingers on her shoulder. She couldn't hide — not dressed in white in a dark forest. She could only run.

And *fight.*

She'd make a good fight of it, hold him off as long as she could, every second was time for the girls to get far away.

Jack had called her bright red fingernails "claws" that day when she hopped into his car after she'd had them done at the nail salon.

The memory welled up out of her soul.

"YOU PLAN on using those on me?"

The smile on his face actually looks comfortable there. Even when they were children, he was solemn, sober, and now she understands why — how could she possibly have been stupid enough to believe his ridiculous stories about where he got all those black eyes and split lips? Well, she'd make it up to him, she'd spend her life giving him ten days of happiness in exchange for every day he'd been in pain.

"You do know that's assault with a deadly weapon." He leans over and kisses the tip of her nose. "And on a police officer, too. A class C felony. They'll haul you off to Danforth—"

Danforth Correctional Facility was the last of a string of prisons where her father, the infamous Billy Ray Hawkins, had spent twenty years for growing marijuana. Her testimony had put him away.

Jack must see the color drain out of her face. She's so surprised by the intrusion of ugliness into the bright sunshine of her day, of her whole life now — that she can actually feel herself go pale.

"Becca, I'm sorry. I didn't mean to—"

She puts her fingers to his lips, wants to tell him it's okay, that she understands, that she is totally overreacting. But she can't because she doesn't have enough air to speak. And because they'd agreed in the very beginning not to do that. Not to call anything an overreaction. Given the damage that facing down a fifty-foot demon from hell had done to both their psyches, particularly hers, any and all feelings were from that point forward and forever afterward to be deemed valid and appropriate.

"Did a body surface?"

Not any particular body. A whole cemetery full, a montage of images from her childhood.

Her father liked to leave the bedside table lamp on … so he could see.

Then she feels her eyes well with tears. Jack takes her tenderly into his arms and holds her tight, rocking her back and forth and whispering words that aren't words into her hair.

"It won't always be like this," *he says tenderly.* "It won't always be a take-your-breath-away hurt."

Then he releases her, holds her away from him and looks deep into her eyes.

"I'm not trying to put lipstick on this pig. You're never going to forget. All we can do is wrap the awful up in wonderful memories, wind them around and around it, thicker and thicker for years, until it's buried so deep … you know it's there, but you can't feel the pain anymore."

SHE AND JACK were supposed to be getting married today!

A sound like a bull running through the forest was right behind her now. His stink rose around her like a miasma of … *what?* Dead bodies.

She lurched forward with all her strength, her breath screaming in and out of her lungs, stumbled as a gray wall suddenly appeared out of the fog and became the huge trunk of a tree.

When she felt his hand touch her arm, she made it another few steps or so before she tripped. Reaching out, she caught herself with the tree, smashing her cheek into the bark, the woodsy aroma momentarily covering the reek of his nearness.

His fingers tightened in a vice on her shoulder then and she knew the chase was over. She'd never get away from him now, not again, not even with Andi there to trip him when she shoved.

The pursuit was over. The fight had begun.

She whirled around with her right elbow sticking out, catching him on the chin with the point of it. His grip on her shoulder loosened and she continued the spin around until she was facing him. Then she reached up, grabbed his face in her hands and dug her thumbnails into both his eyes.

JACK RACED off into the woods, brandishing the torch, totally disregarding the fact that the torch was a gigantic "Shoot Me" sign, flashing in red and yellow neon.

He should have been approaching the situation quietly, too, not barging into whatever was going on like a rhino into a tea party.

He tried to care about those things, but the burst of adrenaline fear that surged into his system at the sound of Becca's voice had propelled him forward with the force of a nuclear missile. The rocket fuel of his fear would carry him all the way to his target — who would drop him in his tracks and still murder Becca if he didn't *get a grip!*

It took every speck of will he possessed, every ounce of self-control, to stop running, to stand still, to think!

He didn't even know the direction the sound had come from, for crying out loud. How did he expect to save Becca from whatever terror had forced that cry from her throat if he didn't even know where she was?

Think!

Becca and the girls had been on their way to the car when something happened.

The girls!

Andi and Ariel. If Becca were in some kind of danger, so were they!

He honestly didn't think he could be more frightened but the prospect of the "crazy people in the woods covered in blood" hurting those children — *precious* Andi — almost clamped such an iron grip of fear around his chest that he couldn't get his breath.

Think.

Being on their way to the car narrowed the search area somewhat — but there was still a lot of forest on both sides of the pathway for them to get lost in and he had neither the time nor the skill to go to the path and try to see if he could locate tracks.

What could he do? How could he find them? And there was *no time.*

Becca had sounded so terrified. He had seen her frightened often, too often. That day in the forest when the Bad Kids had kidnapped her, the look of fear on her face had broken his heart and sent blind rage through his body like an electric shock.

But he couldn't do anything to help her that day. He had tried, but he'd been no match for the superhuman power of the Bad Kids possessed by demons. He had failed, had sat in the dirt and watched them take her away.

CALL yourself a cop and you can't even help the woman you love? What kind of man are you?

IT WAS like someone had whispered in his ear. And it was true!

He felt the same sense of helplessness. He couldn't help her then and he couldn't help her now — indeed, was probably already too late to do her any good even if he knew where she was — which he didn't.

Daniel's description of walking into the sanctuary and seeing his Emily sprawled on the floor in a puddle of blood took his breath away. Noooooo. Becca was going to become his wife.

No, she's going to die and it will be your fault.

"HELP!"

He sobbed the word out loud. Or maybe he only thought it. He didn't know for sure, but he did know it was a prayer and he hadn't prayed since the day in the tunnel when he'd told God he had the wrong man. When he'd told God he didn't trust him, didn't even like him.

"I have to find her. *Please!*"

There was a sudden rustling sound in the bushes only a few feet away and he whirled toward it, raising the rifle into position, his finger inside the trigger guard.

"Uncle Jack! I knew you'd come."

A child's voice. He released the pressure he'd begun to apply to the trigger as the little girl burst out of the bushes where she must have been hiding. Jack's heart breathed her name in a sigh of relief — *Andi!*

Thank you, God. That was a prayer, too.

Ariel trailed along behind her, looking very small and frightened.

"The Ugly Man grabbed Becca but I made him fall down so she could get away and then he grabbed me—"

The child was babbling.

"Andi, where is she?"

"I don't know … it's so dark, I can't see and neither can Becca."

"I'll show you," said Ariel and darted off through the undergrowth like a baby rabbit. Jack followed with Andi on his heels.

They wound through the trees, the light from Jack's burning stick dancing off tree trunks when they materialized out of the darkness. Ariel stopped, unsure now. She pointed. "I think it's that—"

A growl, a cry of pain and rage tore through the foliage. *Close!* Jack could follow the sound.

"Stay here!" he told the girls, and continued toward the grumbling roar it was hard to imagine came from a human throat.

Thrusting the torch out ahead of him to light the way, Jack stumbled into a small clearing.

Becca!

Her white dress shone like a lighthouse beacon. She was backed up against a tree, cowering. A man stood in front of her, his hands on his own face, roaring in rage.

Jack took two more steps out of the trees, dropped the burning stick on the ground, lifted his rifle and fired three rounds. All body shots. He wasn't close enough to attempt a head shot. The first bullet caught the man in the side, spun him around and Jack planted the next two bullets in his chest.

The man staggered. *But he didn't fall!* Three shots from an M4 and he didn't go down!

He screamed, though, so he must have been hit. Reaching out like a blind man, he grabbed at Becca but she ducked away. Jack fired two more shots that had no more effect than the first three.

What the …?

The man was lurching around like he couldn't keep his balance, his hands on his face, shaking his head. In the flickering torchlight Jack caught only a glimpse of the man's face when the first bullet spun him around, and Jack recoiled in horror. No wonder Andi had called him the Ugly Man. Then he realized the guy couldn't see. Where his eyes should have been were holes gushing blood and gore down his cheeks. Making a sound more feral than human, the man turned with a jerky-jerky movement and made for the trees.

Jack took one step to follow him, to finish him off … but how would he kill him when he caught him?

The man vanished into the darkness of the woods.

Jack raced to where Becca crouched on the ground, her eyes wide with horror, shock, joy, relief, surprise—

Kneeling, he wrapped his arms around her, held her so tight against his chest he was sure he was choking the life out of her. But he couldn't seem to let her go, just held her, whispering words that weren't words into her hair.

He couldn't hear the sounds of the man staggering away through the trees, crashing, blundering sounds. He should have heard them, but instead, he heard only silence.

Chapter Thirty

THERESA CONTINUED TO PRAY, the kind of prayers that don't have words. And it was a good thing that she didn't have to put words on 'em, that God heard her in ways didn't need words because she was having trouble forming words. And focusing. And making sounds.

She felt like she was somewhere between being awake and aware and being unconscious. She couldn't feel them cold rocks underneath her no more and that was a good thing, too. No, it was a bad thing if she couldn't even feel her own self.

She shook her head to clear it, only it didn't clear. She thought of a bottle of salad dressing — the oil's all together, solid-like, with the vinegar separate . But when you shake the bottle, the solid layer of oil comes apart into little gobs all floating around in the vinegar. Her thoughts was them gobs of oil — just floating around random — all shook up from each other so she couldn't put any of them together in something solid that made sense. Her whole self was like that, really, just floating around in the world but not really there, connected.

She wasn't cold no more because you had to be able to feel your own self to be cold. It was just her head now she could move and look around and hear some, but everything else below her neck had disappeared. She tried to scratch her nose but her hand didn't do what her brain told it to do. That couldn't be good.

She was lying down in a cave at night and it was hard to get any darker than a cave. But somehow it *was* getting darker, like somehow the darkness was growing inside her and it didn't matter how bright it was outside. The flickering light from the campfire above that she'd watched dance on the pile of rocks and hunks of building on top of her was getting dimmer.

She knew the fire wasn't going out. *She* was going out.

The fire wasn't dying. She was.

JACK HELD Becca to his chest, felt her heart fluttering, not individual beats but the sound of a hummingbird's wings. She felt so fragile, like she might shatter into a thousand tiny pieces of colored glass. She'd always seemed fragile, small and defenseless. He had no memory of that time when they were children that she stood up to the efreet in the cavern. He'd seen it, but the memory was gone. Little Becca and the towering angel, surely as beautiful and magnificent as Andi's had been when it rose up to face the mighty demon. He had imagined it so many times it had become an artificial memory, like he had actually seen it.

Jack called out to Andi and Ariel, told them it was safe now and two little rabbits emerged from the nearby bushes. Andi picked up the burning stick Jack had dropped as she approached. Little girls in white dresses and oversized men's jackets.

Then Jack remembered he still had his phone in his pocket. It might not function as a phone, but it still turned on, at least it had when he'd shoved it down into his pants pocket a lifetime ago when he'd started up the mountain.

He let go of Becca to get it out of his pocket but she continued to cling to him, her arms around him, holding him fiercely — as if the strength of her grip alone would keep him from ever being taken from her side again.

When he drew the phone out and thumbed it on, she finally let go and stepped back, the glow of the screen lighting her up, a pale apparition on the black background of the night.

He tapped the flashlight app and turned it toward the trees where the man had retreated, searching. He saw no one, and what he would have done if the man had been there, he didn't know. Bullets hadn't even slowed him down.

Jack had *shot* him. Five times.

"I blinded him," Becca said, "put out his eyes." She was searching the dark woods where Jack's flashlight app lit the trees. "He couldn't see … so how did … how could he get away through the woods if he couldn't see?"

He swung the flashlight beam back toward Becca and saw movement on the ground next to her.

What in the world—?

Bugs! Worms! Maggots! Squirming in a writhing pile on the forest floor.

Becca gasped when she saw them, muttering something about "the smell" but he missed it.

"He could have killed me," said a little voice out of the darkness. Andi. Jack had almost forgotten that the little girls were standing only a few feet away.

"Do you mean he *caught* you?" Becca was horrified. "And you somehow got away?"

Andi nodded. Becca held out her arms and Andi and Ariel rushed into them. From the comfort of Becca's embrace, Andi continued.

"But I didn't get away. He let me go. He caught my foot when I tripped him. He was right on top of me and he was going to kill me and then … I don't know … he stopped and just looked at me. Then he tried to talk. His mouth was all messed up and maybe he didn't talk with it because he almost couldn't. And then he let go of my foot, got up and ran after Becca."

Andi pulled out of Becca's arms and held out something on the palm of her hand.

"He dropped this. He was on his hands and knees, leaning over me, and it fell out of his shirt pocket."

It was a heavy gold ring. There was no stone. The top of the ring was flat with a shield shape surrounded by leaves. Beneath the shield was a single word: Harvard.

It might have been only the second one of those Jack had ever seen. The first had been on the hand of Jeff Kendrick, which he had only noticed because Daniel had pointed it out to him once disdainfully when they were all sitting together in Theresa's living room.

"Wearing a high school class ring tells everybody: my life peaked at seventeen and I'm going to die in the same town I grew up in," Daniel had whispered into his ear. "But if you need to advertise the fact that you went to Harvard on your finger, you are definitely doing life wrong."

As a matter of fact, Jeff's had looked a lot like this one.

Jack felt a greater chill than the already frigid air blow on the back of his neck. He took the ring from Andi and examined it in the glare of the phone's flashlight. A year was engraved on the side of the ring: the class of 1997. So was Jeff's.

Whoa, Nellie. Jeff Kendrick was dead.

"He just … let you go?" Becca asked. "Didn't try to … he had a knife."

"Oh, he was going to kill me. He raised the knife up over his head, you know, like you do when you're going to stab somebody. But then he just looked at me and lowered the knife back down. That's when he tried to talk."

"What did he say?" Jack asked.

"I don't know. All I understood for sure was my mother's name."

Jack stopped breathing. "Emily?"

Andi nodded. "Uh huh. And maybe something like 'little girl.'"

The words came out of Jack's mouth before he had a chance to think them.

"'Take good care of *Emily's little girl*'?"

"Yes! That's it. How do *you* know what the Ugly Man said?"

THE WHITE-HAIRED MAN removed his sunglasses then and looked Daniel full in the face.

To look into those eyes was to look into a yawning black pit of evil and depravity. They positively glowed with malice and hatred. But the brown orbs were more than windows on an interior filled with an anger and hatred and malicious intent. There was intelligence there, too. Cunning. Craftiness. And the kind of brazen confidence only the very powerful or the very delusional possessed.

Hold the look for more than a second, though, and you saw deeper than that. Layers deeper, an elevator plunging on a broken chain and the other floors fly by, each uglier and darker and scarier and more evil than the last.

Continue to hold that look at your own peril because there was much, much more beyond that. Utter despair, desolation and ruin as far as the eye could see — a barren wasteland devoid of all hope. A wave of hopelessness washed over Daniel and he felt a cold blanket of endless depression settle over him. All effort was futile. All thought was purposeless. Nothing and nobody mattered. The faces of loved ones appeared and then were expunged from the heart and mind — the images shriveling up like parchment in a fire or merely vanishing slowly, wiped off his consciousness with a cosmic eraser.

Jack.

Crock.

Theresa.

Andi.

Andi! No!

Daniel wrenched his gaze out of the grip of the Chosen One with a strength of will he had no idea he possessed. Nothing … *nothing* was going to take Andi from him.

And the spell was broken … at least it had felt like he'd been in some kind of altered state, some kind of trance, because suddenly Daniel was aware of his surroundings again, of being on his knees, the chunks of gravel punching through the fabric of his suit pants, the cold breeze ruffling his hair, the lump on the back of his head making its presence known with heartbeat bursts of pain.

But the man looking down on him was no longer larger than life, and as he broke the stranger's gaze his own eyes passed down over his white-bearded face — and stopped. Hung there on a nail. He stared then. Not because he had been willed to do so. He stared because he couldn't believe what his eyes were telling him.

There was a mark on the man's cheek. Beneath his left eye.

Becca's voice came from a long way away, not just in distance but in time, as if she were speaking to Daniel from that summer when they were twelve years old.

THE THREE MUSKETEERS are sitting under a tree in a meadow with flowers in it. Sunflowers. They have spread out a blanket on the ground and have taken out their lunch from the picka-nick basket he and Jack had made for Becca in shop class out of a five-gallon gasoline can.

"I asked him once about it and he said it wasn't any of my business so I never asked again," Becca said. "But one night when he was drunk he grabbed my arm and pulled me up close, inches from his face and made me look at it."

"'See this here teardrop tattoo. It's on the outside, but it reminds me they's always tears on the inside where people can't see. I got it for other people to look at — to let them know they'd be crying a river full of tears if they ever crossed me.'"

THE TEARDROP TATTOO. The day he and Jack went to Danforth Prison to ask Billy Ray where to find Becca, Daniel had noticed that the tattoo was still visible on his face.

He had wondered at the time why that old mark under his left eye was the only tattoo on his face — since every part of his body you could see was covered in full sleeves. Clearly he'd been the canvas for more than one tattoo-artist cellmate over the years.

All the other art made the lone tattoo on his cheek stand out, faded but distinct. An aging medal of distinction.

What Daniel was looking at was Billy Ray Hawkins's tattoo. His breath did freeze in his chest then, a solid glacier of icy terror. It couldn't be! He had watched Billy Ray die! He had fallen, vanished into the crack in the floor in the cavern, knocked off his feet by Jeff Kendrick.

When his eyes shot back up to meet the white-haired man before him, the man spotted the recognition in them. He threw his head back and roared with laughter a second time.

This man couldn't be Billy Ray Hawkins. Billy Ray was dead.

❧

THE UGLY MAN couldn't be Jeff Kendrick. Jeff was dead.

Of course, that would explain why Jack's bullets hadn't stopped him. Hard to kill a man who's already dead.

"I *didn't* know the man said that to you," he told Andi. His voice was level. Not a good sign — a level voice. "Your daddy told me that a man said those words to him once, when he was in the cave and Billy Ray was threatening to cut his head off."

"Jeff Kendrick?" Andi asked. "But I thought Jeff Kendrick died in that cave."

"So did I." His voice shook then. Good. It was reassuring to know that his own response to the situation was *normal*, given that absolutely nothing else going on around him was. Finding out a dead guy was up walking around was — what? Shocking. Stunning. Staggering? All of the above — and if it didn't upset you, that would definitely call into question your own sanity. But then, how could you possibly be sane and countenance even the possibility that a man who was dead … *who had been dead for months* … suddenly wasn't anymore?

Becca was shaking her head *no*, a look of horror and

astonishment on her face, obviously emotionally backing up from that conclusion so fast she could have tripped over her own feet.

"How could …?" She started to physically back away then, shaking her head. "No, it couldn't be … It's not Jeff Kendrick. It's not! It's … somebody else."

"Who?" Jack didn't want to contradict her. He wanted to agree with her, that it couldn't be Jeff, that it was somebody else.

"I don't know! He found the ring or stole it or … bought it. He wasn't wearing it, just had it in his pocket." Not a lot of Harvard class rings for sale on eBay, but Jack didn't say that. Becca's voice was getting higher and reedier. "How would I know who it is? I just know who it's *not*. It's not Jeff Kendrick."

Well, since it wasn't Jeff, it had to be some random somebody taking a stroll in the woods who just happened to have a 1997 Harvard class ring in their pocket, that's all. Shoot, there were probably dozens of folks in these hills who'd graduated from Harvard. And who also killed indiscriminately but *let Andi live*, a man who knew what Daniel had told only three people in the world — Theresa, Jack and Becca.

"Who else—?"

"No!" Becca yelled, her beautiful face contorted. "It's not! No, no, no!"

The last "no" trailed off in a wail and she clamped her hands over her mouth and stared wide-eyed at Jack.

Then he got it. Realization hit him all in a rush, all the harder for the fact that he should have seen it all along. Jeff Kendrick and Billy Ray Hawkins had died together in that cave last fall. Now, Jeff Kendrick was — what? Alive? No, just *back* somehow. And his "return" begged the question — was Billy Ray numbered among the not-dead, too?

Then her wailing cut off like she'd flipped a switch.

"Jack, you're hurt!"

The flashlight beam from the phone had briefly lit his leg and Becca'd seen it.

She forced him to point the beam at his injury, sucked in a gasp, then reached under her skirt to her petticoat and began to rip the fabric, tearing the pieces into bandage-sized strips.

"I can see," Andi said, her voice small. "So can you." Becca's head snapped up.

Ariel had led Jack to Becca because Andi couldn't see. She'd said Becca couldn't see either, but clearly she could now.

"Yes, I … I don't know when I—"

"It was after you screamed. I was trying to keep up with Uncle Jack, running with Ariel through the trees. And then the dark … the mist … it went away."

Becca didn't say anything else, just went back to bandaging Jack's leg.

"You couldn't see and then you could and—" he began.

"I blinded him," she said, without lifting her head. "Put his eyes out."

"Are you saying … that as long as he could see, you couldn't. But when he …?"

"I don't know what I'm saying," she snapped. "Just hold still."

THE WHITE-HAIRED MAN burst out laughing again. Now was the time, before he leveled the power of his voice on the mob and the stampede started.

Linc's plan was pathetic, he granted. But when pathetic

was all you've got, you go with it. Linc would bluff. He'd drop the white-haired man if he had to — probably would — then Bob Huddleston, the big guy who had carried Daniel through the woods, followed by Jim Hayes, who'd convinced Jonah Ballard to bring Daniel back with them instead of killing him on the spot.

He didn't have a clear shot at Jonah in the crowd or he'd have dropped him, too. Surely that'd make an impression. Rapid fire, one, two, three.

In theory at least, that should convince the others they would suffer the same fate unless they let Daniel go. Of course, then he'd only have rounds enough for thirteen more, but even though these people were familiar with guns, what they used were hunting rifles, shotguns, .30-06 deer rifles and .22's. Linc's Glock was puny by comparison, but every gun appears big when you're looking down the barrel of it. He doubted anybody in the crowd would recognize what kind of gun it was, and thanks to television cop shows and movies, people never thought about a weapon's ammunition, since James Bond and the make-my-day types not only never counted their own shots but never ran out — even though they also never reloaded.

Linc stood up suddenly behind the bush, then stepped to the side of it so the people could see him clearly — take note of the uniform and make no mistake about who he was. He had his pistol aimed at the white-haired man's chest.

At the sight of him, the crowd jumped back. That was a good sign. The white-haired man didn't appear either startled or alarmed. That was not a good sign.

"That's enough," Linc said. He was matter-of-fact, had learned over the years that if you had to *act* menacing and dangerous you probably were neither. "Nobody's chopping anybody's head off."

He spoke to Daniel. "Daniel, you're coming with me."

When Daniel started to rise, the man reached out a restraining hand and put it on his shoulder.

"And you are?" he asked Linc.

"Caverna County Sheriff Hezekiah Lincoln. And you are?" Linc kept his gun leveled at the man's chest.

"I am the Chosen One and you are interfering with a religious ceremony. Last I checked, the First Amendment of the Constitution guaranteed freedom of religion in this country."

"Last I checked, premeditated murder was a capital offense in this country."

"The laws of God are higher than the laws of man."

This was dragging out too long. Every second gave the crowd a chance to get over their surprise, to calm down … and maybe time enough to start doing a little math.

"I'll say this one time," Linc said. "Let him go."

The man didn't take his hand off Daniel's shoulder.

Chapter Thirty-One

WELL, now here was a twist the Chosen One hadn't seen coming. The county sheriff had come uninvited to his little party, too. Who else was out there wandering around in the woods — Elvis?

What to do, what to do?

They could kill him, of course. A Glock 22 .40 caliber holds sixteen shots, if you load one in the chamber. And the minions would get to him before he had a chance to kill more than half a dozen of them. The rest would literally tear the sheriff limb from limb if that's what the Chosen One told them to do.

There was a certain thrill to that notion. He'd always wanted to off a cop. He'd done a prison guard, once, slipped a shiv into his belly when no one was around to see and nobody suspected a thing because he was, after all, a model prisoner. He'd even managed to frame Big Al Conklin for it and that part had been almost as much fun as killing the guard — waiting for the lights to dim in the cellblock because it took a lot of juice to fry a man.

Sharing in the group murder of a cop would definitely

solidify his troops. Besides that, he'd still have Daniel Burke to play with and that had already been so much fun. Before it was over, Daniel Burke would be pleading for death, just like Theresa Washington's son Isaac had before he'd cut him up — alive — with a chainsaw. Making Daniel Burke beg, that was worth the price of admission.

But killing the sheriff might not be the wisest, shrewdest option and the Chosen One had to think strategically now here at the beginning, position himself for what was to come. If they let the sheriff go, that would solidify the troops, too — maybe more than killing him. They were all still functioning under the delusion that there would be no consequences for their crimes, that they'd never get caught — because Judgement Day would intervene and the God of the Universe would pardon them from their sins, so let it be written, so let it be done. If the sheriff lived, he could tell the world about what they'd done. There'd be no going back then.

Couldn't very well abandon a cause once the law knew you'd committed murder for it. Besides, the Chosen One didn't want to lose followers, the first crop, the blood-drenched super-fans.

And Daniel Burke! What a *delightful surprise,* a tiny sip of the frosted beer mug foaming with power, retribution and revenge he would one day drink from deeply, drain to the last drop. Daniel would still be around later. If Daniel somehow got killed in the crossfire, the Chosen One would never find out what in the Sam Hill he'd been doing out in the woods dressed up for a funeral!

Let him go, let them both go. For now.

"Now, Sheriff, can we talk about—"

Shock and awe.

Linc fired. His first round caught the white-haired man in the center of his chest, knocking him backward. Linc instantly swung the gun barrel around to Bob Huddleston and sent a bullet into his chest, too, and blood squirted out like he'd hit a water balloon. His third target had had time to turn and run and Linc shot Don Cowdrey in the back. He fell into the arms of Lauren Clough, knocking her down. She screamed, began to shriek,

"You shot him! You shot the poor man *in the back.*"

Her righteous indignation over such an egregious transgression of civil behavior rang a little hollow, given that she'd bragged about hacking a defenseless groundskeeper to death with a meat cleaver.

Daniel had leapt to his feet after the first shot and ran toward Linc, right into the line of fire so that Linc wouldn't have dared to take another shot even if he'd had one. He blocked Linc's view for a moment so Linc didn't see the man get up, if, indeed, he had ever fallen down. The next time he saw the white-haired man, he was standing, watching Daniel go. There was no blood on the front of his shirt from the bullet wound.

How could he possibly have missed from this distance? No, he didn't miss — the man staggered. But why wasn't he dead?

He and Daniel backed away a few feet, far enough that with one step they'd be hidden from view by the bushes.

"Follow us and I'll pick you off one by one, by one."

Well, one by one, anyway. At some point he'd have to throw the gun at them.

The two stepped out of sight, and the sheriff grabbed Daniel's arm and whispered, "This way!"

Instead of turning into the woods, they ran as fast as they could just out of sight of the building all the way to the back side of it. Then Linc instinctively held up his hand in a fist, which Daniel must have known from hanging around Jack's SWAT team meant stop. They waited. There was no sound of pursuit. The Chosen One was talking again to the crowd but from their position they could only catch his voice, not what he was saying. Linc put his finger to his lips, then lead Daniel in a diagonal line that took them into the woods to the top of the ridge.

CROCK HAD TAKEN off his shoe and used his sock to bind up his injured hand. He couldn't imagine that a stinky sock could be good for a wound like that, but bleeding to death could ruin your whole day. He had watched the spot where Jack had run off into the woods for as long as he could see the speck of light from the torch. Then the woods went dark again.

At least it was a clear night and there was a full moon. Of course, it couldn't possibly be night yet, couldn't be more than four-thirty, maybe five o'clock in the afternoon. It was, however, indisputably *dark* and there you have it. The moon was full, though a gigantic harvest moon on the Fourth of July, casting light so bright Crock thought he might be able to read the ingredients label on a bottle of aspirin, if he'd had a bottle of aspirin. And right now he'd give his kingdom for an aspirin. He couldn't seem to take his eyes off the moon. How could a big old yellow moon lighting up the sky look sinister? It managed.

In the moonlight, he could see the carcasses of the dead coyotes out beyond the light of the bonfire. He saw one of them move nearby, grabbed a hunk of firewood with his good hand, staggered to his feet, lurched toward the beast and clubbed it to death before it could come around totally and remember that killing the old man by the campfire was on his to-do list.

Then a wave of dizziness washed over Crock and he collapsed back on his easy-chair rock. He was almost grateful for the pain in his hand. It helped keep his mind focused and tethered to the right here, right now. If he let it wander out there trying to guess what might be happening to the others, the pain of those possibilities hurt way worse than where a coyote had savaged his palm. Jack, Daniel and Linc had agreed to be back before dark, and sundown had come and gone a long time ago. They didn't likely stop off for a beer on the way home. They would have shown up if they could have — which meant they couldn't. He had told himself that the girls had made it to the car and were safe there. Clearly, Becca wasn't in the car — she was out in the woods screaming. So where were Andi and Ariel?

Unfortunately, he didn't have to guess what was happening to Theresa. She was right here and hadn't been really coherent for — how long? He instinctively looked at his wrist. Even his wind-up watch had stopped. So much for takes a licking and keeps on ticking. He'd kept her alert and engaged in conversation for as long as he could. But then he'd gotten busy with the coyotes. The contemplation of being ripped to pieces by wild dogs had more or less demanded his full attention and had driven thoughts of Theresa out of his mind. But as soon as Jack ran off, Crock called out to her to ask how she was doing. She didn't answer at first and when she did it was worse than no answer at all.

"Bishop? Is that you?" Her voice was weak and trembly.

"No, Theresa, it's me, Major Crocker." That's what she usually called him. "How's the weather down there?"

"Where's Bishop?"

"He's not here."

"Well, go find him, then. He done left me stuck here and I need to get home and make supper."

"Can you move — wiggle your toes?"

"What kind of question is that? Can *you* wiggle *yours*?"

There was some life in that at least — a hopeful sign. But she didn't tell him about her toes.

"I'm good on toes. Fingers, not so much. Wiggle your toes for me, okay?"

She didn't answer.

"Theresa …"

"Wiggle your own toes!"

She said nothing at all after that. He kept trying, calling out to her, trying to get her to reply, but there was no response from the depths of the pile of rubble.

Then he saw a small flashlight beam and shapes appear out of the woods and his heart leapt into his throat. *Crazy people covered with blood.* Jack had taken the rifle with him. What Crock had by way of defending himself was a handful of nothing, *in only one hand*. It felt too pathetic to grab a stick from the pile of kindling to fight them off, and he wouldn't make it twenty feet if he made a run for it, so Crock did the only thing he could do — he stood his ground. Well, *sat* his ground. Death-by-crazy-person beat being eaten alive by savage dogs, so he'd take that. When the shapes stepped into the glow of the campfire, he was glad he hadn't been standing because his legs would have collapsed out from under him in relief.

All of them — the girls, Jack, Becca — *alive!*

Becca was wearing Jack's suit jacket and had his arm around her shoulders, helping him limp along. Her hair had come loose on one side from the bun of curls and was dangling in her face. The little girls were scratched and dirty, looked like they'd gone out to play in their Sunday dresses and their daddies' suit coats. Jack looked like death on a cracker. All in all, they were the most beautiful sight Crock had ever seen.

Becca immediately dropped to her knees beside the pile of rubble and called out, "Theresa, how are you doing?"

Silence.

"Theresa?" That was Jack as he focused the beam from his phone flashlight into the pile of rubble. It lit nothing beyond the closest rocks and beams, actually made it harder to see down into the depths. In growing alarm, he called out again, "Theresa, talk to us."

More silence.

"She hasn't said anything in a long time," Crock told them, as the others cried out her name.

Andi's "Theresa, *pleeeease* ..." broke Crock's heart. Then the little girl stood and looked around. "Where's Daddy?"

"He's not back yet," Crock said. "He stopped to pick up a milkshake for you but they were all out of chocolate and—"

Movement again flickered outside the firelight, and Crock was cheered to see that Jack hadn't lost a step to his injuries as he whirled around with the rifle leveled.

"Stop right where you are," he called out. "Don't move or I'll—"

"We come in peace," came a voice from the darkness.

"Daddeeeee!" Andi cried and raced toward the approaching figures.

At that moment, Crock thought he might just be about as happy as he was ever likely to be.

Daniel, with Andi wrapped around his leg and Linc beside him, appeared — at least in the firelight — to have fared better than the others.

"… not saying anything," he heard Andi babbling to her father. "We called and called."

Daniel called down into the hole in the ground that only hours ago — how *many* hours was up for grabs — had been a chapel in the woods. He got no more response than the others.

"Nobody's going to come to our rescue." Desperation and frustration knit together in Becca's voice. "*We've* got to get Theresa out of there *now!*"

The clock was ticking. Eventually, Theresa would go into shock … if she hadn't already. But if they *could* have gotten her out somehow — without killing her in the process — they'd have done it already. There was no way—

"I think I know a way," Jack said. Everyone looked at him in surprise and he turned to Daniel. "Actually, it's not my idea. The plan is Daniel's."

THE IDEA HAD COME to Jack when he was in the woods holding Becca tight to his chest, unutterably grateful that she was alive and unharmed. He'd been remembering the moment of terror he'd felt when the chapel suddenly collapsed and he'd thought Becca was in it. A few horrifying seconds of living nightmare had twisted reality out of shape and images had flashed across his mind like racing comets. A red dress falling from a building. A white dress buried under one. The horror had so taken his breath away that he was aware of nothing else, and no other thought penetrated his consciousness.

But some part of his trained-observer's brain catalogued facts the rest of his brain had been too preoccupied at the time to pay attention to. Fact one: seconds before the building fell into the sinkhole, they'd felt the ground shake, just a little, easy to dismiss. Fact two: he'd seen something odd in the forest when they felt that first warning shake. He'd seen trees *moving*.

"This isn't the only sinkhole around here," he said. He pointed toward the woods to the east. "I saw trees over there shake right before the building fell. The trees were moving because the ground was falling out from under them, too."

Becca wasn't following. "I don't get what that has to do with—"

"If there's a sinkhole over there, the ground collapsed into a cave … right? These caves *connect*."

Daniel took Jack's thought and kicked it through the uprights.

"If we can get into the cave system through that sink-hole, we could *go through the caves* to get to Theresa! Get her out from under the debris — from the bottom — instead of trying to move debris off the top."

"You told me those caves were like a rabbit warren," Crock said. "A hopeless maze going every which way … that nobody ever went into them because they'd never find their way back out."

"Daniel figured a way around that when we were kids," Jack said.

"But when I suggested it, you said that spelunkers weren't lining up to explore the Caverna County caves and there was a *reason* for that!"

Clearly, Daniel remembered that day, too — the day their childhood ended.

It had been the day Bishop had dropped the Three Musketeers off in the woods to hunt for ginseng. The first part of that day — before Becca watched the Bad Kids kill a fisherman and they kidnapped her, before he and Daniel had gone up against demons who'd hijacked human bodies — those few precious minutes had been the last Jack, Daniel and Becca spent as children. The whole rest of their childhood was stolen from them, their innocence gobbled up by evil.

JACK IS WALKING beside Daniel in the woods, listening in what he hopes looks like rapt attention to what Daniel is telling him, details of Daniel's grand plan to do what nobody had ever done — draw a map of the hundreds, no, probably thousands of miles of interconnected caves beneath Caverna County.

"Of course, it'd take a lot of rope," Daniel says, "but you could go out to the end of a piece of rope, draw a map of how you got there, then move the rope—"

"It's like a honeycomb," Jack says. "Layers and layers going down nobody knows how far."

"We'd start with the top level and then—"

"—and then fall through to the next level or the next, break a leg and get stuck down there. That rock's unstable. The water's still dissolving the limestone."

"Yeah, but—"

"How can you draw a map of something that's constantly changing? One minute, there's a cavern and a wall. And the next time you go in, the wall's gone and it's two caves. You don't see a long line of spelunkers itching to crawl around in the caverns, Dano, and there's a reason for that."

"So you think it's a dumb idea?"

"Well …" It's really hard to lie to Daniel. Even if you were a good liar, he could spot it. Jack suspects that's because Daniel probably hasn't told half a dozen lies in his whole life, and that included the ones you had to tell about the ugly scarf your aunt sent you for Christmas or when some lady in a store wanted to know if a dress made her look fat. "Not dumb, exactly, just—"

"Shhhh," Daniel says. "Listen."

THE SOUND DANIEL had heard was Becca's dog barking. McDougal had led them to the Bad Kids and Becca and the nightmare of the rest of that summer when they were twelve years old, the summer that changed all the years that came after it.

"Daniel's plan was to use rope to find your way back out of the caves but a variation of it might work now. We won't be dealing with layers and layers of caves to find Theresa. Both the sinkholes would have dropped whatever was above them down into the cave just underneath the surface of the ground. Linc, Daniel and I could go in and find Theresa — the sinkholes probably aren't more than a hundred, maybe a hundred fifty yards apart."

He took a step toward Becca, shoved his hand down into the pocket of his suit coat that she was wearing and pulled out the tie he'd stuffed in there, the one Theresa had knitted for him.

"We'll use *this* to find our way out. Theresa bragged to me that she used two skeins of yarn to knit it — at about two hundred twenty yards of yarn to a skein, that's a length of yarn roughly four football fields long and the sinkhole in the trees is right over there."

"And if that's not enough, there's Theresa's knitted purse — it's *big*," Andi put in. "And *we* have purses, too."

"Once you locate her, how are you going to get her out from under all this stuff?" Becca asked.

"I don't know. But this is the only card we have to play. All we can do is hope that whatever has her leg pinned down is something Daniel, Linc and I can shove out of the way without bringing the rest of the thing down."

"Even if you do get her out from under all this stuff,

how are you going to get her back to the surface?" Crock asked. "Theresa's a big woman and she might be hurt."

"You could make a stretcher." The voice was Ariel's, who had remained so quiet through everything that had happened it was easy to forget she was even there. "Use two tree limbs and the train from Becca's wedding dress."

Out of the mouths of babes.

Chapter Thirty-Two

THE NEXT SMALL voice that silenced the adults wasn't Ariel's. It was Andi's.

"I'm going down into the cave with you," she said.

They all turned to look at the child.

"No, baby," Daniel told her, "you're staying right here. The roof of that cavern is unstable and might come tumbling down on—"

"Miss Theresa needs me."

Deja vu all over again. Andi had said that the day she'd visited Theresa in the hospital after Theresa'd been attacked by rats. Jack had no idea what the two of them had said to each other that day, but Theresa had been in a very dark place and Andi had talked her off the ledge.

Daniel's eyes found Jack's and locked there, his look pleading with Jack to offer him a way to say no. Daniel absolutely, one-hundred-percent did *not* want Andi to set foot in a cave — not in *any* cave, not today or tomorrow or ever again!

Jack loved Andi so much he'd often wished she was his daughter, but right now he was grateful she wasn't. He gave Daniel a noncommittal shrug. This was Daniel's decision and he'd have to make it. Andi was his little girl.

No one else spoke. Andi merely stood there, looking up into her father's face. Jack could only imagine the war going on right now in Daniel's heart. Love and fear all tangled up with the inescapable suspicion that maybe Andi was *supposed to* …

"Okay." Daniel turned his face away. Maybe he was crying.

Armed with the rifle, Linc and Daniel hurried to the cars to bring back the train, the knitted purses and anything else that might prove useful. While they were gone, Andi and Becca poked around on Jack's tie until they found the thread that would set up the unraveling process, pulled out about a foot of yarn and stopped. Andi was to be the official un-raveler. They'd leave the tie intact, unraveling it as they went so the yarn wouldn't get tangled.

Crock was left with Ariel — and Becca, who'd demanded to go along until Jack kindly pointed out that she couldn't clamber around in a cave in a wedding dress. Jack figured he and the others weren't likely to be attacked in the cave by blind crickets so he handed the rifle and tactical vest with extra ammunition to Crock, who would have trouble shooting with an injured hand. But if something came along that he had to shoot, an injured hand would likely be the least of his problems.

"No more Mr. Nice Guy," Crock said, his voice uncharacteristically grim.

Jack agreed. "If it moves, shoot to kill."

IT WOULDN'T HAVE BEEN hard to find the sinkhole in the daylight.

But the daylight … wasn't playing well with others right now and night had come. There was a full moon — which shouldn't have risen into the sky for several hours after dark. Daniel couldn't recall noticing it rise at all, as a matter of fact. It wasn't there … and then it was, a big bright yellow moon. They were grateful for the light, though. With their eyes adjusted to the darkness, it was easier to find their way using moonlight, keeping the flashlights turned off. In the odd pearly-light, Daniel, Jack, Linc and Andi headed out in the direction Jack saw the swaying trees — and just kept going, hoping they wouldn't pass the sinkhole without seeing it in the moonlight.

Jack was limping, but walking better than he had when Daniel first saw him. From the back, Daniel could see that his shirt had bloody rips all the way down. As an EMT, Linc had pointed out that both Jack and Crock's wounds needed *treatment*, needed to be cleaned and disinfected from the meager supplies of the first aid kit in his cruiser. But there'd been no time for that, so Linc readjusted the field dressing on Jack's leg, using fabric from Becca's dress and binding it in place with duct tape, and replaced the pressure bandage on the puncture wound in his upper arm.

Becca said she'd see to Crock's wounds and it was clear to everyone that the major's hand injury would need more than the first aid either Becca or Linc could provide.

About half a mile from the chapel, the forest floor suddenly opened up in front of them. The sinkhole wasn't nearly as large as the hole that had swallowed the chapel. Apparently, the chapel had been built above an open cavern like the one Billy Ray had used to bury his boxcar. But if that was the case, it was surprising the chapel hadn't fallen in years ago. Of course, maybe it fell now because *it had help*.

When the forest floor had dropped into the hole in

front of them, it had taken two large trees with it. A couple of nearby trees were leaning where the ground beneath them had collapsed on one side and yanked at their roots. They switched on the powerful flashlight from Linc's cruiser and quickly discovered that there was a slope of dirt they could climb down and an opening at the bottom that led into the cave system. That was no small thing. The cave roof could have done what it had done beneath the chapel — dropped away, leaving a gaping hole you'd need a rope to climb down into. Or the bottom of the sinkhole could've been blocked up the cave at both ends, leaving no entrance. In fact, it was almost as if the sinkhole had been *specifically shaped* to provide them access, like … No, Daniel couldn't go there. If it had been shaped … who'd shaped it? Or *what* had shaped it? He had nowhere in his mind to process those considerations right now.

It was simple enough for the four of them to clamber over tree roots, patches of slippery dirt and rocks to get to the bottom. How would they get Theresa up that slope to the top? One problem at a time.

Without pausing for discussion, they each climbed down through the hole into the cave.

Back in a cave. Again. With Andi.

Daniel had sworn as soon as he stepped out into the autumn night air after they'd challenged and banished the efreet that he would never, under any circumstances, *ever set foot* in a cave again. Yet here he was, holding tight to Andi's hand, following along behind Jack — whom he suspected had made a similar vow that day, too.

Everyone except Andi had selected sticks from the pile of kindling beside their campfire and when they got into the cave, Linc lit the tip of each one with the Bic lighter. The burning sticks wouldn't last long and didn't provide a whole lot of light, but in the absolute darkness of a cave they provided enough illumination to see a way forward. They were saving the batteries on the two flashlights — Linc's powerful one and the pitiful little one in Theresa's glove box, using them only when they absolutely had to. Daniel had phones in his pocket, too, but once they drained the power using the flashlight app there'd be no recharging them. Becca had kept one — to use to dial 911 if they ever got cell coverage again.

When Linc went to his cruiser for the flashlight, he had dug around in his trunk to find anything else they might need and he'd discovered a lone road flare that had rolled behind the spare tire. He searched the other vehicles, too and gathered up any and everything that might be useful. They were saving that last flare to use for light once they found Theresa.

The cave was small, which Daniel knew must be giving Jack's claustrophobia fits. Linc was in the lead with the largest burning-branch torch. In his other hand, he carried Theresa's purse that contained the train to Becca's wedding dress, the last flare, and two rolls of duct tape out of Jack's trunk. Next came Jack, carrying one of the stripped tree limbs they'd use to make the stretcher. Daniel carried the other. He and Andi brought up the rear with Andi carefully unraveling Jack's tie. She carried her own purse by a strap around her neck and had stuffed Becca and Ariel's purses inside it, just in case the tie didn't provide enough yarn. They'd tied the bright green yarn dangling from Jack's tie securely to a branch of one of the upturned trees at the opening of the sinkhole and she had been feeding it out as the tie unraveled while they walked.

Daniel absolutely forbade himself to look back, not even once. If he ever started looking over his shoulder, he'd started imagining he could hear What Comes Behind, the tangle of spiders and snakes that had sealed them into the cave when they were children and had parted like leaves before a leaf blower for Daniel last fall when the angel's light struck them.

The cave led downward for the first fifty yards or so, twisted one way and then another, and soon Daniel was hopelessly confused, uncertain if they were even traveling in the right direction. It became clear quickly that the distance between the two sinkholes might be half a mile "as the crow flies" but by the circuitous route of the cave, no telling how far it might be. Linc seemed to have a better sense of direction than most. Whenever they passed other passages, he'd pause only briefly and then continue.

"Do you feel it, Daddy?" Andi whispered.

"Feel what?"

"How warm it is, only it's not really. I mean, it seems warm down here in comparison to the cold up above, and it should be the other way around, shouldn't it?"

He dodged the question because the answer begged other questions he didn't want to be asked.

"Are you warm enough in my jacket?" Not that he could have done anything about it if she wasn't.

"Why is it so cold, Daddy?"

So much for avoiding questions he didn't want to answer.

The image came to mind of a soup can display he'd seen last week in the small Kroger grocery store in Harrelton, a suburb of Cincinnati where he and Andi lived. It had been built from the floor up to about six feet tall as a pyramid, cans stacked around and around in smaller circles to the top. Take out one of the cans on the bottom row — it might take two or three — and all the cans stacked above it would come tumbling down on your head. It seemed to Daniel that discussing the extraordinary cold with Andi — coupled with everything else that had happened since the wedding music started in the chapel ... how long ago? Who knew? — would be yanking out one of those cans. All the other craziness would come crashing down, whacking him on the head, forcing him to acknowledge to the others what he'd only a few minutes ago acknowledged to himself. All the crazy stuff was demonic, evil gone berserk, and all of them — all the usual suspects from battling demons in the past — were right here in the middle of where that evil was coming into the world.

Theresa and Bishop had taught him, and life in the demon-lane had confirmed it time and time again over the years — there's no such thing as a coincidence. They were *here*. *Now*. All of them. There was a reason for that.

He was spared having to answer Andi's question when Linc, at the head of the procession, stopped.

The tunnel had been angling steadily upward, or at least it seemed to Daniel that it was. But the roof wasn't angling with it. In the past — five minutes? Five years? — the taller among them had begun to stoop over a little to avoid hitting their heads.

He didn't have to ask what was up. Just ahead of them, the tunnel split. They'd passed other openings off the main tunnel as they walked along, but it had been clear they were in the biggest one — the one that, theoretically, at least, had collapsed when the earth shook, opening up sinkholes along its route. One of them had been the one they'd entered through in the woods. Hopefully, the chapel had collapsed into another.

He gestured toward the forked tunnel. "Both of these are going in the right direction. What do you think?"

"The one on the left," Andi said without hesitation. They all turned to look at her.

"How do you know that's the right one?" Jack asked. His voice was breathy. And he was sweating even in the cold. It must have been torture for him to be here, closed up like this, yet here he was. Daniel had always admired his courage but never more than he did right now.

"It's the one Gandalf would take."

That was a conversation stopper.

"You know, when they're in Moria and Gandalf is leading them with that lighted staff and the cave forks and he can't remember which tunnel to take."

Daniel had read the whole Lord of the Rings series to Andi when she was younger and had watched the movies with her. But he still had no idea what she was talking about. Jack probably didn't know who Gandalf was.

She looked from one of them to the other. Nothing.

"When they figure out Gollum is following them …?"

Still nothing.

Andi was too polite to roll her eyes, but he knew her well enough to know that's exactly what she wanted to do.

"Gandalf sniffs the air. And they take the tunnel where the air 'doesn't seem so foul.'" She paused. "Don't you smell it?"

Daniel had read somewhere that children could hear some frequencies grownups couldn't but he didn't know if the same thing applied to the sense of smell. When he stood still and concentrated, though, he got it, too. Through the tunnel on the left you could smell cool, fresh air.

"I think you folks need to start calling out to Theresa, now," Linc said. "It'd be easier to follow the sound of her voice than to sniff our way there."

"Theresa," Jack called. "We're coming for you."

"Theresa!" Daniel called. "Where are you … Theresa?"

Nothing came back to them from the dark cave ahead but silence.

SOMEONE WAS CALLING HER NAME. The voice was coming from a long way off, so far she could barely hear it. But that didn't matter. She wasn't planning on answering even if they'd been standing right beside her. Theresa Washington was busy. Dying had a way of taking up all your attention.

She'd been near getting killed other times in her life, the most recent when Cole Stuart duct-taped her to a chair in a burning warehouse and if hadn't a'been for Jack and that angel, she'd have gone on to meet Jesus right there and then. But that wasn't her time.

This was her time.

Daniel had told her about being tied up in the dark with Jeff Kendrick, knowing he was going to die as soon as Billy Ray returned. *Billy Ray!* If ever there was a man needed to go on to meet the final judgement and suffer the consequences of all the things he'd done, it was Billy Ray Hawkins! Daniel'd said that knowing he was going to die had called into question everything he believed or said he believed, stripped away all the pretense and got down to what really mattered. What mattered was *love* because love proved there was ultimate good. And if there was ultimate good, then everything he'd been telling people about God and Jesus all those years had been right. He hadn't believed the words when he'd said them, but that didn't make them any less true when they come out past his lips into the ears of all them people in the pews. Theresa suspected that what Daniel had said, whether he'd meant it at the time or not, had had a profound effect on the lives of thousands of people.

Here at her "moment of truth," she was relieved to discover she didn't have any doubts to overcome. She'd been walking with the Lord up close for most of her life and he'd been there for her every step of the way. She wasn't left, here at the end with nothing to wonder about. She was gonna die. She was gonna go to Heaven. She was gonna see Jesus — face to face!! And later on, she was gonna get to see Bishop and Isaac, too.

Theresa, can you hear me?

Another voice. She ignored it just like she done the first one. Nothing important. Nothing important at all.

Isaac. Oh, to see Isaac again. The ache in her heart for that boy had healed over some in all these years, but it was still there, a soul wound that went all the way to the core of who she was. If she picked at the corners of the scab over that wound just the least little bit, the pain would come roaring out and gobble her up. Wasn't gonna be no pain no more now, though. Jesus was gonna dry every tear from her eyes. Living on this earth was fine indeed, but living in Heaven was gonna be a whole lot better.

She hadn't been aware of any part of her body in a long time now, even her nose had stopped itching. Nothing hurt or felt cramped anymore. Nothing felt at all. She noticed her breathing beginning to fail. The breaths still come, but slower now. Each one a deep heave in and a sigh back out. She closed her eyes. What she could see outside was nothing but rocks and dirt and timbers. But inside her eyelids … Oh my, inside her eyelids a party was just beginning and she was the guest of honor. It was bright and warm, sunny, with a breeze caressing her cheek where she'd scratched it, but it wasn't hurting no more.

She felt herself slip her moorings at the dock of life, almost heard them dropping with a plonk sound into the water. Her ship began to ease out to sea. Beyond, on the horizon, was a brightly lit place and there was a sound … was that music? Oh my, it was so beautiful it almost hurt to hear it, like maybe her ears wasn't holy enough to hold such a sound.

And laughter.

There was laughter in the light.

She smiled.

Theresa sighed out a breath.

She didn't draw another one back in.

Chapter Thirty-Three

"SHE'S NOT BREATHING," Linc said.

Jack felt like he'd been hit in the chest with a wrecking ball.

No!

"Does she have a pulse?"

There was a pause that seemed to last for a hundred years.

"No." Linc was trying to sound professionally dispassionate and failing miserably. "Not that I can find."

Linc was the only one of them who had gotten close enough to touch her. They'd followed the clean air and ever-brightening glow of the campfire's light to the spot where the earth above the cave had come crashing down into it. Then they'd flipped the switch on Linc's flashlight and could clearly see Theresa lying on her back in the debris only about twenty feet away. The afghan was pulled up snug under her chin, so they couldn't see much of her body, but there were broken timbers and pieces of stone all around her and a wooden pew lying crossways across her from the waist down.

From inside the cave, you could see that the area that had given way beneath the chapel had been a large chamber — much like the one where Billy Ray had knocked out a hole in the roof with a backhoe to lower his boxcar down inside. Just getting to Theresa would be tricky, though gratefully she was near the edge of the debris pile closest to where it opened into the cave.

Linc had lit the flare and cave shadows had leapt back from the light.

When Becca saw the flare light from above, she'd called out, wanting to know how Theresa was. Jack hadn't been able to answer.

Theresa had not responded when they'd called out to her and they had forced themselves not to panic, to study the debris pile before they touched anything. Moving something, anything could dump the rocks and timbers above down into the hole. Then Linc had dropped to his belly and began to crawl. And Jack understood that it was Linc who'd taken the initiative because he and Daniel were nailed to the floor where they stood, fear and dread holding them so firm it would have taken a jackhammer to break them free.

Linc had gotten close enough to Theresa to reach out and touch her hand. And her wrist ... that didn't have a pulse.

They had come too late.

Jack looked at Daniel and saw the same look of total desolation on his face he was sure Daniel could see on his own. Theresa couldn't be ... dead. Though she had only come back into their lives a little over a year ago for the first time since they were children, Jack couldn't countenance a world and a future without her. He was sure Becca couldn't either.

And *Andi!*

He turned toward the child.

She was gone.

~

THIS WAS one of those times that you didn't ask for permission before you did something — because if you asked, the answer would be no. Andi hadn't ever defied Daddy outright, at least not that she could remember. But she didn't think it was defying if you did something before he had time to tell you not to. Maybe it was, but she was willing to go with that.

Daddy would say it was too dangerous. He'd say the pile of rocks and stuff might fall down on her head. He'd tell her to wait. And she couldn't wait. She didn't understand the sense of *right now* that filled her chest, any more than she understood when the walls of her room vanished and huge shapes appeared to her that were so big they'd never have fit in there. Sometimes it seemed that she really didn't understand much of anything at all. But she was only a little girl and she didn't think it was her job to understand. She was just supposed to listen and do. She knew she didn't have time to wait. Theresa didn't have time for Andi to wait, either.

So she stepped quietly back to the cave wall, ducked down behind a big piece of rock from the chapel, and began to work her way carefully into the maze of rocks and boards. She wasn't very big and managed to squeeze through small openings where none of the others would have fit. She'd almost gotten all the way to Theresa before anybody noticed what she was doing.

"Andi!" Daddy called. "What are you doing? You can't—"

"I'm little and I fit and you don't and I have to talk to Theresa."

"You can't talk to Theresa, honey." There was an awful wooden quality to his voice. "Miss Theresa can't hear you. She's …"

"No!" Andi cried.

She knew he was going to say dead! And she couldn't let him say it because if he put the word out there into the world and they heard it, that would make it true. And it *couldn't* be true. Andi couldn't let it be true.

Theresa was still about six feet away and Andi just had to scoot under one more rock. She slithered under it and came out into a small opening right beside Theresa. She touched her hand and it felt cold. Then she leaned up next to her face — she wasn't breathing, Andi could tell that even though she was trying not to know it.

Andi squeezed her eyes shut and tears squirted out anyway. Where was her angel? If Princess Buttercup were here — but she couldn't come here, she'd said it was too dark. But no place was too dark for God.

Don't take her now. Please, don't. If she goes away, all this badness is … it's going to take over. It's going to win.

She stroked Theresa's cheek, put her lips close to Theresa's ear and whispered fiercely, "Miss Theresa, come back!"

Andi knew where she'd gone. She knew what she was asking of Theresa, how *hard* it would be. But she asked anyway.

"Please. We *need* you."

Then it was quiet. It was the kind of absolute silence that only existed in a cave. Theresa wasn't the only one not breathing. None of them were. In fact, it seemed to Andi that the whole rest of the universe was holding its breath, too.

DANIEL HAD STOPPED MOVING and breathing and thinking when Andi stroked Theresa's cheek. When she leaned over and whispered into her ear, the familiar video played on the screen of his mind.

HE AND EMILY are beside the little girl in the hospital bed who is so white, so white, and so still, her little hand cold and unmoving.

The whole world has swollen into a single sound. A heart monitor beeping slower and slower. It beeped … it beeped … then the beep becomes a single, long buzzing sound. Daniel looks at the monitor and sees not mountains and valleys anymore but a single, flat green line.

Emily sucks in a horrified gasp. There's no air at all in the room to breathe even if Daniel could. The buzzing sound cores into his soul.

Jack is here. He speaks into the silence, his voice soft, gentle, a whisper on a breath. A single word: "Andi."

The monitor begins to beep again. Not the languid, turgid ever-slowing rhythm from before, but crisply, briskly. Beep. Beep. Beep. Beep.

THOUGH ANDI WAS BLOCKING MOST of his view so he couldn't see Theresa's face, he could see the rest of the upper part of her body snuggled up tight in the afghan. He should have thought his eyes were playing tricks on him, that he wasn't seeing what he thought he was. That it was just wishful thinking. Shock and grief could alter your perception of reality.

That wasn't what was happening now, though. He knew what he saw was real. The afghan covering Theresa's chest moved up, just a little. Back down and up again.

JACK COULD TELL from the look on Daniel's face that he'd seen the same thing Jack had.

So had Linc, the only one of them totally unprepared for the sight. For a fleeting moment Jack considered the amount of power and mystery they had brought into the man's life in just a few months, how they had pulled back the curtain an inch or two and given him a glimpse of the *real* world. He'd handled it better than most, but Theresa breathing again — it might have been a bridge too far.

Linc's eyes had grown so wide the white showed all around. He had reflexively moved back, pulling away from what couldn't possibly be happening but was. He'd been on his belly on the ground, and when he pulled up to his hands and knees and lurched backward, the motion shook the debris pile and it began to shift. Timbers creaked and moved, pieces of stone tumbled out of place and fell, dust sifted down in a fine mist. For a breathless moment, it looked like the whole pile was going to come tumbling down as the cloud of sifting dust obscured everything. But the pile held, though parts of it had moved. One of those parts was the wooden pew stretched across Theresa's body. A rock must have fallen on the other end of it because it lifted up into the air about a foot and shifted sideways.

Theresa was no longer pinned down. She opened her eyes, looked up into Andi's face and said something too soft for him to hear. Jack felt the smile on his face — when had *that* happened — and heard a noise like soft laughter coming from his own throat. That's when he realized that the lead ball of fear and grief in his belly was gone. He took in a deep breath and let it out deliciously slow.

Now, they just had to get Theresa out of here!

Some time later, they were struggling to maneuver the makeshift stretcher loaded with Theresa up the slope of the sinkhole in the woods where they'd entered. How long it had taken to free her and carry her out of the cave was impossible to tell. Jack had finally accepted what Theresa had suggested earlier — time was broken.

Getting her free of the debris had been simpler, though just as difficult, as he'd thought it'd be. After much discussion and analyzing, and a couple of plans were proposed and rejected, they had gone with the one that involved the least contact with the pile of debris. They wouldn't try to move it to get to her — that had been one plan. The men wouldn't try to clamber into it to free her, either — that had been another. Instead, Andi had wiggled through small spaces under the pile, dragging one end of Becca's train along with her. Then she'd pulled in more and more fabric, stretched it out beside Theresa and after a considerable amount of wiggling and adjusting, she'd gotten Theresa rolled over on her back on top of it. Then the men took the other end of the train and pulled. Theresa slid feet first out from under the pew that had held her captive with only inches to spare, passed beneath timbers none of the adults would dare have crawled under, and out from beneath the final rock with only minimal grunting and straining from Jack, Daniel and Linc.

Once Theresa was free, Jack knelt beside her. Her breathing was regular, calm. Her pulse was steady. She appeared to be merely asleep, not unconscious, like she'd open her eyes in a moment, stretch and ask where was her morning coffee.

He started to speak to her, but Andi touched his arm and shook her head. Andi didn't think they should disturb Theresa and the little girl's authority was more than good enough for Jack.

The stretcher formed with the train, two limbs and a whole lot of duct tape worked fairly well, though they had to stop a time or two to adjust the cloth where it'd slipped. Theresa was heavy, no way around that, and the men rotated out of carrying positions or they wouldn't have made it at all. The final push up the slope had been grueling and they paused on the edge of the sinkhole to get their breath. But only for a minute or two. Jack didn't believe Theresa was in as good a shape as she appeared to be. She could be badly injured for all any of them knew. Car wreck survivors walked around on broken legs or with broken backs. She needed to get warm by the fire, get something hot to drink, and wrap up in the afghan.

And Linc needed to get back to the fire to see to Crock's wound.

Then they'd have to figure a way to get Theresa — and the rest of them — to civilization.

WHILE LINC DID first aid on the wounded, he told the others about seeing Daniel's capture and following the kidnappers to the church. Daniel rummaged around in his head for words to use to tell them what he'd seen. He hadn't even figured out how to think about it himself yet, let alone share it with others. He had spent the whole way back through the woods to the chapel trying to jam what he had seen into the shape of his understanding of the functioning of the universe. Nothing fit.

It wasn't Billy Ray. It was somebody who *looked like* Billy Ray, who had a tattoo like Billy Ray.

Right. And who also knew what Billy Ray had said to him and Jeff about beheading that day in the boxcar. *The exact words.*

Okay, it *was* Billy Ray and he was alive. Billy Ray hadn't been killed in the fall after all.

Right. He'd tumbled hundreds of feet down into the darkness of a crevice and — what? Landed on a cotton ball? Was just knocked unconscious and woke up later and climbed out? Up hundreds of feet of smooth rock face? And on the way up, his hair turned white and grew a foot. Oh, and his voice changed, too.

More than his voice, though — his whole … demeanor was different. He wasn't the snarky, sneaky, mean little rat man he'd always been. But he wasn't possessed, either, or at least Daniel didn't think he was. There was not some other being, some soulless evil pulling the strings on a puppet Billy Ray devoid of all personality, minus all his Billy-Ray-ness. Daniel and Jeff had watched Billy Ray lose his mind in the cavern as he was preparing to behead them, could see that he was no longer rational by anybody's definition of sanity. The man with white hair and a white beard wasn't *irrational* — crazy, yes, but infinitely lucid and not in a "supernatural" way. He was Billy Ray … but Billy Ray on steroids. Billy Ray intensified. Billy Ray with the volume turned up so loud it blew all the glass out of the windows. There was an aura of power there, but more the power of the evil that had always been a part of the man — turned loose and given a motorcycle and a dose of meth.

And that evil was *attractive!*

Daniel didn't consider himself an expert by any means, but with his limited knowledge and understanding he didn't see possessed people as attractive. Chapman Whitworth had been mesmerizing, hypnotizing — but he'd also been perfectly possessed by a demon prince he'd summoned into this world. If you got near him, were physically in his presence not just watching his image on television, you could sense, sometimes even see, the demonic presence only barely contained by the physical body. And you were *terrified* of it. He wasn't a man all the little boys wanted to grow up to be. The Bad Kids had been possessed against their wills and they didn't have a posse of fawning admirers who wanted to emulate their every thought and move. Possessed people were scary! Even those like Daniel who didn't have the knowing sensed the foreign being dwelling inside, calling the shots. And that monster was horrifying.

A possessed person might coerce someone, or a group of someones, to follow him by the sheer force of the terror he engendered. Billy Ray's power was different. He wasn't coercing all these people to go out and hack apart perfect strangers. It wasn't fear of him that drove them. They were *mesmerized* by him. Not by Billy Ray, but by the evil that was as much a part of who he was as creamer poured into a cup of coffee.

Billy Ray could convince others to do what he wanted, he could bend them to the force of his will so they wanted to do it. It was as if the evil that resided in Billy Ray's heart called out to the evil in the hearts of others, linked up with it, made it a willing slave to the greater evil inside Billy Ray. Billy Ray was badder than bad, and bad people responded to that, resonated with that, wanted to emulate and follow it.

Billy Ray was leading a group of otherwise normal

people in a crusade of bloody violence and they were following along, jumped when he said jump and carried out his will because it was like their own, but worse.

"... Daniel?"

Becca was speaking to him, in the tone of voice of one who was repeating what they'd already said. Maybe said a couple of times.

"Daniel, are you all right?" she asked.

The concern in her eyes warmed his heart. If only he didn't *care*.

"Actually, no, I'm not all right. I am all wrong, as a matter of fact." He stopped, started over. "I don't know how to say this."

"Try just blurting it out, son," Crock said, a little breathless from the pain in his hand. They had to get medical attention for him, and for Jack, too. Soon! "No sense walking around with a fart in your spacesuit."

"The white-haired guy, the Chosen One, Linc shot him, point blank range. But he didn't ... it didn't hurt him. He didn't bleed or fall down."

Becca sucked in a gasp and suddenly looked as frightened as she'd looked that day when they found her with the Bad Kids in the woods. Tears sprang to her eyes and she reached to grab Jack's hand, but he drew her to his side instead, his arm protectively around her shoulders.

"I shot the guy in the woods, too. With an M4. Put five rounds in him, close range. He didn't go down either." Jack tossed something at him, a small shiny object, and Daniel caught it. "He dropped this."

Daniel looked at the Harvard ring and couldn't breathe.

"Are you telling me two police officers shot perps less than twenty feet away, took what — almost a dozen shots? — and *missed?*" Crock said.

"No," Jack said carefully. "I'm telling you I *didn't* miss. I know I didn't miss."

"I didn't miss either," Linc said softly.

"Then how in the Sam Hill—?" Crock didn't have enough air to finish and it had nothing to do with how bad his hand hurt.

Jack's voice was barely above a whisper, tight with tension and awe and fear. "I don't think it's possible to kill someone who's already dead."

Chapter Thirty-Four

WHEN THERESA FIRST CAME BACK, she kept her eyes closed because to open them was to let the world in and the light and music would fade. It was fading anyway, of course. She'd been so close, so near she could see, smell and hear its exquisiteness. And then she had come back. She couldn't exist in both worlds. She had to let one of them go. She knew that, but not yet. Not quite yet.

And so she *slept*. Though she was aware of what was going on around her, of being carried and the warmth of the fire, too, she had purposefully not engaged with this world.

But it was time now and she knew it. Couldn't keep hanging on. She was in this world and she'd come of her own free will and she had to own it and do what she'd come back to do. Which was … She thought she knew, but was absolutely sure of only one thing — she'd find out what she needed to know when she needed to know it. Right now, it was enough to know that she was here with those she loved to help them. And that meant she had to wake all the way up.

Just not quiiiite yet. She lay there for a time more, basking in the warmth of the fire, feeling Becca and Andi patting her lovingly, like you'd unconsciously pat a baby asleep in your arms.

She listened to the stories.

Hearing Crock say, "Are you telling me Jeff Kendrick and Billy Ray Hawkins somehow ... resurrected?" brought her all the way back.

When she spoke, they all jumped in surprise. Surprise that she'd actually said something, and she suspected equal parts of surprise that she didn't sound like she was at death's door. She had been. Oh my yes, she had. She'd knocked and it'd opened and she'd stepped through ... but stepped back out before it had time to shut behind her.

"Ain't but one person ever walked out of the grave and that was Jesus Christ," she said, and her voice wasn't the faint airy voice of a person didn't have no life in them. She was loud and firm. "He's the only person ever resurrected. You's confusing resurrected with re-activated. Them two things ain't the same a'tall."

"Theresa, are you all——?"

"How are you feel——?"

"We thought you were——"

"Stop fussing over me like I's a baby chick and you's the hen that laid the egg I just come out of," she said, a little grumpier than she'd intended. Well, they just needed to cut her some slack. She'd had a bad day. "I'm fine. But you ain't fine if you think God goes around resurrecting folks like pulling rabbits out of hats."

"It was Billy Ray," Daniel said. "I can't explain it, but I know what I saw."

"That man in the woods tried to kill everybody *except Andi*," Jack said. He looked at Daniel and held out his hand and Daniel tossed him something, a ring. Jack held it up.

"Harvard class of 1997." He kept looking at Daniel and said the rest carefully, like he knew hearing it was gonna hurt. "The man only said one thing: 'take good care of Emily's little girl.'"

Daniel looked like he was going to throw up.

Becca was staring into the fire, digging into her own upper arms with her fingernails, her face the color of chalk. "Daddy's alive?" She turned to Daniel, too. "Is he? Are you sure, Daniel?"

"Ain't neither one of them alive," Theresa said. "But they ain't dead, neither." She held up her hand before anybody had a chance to speak. "And the first one of you says the word 'zombie' to me had best remember all them times when you was little and I washed your mouths out with soap."

Actually, she'd only done it once. To Jack, for cursing. Daniel never did anything meriting soap in the mouth.

The sheriff looked at her, pleading with his hound-dog eyes.

"Do you understand what's going on here, Mrs. Washington?" he said. "'Cause I sure don't. I'm so far out of my comfort zone UPS don't deliver."

He paused.

"Were you …? Did you …? And the others, Billy Ray and Jeff? If you say they aren't alive and they also aren't dead — what are they?"

"I never claimed to know what they *are*," she said. "The only thing I know for lead pipe certain is what they *ain't*. I don't understand most of it my own self." She took a breath, listened to a night devoid of night sounds, heard only the crackling of the fire. "Jeff and Billy Ray's bodies died. They fell down in that hole and the fall killed them. Had to. And their souls … that's what I don't know about. They fell down where the veil between this world and the darkest pit of the spiritual realm is so thin … I don't know what happens to a man whose soul don't belong to God — and theirs *didn't*, neither one of them — and whose body dies there, in all that evil."

She said nothing else and silence rushed in to fill the void left by her words, crashed in like the water of the Red Sea surging back into its banks.

"Theresa was gone and she came back," Andi said thoughtfully. "So did I."

"You'd stopped breathing and your hearts stopped beating, but your bodies hadn't shut down yet," Jack said. "Your souls left your bodies and then came back while your bodies were still functional. Billy Ray and Jeff … after a fall like that there couldn't have been much left of their bodies to come back to."

"The Ugly Man's face …" Andi stopped, then started again. "It was *awful*. It was all broken up, smashed, looked like a Halloween mask."

"Maybe he … *landed* on his face," Daniel said, and Theresa remembered how dashingly handsome Jeff Kendrick had been … when he was having an affair with Daniel's wife, Emily.

Daniel held out his hand to Jack, who tossed him the ring. Without a word, Daniel drew back and threw the ring out into the darkness.

"We're chasing our own tails trying to figure out how it happened," Linc said. "Seems to me, the more important question is what they're doing here. Billy Ray and Jeff — what do they want?"

"Evil is its own imperative," Daniel said.

"Sounds like some'm out of a theology class," Theresa said.

"Actually, I think it was Bishop who said it. But the point is that evil only knows how to be evil. However they were reanimated, reactivated, recharged, put the batteries back in — whatever — Billy Ray and Jeff don't have a shred of humanity left in them. They will do harm, cause pain and suffering, any way they can because that's all evil knows to do."

"I hate to be the one to dump a bucket of cold-water reality on all this metaphysical palaver," Theresa said, "but it's dark — when it hadn't ought to be, and it's cold, when it also hadn't ought to be. Some of us is hurt, all of us need shelter and something to eat and drink. I think we ought to be worrying about fixing what's broke. Figuring out how it got broke and why will wait."

Theresa sat up then and started to rise before they all joined in a reflexive communal, "No!"

She didn't argue with them, just settled back and said, "Ain't nothing wrong with me that was caused by falling into that hole. But I come back to the body I left and it wasn't in great shape when I left it. I got a bad knee and a bad back, but I walked into that chapel under my own steam and would have walked back out if it hadn't collapsed. They's folks here in a lot worse shape than me." She looked from Crock to Jack. "How about ya'll fuss over them." She looked up at Becca and held out her hand for help standing. "I done wet myself once and I ain't gonna do it again. Let's you and me go find us a bush."

IT WAS obvious Linc had already given considerable thought to their predicament and their options.

"I think we need to make for Brewster Academy," he said.

Jack knew the private school for the upper crust was several miles past the lane leading to the chapel, but he had never been there, had never wanted to go after his association with the Bad Kids when he was twelve — six boys from the academy who were possessed by demons. Few people from Caverna County ever set foot on the grounds. The rich and famous helicoptered their kids in or they drove through town in limos with blacked-out windows, journeying back in time and place to the academy that had been built as a monastery in 1805 by Trappist monks from England. The architecture of the original structures was reminiscent of Alnwick Castle, in Northumberland, England — which was used as a set for the Harry Potter movies. After the movies came out, locals took to calling the place Hogwarts.

"This weekend is Brewster's Family Weekend," Linc said. Jack knew what that meant, too. The ranks of students and faculty would be swelled by all sorts of "dignitaries" who weren't usually on the campus — the kind of people who were either rich, famous or both enough to park their kids in a fancy private boarding school while they jetted off to wherever. There was absolutely no telling who might be there. "We could get help — medical attention, phones." He paused. "It'd be safe there."

"The academy isn't terribly far from here," Daniel put in. Walking the length of a football field sounded terribly far for Jack right now, and Theresa ... and definitely for Crock.

"Yeah, but between us and them is Camelback Ridge," Theresa said.

It was the highest point in the county, almost 3100 feet, towering more than a thousand feet above any of the surrounding mountains. Though the change in elevation would be spread out over several miles of winding road, it would still be daunting. And none of them was in any shape to go hiking. Still, the academy was the obvious place to go.

"I say we need to eat something 'fore we set out."

They hadn't eaten since breakfast that morning. Though that was an indeterminate number of hours ago, their empty stomachs didn't need a clock.

"What we got to eat is chips, dips, snacks, lemonade, wine, champagne … and wedding cake."

And so they had a picnic of sorts, trying to put a good face on it for the sake of the children.

Some jolt had caused an avalanche of icing on one side of the huge wedding cake so the whole structure looked to be in danger of falling apart. There was only the silver cake spatula to cut and serve with, hunks of cake on paper plates balanced on their knees as the wedding party sat around the fire on pieces of broken wall or beams from the collapsed chapel.

Jack gave the first piece to Becca.

"I think you're supposed to shove that piece in my mouth and I'm supposed to do the same with yours," he said, keeping his voice cheery with enormous effort. "And we *will* do that one day. We're just going to call this the official Jack and Becca Wedding Dry Run. As soon as we get out of this, we'll have the beautiful ceremony, complete with all the trimmings" — he cast a look at Theresa — "and you can get as foofy as you like."

"I just want to marry you," Becca said and Jack almost lost his composure. "I don't care about the wedding."

"I do. You deserve the most beautiful wedding in the world."

After they ate all anyone wanted, they washed off sticky hands with Perrier-soaked strips of Becca's wedding dress train. Then they set out through the darkness down the lane toward the road. They took the remains of the train with them in case they had to make a stretcher for Crock or Theresa.

There was something absurdly freeing about not knowing what time it was, coupled with an understanding that time was "broke" so it didn't matter anyway.

How long did the trek to the top of the ridge take? Pain and blood loss had clouded Jack's thinking, but when he reached the conclusion that the amount of time it took was different for each one of them, it had the ring of truth. Impossible, but true.

The last hundred yards or so to the picnic area for tourists on the ridge overlook seemed to Jack to take longer than all the other miles they'd traveled put together.

They all collapsed, exhausted, on the benches. Linc checked the bandages on the injured, and told Jack softly that, "the major's hand don't look good. And neither does he."

Sunrise seemed to come out of nowhere. Almost abruptly. Not a gentle transition from darkness to light, but a jarring jolt from night into day. The sun was just cresting the horizon, still down below the eastern mountains. It appeared first as only a pale, pink-yellow glow on the black sky, extinguishing the stars. Then day spread out in defuse light that only painted the tops of the tallest mountains and left the valleys and hollows in shadow. From the overlook, they could make out the dark outline of Brewster Academy below them in the distance. Emphasis on *dark*.

Jack exchanged an alarmed look with Linc. There should have been *some* light down there. Not a single spark likely meant there was no electricity. And if the electricity there didn't work …

Andi didn't scream exactly, just made a frightened cry and they all turned to look at her. She was facing north, so the sunrise lit only one side of her face, creating shadows in the dimples in her cheeks and sparkling her cinnamon freckles.

She looked terrified.

"Can you see it?"

"See what, sugar?" There was apprehension in Theresa's voice. When Andi Burke saw things you didn't see, it wasn't usually a pretty sight.

"I see it," Becca said, her voice a mixture of awe and horror. "It's like a black tide."

Andi and Becca were staring at the northern horizon as it was lit by the sun rising in the east. In that sunrise glow … what was that? Jack could see something, too. A black cloud, a mist oozing, moving south.

The horizontal beam of light slicing across the landscape from the eastern sunrise lit the cloud and made it visible, the way a beam of sunshine lights dust motes hanging in the air that you couldn't normally see.

"It's evil." Theresa's voice was so soft she was almost inaudible. "It's evil spreading out in a wave of darkness."

Jack saw Linc doing as he was doing, head on a swivel, looking 360 degrees from their high vantage point. Their eyes met and the look on Linc's face confirmed he'd seen what Jack had seen.

South of where they stood — in the direction of "civilization," the air was clear. But spreading out from the north toward them was a gathering darkness. Camelback Ridge sat in a pool of gray mist, the front edge of the flood. But ever darker waves of darkness flowed toward them.

"Them twinkling lights in the dark, thousands of them … maybe millions of them, blinking on and off, making a sick yellow glow. Them lights, they's demons."

"I can't see anything," said Crock, his voice thin and pain-sharpened. "No wait, yes, there." He coughed, some sound between a gasp and a gag. "I'm not sure I'm seeing this with my eyes, but that tide spreading out is filth, sludge, putrid."

Crock took a couple of steps to the side and lost his wedding cake into the grass.

"What is it?" Ariel asked, the fear in her voice making it plain she could see it, too. "Are demons making it dark outside?"

"No," Becca said. "Demons aren't *causing* the darkness. Demons *are* the darkness."

"There are so many of them, they're so thick ..." Andi's voice seemed to grow smaller with every word. "It's like they're absorbing the light or eating it or something."

"Ain't eating it," Theresa said. "Light and dark can't exist in the same place at the same time."

Linc's voice was the only one that sounded strong and firm, probably because he wasn't fending off the memories the rest of them were.

"I figured it out when I was in Grant's Crossing. All the screwy things — the fish, the cattle, the pumpkins and vines and birds — put pins in a map and you'd see it. The area is getting wider as it spreads south from ..." He paused, and in that silence, Jack heard his words before he spoke them. From the look on Daniel's face, he did, too.

"The evil is spreading south from Moonstone," Linc said.

Moonstone was the place near the river where a cave opening led down into the bowels of the earth to the spot where the efreet had entered the world.

~

ARIEL'S VOICE cut through the silence.

"Look over there." She pointed in the opposite direction from the black tide, where light from the rising sun now lit the distant highway, Route 15, that ran between Bradford's Ridge and the interstate. It took Theresa a moment to realize what she was pointing at.

Cars.

Cars were driving down the road.

Theresa didn't have to be a psychic to read Jack's mind: he was seeing that as their way out.

"I don't know how long it will take us to get there," he said, gesturing toward the road. "But at least it will be in the daylight."

"So you sayin' we'd ought to go that way?" Theresa said.

"Of course we should. Civilization. Cars that run. Remember those? Phones that work. 911!"

He gestured toward the outline of Brewster Academy, directly in the path of the coming black tide.

"We're going the wrong way."

Andi had followed his glance.

"But … they're about to get swallowed up. Shouldn't we …?"

"And I'm sorry about that. I really am. But right now I'm more concerned about all of you. Just because we happened to be here—"

"You think this was a *coincidence?*" Theresa shook her head. "You know well as I do they ain't no such thing as a coincidence."

In the silence that followed, she looked each one of them in the face, one after the other, then spoke to them all.

"You think we here *by accident?* We just happened to come along at the same time as all this awful stuff started happening? One-millionth customer gets a year's supply of Drano?" She made a humph sound in her throat. "When

God goes to this much trouble to show you bad stuff, there's a *reason* for that — and the reason is he intends for you to do something about it."

"And what could he possibly intend for us to do about" — Daniel made a helpless sweeping gesture that encompassed everything — "all this? We don't even know what it is."

Jack lost it.

"Becca and I came here to get married. *To get married* for crying out loud." His voice almost broke. "We weren't looking for trouble — shoot, if we'd known, even suspected there'd be anything like ... we'd never have set foot in Caverna County."

"I know it's hard, sugar, preparing for the best day of your life and ending up living the worst."

"I know I sound like a little kid, but I don't care. *It's not fair.* We've all been through enough! Through hell — *literally.* Can't God pick somebody besides us to go on this little adventure?"

His anguished face twisted with such a mixture of emotions — anger, grief, disappointment, fear — that it about broke Theresa's heart.

"Why us?" he whispered.

"Why not us?" The voice came from behind him and he looked around, startled. Becca.

"I hear folks sayin' all the time that somebody's had 'more'n they share of heartache or pain.' You think that's the way the universe works? That you got this allocation of bad stuff and soon's you live through all of it, you's free and God'll punch your ticket and ain't nothing else bad ever gonna happen to you? Or maybe it's that you think you *earned* a break, that you done such a grand and wondrous thing for God by getting rid of that efreet, now he *owes* you a happy life?"

Jack's shoulders slumped.

"That's one of the things I've always *hated* about religion," he whispered. "There's *always* an explanation. Even if the explanation is that God doesn't owe you an explanation."

He looked up into her face, anguish distorting his.

"Doesn't anything ever dangle, Theresa? Aren't there ever any loose ends? God's good and we're not. God's right and we're wrong. Nice and neat, tie it up in a bow, badda boom, badda bing, game over."

"Absolute truth don't leave no room for loose ends. Two plus two is four. Always, every time. That's 'cause God made it — cause that's his nature. That hadn't ought to make you feel bad, Jack. That ought to mean you can just relax, knowing they's things you can absolutely depend on — you might not like some of them, but you know they ain't never gonna change no matter what."

Jack was struggling.

"If we make for the road, we could get a ride and be out of Caverna County before sundown. And we would never, *ever* come back again for the rest of our lives." He shook his head. "But you're saying we should stay? We're *supposed* to be here?"

"I think we got to stay." Her voice got softer. "'Cause what's happenin' … might be *it's our fault.*"

"*Our* fault?" Jack was incredulous.

"While the rest of you was out riskin' your lives, I was just lying there, buried under that church. Had me a lot of time to think."

She wasn't rightly sure how to explain it because she didn't totally understand it her own self. But Bishop always said that sometimes you don't know what you're thinking until you hear it come out of your mouth. She hoped this was one of them times.

"God established natural laws when he created the universe — gravity and the like — that held the world together. Without 'em, wouldn't nothing work. Remove 'em altogether, and the whole universe would fly apart."

"Like … that cows won't hurt you," Andi said, and Theresa suspected her little mind had already got to the end while Theresa was still just on her way.

"God invented the beautiful patterns of starlings flying wingtip to wingtip in complicated formations man wouldn't have figured out with a hundred thousand computer-generated models.

"Yet them birds flew right into the ground. And all them fish — they was turned completely wrong side out. Them cows attacked! All that went against the natural laws of the universe."

She watched wonder and horror spread over Andi's face and knew for certain she'd arrived.

"The angel said she couldn't come with me," she whispered so softly maybe only Theresa heard. "The darkness hates the light."

"So I lay there, trying to think what could cause the natural laws of God to stop working."

The answer scared her worse than she'd ever been scared in her whole life — even worse than facing Chapman Whitworth, who was controlled by a demon, a monster prince of demons.

But it was only *one* demon.

What if there were hundreds of them, thousands, millions?

How could that many demons have got loose in our world?

Theresa thought she might know the answer to that, too. But the possibility was so awful she kept backing up from it, trying not to see.

"What's happening, Theresa?" There was desperation in Jack's voice. "Why—?"

"The veil … the fabric that separates hell from the earth. They's places on earth where it's real thin, like almost not there at all."

"Bishop told us about that," Daniel said, his voice airless. "He said his grandfather had told him that Caverna County was one of those places. That's why bad things happen here so often."

"Yeah," Linc said. Just the one word, but it was a confirmation that what she'd said explained a reality he'd experienced.

"The efreet and all them other demons that was with it — they come through that fabric, was summoned into the world by Chapman Whitworth."

"But the demon's gone." Jack's voice almost broke with wanting his logic to matter and knowing it didn't. "We sent it back to hell!"

"Uh huh, back to hell *through that fabric*."

She had to pause, to gather her strength. Every word felt like a boulder she had to lift up out of her soul and heave out into the world.

"I believe that when you drove that efreet out of the world, somehow … it ripped the veil. *Tore a hole in it somehow.*"

Becca and Ariel both squeaked out little screams thin as paper cuts.

"Wouldn't we have *seen* that?" Crock asked.

"Was you lookin'?"

"Why now?" the sheriff asked. "That was last fall, eight months ago. Why—?"

"The hole it ripped … I think it's gettin' bigger. The evil comin' out is tearing it wider. And they comes a point when …" She stopped, thought. "You know how when you cut into a watermelon, stab it with a big old knife and—"

"And you don't have to keep cutting to slice it open." The words were Sheriff Lincoln's. The voice was somebody she didn't know. "Eventually, the crack *runs out in front of the knife.*"

The silence that fell then, as realization come into the hearts and minds of all of them, felt like the whole universe was a tomb.

"This is that," Linc said. "That's what's happening."

Theresa nodded, found she didn't have enough air to form words.

"And what are we supposed to do about it?" Daniel asked.

"I ain't got no idea, sugar." She shook her head. "I just know that's why we here."

THE END

Epilogue

THE CHOSEN ONE looked at the creature standing before him, wallowing around in his mind the news it had brought. The thing had gone out looking for Morag Heywood. But he'd found a prize instead. The golden egg. The brass ring.

Becca.

The Chosen One shivered at the power she still had to move him.

Becca, *here.* Within his grasp.

He chuckled at the monumental stroke of good fortune. Not a full belly laugh, but real, authentic — almost human.

It was all working out far better than he'd ever imagined.

He turned his attention back to the thing in front of him.

"You're no good to me blind," he said.

Reaching up to his own face, Billy Ray dug his right thumbnail into his left eye socket. Pushed it deep until the eyeball popped out into his palm with a squishy sound. He

404

picked it up, held it between his thumb and index finger and then fit it into the empty left eye socket in Jeff Kendrick's ruined face, had to wiggle it around some to make it fit.

He stepped back, moved his hand back and forth in front of the face and watched the eye track.

It would do. Yes sir, it would do just fine.

A Note From The Author

Thank you for reading *The Fault.*

If you enjoyed this book, would you please consider writing a review of it on your favorite bookseller site so other readers might enjoy it too? Just a couple of sentences. That would mean a lot to me.

Thank you!

Ninie Hammon

About the Author

Ninie Hammon (rhymes with shiny, not skinny) grew up in Muleshoe, Texas, got a BA in English and theatre from Texas Tech University and snagged a job as a newspaper reporter. She didn't know a thing about journalism, but her editor said if she could write he could teach her the rest of it and if she couldn't write the rest of it didn't matter. She hung in there for a 25-year career as a journalist. As soon as she figured out that making up the facts was a whole lot more fun than reporting them, she turned to fiction and never looked back.

Ninie now writes suspense--every flavor except pistachio: psychological suspense, inspirational suspense, suspense thrillers, paranormal suspense, suspense mysteries.

In every book she keeps this promise to her Loyal Reader: "I will tell you a story in a distinctive voice you'll always recognize, about people as ordinary as you are--people who have been slammed by something they didn't sign on for, and now they must fight for their lives. Then smack in the middle of their everyday worlds, those people encounter the unexplainable--and it's always the game-changer."

Also By Ninie Hammon

The Saved

The Unexplainable Collection

Five Days in May

Black Sunshine

The Based on True Stories Collection

Home Grown

Sudan

When Butterflies Cry

The Knowing Series

The Knowing

The Deceiving

The Reckoning

The Fault

Stand-alone Psychological Thrillers

The Memory Closet

The Last Safe Place

www.ingramcontent.com/pod-product-compliance
Lightning Source LLC
Chambersburg PA
CBHW010520100726

47903CB00011B/2835